ROSE COLLIS, COMM

in Wimbledon in 1959, and

previously worked in fring

singer, songwriter, musicia

forming extensively through the UK and Europe, including the Edinburgh Fringe. She lists her most memorable roles as a two-legged teenage "Toto" in *Dorothy's Friends*, an 80s reworking of *The Wizard of Oz*, a revolting lesbian extra in Derek Jarman's *Edward II*, and a member of the world's first lesbian and gay ceilidh band.

She began her career in journalism in 1985, and since then her articles and reviews have appeared in over 30 publications on both sides of the Atlantic, including the *Independent*, *Time Out*, *City Limits*, *The Bookseller*, *Diva*, *Gay Times* and *Xtra* (Canada). This has led to her interviewing Sinead O'Connor in the back of a van; defeating "Bea" from "Prisoner Cell Block H" during an intensively competitive game of Trivial Pursuit; and getting Melvyn Bragg to admit he placed a bet that Labour would lose the 1992 election. She has written sleevenotes for albums by Elton John and Dusty Springfield and is a contributor to the Oxford University *New Dictionary of National Biography*.

She is the author of several critically acclaimed books including *Portraits To The Wall* (Cassell 1994) and *A Trouser-Wearing Character: The Life and Times of Nancy Spain* (Cassell 1997).

She has made numerous TV and radio appearances, including Woman's Hour, GLR and Talk Radio's Lorraine Kelly Show, and was one of the team who produced *Framed Youth* (C4), winner of the BFI Grierson Award for Best Documentary of 1984.

Also available

The Mammoth Book of Ancient Wisdom
The Mammoth Book of Armchair Detectives & Screen Crimes
The Mammoth Book of Arthurian Legends
The Mammoth Book of Battles
The Mammoth Book of Best New Horror 99
The Mammoth Book of Best New Science Fiction 12
The Mammoth Book of Bridge
The Mammoth Book of British Kings & Queens
The Mammoth Book of Cats
The Mammoth Book of Chess
The Mammoth Book of Comic Fantasy
The Mammoth Book of Dogs
The Mammoth Book of Erotica
The Mammoth Book of Gay Erotica
The Mammoth Book of Heroic and Outrageous Women
The Mammoth Book of Historical Detectives
The Mammoth Book of Historical Erotica
The Mammoth Book of Historical Whodunnits
The Mammoth Book of How It Happened
The Mammoth Book of International Erotica
The Mammoth Book of Jack the Ripper
The Mammoth Book of Lesbian Short Stories
The Mammoth Book of Men O'War
The Mammoth Book of Mindbending Puzzles
The Mammoth Book of Murder
The Mammoth Book of New Erotica
The Mammoth Book of New Sherlock Holmes Adventures
The Mammoth Book of Nostradamus and Other Prophets
The Mammoth Book of Oddballs and Eccentrics
The Mammoth Book of Private Lives
The Mammoth Book of Seriously Comic Fantasy
The Mammoth Book of Short Erotic Novels
The Mammoth Book of Sports & Games
The Mammoth Book of Tasteless Lists
The Mammoth Book of the Third Reich at War
The Mammoth Book of True War Stories
The Mammoth Book of Unsolved Crimes
The Mammoth Book of War Diaries and Letters
The Mammoth Book of the Western
The Mammoth Book of the World's Greatest Chess Games

The Mammoth Book of

LESBIAN EROTICA

Edited by

Rose Collis

ROBINSON
London

Constable & Robinson Ltd
3 The Lanchesters
162 Fulham Palace Road
London W6 9ER

First published in the UK by Robinson
an imprint of Constable & Robinson Ltd 2000

A copy of the British Library Cataloguing in Publication data is available from the British Library

ISBN 1-84119-077-2

Printed and bound in the EC

CONTENTS

ACKNOWLEDGEMENTS

I would like to thank the following for their kind assistance, support and co-operation:

Peter Burton; Frederique at Cleis Press; Stella Duffy; Jeff Lazarus, Stokrose Publishing; Laurin McKinnon, BlackWattle Press; Sally McMahon; Sue O'Sullivan; Mark Peters; Nina Rapi; Gillian Rodgerson; Lawrence Schimel; Birgit Scheuch; Dorothee Winden.

And thanks to all the writers who took the time and trouble to send their stories for consideration.

The Mysteries of the Psitticine Orgasm © 1998 by Thea Bennett. Reproduced by permission of the author.

A Feather © 1998 by Susannah Marshall. Reproduced by permission of the author.

Virtual Femme © 1998 by Urszula Dawkins. Reproduced by permission of the author.

Vanilla © 1998 by Maisie Langridge. Reproduced by permission of the author.

A Place For Us © 1998 by Karen X Tulchinsky. Reproduced by permission of the author.

Sweet Violet © 1998 by Ruby Vise. Reproduced by permission of the author.

Visiting © 1998 by Susan Stinson. Reproduced by permission of the author.

Having Your Cake and Eating it © 1998 by Amazon. Reproduced by permission of the author.

The Cake Maker © 1998 by Stella Duffy. Reproduced by permission of the author.

Diesel Donuts © 1998 by Isla Jule. Reproduced by permission of the author.

Tea and Sympathy © 1998 by Stephanie Sellier, from *Fresh Out Of Hell*, Konkursbuch Verlag. Reproduced by permission of the author and Konkursbuch Verlag.

Hungry Love © 1998 by Ava Hines. Reproduced by permission of the author.

Still © 1998 by Mary-Kate Kelly. Reproduced by permission of the author.

The Wet Room © 1998 by Rosa Riley. Reproduced by permission of the author.

Fiskar © 1998 by Patience Agbabi. Reproduced by permission of the author.

Table Manners © 1998 by Ros Marinus. Reproduced by permission of the author.

Red Rock © 1998 by Lorna Stucki. Reproduced by permission of the author.

Sleeping Passions © 1998 by Deborah Caplan. Reproduced by permission of the author.

Light and Darkness © 1998 by Isabelle Lazar. Reproduced by permission of the author.

The Intransigent Presence of Paradox © 1998 by Maya Chowdhry. Reproduced by permission of the author.

Starlit Fingers © 1998 by Berta Freistadt. Reproduced by permission of the author.

Litany of Remembrance © 1998 by Sovereign Muse. Reproduced by permission of the author.

One Size Fits All © 1998 by Eileen Finn. Reproduced by permission of the author.

Josie's Restrooms © 1998 by Nina Rapi. Reproduced by permission of the author.

Clash of the Titans © 1997 by Karlyn Lotney, first published in *Gone Is The Shame*, Masquerade Books, 1997. Reproduced by permission of the author.

Homage To Vi © 1998 by Heather Murray. Reproduced by permission of the author.

Cocktease © 1998 by Deborah Kelly. Reproduced by permission of the author.

The Weekend © 1998 by Alex LeQuesne. Reproduced by permission of the author.

All She Wanted © 1998 by Debra Diana Blue. Reproduced by permission of the author.

Petra and Other Identities © 1998 by Carolyn Gammon. Reproduced by permission of the author.

A Story for Louise © 1998 by Julie MacLusky. Reproduced by permission of the author

Last Time © 1998 by Jo Fisk. Reproduced by permission of the author.

Speaking In Tongues © 1998 by Emma Donoghue. Reproduced by permission of the author.

I've Seen Her Before © 1998 by Twiggy O'Connor. Reproduced by permission of the author.

Piracy © 1998 by Rebecca Rosenskjøld. Reproduced by permission of the author.

A Struggle For Peace © 1998 by Mercia Schoeman. Reproduced by permission of the author.

Summer's Coming © 1998 by Julie MacLusky. Reproduced by permission of the author.

Carol © 1998 by Kathleen Bryson, extract from the novel *Mush*. Reproduced by permission of the author.

One Night In Paris © 1999 by Jill Gardiner. Reproduced by permission of the author.

All Of It © 1998 by Joan Nestle, excerpt from *My Cancer Travels*, from *A Fragile Union*, Cleis Press, 1998. Reproduced by permission of the author and Cleis Press.

Thai Silk © 1998 by Bente Clod, first published in *Ex hibition*, Stokrose Publishing, Copenhagen. Reproduced by permission of the author and Stokrose Publishing.

A Wine-Dark Night © 1998 by Boz Thomas. Reproduced by permission of the author.

The Missionary Position © 1998 by Astrid Fox. Reproduced by permission of the author.

INTRODUCTION

Mainstream society has always had a problem with lesbians and sex: the idea of women holding hands and reading poetry to each other was about as far as tolerance went. But the merest hint that they were more interested in each other's pants than pentameters often resulted in poetic injustice.

Most people will know the old, apocryphal story of how Queen Victoria stopped lesbian sex being outlawed because she couldn't see what there would be to outlaw. However, fewer folk probably know that an attempt to criminalize lesbians was made in 1921. The main purpose of the Criminal Law Amendment Bill was to raise the age of consent to sixteen and increase punishment for brothel-keepers. But an amendment was included to outlaw "any act of gross indecency between female persons"; the reason given for this clause by one of its supporters, Sir Ernest Wild QC, was that "it [lesbianism] debauches young girls, and it produces . . . insanity". The amendment was overwhelmingly passed by the Commons, but eventually thrown out by the House of Lords. One of the peers, Earl Malmesbury, opposed it on the grounds that "the more they advertised these vices the more they would increase".

Six years later, the obscenity trial involving Radclyffe Hall's *The Well Of Loneliness* demonstrated only too well the opposition to all-female "vices". A book could be booed, banned and burned for "and that night they were not divided". Happily, in 2000, we can be a tad more explicit, though bookshops can still be subject to prosecution – or should that be persecution – for stocking erotic titles, as Britain's *Gay's The Word* and Canada's *Little Sisters* could bitterly testify.

The portrayal of lesbian sex on the printed page has come a long way in seventy years, and the arguments about the desires and dangers involved in making lesbian erotic material more widely available have surfaced regularly during that time. Should our sexual experiences, secrets and fantasies run the risk of falling into the wrong hands? In 2000, the current climate seems to be that it's a risk well worth taking and the more, the merrier. Hence, *The Mammoth Book Of Lesbian Erotica.*

I took a number of decisions very early on in the process of compiling this anthology. Unlike similar collections, it would not just feature stories from the UK and the US, and the authors would not include all of the usual suspects – this should explain why some erotic writers you might expect to see in a collection like this are not. I also wanted to approach certain established authors of quality fiction, not "known" as exponents of erotica, to see if they fancied doing a little genre-hopping. There would be no set "theme" or "subject" for the stories, and no upper or lower word limit. Finally, as far as was humanly possible, given deadline and budget limitations, many of the stories would be new and previously unpublished.

It is all these reasons, and more besides, which I believe set this anthology aside from others in the predominantly US-dominated lesbian erotica market. It will also, I hope, give some hope and encouragement to writers for whom the UK-based publishing opportunities for such material are lamentably few and far between. Since Sheba's two volumes of *Serious Pleasure*, there has been virtually nothing produced from Britain to fill the subsequent, and substantial, gap.

And, happily, there are some other positive signs: Diva Books, an offshoot of the popular UK lesbian magazine, launched its first volume of erotic writings, *Batteries Not Included*, solely on the theme of sex toys, in 1999. Virgin Publishing also launched *Sapphire*, a series of full-length erotic lesbian fiction, edited by Kathleen Bryson, who makes an appearance in this anthology.

It's not as if there's no demand: during the time it took to put this book together, *Diva* magazine carried out an extensive reader's survey on love, sex and the whole damn thing. Amongst its revelations was the fact that nearly a quarter of those who took part in the survey read erotic stories on a regular basis, while over half read them "sometimes".

No one volume can adequately represent all corners of the globe, but we've had a go: homegrown stories come from all over England, plus Scotland, Wales and Northern and Southern Ireland. There are also stories by writers from the US, Canada, Australia, New Zealand, South Africa, Germany and Denmark. Stories are set in varied geographical locations, too: Iceland, Thailand, Australia, Paris, Africa, Hawaii.

One of the most frequent questions asked by prospective contributors about this book was "what do you want the stories to be about?". The answer, of course, was "Whatever *you* want them to be about – see where your imagination takes you". Many writers were both relieved and enthusiastic when told that their stories didn't have to be entirely serious in tone, nor did they necessarily have to have a sex scene in them!

Another aim of the anthology was to introduce a fair number of new writers into the genre, and so we're particularly pleased to welcome all its debutantes and wish them more passion to their pens and PCs.

One of the real eye-openers in putting this anthology together was discovering the way that lesbians – and lesbian writers in particular – have cottoned on to the potential of the Internet and are using it to good effect. Through the wonders of the Web, it was possible for me to contact a wider range of authors than would previously have been possible. For instance, a notice on the lesbian writing website *Sapphisticate* yielded a healthy number of submissions from writers previously unknown to me. BlackWattle Press, the Australian lesbian and gay publishers, were able to forward an e-mail message to all of their relevant authors, as well as posting it on their own website. But most exciting of all is the development of lesbian writers' groups around the world, swapping news, views and advice electronically. This has also proved a highly efficient method of unearthing good new writers from more than one country.

It's also been immensely satisfying that established writers, well-known in their different fields of literature, including full-length fiction, biography, poetry and drama, have wanted to be part of this anthology. Undoubtedly, there will be many pleasantly surprised to find the names of Emma Donoghue, Stella Duffy, Susan Stinson, Patience Agbabi, Nina Rapi and Maya Chowdhry included here.

What is regarded as erotic is, of course, entirely subjective. It can be, as Blondie sang, spending an hour watching someone shower. And why not? The presence of water in dreams, it is said, represents sexual desire – which is a little worrying, given that my most common recurring dream involves a huge tidal wave rushing towards me, and everyone else, on a beach. I run around trying to warn people, shouting "Can't you see what's coming?" But they remain oblivious – so clearly, size doesn't really matter.

It's all a matter of taste – in more ways than one. One thing seems to be consistent, though: food and drink play a large part when we want to enjoy other pleasures of the flesh.

Wherever two or more lesbians are gathered together, the consensus on sexy food seems to give the thumbs-up to cream, Greek yoghurt, cherries, mangoes, strawberries . . . and avocados. Now, quite why these always feature highly on such lists has been a mystery to me – but, hey, if greasy, tasteless, green globules are the food of your love, then play on . . .

By the time Daphne Adams finally marries her madam, you'll have sampled a vat's worth of wine, plus a fair amount of tea and coffee, and the odd beer and bottle of champagne.

You'll also have worked your way through doughnuts, pizza, garlic bread, chocolate cake, popcorn, cheese, oranges, baked chicken, corn on the cob, potato salad, and a sweet rice-cake.

Crikey, never mind the sex – that little lot should be more than enough to satisfy anyone's appetites.

But if food and drink continue to be vital to our sexual lives, then it should come as no surprise to see another lesbian passion – animals – popping up throughout this collection. Dogs, cats, parrots, mice – they all have supporting roles. Even a frog gets a brief look-in.

Virginia Woolf said, "Women alone stir my imagination" and imagination certainly doesn't seem to be a problem for lesbians, as lovers or writers. What the *Diva* survey revealed appears to be backed up by many of the stories in this collection, especially when it comes to unorthodox places for having sex.

Somewhere in this world are women who have gone for it on cliffs, in trains and buses, a wheelbarrow, toilets, phone boxes and, spookily, a changing room in an Edinburgh clothes shop. Any relation between this real-life event and those outlined in Eileen Finn's story are purely coincidental . . .

In this anthology, women also go for it in the toilet, in the shower, in a changing room, in the back of a van, in a garden, on a sofa, in every room in an entire house, at an Icelandic spa, against a fridge, in a taxi, in a mouse-suit – oh yes, and sometimes, in a bed. As Alfred Kinsey himself once said, "The only unnatural sex act is that which you cannot perform", and there are some performances throughout this collection which merit applause – if your hands aren't otherwise occupied, that is.

And so, dear reader, hopefully having whetted all your appetites, here is a brief guide to what lies waiting for you between the sheets of this book:

In Mercia Schoeman's *A Struggle for Peace*, love and passion are set against the social and political turbulence of South Africa as it moves away from the evil and injustice of apartheid. In Bente Clod's *Thai Silk*, set in the heat and humidity of an Asian climate, two lovers on holiday discover the Thais that bind. *All Of It* by Joan Nestle expresses the possibilities open to you if you are prepared to explore new territories, and Jill Gardiner is in hot pursuit of the most beautiful bottom in Brighton during *One Night In Paris*.

Maisie Langridge's *Vanilla* reminds us what a delicious flavour it can be. Ava Hines' *Hungry Love* sees dinner for two leading to a sumptuous helping of afters. In Mary-Kate Kelly's *Still*, a dull lunch is enlivened by a bit more than a dab of mustard. Stephanie Sellier's *Tea And Sympathy* explains why, though you might think it would be simple to have a quick cuppa in your own flat, it's best to remember your flat-mate's proclivities . . . In Ilse Jule's *Diesel Donuts*, women really do get to have their cake and eat it, a theme also pursued by Amazon in *Having Your Cake And Eating it*, where pink champagne and chocolate cake leads to other sorts of gorging – as well as slipping in a plug for the very book it appears in! And in Stella

Duffy's mouthwatering *The Cake Maker*, Natsuki enjoys more than just a sweetmeat with her warrior woman. After this, who needs Xena?

The excitement and pain of lost love is beautifully held in Berta Freistadt's *Starlit Fingers* and Karen O'Brien's *Litany Of Remembrance*. Jo Fisk's *Last Time* show how love and lust don't always end at the same time.

Twiggy O'Connor's *I've Seen Her Before* shows how, if you wish hard enough for a dream lover to call your own, she might just appear! Astrid Fox's *The Missionary Position* proves that God does, indeed, move in mysterious ways and while reading Karlyn Lotney's *Clash Of the Titans*, you might want to have a tape of Cole Porter's *You're The Top* playing, to set the right mood . . .

Creature comforts are everywhere: in Shari J Berman's *Welcome To The Big Island Big House*, part of *I Do! The Quarantine Chronicles*, a dogs' quarantine kennel in Hawaii is the backdrop for love – and not just for humans.

In *Nightmare On Easter Road Pt I* by Marjory Smith, cats have supporting roles, in what almost becomes a lesbian take on *La Ronde*. *Virtual Femme* by Urszula Dawkins celebrates the animal passion that lies sleeping in all of us. Mary Gerideau's *Marvin The Mouse* is a tail tale, set one hot summer, where a costume mouse-suit provides one of the most unusual settings for a close encounter I've ever heard of. Winged creatures feature literally and metaphorically in *A Feather* by Susannah Marshall, and Thea Bennett's *The Mysteries Of The Psitticine Orgasm*, which shows that Polly's not the only one who thinks she's a pretty parrot.

And they called it puppy love, just because they're in their teens. Karen X Tulchinsky's *A Place For Us* sees two teenagers in love come full circle after a decade's separation, and Ruby Vise's *Sweet Violet* captures the illicit excitement of young lust that has nothing to do with Donny Osmond. The writer in Emma Donoghue's *Speaking In Tongues* finds erotic echoes from her own youth reverberating when she gives a lift to a young woman.

Never mix work and pleasure, goes the old adage. But try telling that to some girls: *Petra And Other Identities*, by Carolyn Gammon, sees the mysterious Frau Klein taking the employer–employee relationship a stage further to find out about "women", a theme not dissimilar to Debra Diana Blue's *All She Wanted* and Alex LeQuesne's *The Weekend*, where two colleagues put in some serious overtime together as one decides to develop their very inter-personal skills. Kathleen Bryson's *Carol*, an extract from her novel-in-progress *Mush*, also shows that newcomers are not backwards in coming forwards.

George Michael got flushed out when he took a quick toilet break in LA, but some of our authors reveal that there can be more fun in the women's room. In *Light And Darkness* by Isabelle Lazar, a bar-room encounter results in a little more than nose-powdering in the ladies' room. Nina Rapi's *Josie's Restrooms* is a video-diary monologue by a butch toilet attendant about her sexual experiences and fantasies, which you'll want to spend more than a penny to share.

Hopefully, there's enough moisture splashing around elsewhere to slake the thirst of any water babies: the tide is high down by the lazy river in Lorna Stucki's *Red Rock*; enter Rosa Riley's *The Wet Room*, and you'll be bathing in the sex/water metaphor; and Susan Stinson's *Visiting* sees an aunt's revelation to her niece in a boat creating waves of resonance.

We know there are plenty of you who are familiar with the pitfalls and pleasures of personal ads in *Diva*, the *Pink Paper* et al. So, it's hardly surprising that this has also emerged as a favourite theme in a good number of the stories submitted –

and, if the experiences related in them are anything to go by, all that money being spent on 0898 numbers isn't being wasted. In Patience Agbabi's *Fiskar*, a contact ad leads to an encounter of the moist kind in Iceland and *Table Manners* by Ros Marinus also emphasizes that when you answer personal ads, life doesn't always have to be a beach.

In *Sleeping Passions* by Deborah Caplan, two lovers settle down for a quiet night – in their dreams. Boz Thomas' *A Wine-Dark Night* brings together popcorn, a fellow worker and memories of childhood. Eileen Finn's *One Size Fits All* combines the twin pleasures of shopping and fucking; Heather Murray's *Homage to Vi* gives off good vibrations – who said diamonds are a girl's best friend? – while Rebecca Rosenskjøld's *Piracy* is a jolly roger.

The characters in Maya Chowdhry's *The Intransigent Presence Of Paradox* enjoy what you might call a quantum leap, and Deborah Kelly's *Cocktease* gives one option of what to do when you've got a man by the balls.

And then, topping (in a manner of speaking) and tailing this eclectic collection, Daphne Adams' *I Married Madam, Pts I And II*, follows the adventures of two friends who go a-hunting, with one of them using her unfeasibly long nipples as an ice-breaking line. Well, it worked for her, so you never can tell.

Lily Tomlin once said, "There will be sex after death, we just won't be able to feel it" – which seems to be the best endorsement of having a healthily active love life while we can. And so, as the Earl of Malmesbury most certainly would not have said in 1921 – may your "vices" increase.

I MARRIED MADAM PART I

Daphne Adams

"Zomtimes I ver rubber, zomtimes I ver ledder", she said, in best Dietrich-clipped English.

"Oh, really? That's nice," Anna replied inanely, trying not to moan with pleasure from the pressure being applied to her clitoris by the woman's groin.

"Move closer, mooove your body real close," the music crooned. She looked coolly into Anna's eyes and flicked her tongue out like the lounge lizard she really was. When it rasped lasciviously down the soft flesh by Anna's left ear, it took all her self-control not to drag this gorgeous woman from the dance-floor and yank her upstairs into the club's (unusually clean) toilets so that she could do outrageous things to her torso with her tongue.

Doing it in the loo wasn't terribly erotic, Anna decided. She could do much better than that, if only she could think of something sexy to say. She searched the darkest recesses of her brain for inspiration and, in the heat of the moment, out it popped.

"I might have small tits, but I've got the longest nipples ever!"

Nothing stirred in her dance partner.

Undeterred, Anna pulled away from their clinch to gesture with thumb and forefinger: "When erect, they're THIS long!" Anna showed an impressive gap of at least an inch. "Really, I have," she added forlornly, in the voice of someone who knew they'd gone too far, but hadn't the sense to shut up.

Anna's "Prussian Peccadillo" raised her right eyebrow in a quizzical gesture which had all the hallmarks of Jack Nicholson's "devil-look" before she . . .

Anna threw caution to the wind, pressing her body back against the woman's muscled torso.

". . . 'Til we feel like we're reeeally making louuuve," the record climaxed. Just as Anna was about to follow suit, her dark, sultry suitor walked briskly off with a "Zank yew" thrown back over her broad shoulders. Anna stood swaying in her wake.

Anna made as dignified a job of walking back to her table as she could. There, her best mate Joan met her with a chortling fit so violent she sounded like a pig with sinusitis.

"Oh, darling, you're not going to believe it," Joan hiccuped in her posh Camden School For Girls accent. "You'll never guess what her name is. M . . . M . . . *Marlene*! . . . and she's from *Berlin*!" she barked, before collapsing into paroxysms of nasal snorts and table-banging.

"Let's go," Anna snapped, not knowing how she could possibly be insulted further that evening. She angrily stuffed her ciggies and lighter into her jacket pocket and trundled towards the Angel's Heart Club's pink neon exit sign. Joan meekly followed at a respectable ten paces; she'd just spent her bus fare home on that "one last pint for the road" and now desperately needed to get back into Anna's good books, otherwise a cold, damp eight-mile walk back to Lickey End, near Cockfosters, beckoned. The vomit-fumed warmth of the night bus seemed like a luxury charabanc in comparison.

Suddenly, a bony, bejewelled hand reached out of the darkness, picking and clawing at Anna's arm like carrion tucking into ripe flesh. She turned, alarmed, as her exit from the club was barred.

"For you," the barmaid said, thrusting a yellow Post-It note under her eyes. Anna thought that, with her yellow-dyed hair and puppy-brown eyes, the woman bore an alarming resemblance to Margerita Pracatan. She hoped to God she wouldn't start warbling "I will surbibe . . ."

The note (written in biro) read: *Marlene. 0181 999 9674. XXX.*

"Three kisses. Not bad. That's what you wanted, kid, isn't it?" Joan asked.

After a respectable silence, she nodded and waited patiently for Joan to broach the subject of how she'd settle the ten-pound bet she'd just lost.

Life and the universe began for Anna and Joan when they tired of the North London Lesbian scene (and, in Anna's case, of her North London lesbian girlfriend, Vicky). It wasn't that she didn't love her partner of nearly five years, but it was in a way that defied any word in the English language. "Sister" or "friend" didn't come anywhere near. Perhaps, as they hadn't made love for so long, "companion" was the most apt description. Even when they'd been fresh in lust during the time when most couples are "at it like rabbits", it seemed as if their love-making had only occurred in months with a "y" in them. Anna knew what it was. They were suffering from "lesbian bed death", according to the magazine article she'd read somewhere recently. Even in midsummer, Anna would jump into bed, pyjamas buttoned up to her chin, a subtle indication that she was as physically available to Vicky as a clam shut tight in its shell. She dreaded that microsecond just before Vicky put out the light. Would she turn and give Anna's shoulder a "how about it?" squeeze?

The last time this had happened, Anna had lain there inert while Vicky had lightly brushed her cold skin with her lips. When they reached her nipples and worked them slowly erect with a writhing tongue, Anna had cried silently. The only outward sign of her inner misery was a large, saline tear sac which rolled exquisitely down her cheek. She mourned her freedom, frustrated by her feelings of domestic entrapment. She was shamed that her body reacted positively to a touch she found near-abhorrent. She was sad for the person she loved and had promised to be with forever. She now knew that she would break that most solemn oath.

Her liberator was Joan, the "Old Trout" and propper-up of bars throughout North London since the Gateways had closed some ten years before. Joined by fate (Anna didn't know anyone else on the scene) and circumstance (they were both fed up of their sleazy local), they planned to leave "Base Camp" at the earliest justifiable opportunity. Why? Because it was the "usual" drag bar full of life-sized mug-shots of long-forgotten style-queens hung against flock wallpaper impregnated with the faint odour of poppers. The toilets were disgusting – to market them as something from a bygone gay age was insulting to the past. Their black plastic seats hung askew with shame. Toilet paper was a scarcer commodity than gold and, when it was found by a lucky prospector, managed to wind its way all over the wet floor in a pattern the Andrex puppy would be proud of.

As "early-middle-aged-somethings" (Anna was thirty-five, Joan pushing the wrong side of fifty) they weren't old by anyone's standards, but the baby-dykes seemed to be getting younger by the week. Worse still, they would keep knocking back copious amounts of illegal substances, then lurch onto the small stage to gyrate alarmingly like gross parodies of Madonna in her "Like A Virgin" phase.

"Bloody disgusting," said Joan, drawing on her legal substances (liquorice paper roll-ups and a bottle of Grolsch) as one rather damp and enthusiastic gal whipped off her top, sweaty boobs gyrating to the techno-crap rhythm. Joan gesticulated:

"ONE: I can't bear DJ Rosemary's silver lamé curtains. TWO: If I approach any of these bints, I'll be accused of paedophilia. THREE: If Gerry waters my lager down any further, the gnats won't even be able to piss in it. FOUR: The last "woman" you fancied in here turned out to be a transvestite called Daisy, when you finally got the balls to go over and chat her up. FIVE: When I said that the early seventies fashions I wore would "come around again one day and I'd be trendy", I never ever expected it to really happen.

"Remember the saying about when all the policemen get younger? Well, my angel: 'Unto each man comes a day when his favourite sins all forsake him And he complacently thinks he has forsaken his sins . . .' In relation to the fairer sex and me: not bloody likely, I'll say! I want to die with my sins on my lips!"

In order to accentuate this deep spiritual point further, Joan hitched up her home-made flares (made from a material not dissimilar to the floral pattern of her lounge curtains). She ran her hand through her Bay City Roller hairstyle, raised her right fist in a Communist salute and, looking alarmingly like a little grey-haired Gonk, stated boldly: "Next week, my angel: South London awaits!"

* * *

Friday night (the next week) involved an abortive visit to a club in Victoria where a drunken ginger-haired diesel-dyke squared up to Joan and used the strangest chat-up line ever: "I was in a cell next to Rosemary West."

For once, Joan couldn't come up with a witty response.

"Thing is, angel, I found her fascinating," she enthused in rich plummy tones to Anna, after the magnificent event had occurred. "I was speechless because she had these riveting tattoos of naked women etched around her neck. When she spoke, the muscles in it bulged and they kind of danced . . . Hope you don't mind, but I got away from her by saying we were an item."

As Anna beat a hasty retreat home, she barely managed to avoid the "I'm-going-to-make-a-Voodoo-doll-of-you-when-I-get-home-and-stick-pins-in-pain-maximizing-places" glare given to her by her lovesick thwarted rival.

Friday night (the week after) in a Charing Cross bar also ended with thunderbolt speed. By the time Joan had circumnavigated the prissy dancing queens, with fingers jabbing into peoples' eyes, very little lager was left in the plastic glasses she'd clutched possessively to her bosom.

"Bugger!" She flopped down onto a stage doubling up as seating. "Nearly five quid a pint. Would you believe it, angel?"

When Joan stood up a few minutes later to shake her arthritic legs, Anna hissed, "Trousers! Black mark, right buttock!"

Joan inspected her "Saturday Night Fever whites". "Oh, me 'John Travoltas'," she wailed, spitting into her hand and rubbing it over the cowpat-shaped stain. She was moving like a line-dancer with a bad dose of crabs and Anna, choked with laughter, began to draw attention to her pal's antics.

Joan stopped in her tracks and eyed Anna venomously.

"That's it! I shall retreat to the water closet. Having undertaken a repair job on my arse, I shall return. For your distinct lack of moral support in my hour of need, I expect a fresh, full pint awaiting *moi.*"

Joan trotted off. From the most surreptitious hiding place in the club (behind the cigarette machine), a chunky leather-clad arm grabbed her by the throat and swept the irascible rogue off her feet.

"Oh, shit. Mad Morag." Anna watched as her friend's fragile form was thrust against the wall and smothered in kisses by an obese Celt dressed in sado-masochistic attire.

Mad Morag had been a go-go dancer in the 1960s. She had earned her handle by infamously whipping off her cheesecloth shirt on "Top Of The Pops" (when "Chirpie Chirpie Cheep Cheep" was playing, no less). Revealed: her pendulous breasts, swaying in time to ". . . last night I heard my Mamma singing a song . . ."

She had of course been ejected from the set at the most opportune moment a live television show could present, and had gained immortality as one of the first Streakers To The Masses.

Joan had previously had a bit of a "thing" for Mad Morag.

"The best sex ever, darling," she'd emphasized one night, propped against the main bar of "Base Camp" and waving her cheroot dangerously close to Anna's eyes.

"Really?" Anna simply couldn't imagine how the nine or ten stones' difference in weight between them could be translated into any kind of interesting sexual position.

But their affair had infamously gone on for some time – until, that is, Mad Morag got a hankering for her past.

When she revealed her latest acquisition (a studded leather halter from a sex shop down Camden Market), Joan confided to Anna: "My pash was sucked from under me. To tell you the truth, I felt like an old nag with one last chance to have a nibble from a nosebag. It really put me off."

The more Joan avoided her trussed lover, the more Mad Morag found her a tease. Incidents like this "alien abduction" happened occasionally as a result.

Just as Anna was beginning to give up all hope, Joan skedaddled past her in the direction of the fluorescent exit sign, shouting: "If we don't go now, I'm never coming out with you again! I shall also publicize to your boring excuse for a girlfriend that you have been seeking a series of clandestine bonks with women who prefer champagne to snakebite. Now let's see where your loyalties lie . . ."

Friday night (the week after that) saw the intrepid duo wandering round the backstreets of Waterloo.

"Do you realize," asked Joan laconically, "that if we ever find this rat-hole, we're going to have an absolute swine of a time getting home from here at 3 a.m.?"

"Mmm," Anna replied, hell-bent on finding their "Holy Grail" and seeing what it looked like before making up her mind she didn't like it.

"Pit-stop, my angel!" her friend commanded.

Anna said nothing, somewhat surprised at being hauled into a dingy pub when they were less than a few hundred metres away from their destination (a women-only club for the discerning dyke).

"Dutch courage," Joan explained as she ordered two pints. Anna was inclined to agree with her. After their long journey, it might be worth recharging their batteries.

She surveyed the pub's surroundings. Bathroom and kitchen sinks were plastered into the ceiling and walls at oblique angles. Anyone above six feet tall was likely to be nutted by swinging plugs on chains or, if they tried to escape, suffocated in broken fishing-net swathed around the grimy walls. It was too surreal for words. She hoped the atmosphere at Angel's Heart would be less uncomfortable.

"Not the kind of place to get pissed in, is it?" Joan remarked tremulously. "I get the whirlies in here without supping an iota of booze, just from looking at the decor."

"Not the best choice of watering-hole you've ever made, Old Trout," Anna replied. "I don't like it here, either. I feel like something horrid's going to happen if we stay much longer . . ."

"I know. Me 'gonads' are flipping, too. Let's drink up."

"Where the hell are we?"

"Where indeed?" Joan looked around. They were standing in front of a glass door next to a Mexican restaurant, so kitsch it put the "tac" into "tacos".

"Oh, is this it?" The club's main marketing tool was a white cardboard sign sellotaped lop-sidedy to the door. It read: ANGEL'S HEART.

"Looks like it," Anna said grimly, pressing on a white-nippled plastic doorbell.

"If the ambience is like the bloody outside, we should abort mission before we pay," Joan stated.

Anna nodded as she watched a shape in the glass looming ever-nearer, with an asthmatic huff sound-effect thrown in. The door was wrenched open by a large woman dressed from neck to ankle in black cottons, which accentuated beautifully her flabby neck and knees.

Anna shuddered as she looked past her down a narrow flight of burgundy-carpeted stairs flanked by red velvet walls.

"Welcome to Angel's Heart," the woman bowed and said in her best East End.

"Beam me up, Scotty," Joan whispered. "Next thing she's going to tell us is that her name's Ange."

"Come in, girls. Follow me! By the way, me name's Ange." She swept regally down the stairs, followed by her "subjects", who were trying so hard to avoid a hysterical outburst that they were choking with the effort.

"It's so . . . red." Anna gazed around her, searching for an inspirational adjective.

"Just like being in Gabriel's bloody atrium," Joan sighed. Anna looked confused. "Angel's Heart! Oh, bloody hell. Never mind. You pay, I'll find the bar." Joan beavered off.

Having coughed up the entrance fee, Anna followed her friend through glass doors. To her surprise, a cosy room awaited her, coloured aquamarine instead of the downmarket bordello style she'd been expecting. Tiny, bright-hued *poissons*, with bubbles floating from chubby lips, chased each other along walls which joined to form an intimate dancefloor.

Joan had, no doubt, already demanded in crisp Queen's English a bottle of plonk for consumption, for as Anna joined her a bottle of Pinot-Grigio arrived in the claws of a bird-like woman who looked and dressed like Edith Piaf.

They were pointed towards a small round table close to the dancefloor. It was covered with a crisp white tablecloth, a bowl of peanuts and a lit, lemon-scented candle.

"Fiver each to get in," Anna said.

"Nine for the wine," Joan replied, almost square with her pal.

Piaf ambled across. One leg seemed shorter than the other, Anna noted. The fake chanteuse placed two glasses on the table, poured a little of the chilled wine for Joan to taste, and waited patiently for her response.

After more quaffing and squelching than Jilly Goolden could ever muster, Joan nodded her approval. The bottle was deposited in an ice-bucket, neck wrapped in a linen serviette to keep delicate fingers dry.

"This place is going to be a soupçon interesting!" Joan

opined. "So far, everything seems to be in our price range, even the women . . ." She gave her "Mephistopheles look" (a raised right eyebrow, designed to make her look jolly clever and mysterious) to a rather well-dressed woman, and got a nod and a wink in return.

"Surely not? Gawd . . ." Joan shrieked. "A response. I'm in Heaven."

One hour later, the Pinot-Grigio bottle lay upside down in its slushy bed of ice. Joan staggered from the dancefloor for the umpteenth time with a smile so beaming it made her yellow nicotine-stained teeth look white.

"Do you know, angel, the DJ is actually playing records. Lovely vinyl. If I dance on a specific spot, I can make 'Doctor Kiss Kiss' jump. I never liked that song." She lurched off, muttering, "Must pee. More wine . . ." Anna sat totally absorbed in the music. It was a long time since she'd heard "Young Hearts Run Free". Piaf arrived, nodded, deposited an opened bottle in a fresh ice-bucket, and removed the dead one.

But the end of the song was cut short by a whooping and howling which rose to such a crescendo that the noise bounced around the walls and drowned out sensible conversation. Anna craned her neck to see what the object of the hullabaloo was. She saw a tall, swarthy, Germanic-looking woman dressed in full army uniform descend the final few steps into the club. She doffed her peaked cap with theatrical aplomb to great applause. Anna was fascinated by her. It was as if she had entered a tunnel and all life existed outside of it apart from this chameleon, standing before her in close-up. Whilst the woman seemed brashly confident, Anna sensed an undercurrent of brittleness emanating from her, an aura like Judy Garland exuded in her final years. She overheard one woman remark: "Beautiful, but too much of a handful for most."

Not for the likes of me, thought Anna. If only I had the confidence to approach her, I . . . I . . . She closed her eyes and imagined the feel of the coarse wool of the uniform against her warm skin. The woman would keep her hat on, of course, whilst Anna slowly peeled away each article of clothing: belt . . . gloves . . . tunic . . . waistcoat . . . shirt; like removing the leaves from an artichoke one by one. She was turning herself on as she fleshed out the fantasy. When all the leaves were removed, she'd be left with the furry, succulent centre. Just as Anna was really getting off on the imagery, she heard Joan's Queen's English voice in her head:

"Drinking from the fur cup, darling?"

The fantasy was ruined, replaced by Joan's "interesting" way of describing cunnilingus, arrived at one evening when she was at her most pissed and unattractive.

On cue, Joan flew at the table. She grabbed the neck of the Grigio and slugged back a mouthful of wine so vast it made her splutter.

"What the . . . ?" Anna was dumbstruck.

"You'll never guess what's . . ." Joan took another draught. Anna wrenched the bottle away.

"Sergeant Major!" barked Joan.

"Who?"

"That woman, the one in the uniform."

"What?" Anna was incredulous.

"She hit me!"

"What?"

"With her riding crop."

"*What?*"

"You're not listening. *Sergeant Major hit me on my right buttock with her riding crop as I was leaving the pissoir.*"

"Why?" Anna drank a glass of wine straight off, lit a Dunhill, and stared at her friend.

"Probably for fun, darling. She did have a nasty glint in her eye at the time. It was just the shock of it, that's all." Joan started giggling.

"Mind you . . . I did manage to have the last laugh once I'd recovered. I squared up to her and I said, in my best Peggy Mount voice: 'If you want to thwack the other one, sweetheart, all you have to do is ask." I think that's the first time she's had someone have the last word. Madam was impressed.

"I'll lay a bet on with you," Joan added, conspiratorially. "I reckon she's your type. She'd push you. Just what you need. But you haven't got the guts to tackle her. I'll bet you ten quid that by this time next Friday you haven't even got her phone number, let alone have had a dance with her!"

So the Old Trout was becoming devious, Anna decided. What a clever ploy to avoid paying back the bus money she'd subbed her the last two Fridays. She revelled in the challenge. After all, it could prove an incentive to get to know this woman who made her "gonads" leapfrog.

"You're on!" she announced. She spat in her hand and held it towards Joan's surprised face, waiting for their deal to be struck.

MARVIN THE MOUSE

Mary Gerideau

I feel very strongly that I should be allowed to say a few words in my defence. I realise of course, on the face of it, that what happened seems the stuff of farce. But haven't you ever been in a situation that has spiralled slowly out of control? By the time you realize what is happening, there you are, crashed in flames, flat as a pancake on the ground. You have, to coin a phrase much loved by my late mother, fallen quite flat.

I suppose it would be true to say that it all started with my fur fetish. I do realize that this is not a politically correct fetish although, now I come to think of it, maybe no fetish is. And I would like to make one thing plain from the start: I do not condone blood sports or mink farming, it's just that I have always loved fur. I very much prefer it on the correct animal. I do myself live with several cats and a hamster. Put simply, furriness in all its manifestations turns me on. This was one of the reasons that I decided to take the job as Marvin the Mouse, the mascot of the Festival of One Hundred Cheeses, in the food hall of a very well known West London department store, this summer. It was the fur, and by happy coincidence I am also partial to cheese.

That year I had been resting for longer than was comfortable. The great advantage of dressing up in a mouse suit, I thought, was that I could retain my anonymity and therefore my dignity, earn some money, and hopefully eat some cheese. I would not have done it, if for one moment I had thought that, as a consequence, I would be plastered across the Tabloid Press, and that my picture would end up in the *National Enquirer*. I did not tell any friends or relatives about the job. My friend Gerry, under pressure from the DSS, once took a job as Father Christmas at a large toy shop, out on the North Circular. He thought he was safe, because no one in their right minds would travel all the way to Arnos Grove just in order to laugh at him. He told people. As a consequence, a steady stream of friends and relatives came visiting. They then stood around in small groups not far from his grotto and sniggered as he struggled to be nice to small children.

Unfortunately, both for the cheese and me, the job also coincided with the hottest week of the year. That year there had been no summer, and people were still suffering from the S.A.D. that they should have shed in May. Then, in the second week of August, it got hot. Not 75°F hot, you understand, but 95°F hot; salmon-pink, sweat dripping down the back of your ears, no breeze at all – no, not one tiny bit – stinking hot. And naturally, everyone stopped complaining about how there had been no summer, and started buying up electric fans and muttering about global warming.

By mid-August, most of my friends had left London and were on holiday. I had no money to go anywhere, so I stayed with the tourists, kicking my bank statements under the door mat, and thinking about, but not daring to, cut up my credit cards.

I was pleased to get the audition for Marvin and, even though I say it myself, performed a jolly cheese-loving mouse to perfection, saying, "I love tortellini mascarpone", with an impressive Italian accent. There was only one problem.

"What about your tail?" the man said.

"Ah," I said. "A hamster has no tail."

"You're a mouse."

"Yes, I know that, but I have a hamster. I've been watching my hamster for acting tips."

"I used to have a hamster when I was a boy," he said, wiping sweat from the end of his nose.

"Very stupid."

"What?"

"Hamsters: always walking off the edge of things."

"Yes."

"When I'm in the suit, I'll have no problem with the tail, 'cos I'll have it, won't I?"

"I suppose so," the man said, lugubriously. "You seem to have the gist of it. Really, it's all about having a passion for cheese."

He leant forward on the table and ran his hand through his hair, staring at me intently.

"Do you have a passion for cheese?"

"Where's the suit?"

"Mouse suits will not be available until the day; they're expensive to hire."

"Won't I need time to get used to it?"

"You'll have to do the best you can."

"Does that mean I've got the job, then?"

"I suppose so."

* * *

The morning of my first day in the new job, I got up early, filled with enthusiasm. I will be the best cheese-loving mouse they have ever had, I thought. But, somewhere in me, I suspected that the job I had accepted was reflective of a certain desperation on my part. So I did what I always do in these circumstances: I reached for erotic lingerie. I might be dressing up as a fat sexless rodent, but there was no reason I could not wear my black silk and lace Perla underwear; no reason at all. Then I pulled on a pair of shorts and a T-shirt, shuffled my feet into my deck shoes, and taking a last look at my snoring, cotton wool-covered hamster, headed for the door.

When I arrived, there was panic back-stage because the fridges, which had been housing the cheeses overnight, had broken down; the smell was extraordinary, and many of the cheeses looked as if they might walk into the food hall unaided. My mouse suit was hung up, being groomed by a woman I had not met before, and I went over to introduce myself.

"Hello," I said, "I'm the inside of the mouse."

"Hi," she said. "Laurie."

She was tall and rangy-looking, had short blonde hair, and grey eyes. I could not help noticing that she was wearing a pair of shorts exactly like those worn by John Mills in *Ice Cold In Alex*, one of my favourite films. Her black leather belt had a silver nugget on the end, which hung down, catching the light as she moved. Into her shorts was tucked a black sleeveless vest, which exposed well-muscled brown arms and shoulders.

"There's been a slight mistake," she said. "The mouse is bigger than we thought. We asked for a medium and they sent us a large."

"I'm sure it'll be fine."

"I'm your dresser."

"Oh, no need, I'll be fine."

"No, they're really difficult to get into."

I shrugged.

"It's going to be very hot. You should take off everything but the bare essentials."

"I'll keep on the T-shirt and shorts."

"I wouldn't. Last weekend, we had a guy who did that. The suit was boiling. He passed out and had to be put on a drip."

"Right."

I kicked off my shoes, dropped my shorts and then tugged my shirt over my head.

"Hmmm," she said, looking me over and smiling. "Going on somewhere later?"

"Chance'd be a fine thing," I said, hands on hips, trying to be nonchalant.

"Shame," she said.

"So," I said, attempting a businesslike tone. "How do I do this?"

"Suit first, then the feet, the hands and finally the head."

Maybe I was imagining it, but I'm not sure that all the physical contact that followed was entirely necessary. By the time I was finally inside, I was very hot indeed. The mouse feet were huge, and wearing them made me feel like a furry glam rocker.

"I've never been very good with heels," I said, stomping about, trying to keep my balance.

"Now the head," she said.

I was supposed to be able to see out of the mouth but, because the head was so big, it kept slipping forwards, obliterating my vision.

"Hrglmph . . ." I said, trying to adjust it, and promptly tripped over my tail, and fell onto a table covered in runaway cheeses. I staggered backwards and rolled onto my back, lying there like a beetle, struggling ineffectually to get up. Somewhere off in the distance, I heard hysterical laughter.

"For God's sake help me," I yelled, tugging at my head, "Or I'll suffocate in here."

Still laughing, she got me to my feet.

"Sorry," she said.

I was to have one hour on, then one hour off, because of the heat. Laurie lead me out into the food hall and, for the next hour, I handed out leaflets, was nice to small children and tried to keep my tail out of trouble. The sweat streamed down my body, into my mouse feet and claws; my suit got soggy. But there was no doubt at all that the fur was really turning me on. I thought about Laurie and my forthcoming break.

"Perhaps we could go somewhere and get a cup of coffee," I said, once she'd helped me get the head off.

"Coffee," she said frowning, leading me by the hand, still in my mouse suit, towards a large walk-in larder.

She unzipped the back of my suit and climbed inside. I felt her body against my back, her hands moving down my sides and over my hips. She ran them along the front of my stomach and then slowly along the insides of my thighs. I groaned, leaning back against her, feeling the cold metal of her belt, and her hands came back up my body to my breasts. Cupping them, she felt for my nipples through the silky fabric, squeezing until they were hard under her hands. She pulled up her shirt and I felt her breasts, soft against me. I was so wet and hot it was unbearable, but I couldn't move or turn round. Her hands ran down my back, moving under the silk covering my arse. Slowly she spread my cheeks, one finger circling my arsehole, the other one rubbing me through the silk. My knees were trembling, my legs starting to buckle, and the heat of her mouth was on my neck. Then, just as I thought I was going to come, she stepped back from me and zipped up the back of the suit.

"Your break's over," she said.

"What?"

"Time to go back to work."

"Your kidding, aren't you?"

"Never heard of delayed gratification?"

"No, I fucking well haven't."

I was cross, I was really cross. The next hour did not go well. An elderly gentleman tripped over my tail and threatened to sue the store. I decided I had gone off her in a big way. I would be cool and dismissive when next we met; I was not a happy mouse. I was hot to trot in my mouse suit, and the charms of saying "I love gorgonzola," were wearing off fast.

When I struggled bad-temperedly through to the back, after my second hour was up, she was leaning against the wall, smiling.

"I wondered if you'd like a shower. It's the MD's, but it's August and he's away. There's hardly anyone on that floor."

"Yes," I said immediately, feeling faintly slutty.

We had to travel up part of the way in a public lift, crammed with people. It was one of the rules of the job that I wasn't allowed to take my head off in public; it would shatter the illusion, they said. We eyed each other from either side of the lift. Or I eyed her as much as I could, wearing a huge furry mouse head which was one size too big for me.

In the shower she helped me undress, her hands hot against my breasts and between my legs. I pulled her to me, tugging open her belt, undoing the buttons of her shorts. I was expecting boxer shorts, I think, not black silk and lace Perla lingerie.

"Well, well," I said. "Going on somewhere later?"

"Chance'd be a fine thing," she said, laughing.

"Shame," I said, kissing her, my tongue running over the outside of her teeth, her nipples hard between my fingers. I pushed her back against the walls of the shower, and she winced as the cold tiles touched her back. She reached behind her and turned on the shower, and water came gushing down between our bodies and into our mouths. I ran my hands down the front of her body, then slowly peeled off her panties, relishing the silky sensation of satin, the roughness of the lace. I knelt between her legs and licked her, my fingers working deep inside her, opening her up, and she came with a groan, her hands gripping onto my hair, her body soft and succulent against my mouth.

She leant down and drew me up to her, and I was eager for the salty taste of her on both our lips.

"Hey, look what I've found," she said, waving a bar of soap at me.

She pushed me away from her, and stood there rubbing the soap between her hands, her eyes caressing my body. My mouth was dry, my heart thumping inside my head. She started with my breasts, lathering them with soap, until they were tight purple knots, then she turned me towards the wall and soaped my back, my neck, even my scalp, until every part of me felt slippery under her hands. She nudged my feet wider apart, spreading the cheeks of my arse and at last I felt a finger stroke and then gently push into my arsehole. I gasped, bearing down against her, groaning uncontrollably. The finger slid in and out, slowly at first, then faster and faster, the looser I became. With her other hand she entered my pussy.

"Touch yourself," she said, "My hands are full."

And I did, sliding my fingers over my swollen clit, and she fucked me harder and harder, and I came convulsively, gasping, spread-eagled against the wall, my cheek cold against the tiles, her fingers filling me.

During my final hour, I laughed when my tail was tugged, and took trouble giving tourists detailed explanations on how to get to the other side of town. I also allowed an elegant Italian man to put his arm round me, and have his photo taken. My undoing, however, was the elderly woman who dropped her umbrella. Now why she was carrying an umbrella when it was 95°F outside is anyone's guess – presumably she was pessimistic by nature, but drop it she did. I bent over to pick it up, and bingo, the back of my mouse suit split. In the normal course of events this would have been fine, slightly embarassing for sure, but not a total disaster. But unfortunately I had discarded my underwear in the shower and was butt naked. It also happened that a rather bored, but cheese-loving tabloid photographer, was standing right behind me when the split occurred. So now you know the full story. I am Marvin the bare-bottomed mouse, who appeared in several tabloid newspapers, on the 16th of August this summer. I got the sack, of course. Laurie apologized; she said she knew the zip was a bit iffy, but hadn't got round to mending it. It's a shame, really, because I liked the job; or maybe, on second thoughts, it was the breaks I liked. Whenever I smell a good ripe cheese or see a mouse, I think of her fondly – very fondly indeed.

WELCOME TO THE BIG ISLAND BIG HOUSE

Shari J Berman

"Ow!" The dangling catch on the fence missed my left eye by millimeters. That was close. Maybe I would have seen it if I were a few inches taller.

"Come on, girl." I closed the gate to the yard behind us. Rainbow scampered through the next open door entering her private run. I carefully shut us both inside. The family that does time together stays together. "I hope I didn't embarrass you, Rainy. Most of your cellmates standing on their hind legs are taller than your fearless mistress!" Rainbow put her paws up on my thighs. I reached down and scratched her ears. "Thanks. I know true devotion when I see it."

"I'm coming, baby!"

I jumped at the voice behind me. I didn't recognize it, either.

I had met most of the other owners on Rainbow's cellblock. It had to be someone for the new dog on the other side of Rainbow. It was my third visit. Rainbow and I had developed a specific pattern of cell and yard time. Rebecca, the kennel owner, had mentioned that Rainbow had a new neighbor, but I hadn't gotten around to checking out the new dog yet.

I turned around, but missed seeing the woman pass the back door of Rainbow's run. The dogs now shared a wall that was solid from the back gate up until the last two feet in front. The bottom of that last section was concrete with chain link for the upper six feet and some open space above that. I looked around at our enclosure. It was roomy enough, but grim nonetheless. Maybe I should take pictures and send them to my friends who acted a bit envious when I told them I was moving to Hawaii. Surely this was a seldom-photographed scene from paradise!

"I know, sweetness, life in this pooch penitentiary is such a hardship."

Was she reading my mind? The woman's voice had a deep 900 number quality to it. I could imagine her answering the phone: "Hi, my name's Melissa, just listening to me talk is enough to send you over the edge!" I had gooseflesh. Would that voice work for me? Perhaps. Maybe real phone sex women are subtler; it's not like I've actually called one . . . I've only seen the operators standing by on cable TV commercials.

I tried not to listen in on this woman fawning over her dog, but the wall didn't even go up to the ceiling. I needed an activity; so, I bent down and swept some of Rainbow's dog food nuggets off the concrete floor and back into her food bowl.

"How about some cookies, doll?" For a split second, I thought she was talking to me. "Be right back," she informed the dog. Again, the tone she used with the dog bordered on seductive. I began to draw a picture of them in my mind. I could see them clearly. The woman was a platinum blonde with three-inch fingernails painted blood red and the dog was a French Poodle with bows everywhere.

Once more, she shot by so quickly that it was impossible to tell if she looked like her voice. A chorus of barks followed her out of the quarantine area. The noise subsided as the sound of the woman's footsteps dissipated.

Relieved at the reprieve from the audible canine excitement, I plopped down in the plastic garden chair that adorned Rainbow's space. It was a feeble attempt to make the place homey. Knowing Rainbow, she probably slept on the chair, instead of the fluffy mat on the floor. My trusty Norfolk Terrier curled beneath my chair and set her jaw on my foot. "You're entirely too cute, Rainy," I told her. Rainbow sighed and closed her eyes. Okay, maybe I get a little mushy with my pet, too – but only in complete privacy.

I opened the novel to the dog-eared spot and began to read. I had finished a mere page and a half when the clattering of the run next to us once again jolted both dog and owner to attention. I figured it was sexy-voice's dog jumping against the back fence of its run – the woman must have struck up a conversation with one of the staff members or something, because she could have bought some biscuits and come back and forth ten times in the time she'd been away. Her dog was going nuts. Based on the vibrations, this was no poodle.

Actually, every dog in the place was barking fiercely. Rainbow was more than slightly agitated. I stooped to pet her and before I could turn again, that woman was back inside the run next to us feeding her dog the promised snacks. I listened to her talk to the dog again. I was amazed that she'd managed to get back there without my having a chance to eyeball her. Maybe she wasn't a 900 operator; maybe she made porn flicks – *Deep Throat*, *The Ninja Prison Matron*.

Curiosity was killing me. I stood up and walked to the

exposed end of Rainbow's run where the dogs shared a fence. I glanced through the links at the adjacent run. The mystery woman was in plain view; I was flabbergasted. This cooing creature was tall, solidly built and had short, cropped gray hair. She was wearing very dark sunglasses. Her darling baby dog was a strapping chocolate Labrador Retriever. Eyeing them for real felt like a cross between *Gulliver's Travels* and *The Twilight Zone.*

I completely forgot myself. I was drawn closer to the fence links to look at the pair. The Lab had quite a few gray hairs in her muzzle. Perhaps the idea of people resembling their dogs was true. For my money, however, the woman looked much tougher than her dog.

It doesn't take much to make Rainbow jealous and I was crossing the line big time! Rainbow stood on her hind legs behind me, but she was too short to see over the two feet of concrete that supported that chain link fence. All right, the irony wasn't lost on me. I grinned. I could see a resemblance between my dog and myself at that point.

Rainbow gave up trying to get a peek over the wall and she paced back and forth between the front and back fence doors, where she could see out clearly. She was on alert to get a glimpse of the newcomers the next time they went by.

"Sorry it took me so long, angel. You have to settle for grocery store confections. I can barely afford the Hawaii relocation, let alone the gourmet morsels they sell in the shop here."

That's for sure. Not to mention the balance that has to be paid to get you out of prison at the end of all of this. Ah-ha! That explained it; she'd gone off to the grocery store.

"Hell, we may be quasi-destitute, but we've got each other!"

Both the sentiment and the two-dollar expressions amused me. I chuckled. The woman looked up at me. I'd been acting like I was watching TV . . . I thought I could see her, but she couldn't see me. I backed up self-consciously. She nodded at me and we mumbled greetings. I knew, despite the shades, that she was looking at me. It was a bit of a turning point; she stopped cooing and I stopped staring.

I moved away from the fenced part and fiddled with Rainbow's toys. In a few seconds, the woman unlatched the forward fence and she and the dog headed to the visiting yard. Rainbow finally got a glimpse of both of them and woofed as they went past. I returned to my book. When I read the same paragraph three times, I closed the novel.

I leaned back in the chair and shut my eyes. Rainbow remained at the edge of the run, waiting for the newcomers to return from their playtime. Driving back and forth to the kennel from my new place on the other side of the island was turning into a full-time job. I was exhausted. I worked to clear my thoughts, drifting in and out of sleep. When I awoke, I realized that I had had some vague dream about the woman with the Lab.

I stood and stretched. It was quiet next door. "I'll be back in a while, Rainbow," I told her, easing out of the enclosure. I couldn't help myself; I poked my head over and looked in at the neighbor. The Lab was napping. I stood on my tiptoes and peered at the chart on the clipboard attached to the fence. It said that the dog's name was "Candy" and the owner was Marilyn Bartlett. Marilyn? Hmm . . . Well, maybe the voice.

I decided on an early lunch. Local food was easy to find, cheap and didn't require a dining companion. I asked for a fish sandwich at the order window of the drive-in and sat down to wait. Before my sandwich was cooked, the crowd under the pavilion of picnic tables multiplied – the smoke and the noise were overwhelming. When my order was called, I inched away from the main eating area and headed for the overflow tables in the back. I made a beeline for an empty one. As I set my sandwich and drink down, I noticed the woman at the next table.

She stood. "Hi. We seem to end up next-door neighbors everywhere we go! I'm Bart."

Bart? "My name is Kimberly." *Of course: Marilyn Bartlett – Bart.*

Bart tossed a sandwich wrapper into a trashcan and loomed, soft drink in hand, over to my table. Not sure what my next move should be, I, uncharacteristically, batted my eyelashes. "Mind if I join you?" she asked.

We shared a UV-protected version of eye contact. Bart didn't wait for my answer; instead, she dragged her long legs over the seat of the picnic table to face me. I had no idea why I was watching her so carefully. Maybe it was just curiosity. She was a tapestry of contradictions: high-falutin' vocabulary, sweet voice coupled with the short butch hairdo and man's name. A shudder began from my bare calves and tingled up my entire body.

This was entirely too peculiar. Although I have political problems with the classic categories, I've always pegged myself as a soft butch. I'm attracted to hair tossing, chiffon dress-clad femmes. It was a personal gender bender to be turned on by and making eyes at this edgy butch in black jean shorts. I had a full-blown Q&A going on in my head. Q. Besides all this weirdness, when did I get so shallow? A. Forty-five minutes ago – when you first heard her speak. Q. How can I possibly be interested in her? I've heard her say fewer than ten words that weren't directed at her dog. A. These things aren't logical.

I took a deep breath. Perhaps I wasn't getting enough oxygen. I still was clamoring for reasonable answers. What kind of a relationship could I have with someone like this? It was all wrong. Besides the butch on butch bit, there was the stranger to stranger, pauper with pauper – stop the presses, the "no" list was starting to make us sound eerily compatible. We were two dyke dog nuts subjecting our pups and ourselves to a harrowing experience.

I had felt famished while I was waiting for the fishburger, yet now my appetite had all but disappeared. I nibbled gracefully for something to do with my mouth. Without the food prop, it was likely to hang open and embarrass me.

Bart chatted amiably. She had recently purchased a small working coffee farm to putter in on the weekends. She was a CPA. She had lived in Colorado before making the move to Hawaii. I contributed here and there. When I had first glimpsed the gray hair, I had figured Bart as older than she looked on closer perusal. Her skin was smooth and youthful. She removed the sunglasses and rubbed her eyes. They were pale blue and perhaps the kindest I'd ever seen. I started thinking about how much I would like to reach out and touch her face. Had she been one of my usual pushover femmes, I'd have gone ahead. The fact was that, gentle eyes or not, I was scared shitless of Bart.

For her part, Bart seemed graceful and comfortable in her large frame. She also appeared unaware that I was checking her out. Maybe the short hair was a fashion statement. It hit me like a ton of bricks – *She could be straight, for all I know.* There are some pretty clueless straight chicks around . . . No way . . . Maybe . . . I don't know. When was the last time I had had my gaydar adjusted?

Rainbow

Kim explained stuff to me, but there are just some things that don't make any sense. Why I'm here, for one! They have me in this cage in the middle of this strange place to make sure I don't spread rabies. Now, where would I have gotten rabies? I was born and raised in Kobe. We haven't had rabies in Japan since 1956!

Kim told me she went to bat for me – she even accused the Hawaiian government of Japan-bashing. I would love to have been there when she did that, but she came to Hawaii by herself last summer and left me with Steve and Masaru in Osaka. Sometimes Kim does really ballsy things like telling off government officials. Personally, I think she could have been a terrier in a former life.

Kim tells me that we're in paradise now, but I don't get it. For me, paradise would be a place without doors. There would be endless biscuits and cheese. The squeakers would come back after you chewed them out of the squeaky toys. Big dogs would quake when I barked. This, my friends, is not paradise.

OK, we do have a cool pool to swim in, but we don't do anything but stay in these big cages and run in the yard a few times a day. My life was full before. I went for walks and stopped in parks; I went for rides in Steve and Masaru's car; Kim took me to the yakitori shop sometimes, too. She'd even spring for an order of liver-on-a-stick for me when we went there. Nope, this is far from paradise.

The first few days were kind of interesting. I'd never seen so many dogs in one place before. It's lost its charm, though.

Today was even weirder than the other days. There's a new dog next door and Kim seemed even more on edge about it than I was. She came back from lunch and she was talking to the dog's owner. The next thing I know, they're both in this little place with me gabbing away. I have a decent enough amount of room when I'm alone, but two big people in here is way too cozy. Besides, it's hard enough sleeping with thirty dogs barking, but to have two humans chattering, too, was over the top.

Kim was acting kind of funny. She let the other woman sit in my chair. Now I was gracious enough to give it to Kim, but I didn't say she could let someone else use it. The other woman was calling her Kimberly, so I figured it wasn't anything serious. Kim is pretty particular about who she lets call her "Kim." I assume she and I are close enough for that. I've been sleeping on her pillow since I was two months old.

She let Sonia call her Kim. I'd hear her calling her that late at night. Actually, it was "Oh, Kim; oh, Kim; oh baby; oh, Kim." She'd get louder and louder. It made it tough for me to snooze. Sonia was a slight improvement over Yoshie, who treated me like I was a mouse. If I made a sudden move, she'd jump up on one of the dining room chairs.

I didn't think Sonia liked me very much, either, though. She had all the signs of a closet cat lover. She recoiled and went on and on about how clingy I was if I gave her my usual boisterous greeting when she got home. Heck, I didn't even give her any teeth when I jumped all over her.

If I could talk people talk, I would have told Kim what a wuss Sonia was. As it happened, Sonia met Mariko and Kim was toast. It went back to being just Kim and me at night in our apartment in Kobe.

Where was I? Oh, yeah. Kim brought the dog next door's owner back with her to my cage. By the way, the dog next door's name is Candy – or so she told me. Is that a real name? She barked up a storm before the humans returned. I jumped up as high as I could and finally got another look at her. She responded with some big dog attitude.

We've been doing a bit of gabbing since then and I let her know that I may be small, but I'm tough. I survived the Hanshin Earthquake. I know what kind of stuff I'm made of. You don't know how strong you are until you dodge a dish cabinet full of sake cups, a dozen half-finished pots and various sculptures hurling at you at the speed of light.

Kim's an artist. She sculpts and makes pottery. She had quite a few pieces in progress that January morning. We managed to get ourselves in the door jamb in time to avoid a lot of the stuff hitting us. Our building was pretty strong. The place across the street crumbled. Anyhow, when I told this all to sweet old Candy, she started to howl a different tune.

She backed off after hearing my story, all right. I decided not to hold it against her. She's kind of nervous. I bet she's still tired from her trip here, not to mention the poking and probing they do in Honolulu before they send you to Hilo.

Back to Kim and Candy's owner. It was a bit worrisome from the start. Kim gave her my chair and said that she was used to squatting on the ground from her years in Japan. I knew Kim was showing off, because our place was really Western. Not like the Ishidas' apartment. The Ishidas' own my mom. I was born in their place near Sannomiya Station. As I was saying, Kim and the woman were in here and they talked and talked. Kim called the other one, "Bart".

At one point, Bart reached under her and realized she was sitting on Kim's book. Kim tried to take it back from her, but Bart held on to it. She opened it up and read the line, ". . . she pressed her heaving bosom against him". Then, Bart started laughing.

Kim got that look that humans get because they can't put their ears back like us. Bart said, "Does your boyfriend know you read this drivel?"

"Does yours know you don't?" Kim answered.

Then they looked at one another and both started laughing like hyenas. I have a pretty good sense of humor, but I couldn't imagine what was so funny about that. After the chuckle-fest, Kim started to get up and had trouble with one of her long paws. I guess it's what happens to mine sometimes when I wake up from a nap.

Kim kind of faltered. Bart got out of the chair and caught her. Then, Bart held her up against the wall and they had their faces really close together. I suppose they were sniffing each other, or whatever people do to figure out what they're up against. The next thing I knew, Bart had her mouth on Kim's. It reminded me of stuff Sonia would do before the "Oh, Kim" chorus.

People: what a species! At least this Bart likes dogs. What kind of name is Bart, anyway? It's even stranger than "Candy". I thought "Bart" was only used for cartoon characters.

Next, Kim and Bart started talking about dinner. This sounded like a great idea, since they've got me on one meal a day in this godforsaken prison. Kim patted me on the head and said she'd see me on Saturday. My question was . . . why did she come back here this afternoon? She hardly looked at me!

Bart went into Candy's cage and said a bunch of gooey stuff and they both left. It's quiet here now. Very quiet. Too damn quiet. Where is everybody?

Bart

I looked down a couple seconds ago and saw that my knuckles were white against the steering wheel. What was I thinking? Dinner was sounding like less and less of a good idea. By the time we were finished eating, it would be late. I have a cottage rented at a bed and breakfast, but Kim would have to drive two and a half hours back to Kona. Unless . . . no, that's even more ridiculous. Where has my common sense gone? It was my strongest ally.

How did I get myself into all of this? There are thousands of unknowns. I'm a worrier. I admit it. I've had this full head of gray hair since I was thirty-five and I earned every strand. I'm a world class worrywart. If they gave gold medals, I'd have a closet full. I get uptight about what happened, what didn't happen, what might happen, what could've happened, what will happen, what won't . . . I'm sure you get the picture.

People are my problem, mostly. They scare the wits out of me. I prefer numbers. They stay the same. I've seen women swear their undying love for me on Thursday and then make out with someone else on the dance floor on Saturday. I've had friends promise to be there for me in times of need – who've headed for the hills when I've faced some problems. On the other hand, five times ten is fifty now, before and forever. That's why I'm a CPA, and a damn good one, if I say so myself.

Glenna agrees. That's the reason she asked me to join her in her little firm here. I finished up tax season in Boulder and hopped on the first plane. The new business is in Kona and Candy has to be in quarantine in Hilo. It's quite a trek. They don't call this the Big Island for nothing!

Actually, it's not just numbers; I love words, too. I know that some people find a strong vocabulary pretentious. Most people use the same words over and over, especially vulgarities. Hence, there are three acceptable past tense forms for the verb "to shit," not to mention the variety of compound words. I guess "excrementbrain" doesn't have the same impact. Why call someone "an insufferable ignoramus", when you can imply that their feces have traveled to another part of their anatomy?

I didn't quite reach a level of unabashed participation, but something about Kimberly acted to extricate me from my proverbial shell. I felt extremely talkative around her. She struck me as intelligent with a sense of humor in the snippets that she added to the conversation.

The truth of it is that I had a wonderful time talking to Kimberly. Yes, she spent a good deal of time checking me out. I couldn't maintain steady eye contact. More specifically, I was afraid to look and afraid she'd stop. There was something kind of unsettling about it. Women have given me the once over before, but not like this. She was appraising me the way I usually look a woman over. When a femme is interested, she drops subtle hints. She showers you with sweet talk. She brushes up against you and giggles at your most moronic jokes.

I guess Kimberly is a butch, but a borderline butch. She carries a purse and some sort of amenities bag, for one thing. Yet, she does have a bit of a butch swagger and some I'm-in-charge-bravado. I didn't know exactly what to make of her attention, but it felt very nice.

I teased her about the trashy het novel. She blushed. I had to shove my free hand in my pocket to refrain from stroking her face. The real kicker was when her leg fell asleep. She tumbled against me and we looked at each other. I was out of control and I had to kiss her. I was planning a chaste little peck on the lips. Kimberly messed up that notion in spades. She separated my lips with hers and wriggled her tongue into my mouth.

I sprung into action. I had her against the wall. I had my leg between hers. I was the top – wasn't I? She had her hand on the small of my back and her tongue alternated between pumping against mine and gently tracing the inside of my lips. I usually follow a strict mathematical formula for how far I'll go on any given date, but I had visions of ripping off all her clothes and doing her right in the doggy run. When we opened our eyes and looked at one another, I could tell that she was sharing those thoughts. I don't know the etiquette about all of this, but if two women are going to wrestle for who's on top, I say it best be done without concrete, chain link fence and dog hair.

If we'd gone into the woods near the kennel or consummated this in the car, it would be almost over by now. Always one for gallantry, instead, I invited her to dinner. I'm meeting her in half an hour at an Italian restaurant.

Gas is seventeen cents a gallon cheaper on this side of the island, so I told her I'd meet her at the restaurant at around 5:00, after I got a fill-up. I've never intentionally stood anyone up, but I've been toying with the idea for the past ten minutes. I can't even put my finger on what it is about her. Actually, it's everything. She's an artist; her world is colorful. I'm an accountant; my world is black and white.

As easy as not showing up sounds, I have to go. I'm tingling from head to toe. I've never been much for substances, but I imagine that this is what an addict feels like. I worry that she can't possibly be good for me, but I must indulge. I need to have more of her.

Candy

What an experience! Bart left me in a god-awful cell in Honolulu for two days and then I was carried back to the airport. I was hoping we were going back to Colorado and all of this nonsense was over, but here I am in an upgraded jail. When I got to Hilo airport, two tough women dragged my carrier into a van. I thought I was being kidnapped. They looked a little like some friends of Bart's who drive trucks. It seems, however, that I was just being transferred.

Bart was in and out today. When I woke up after my afternoon nap, Rainbow let me know that her owner and Bart had something going on. Poor Bart! If she were one of us, she'd scratch her skin raw. She's always anxious about something or other. I have to admit that I'm not exactly the calmest creature, myself.

Rainbow says they kissed. Maybe Rainbow tells tall tales. Bart never does that before the third date . . . unless the rules are different in Hawaii.

I wonder what Rainbow's owner is like. She sounded OK.

She talks to Rainbow in a really normal tone, not all dorky like the way Bart talks to me half the time.

They say owners are like their pets. I bet Kimberly is funny. Rainbow is hilarious. She told me that she used to think that all Americans were gay because all Kimberly's American friends in Japan were. Rainbow was born in some Japanese heterosexuals' apartment, but the crowd she hung with changed dramatically when Kimberly bought her. She said, when Kimberly's brother visited, she wondered where his boyfriend was. It turned out he had a wife and two kids.

Rainbow's got more international experience than I do, but she's pretty provincial in her own way. She thought the airplane she came over on from Japan was a big ugly car. I had to set her straight on a lot of those details.

I've spent most of the evening thinking about Bart and Kimberly. Bart did leave in an awful hurry. I hope she brings some good snacks back with her tomorrow.

Kimberly

I managed to wash my face and comb my hair at the mall bathroom. I got to the restaurant ten minutes early, hoping to be seated when she came in, but she'd gotten there first. I figured that I had the long ride back alone in the dark to look forward to, so I drank ginger ale. We were getting stiffer, rather than more comfortable around one another. I didn't exactly understand it. We talked about the restaurant. They had a collection of antique toys at this place.

After we'd exhausted the surroundings, we fell upon a lengthy silent period. I knew we hadn't run out of things to talk about, but I think the temptation of crossing into very personal discussions was high and we were treading carefully.

To break the silence, she came up with "So, Kimberly, what's your last name?"

"Scott," I told her. She was swilling a slug of domestic beer around her mouth, as if it were a fine French wine, at the moment. She seemed to be contemplating my name.

"I know," I offered. "It sounds like a merger between the major toilet paper manufacturers."

That cracked her up. She started laughing and I had to duck to avoid the beer spray. I liked the idea of loosening her up a bit, but my name's a sore subject. I would love to have a more exotic name, like something Slavic, ending in the matronymic – ova, like Martina.

"Your name sounds sophisticated . . . it suits you," she finally said . . . to her fork.

I felt bad for her. Shyness and minimal eye contact like hers would be a real liability for a butch on the make . . . or did some women eat that up? OK, there was me. She certainly had my attention . . . and since when did I give it to a woman like her? I flashed back to the way she'd pressed up against me in the kennel. I guess she lost her shyness at pivotal moments. I shifted in my chair. I figured the polite thing was to ask her for her full name, even though the sneak peek at her dog's chart had given me all that information.

"And what's Bart short for?"

"Marilyn Bartlett."

"Does anyone call you 'Marilyn'?" She reddened at that. I wasn't sure what to make of it. I figured it out – even decades after her death, Marilyn Monroe was a sexual icon and the name carried that nuance. I had, in fact, had those thoughts about her voice. "Let me rephrase: does anyone call you that outside the bedroom?"

She reddened further, which I had not thought possible, and then said quietly, "My mother".

"How about you? Does anyone call you Kim?" she asked.

"Well . . . not fully dressed."

"Do you always flirt so shamelessly, Kimberly?"

I had her attention and the eye contact was there. I shook my head slowly.

We didn't talk much throughout the meal. I managed several dozen bites of something with a red sauce and something else in pesto, but I was hungry for yet another taste sensation. I contemplated telling her that, but I didn't want to have to peel her off the restaurant walls. I sensed trepidation in her and I was prepared to find a dark corner and see to my own needs before the drive back around the island.

We stood in the parking lot for what felt like an eternity. Finally, she put her arms around me. I expected a little peck goodnight. Instead, she enveloped me in a bear hug; she whispered in my ear that she wanted me to follow her back to the little cottage that she was staying at.

"You da butch," I said in my best jive talk. All right, so she was in charge for the moment. When it came to the actual performance, we'd find out whose whatever went where, when. I followed her car past the street leading to the kennel until we got to a residential area on the edge of the water.

After showing me the various nooks of the one-bedroom cottage, she put KLUA FM on the radio in the living room and we swayed to a series of romantic numbers that the hets were dedicating to one another that evening. Ordinarily, I would have been grossed out, but my mind was not on my politics. I know what you're thinking, but trashy heterosexual romances are entirely different!

We had a steady rhythm going, so we just kept moving right through the chatty love song request phone calls and contest announcements. I was pretty tired of dancing and figured she felt the same way, but stopping meant someone had to make the next move.

Not known for my patience, I reached for her belt buckle. She got the message and maneuvered us into the bedroom. We rolled around on top of the Hawaiian quilt, tugging at each other's clothing. Naked at last, we kissed and caressed one another's nipples to puffy points. I trailed my tongue between her breasts, down her stomach and kept going. I felt the muscles in her stomach and thighs tighten beneath me as I reached the reddish fringe. The view was spectacular. I was glad that the lights were still on from the nickel tour of the place. I broke my trail momentarily to get myself closer to the foot of the bed.

"What are you doing?" she groaned.

"Going down on you . . . Marilyn."

Rainbow

Kennel life gets kind of lonely after dark. Nell, the Irish Setter who was in Candy's space before, was a night owl, so we used to confer. She got sprung two days ago. It's not even 9:00 and Candy is already chasing rabbits in her sleep. That is, if she's lucky. That's my favorite dream.

I think I finally stopped having that nightmare where I'm on a leash and the Nakamuras' snooty calico cat lunges at me spitting and hissing. Maybe that's more of a flashback, since it actually happened several times back in Kobe.

It's hard to sleep without Kim, although she is a pillow hog. I tried counting treats, Pup-Peroni, T-Bonz, MilkBones, chicken-basted rawhides, beef-basted rawhides pig's ears, cow's hooves . . . I spent so much time trying to remember what the carrot and string bean flavored chews were called in Japan that I got myself all wound up again. Kim brings lots of stuff when she visits. I guess she feels guilty about leaving me here. It's hard on her, too. Gee, I wonder what Kim is doing right now.

Bart

I let my hips move in rhythm with her tongue. Damn, it felt delightful. I couldn't remember the last time I'd had sex like this. Nora and I had broken up a year ago. There had been a short-lived thing with Eileen, but nothing like this. Was it because I barely knew her? Was this why some people were so into anonymous sex? We were still virtual strangers, yet I was grinding my vulva into her face.

I also couldn't recall being number one to bat. She joked about my being "the butch", but she hadn't opted for me to service her first. I was further confused as she dragged her nails across my ass. Way too long for a traditional butch – was she a butch in femme's clothing or a femme in butch's clothing? Hell if I could figure it out; at the moment she wasn't even wearing clothing. I was way beyond being able to do the math. In any event, she certainly knew what she was doing.

I could feel myself approaching the point of no return. She reached up and pinched my nipple. I heard myself cry out . . . over and over again.

"You sound exquisite, Marilyn," she pronounced.

She had already needled me about my vocabulary. I doubted that she had ever used the word "exquisite" in bed. She was asserting her control over me. I don't know why I felt so competitive, but I flipped her faster than an omelet at the mercy of a master chef's wrist. I rubbed up against her; I tongued every inch of her upper body. I ran my fingers teasingly through her damp mons. I returned the favor. I nibbled at her, I flicked my tongue against her hardened bulb and felt her legs tighten beneath me.

"Eat me, Marilyn. Oh, yeah, just like that."

I'll eat you, Kim, like nobody's ever eaten you before. I slid two fingers inside her. She bucked. Lapping and sucking, I worked her clit over. The pitch of her whimpers became higher and higher. I tickled the back of her knee with my free hand. She rocked more furiously. I increased my pace. I was licking her so intensely that I was getting dizzy myself. She held her breath for a few seconds. I held mine. Was she going to pass out? Maybe I was the one who was going to faint . . .. The silence was followed by a medley of shrieks.

After most of the quaking subsided, I pulled her small body up and held her to my chest. I rubbed my face against her. Her lips sought mine and we kissed and necked for hours.

I woke up at 4:00 a.m. Damn the jetlag. I slipped out from under her and sat in the living room for a while. I realized that I was shaking. I have my rules – granted, sometimes I break my rules. Usually, I don't break so many at the same time. I won't minimize it; the sex was stellar. There's a lot to be said for this butch on butch thing. What could be better than two women who both aim to please? On the other hand, living in a constant state of nausea was not a viable option for me. I was nervous and overwhelmed.

Truth be told, I had enough on my plate. I had just moved across the ocean to the fiftieth state. I had a new business partner to impress. My dog was confined to a cell that was a hundred and twenty winding miles away from my farm and office. The five-hour drive back and forth in the car to see her on a regular basis would sap enough of my strength for the coming month – and then there was Kimberly. It was too much to deal with – what had made me saw the top off this can of worms? Since when did I think with my clit?

I was overwrought with culpability. Jewish and Catholic friends could never understand how a WASP could work up as much self-flagellating guilt as I could. I stood up and walked back to the bed. Kim looked particularly angelic asleep underneath the quilt. It was hard to silently lambast her as my temptress, gazing at this celestial countenance. I shuddered and shook my head in an attempt to grasp what was going on here.

I decided to get some air. I drove to the Safeway and picked up some morning pastries. As I cruised the aisles of the supermarket, I made a long list of why this relationship couldn't work. It started with the way none of it made sense and how we were all wrong for one another. It ended with how we'd just jumped into bed barely even knowing one another. I had it all planned. We'd have coffee and talk. We'd decide to cool it and be friends. After all, our dogs were next to one another in quarantine. We had to be civil about this.

I tiptoed back in. Just as I set the groceries down on the table, she pounced on me out of nowhere. She knocked the wind out of me and one of the bags tipped over. Bent at the waist against the table, I thought about her references to her years in Japan. She obviously had mastered some martial art that lets small people overwhelm us larger folks in a single bound. Her breath was hot against my ear. She had washed her face and I could feel her damp skin through my shirt. "I missed you, Marilyn," she whispered. She was a panther and I was her prey. She pushed against me and I could feel her pump the logic right out of my body.

"I need a shower, Kim," I complained, in a voice much smaller than I remembered my own.

"Take me to the shower, Marilyn," she purred. Off we went, with her clinging to my back like a small child. I almost expected her to say *whee*.

It was a stall shower and we seemed to be at 97 per cent capacity as she dismounted and we got in together. I was aware of her fondling my ass as I adjusted the temperature and turned on the shower. I turned and glanced down at her. With my eyes open and my tired brain functioning once more, I was the one with more innate strength. I lifted her up against the wall, so her feet didn't touch the ground and I held her there with my upper torso against her. She hugged my neck and spread her legs.

I grabbed the bar of soap. It was a fancy olive oil-based cake I had splurged on at the health food store. I rubbed it against her clit and she gasped. "I'm going to clean you up really good, Kim."

"Don't you mean 'well', Marilyn?" she asked.

"If you can still think about grammar, I'm not having the effect on you that I thought!" I let the bar fall to the floor and I began to draw sudsy circles with my thumb. I could barely feel her weight as I held her up against the wall. I must have been pumping adrenaline to beat the band. My head was between her breasts. I found a nipple and got my teeth around it. She was wailing by this time. I felt her nip at the back of my neck. I wanted her to give it up for me. Was the soap and water slowing down the friction? I took my mouth from her breast and separated our upper bodies. I didn't miss a beat as I strummed that soapy mound. I could see her eyes rolling back in her head. "That's it, Kim. I want to see your face when you come . . . take your time. I like having you out of control, up against a wall. After all, I'm 'da butch'," I teased. I saw her muscles clench and she rocked and shuddered against the wall.

I let her slide down, but I held onto her. As I suspected, her legs barely worked. I felt unusually proud of myself. If I had had feathers, I might have strutted. It was at least two orgasms later when I remembered that I had come back to break it off with her.

Candy

I paced back and forth in my area. Where was Bart? I know dogs aren't supposed to be able to tell time, but I knew Bart was late. I focused in on her with my canine ESP. People just think dogs are intuitive, but I see things happening even when I'm not right there. For example, I know when Bart is headed my way in her car. Miles before she gets to me, I can see her looking in the rearview mirror and wrinkling her nose the way she does.

I concentrated. All of a sudden I could see Bart clearly. She was sprawled across a bed sideways. She wasn't wearing any clothes. Someone was on top of her. Bart was groaning.

I barked, involuntarily, at the thought of someone hurting Bart. Bart was sweating. Her head was listing back and forth. I tried to zero in on this place. Why couldn't Bart call for help? "Oh, lord, oh, no, oh, Kim . . ." *Kim?* I marched over to the corner of the cell and took several laps of water. The realization had made my throat dry. Bart was in big trouble, all right. Bart was doing it with Rainbow's mistress. Did Rainbow know about this?

I wanted to tune Bart out now, but ESP isn't like TV. I was forced to watch it. Bart's head was dangling over the edge of the bed. Her legs were shaking. *When are you coming, Bart? When are you coming? You're late, Bart! When are you coming!*

"I'm coming," Bart screamed. That was a relief. Bart had finally heard me. Why wasn't she getting up? Her legs were sticking up in the air. Was she playing dead? That Kimberly creature was grinning at her. *Be careful, you idiot! Don't let Bart fall off the edge of the bed!*

Kimberly was now licking Bart's face. Bart seemed a whole lot more interested than when I do it. Hmpf. *Jeez, Bart. What have you gotten yourself into?* I was suddenly really tired. Humans are just too weird to deal with without a good nap. I hunkered down on the fluffy mat and sighed. *Bart, you've really gone to the people!*

NIGHTMARE ON EASTER ROAD PART I

Marjory Smith

Mantha drew her legs under her in the bed to try and warm her toes and feet, as she watched the shadows of leaves on her bedroom wall, and imagined being a tiger. Edinburgh was too cold, and miserable at this time of year. In the height of summer, it could be the same. Oh, yes, this was the height of summer, she remembered and pondered the cold misery around her.

Suddenly the room was illuminated as her flatmate stood at the open door. "Your friend is on the phone."

Mantha groaned and emerged slowly from the voluminous covers. Slipping on her dressing-gown, she ran downstairs to the phone.

"I'm here!" said the voice on the phone. "I'm back from Durham!"

"What? You've been in Durham? I didn't even know you were away."

"I thought you'd be missing me!" said the voice of Ray with an uncharacteristic ingratiating edge to it.

Ho ho, thought Mantha, what does she want? But also she couldn't help feeling pleased that Ray was trying to be nice. She was usually just trying.

"I hardly see you when you're here so I miss you, then; it makes no difference that you're in Durham," said Mantha, then quickly added, before Ray would decide to take offence, "Are you wanting to see me?"

"Three o'clock at the café."

"OK."

So at three o'clock that afternoon, Mantha was walking into one of the gay cafés. Ray was sitting waiting for her, looking depressed and depressing as was her wont.

"So what were you doing in Durham?" Mantha asked.

"I went back with a woman I met in the pub."

"What? All the way to Durham? You're joking. You're insane," Mantha laughed.

"Nuh, and yes," Ray said unsmiling. "Are you going to buy me a cup of coffee?"

Ray's beautiful almond-shaped eyes followed Mantha as she went for coffees. Ray was determined to be miserable most of the time. Doggedly determined. She saw herself as a very tragic figure, frequently proclaiming to anyone who would listen that she had a death wish. A person with a death wish who patently and incessantly failed to die. (People had been known to offer to do the job for her.) But this only added to her self-perceived aura – more disappointment and failure, more tragedy, more drama. More crap.

Mantha had found out recently that Ray had been the French revolutionary leader, Danton, in a previous life. She had come across a picture in a history book and recognised her beloved's features immediately. Mantha had been fascinated to read of Ray's exploits as the "huge and whoring" one who was described as "free-loving and free-spending . . . a powerful, dissolute, probably corrupt, but immensely talented revolutionary more moderate than he looked." Mantha indeed recognised some of Ray's personality in this description. Now her only worry was "What did I do in the revolution?", for she felt that she too must have been there. She did realize that being guillotined at the order of Robespierre may have had a detrimental and untoward effect upon Ray, even a couple of centuries later, and therefore Mantha tended to be more understanding of her foibles than others who did not know The Truth.

Ray/Danton sipped her coffee and regarded Mantha dispassionately, enjoying to the full the power she undoubtedly had over this woman. Mantha. The type of woman who got personally involved in cat-fights. I mean between actual cats, of the feline persuasion. She would run out, shouting, "Leave that cat alone!" at another, rather startled, member of the same species. She couldn't help it. She couldn't help a lot of things. A creature of impulse, she suffered. She didn't know what she was doing. Her emotions were mangled. And Ray did so enjoy mangling them further, whenever she could.

The hazel eyes of Ray looked over into Mantha's grey-blue ones. The warm eyes wrung Mantha's heart. Ray wouldn't sleep with her any more. Ray did not express affection in any physical way – in fact, never really had – so Mantha was left to wonder, what was it all about? Was this woman a dyke or was she a doughnut? Yes, she was a doughnut. That was the only conclusion that Mantha could reach. So why was Mantha in love with a doughnut? A question none could answer. She couldn't help it.

Tina turned her key in the lock and walked back into the flat. Home. Quiet and warm with friendly green plants welcoming her in the hallway. How glad she was to be home.

She walked into the sitting-room to see her lover Mandy, who was sitting puzzling over something she was writing as the TV (television, not transvestite) chattered in the background. Mandy looked up and gazed at Tina with love, awe and respect, a half-smile coming to the edges of her mouth. For Mandy, the sun really did shine from the orifice at the bottom of Tina's back.

Didn't Tina know it. She looked down at Mandy in the full knowledge of the feelings she instilled in her. But she loved Mandy, too. She nursed her feelings for Mandy now, deep inside herself. They murmured hello to each other. They had a communication problem. All they could do was make love.

Mandy jumped up but Tina raised a hand to stop her. "Turn up the heat," she said. "I want to take off every stitch."

"Off you or me?" asked Mandy.

"Both of us," said Tina as she began untying the laces of her boots.

Mandy breathed a sigh. Soon Tina stood absolutely naked. Mandy looked at her beautiful body; she was so turned on already at the sight of her beautiful Tina. Mandy reached out and smoothed her open palm over Tina, feeling and so softly squeezing. Tina turned around from folding her clothes and folded herself into Mandy's open arms. "I love you," she said softly.

"Ohh," groaned Mandy in the back of her throat, "I love you, too."

Now they were kissing lovingly and sensually, lost in their passion.

The doorbell rang.

They parted their mouths and gazed at each other in horror. The doorbell rang again, this time swiftly followed by a sharp rapping of the letterbox.

"It's f–ing Ray," said Tina. Ray was Tina's best friend, so Tina would let her in. She slung on a towelling robe as Mandy pulled on leggings and a top.

"What the hell do you want? You really pick your bloody moments," snarled Tina as she opened the door.

"I'm sorry," said Ray, looking a bit sheepish and feeling embarrassed. "I didn't mean to interrupt anything."

"Well, you did," said Tina, looking witheringly at Ray before turning on her heel and striding off down the hall.

Ray followed after a moment's hesitation. You never really knew where you were with Tina, no matter how long you'd known her.

"You want coffee?" asked – or, rather, announced – Tina from the kitchen as Ray stepped tentatively into the sitting-room and sat down in an armchair. Mandy smiled at her. Ray blushed, trying not to look at where Mandy's T-shirt was sticking out. Ray shuffled in her seat. She would've taken out a cigarette but she knew Mandy hated them and Tina was trying to stop.

Tina returned and handed cups to Ray and Mandy before getting her own and sitting down, not beside her lover. Tina's intimacy was exactly that.

"Well, what do you want?" she said to Ray. Tina was usually this charming to people. She had given Ray a cup of coffee and that was it, as far as she was concerned: that was as polite as she was going to get.

"It's Mantha," said Ray.

Tina's eyes shot heavenwards. "Mantha," she said. Bloody Mantha.

"She's disappeared," said Ray, with a tinge of melodrama.

Tina burst out laughing "What? In a puff of smoke? So where's the champagne? I'd have thought you'd have been celebrating."

Ray looked at her with tears behind her eyes. "Aye, so would I, but I'm not. It isn't funny."

"I think it's hilarious," said Tina, with no sympathy at all. "What the f— do you mean, she's disappeared? How do you know?"

"Well, she's not at her flat and she hasn't been there for weeks. Her parents say they've not seen her. She's just gone. She's gone." Ray began to sob. Was this love for Mantha she'd never before shown or was it merely another chance for Ray to be the emotional centre of attention? Who could say? Probably not even Ray. Tina certainly couldn't, though she herself felt a horrible twinge of inner concern for Mantha.

"What about the pubs?" Tina said. "Hasn't she been seen there at all?"

"I don't know," said Ray, looking up.

"Well, let's go there tonight and ask people if they've seen her."

So that night saw them trooping off downtown to the gay bars where they did not find the answers they were searching for. Mantha had not been seen there since the last time she'd been out with Ray when they'd argued spectacularly as usual.

Mantha was at home, she was sleeping, she was dreaming, wasn't she? She flew out of the window into the night and right down the side of Scotland until she came to Edinburgh. She recognized it and laughed as she swooped around. Suddenly she saw Tina and Ray staggering home at the West side of the city. She laughed again and flew fast down, right up into Tina's face. Everything was shining and iridescent, luminous. The air around her was pure magic, under a glamour. Tina thought she was seeing a ghost – and the most beautiful woman she'd ever seen. From that moment on she was haunted when the minutes dragged.

"Hi, Tina!" said Mantha, her spirit shining through her eyes. "Bet you didn't expect to see me here!"

She knows my name! thought Tina.

Mantha laughed. "Bet I get home before you do!" she cried gleefully, and flew up again, bounding in the air, over buildings, quick back to Tina's flat. But of course Tina and Ray were still stotting along at the West End, Tina's mind stunned with the face and voice of the beautiful ghost that had just visited her.

Mantha couldn't be bothered waiting around and flew home while Ray tried to understand what in the heck was wrong with Tina now – and if she'd seen a ghost, why hadn't Ray?

Mantha awoke. Tina had kissed her many times in many dreams, something which she had pushed to the back of her mind and tried to ignore. But there she was, popping right up at the front again, worse than ever. The dream demon. She had flown in the bedroom window in the first one and gotten into Mantha's bed, where she kissed her with the most delicious kissing Mantha had ever had, before telling her, "Don't tell me that this is better than anything because I can't handle it." Whereupon she got out of the bed and turned into somebody else. Mantha was horrified by the memory when she woke. Gradually she realised that Tina was something she must face and not try to hide from. Distancing herself from Ray was helping this.

You're so funny, you're so sweet and you look good enough to eat.

I love straight hair, silky soft straight hair, I want to feel it falling through my fingers.

I want to feel it everywhere.

I want to feel your lovely lips, taste your lips, silky soft too, your lovely lips which look like they're just ready to suck something. Something on me hopefully.

You love life, your appetites are strong. You love food, you love drink, you love women. Will you love me too? Are you this good at everything you do?

The following Thursday afternoon, Tina got off work early and was sitting alone in her sitting-room when the phone rang.

"Hello," she snapped into the receiver.

"Tina." Mantha's voice stung through Tina's body. "Listen, I've got to see you."

"What? Where are you? Where have you been?" Tina asked urgently.

"I've been thinking," said Mantha. "Don't tell anyone you've heard from me."

"Thinking? That makes a bloody change. Don't be stupid, of course I'll 'tell anyone'! Ray's really upset."

"Oh, aye," Mantha was sarcastic.

"No, she is; she does care about you really," Tina tried to assure her.

"Well, I don't feel the same any more," said Mantha. "I'm sick of how she acts to me."

"Yeah, she's a pig." Tina had to agree. "But what're you phoning me for?"

"I told you. I've got to see you. I want to talk to you."

Tina smelt a rat, got ratty and slightly rattled. "You're talking to me now, aren't you? What is it?"

"I can't say over the phone."

Tina breathed deeply and attempted to keep her irritation with Mantha under control. She failed. "Don't be so bloody ridiculous! You're not a spy! Tell me, Mantha, or I'll come and f—ing make you!"

"You don't know where I am, and anyway . . ."

The apoplectic resemblance to Basil Fawlty which Mantha incurred in Tina was coming fully to the fore once again as she interrupted Mantha's comments. "I don't care where you are!" she shrieked. "I'll find you! I don't care if you're out in the middle of the sea, I'll get a boat and paddles and row out and batter f— out of you there!"

Mantha laughed, as she took this in the jovial spirit in which it was intended (not). But there were few things more amusing than Tina in a rage. "Come on, then," said Mantha. "I do want to see you. That's why I rang."

"I don't know where you are." Tina's brain reeled as she suddenly knew Mantha was not far away, wherever she was. She was trying to keep calm by telling herself, No I do not want to batter this woman, I just want to sleep with her. But that was not actually a calming thought.

"I'm here."

"You're in Edinburgh?"

"Aye."

Half an hour later, they were sitting opposite one another in a straight café. They didn't want to be seen. Or, rather, Mantha didn't.

"Well?" Tina glared aggressively across the table.

"Don't you know?" Mantha began to have her usual infuriating effect. "Can't you guess?"

"No, I can't bloody guess! Just tell me."

"I love you."

Tina stared at Mantha as if she had suddenly gone bright green. For half a minute she was entirely speechless; then she said, "Nuh. That's a nightmare."

Mantha agreed with her absolutely. Tina was her worst nightmare. And also her wildest dream.

They looked at each other across the table and there was

silence for a few minutes. Then Tina decided. "Come on," she said, and got up. Mantha followed her.

Tina had keys for a friend's flat. She always had somewhere to go. So there they went.

Tina spoke softly, telling Mantha they had all night. They looked into each other's eyes and slowly enjoyed the exquisite moments they had both imagined many times. They amazed each other. Finally, they slept in each other's arms.

When clear daylight invaded the room, the next morning, there were questions in the air. They both knew it but neither really wanted to think about them. They decided to leave before Tina's friend came in so they went to a nearby café where they ordered apple tarts and coffee, their eyes meeting in a pool of love.

Suddenly, there was a shout from across the street. Unbelievably, it was Ray. She had spotted them through the window and was now advancing towards the café at speed.

Mantha and Tina gazed at each other in horror. What the hell were they going to do?

Ray sat down at the table. She surveyed the scene and sensed the atmosphere. She was not as stupid as she looked – which was lucky for everyone.

She looked at Mantha. "So where've you been? I've missed you," she said.

Mantha did not consider that the latter remark had an entirely believable ring to it.

Then Ray turned to Tina. "Have you been seeing her all this time? Tea and tarts! Very nice."

"It's coffee, actually," Mantha remarked, causing Ray to pale with impending fury.

"Don't spoil it, Ray," pleaded Tina.

Ray stood up dramatically as the possibilities of how she

could play the part of tragically wronged, betrayed friend and lover began to occur to her. She walked away. She was hurt but oh, yes, she was going to enjoy this to the full. She was getting in the mood already; she would milk it for all it had. This was a good one.

In such ways did Ray successfully confuse herself as well as everyone else as to what her genuine feelings might in fact actually be.

Mantha and Tina looked at each other.

"She'll be all right," said Tina. As indeed she would.

"Just Mandy to go, now," Mantha commented.

The thought of Mandy depressed Tina now. She groaned and said, 'We'll think about that later."

She should have thought about it sooner, because Ray had. She'd just got to the end of the street when the thought occurred to her. Did Mandy know? If she didn't, she soon would, because Ray was going to tell her.

She got on the next bus up to Tina and Mandy's flat and waited outside. She had a long wait but that did not deter her. She could be very enduring when the mood struck.

Eventually Mandy appeared, and frowned at the sight of Ray in obvious full tragic mode, sitting on her doorstep.

"I was going to kill myself," said Ray, predictably, "but then I thought I owed it to you to tell you."

Oh Christ, thought Mandy, turning her key in the lock. "Look, Ray, Tina's not here," she said.

"Aye, I know," said Ray, her eyes connecting dramatically with Mandy's. "That's why I'm here. I've seen her."

"What? What's wrong? Has something happened to Tina?" Mandy asked worriedly. They walked into the flat.

Ray looked at Mandy. "She was with Mantha," she said, and her meaning was clear.

Suddenly they heard the purr of a car engine and Tina's

tomcat Kelvin sprang to the windowsill, recognizing the return of his beloved Tina.

Tina turned her key and walked in to be greeted by two tense, grim faces. She walked into the kitchen and put on the kettle. "Everyone want coffee?" she called.

"F— coffee!" shouted Mandy. "You been with Mantha?"

Tina walked to the door. "Thanks," she said to Ray.

"Think nothing of it," said Ray.

Tina looked at Mandy. "I'm lovers with Mantha," she said.

Mandy sank to the floor, screaming, and Tina scowled.

Ray got up and announced she had to leave.

Tina was irritated. "Stop screaming, Mandy," she said. "You're frightening my cat."

Mandy cried on.

"Right, that's it," said Tina. "I'm taking Kelvin into the bedroom or you get in the bedroom now; cause I'm not sleeping with you tonight."

"Stop going on about Kelvin," said Mandy. "It's just an excuse."

"No, it's not an excuse, it's a reason. And if you frighten my cat again, I'll kill you."

Mandy screamed.

"Stop screaming, Mandy!!" screamed Tina.

Mandy stormed off to the bedroom. But she soon came back.

"I think we've both forgotten something," she said, grinning fiendishly. "This is my house."

Tina scowled.

Three weeks later, Mantha was moving in, struggling through the door with her cat, Sparko, in a basket.

"Come on, darling," Tina smiled happily, helping Mantha with her things. She frowned quizzically at the sounds emanating from Sparko's cat basket. Kelvin's ears pricked up and he raised his head as he lay on the windowsill. Mantha opened the door of the basket, and Sparko emerged. His eyes met Kelvin's immediately and the atmosphere became electric. Kelvin leapt to all fours, his back arched.

Sparko gazed in amazement at the handsome orange and white stripey tomcat before him. How handsome, he thought.

Kelvin was shocked and in wonder. Sparko had black fur round his eyes which looked like he had kohl make-up on. What kind of tomcat was this?

"Prrt?" asked Sparko. "Prr, prrt?" He was very friendly and eager to become acquainted with this lovely specimen. He advanced towards the windowsill. Kelvin just about fell off it.

Tina and Mantha looked at each other.

"Let's just leave them to it," said Tina as she and Mantha turned towards the bedroom.

An hour later Sparko and Kelvin were sleeping peacefully, curled together in a chair.

THE MYSTERIES OF THE PSITTICINE ORGASM

Thea Bennett

Today, my best friend and loving companion of eight years was taken away in a box.

OK, it was a cardboard box with airholes in the top, and I know it's for the best and it's what she wants; it will make her happy and we'll both be the better for it. But I'm heartbroken and I don't know what to do with myself. How can I go back now to an empty, silent house? With no shrieks of joy to greet me, no passionate French kisses, no welcoming improvisations on the theme of "hello"?

Perhaps I should explain. For the last eight years, my life has been lived firmly under the wing of a bird. I have shared my heart and my home with a cockatoo. My own beloved Poppy. A winged demon, a loving nature spirit, a gremlin, a mimic, a tyrant – a tiny, feathered Tyrannosaur.

When Poppy first came to me, she was just two months out of the egg: a fat, wobbly fledgling still eating baby food from a teaspoon. I suppose she was a sort of substitute child for me and my girlfriend at the time, Anna.

I don't think either of us fully understood the implications of living with a cockatoo. The man in the pet shop told us Poppy was a "corker". We didn't really really know what he meant, but we thought she looked very cute. A tubby white pigeon-sized bird, with a white crest which when raised looked like an exclamation mark. Her bright brown eyes, popping out of her head with excitement as she looked at us, were circled with eyeshadow-blue skin and on each cheek was a glow of pink feathers, like hurriedly applied rouge. As she flapped her wings, bobbing up and down to attract our attention, we could see the vivid lemon-yellow feathers underneath them. And as soon as we tried to turn our backs on her, she wooed us back with squeaky cries of "Hello!" How could we leave the shop without taking her with us?

From the very first, Poppy dominated the household. She ate our chairs, demolished our light fittings (luckily without burning the place down), snipped the metal bits off our bras and threw our dinners on the floor, all to the accompaniment of loud shouts of "Hello!", "What do you think you are doing?" and "Stop that this minute!" She sat on our faces while we slept and shat on our clothes regularly every fifteen minutes while we were awake.

Despite all this, I loved the bird. I just couldn't resist her remarkable charisma, her deep affection and her irresistible comedy. I wish I could say the same about Anna. Under Poppy's onslaughts, my lover rapidly lost her charm, her sense of humour and her sex drive, and within the year she had gone off with another woman. From then on, it was just me and Poppy.

I was a willing victim. Arriving home in the evening to Poppy's screams of pleasure was heartwarming. When I opened her cage door, she would scramble out and snuggle between my neck and shoulder, caressing my cheek with soft beak-and-tongue kisses. When the first ecstasies of welcome were over, she would clean my eyelashes delicately with the tip of her large beak, removing my mascara with the same care and precision she gave to preening her feathers.

The passionate delight Poppy took in these intimacies was at least equalled by the sensual pleasure I enjoyed in handling her. Her feathers had the softest, smoothest texture possible. Her tough, flexible feet, covered in grey lizardskin, had a sensitivity and dexterity that almost amounted to intelligence, and their grasp was as appealing as the clutch of a baby's fingers. Her honey-scented breath was the sweetest of any living thing I have ever encountered.

The communication between us was profound. She understood every nuance of my voice, my expression and my behaviour, and from my touch she could pick up my intention and my mood. It was impossible to lie to her, or force her to do something against her will, but with gentleness I could usually persuade her. Sometimes she bit me painfully, either in play or temper, but she would always nibble me gently again afterwards, as if to say: "I forgot myself, this is what I'm really like. We are friends."

If I was ill at home, Poppy would roost on the bedroom door, keeping one beady eye on me all the time and blowing soft kissing noises at me whenever I woke up and turned over. If the weather was fine at weekends, we would sit in the garden and she would cuddle up in my lap and gaze into the sky with an unreadable, ancient look in her amber eye.

All of this made up our relationship, but finally, there was another dimension too. Sex.

Perhaps it just grew naturally out of the sensual interactions between us. Poppy's busy little tongue, constantly tasting and probing the world around her, was like a very small, grey-gloved finger. But, looked at in another way, it also resembled a tiny penis. Curiously, it was almost exactly the same size as my nipples. One day, as we sunbathed in the garden, Poppy discovered them. She nibbled them greedily and then drew back to look at them with her head on one side, as if to say: "Two tongues, indeed! And just look where she keeps them!"

My breasts in general met with Poppy's approval. She liked to squash herself up against them. But then I suppose a bird is just a big bosom on legs, with its soft, rounded, enveloping feathery front. Sometimes, late at night, I would press my cheek against this softness and imagine the bliss of a minute, naked, cockatoo chick, enfolded in such perfect comfort. So perhaps it was natural that Poppy should feel at home with the bits of my front that were soft and round.

Things began to get complicated in the late spring of Poppy's fifth year. She suddenly became more than usually clingy. If I put her down for a moment, she would rush after me like a demented dowager, her pigeon-toed waddle breaking into frantic hops and bursts of anguished flight. Her demands for cuddles and caresses were endless. And then I discovered that if stroked her vent (a discreet smile-shaped orifice that served her for all functions "down there") her bright eyes would glaze over and she would experience a violent spasm. Before long, I would only have to pull her tail to drive her into a passionate succession of orgasms. As her climaxes grew more intense, her body became rigid with pleasure and she would start clucking loudly like a crazed chicken. I would stop then, partly from concern for her health and partly (especially if we were in the garden) out of fear that the neighbours would hear her. (Something I never worried about with Anna, even at our noisiest.) For Poppy could shudder through climax after climax for as much as half an hour at a time.

All this was our secret. Perhaps Poppy would have had no qualms about discussing my technique if she had had any feathered friends to gossip with. But I felt strangely ashamed and shy about it. After all, are birds supposed to have orgasms? Are people supposed to have sex with birds?

After Anna left, this was often the only sex I had. Poppy's passionate attachment to me meant that it was difficult to spend an evening away from home. I couldn't forget that she was sitting in her cage longing for me to return. And if I ever brought a potential lover home with me, Poppy's burning jealousy made any sort of physical contact between us impossible – her shrieks of rage and evil glares deterred even the boldest of women from cuddling up with me on the sofa.

One great-hearted girl did manage to stay in my life for a few months. Maureen, who worked as a policewoman, was a passionate animal lover, and refused to be repelled by Poppy's poisonous glances and barbed remarks. She was determined to win over my recalcitrant bird, even to the extent of allowing herself to be bitten several times without yelling in pain.

But I think the real secret of Maureen's success with Poppy was the size of her breasts. Maureen was very generously endowed, and it was just too hard for Poppy to resist such an expanse of comfort. Soon, she would ignore me and jump on to Maureen, snuggling up and running her beak back and forth along the edges of Maureen's substantial brassière. Maureen was flattered at first, but when Poppy had to be forcibly prised off her and locked in her cage, the cries of rage that followed us up to the bedroom proved very inhibiting. Even worse were the groans which drifted eerily up the stairs as Poppy echoed our attempts at love-making.

Four months into our relationship, Maureen telephoned one evening. I was in the bath and rushed to pick up the phone, lying naked and damp on the bed. Poppy flew across the room to join me, sitting on my bare belly.

"I think it's time we finished," Maureen was saying. Poppy was looking disapprovingly at my pubic hair and, deciding that I would be better off without it, she suddenly started trying to pluck the hairs out. I squealed with pain and then burst out laughing at the absurdity of it.

"Why are you laughing?" Maureen asked, clearly very hurt that I was responding in this flippant way to her news. I told her what was happening. "Yes," said Maureen, "that's exactly my point. I just can't handle it. You and that bird are just too weird." And that was that. I never saw her again.

Eventually, things had to change. It wasn't so much the lack of human lovers that was getting me down, though that was often hard – but I found that while at work I was worrying about Poppy on her own all day. She was starting to show signs of stress and boredom, and was pulling out her feathers. My vet advised me that she was reaching the age of sexual maturity (as if I didn't know it), and that I should think about getting a mate for her. I put his advice on the back burner, not wanting to commit myself. But then a very interesting job offer came up for me. Deputy art editor on a quality magazine. Long hours, heavy responsibility and lots of hassle, but the kind of hassle that I thrive on. With jobs, as with pets, I prefer the more difficult and challenging. I had a gut feeling that I had to do it. So I went back to my vet.

He seemed very pleased to see me. "I've been thinking about you," he said. "I think I've found a cock bird for your cockatoo. You can get him very cheaply; the owners are keen to get rid of him. Far too noisy and aggressive for them."

Suddenly, the reality of it hit me. I was about to force my dearest friend into a relationship, which might not be up her street at all. I didn't exactly tell the vet about the full extent of my relationship with Poppy, but I told him I was worried that she might be fixated on human beings, specifically me, and that she might not take too kindly to another bird invading her space. I also added that I would prefer to get her a female companion.

He gave me a long, thoughtful look. "Maybe," he said, eventually. "But Goffin's cockatoos, which is what you've got, are now getting rare in the wild. And that means two things. One, we must take every opportunity to reproduce the species, and two, a healthy female bird is at a premium and will cost you five times as much as an unwanted male like the one I had in mind for you. So think carefully. If you take him, you would be doing the right thing by him, because he's in a very bad situation right now – and you would definitely be doing the right thing ecologically. And as for your bird, I think you must give her the chance to reproduce, as she's clearly ready to. Let her make her own mind up about her future."

So I did what a responsible parrot-owner should do and I got Poppy a boyfriend of her own kind so that she wouldn't be lonely any more and she could raise some chicks and ensure the survival of her species.

I couldn't help falling for Bingo as soon as I saw him. It was his large, mournful black eyes. In complete contrast to Poppy, he was and slow and clumsy with years of living in the small cage from which I rescued him. Perhaps his owners had named him Bingo because they bought him with their winnings. They must have loved him to have kept him so long, for his nervousness made him impossible to handle, and his ear-splitting, unpredictable shrieks of loneliness and frustration were unbearable. I hated to think of his long years of incarceration, and I wasted no time in reaching a price with them and taking him home with me.

Poppy loathed him at first sight. She swore viciously at him and at me when I introduced them to each other. Bingo had none of Poppy's agility and confidence. He pursued her ardently around the aviary I had built for them, but he just couldn't catch her. She retreated to the furthest corner, looking daggers at him and at me. If he tried to get too close, she fluffed up to the size of a dinner plate and told him off in her most raucous tones, waving her exclamation-mark of crest at him like an admonitory finger. Perhaps, after so long in my exclusive company, Bingo's maleness and his uncompromising identity as a bird were just not right for her.

Whatever her feelings, I could spare no time to worry over her. I had started my new job, and was drawn into a whirlwind of work and social activity. Waking and sleeping, I was consumed with new ideas, new projects, new people. I fed Poppy and Bingo in the morning, and at night I was pleased to see that, however bad their relationship had been during the day, when dusk fell there was a truce and they always roosted together on the same perch. Things seemed to be settling into a workable routine for all of us, the months passed, and suddenly I realised Bingo had been with us for two years.

Then, the unthinkable happened. Poppy fell in love. First, I noticed that she was not so keen for my attention in the mornings. One Saturday, after a particularly demanding week at work, I felt in need of a cuddle and went to get her out for a few moments. She turned her back on me when I went into the aviary, and bit me when I went to pick her up. Bingo watched with great interest.

Just a few days later, I found the two of them sitting side by side in the daytime and I knew that a sea change was on the way.

At first, it was very hard for me to take, as I watched Poppy daintily and lovingly preening the feathers on the back of Bingo's neck and I remembered the exquisite gentleness of her touch and her bright, kind eye peering into mine as she used to sit on my shoulder.

But, watching the slow development of their relationship, I realized the appropriateness of what was happening. A cockatoo marriage is intense and passionate and deeply sensual. Poppy now had someone who wanted to look at her every minute of the day, touch her whenever possible, be involved with whatever she was doing, and cuddle up to her at night. To say nothing of many hours of rampant copulation, which Poppy of course, adored. Hardest of all for me was when Bingo started to get macho with her. When I went into the aviary, he would push her away from me, and stand in front of her so I couldn't see her, which she accepted without a murmur.

After a few months of married bliss, I noticed that Poppy was pulling Bingo's feathers out. (Like an amiable fool, he just sat there and let her. Ah, love!) My vet advised me that she was wanting to go to nest and make babies, and that I should provide her with a large hollow tree trunk. The magazine I work for was building up to the launch of a new hair-and-makeup supplement, which I was to have sole responsibility for. Somehow, pastel nail polish and rotten tree trunks just don't mix, and I knew that something would have to give. So I offered Poppy and Bingo to the local wildlife park, and they accepted with alacrity, and provided a very superior aviary with two hollow tree trunks and many other amenities. All too soon today, the day fixed for their departure, arrived. And the birdkeeper turned up with two large boxes to take them off to their new home.

At the time, I didn't feel much emotion. I watched them go, and then I set off for work as usual. The day has passed in a mad muddle of arrangements and arguments and office politics. But now it's 6:30 and I don't want to go home tonight. Leaving work and walking to the tube, I feel heavy and tired and empty. The street smells hot and bitter with car fumes. I could have stayed at my desk, shuffling photographs, making decisions, drinking coffee, but now that I can, I don't want to. There seems no point in going to an empty house. I'm free now; I could go anywhere. So, rather than go down into the underground, I keep walking. Maybe to the next station, or perhaps I'll take a bus. Let go, and just take one step at a time.

In the distance, a tall woman walks towards me. Very tall, long bare legs, long neck. She's beautiful, I find myself thinking. I look at images of beautiful women all day, but this one really has it. Proud, strong, elegant. Every line of her body just right. I find myself exhaling a huge sigh of pure pleasure. She's coming closer. There's something else about her, too. A self sufficiency. A little extra bit of fire, of strength. A certain light defensiveness in her step. Could she be a dyke?

She could be; of course she could. A vision of beauty, power and elegance, striding along the pavement towards me. And then the fantasy that I'm indulging in begins to go a bit wobbly round the edges. The vision of beauty starts to have a slight familiarity. She looks a bit like Rosanna, who worked in the post room for a few weeks last winter. Ah, Rosanna . . . And just as the wires in my brain are beginning to short circuit and I'm teetering on the brink of recognition, we meet face to face on the pavement and she pulls her shades off: and, of course, it is Rosanna.

"Hi," she says.

I'm struggling to hide my confusion and embarrassment. It's somehow not done to have a fantasy about someone you know, who you've drunk coffee with in the kitchen and discussed the weather with. Or tried to.

She's looking at me in a friendly way, with her dark yet brilliant brown eyes. A series of flashbacks of her in the office race through my mind. She was there every day but, somehow, I could never quite break the ice with Rosanna. She disturbed me too much. In an office full of hyper-elegant women, her jeans and dilapidated sweat shirts, the heavy tread of her ex-army boots along the corridor as she delivered the mail left me breathless and ill-at-ease. I must have found her beautiful before. Surely, surely I did. But it was just too hard and too odd and too uncomfortable to break the ice in that environment.

"It's weird seeing you here," she says, letting me off the hook. "I didn't recognize you, out of your space."

The power of speech returns to me in a flood. I can go anywhere, do anything now. So I shall.

"Rosanna," I say. Her name slips out so easily. I don't think I've ever spoken it before. Words tumble out of my mouth: "We're like two people from the same planet. But we've both been away so long, we've forgotten how to talk to each other." I can feel a blush coming on and I look down at the pavement. When I manage to glance up I see that, luckily, she's still looking at me and hasn't sped off down the street.

"And, I didn't recognize you because of your legs. I've never seen you with legs before," I say, trying to smile at her.

She grins and says: "They go all the way up to the top, too."

And suddenly, the ice is broken, and we are looking each other up and down, and arranging to meet for a drink later and I'm taking in the fact that she still is just as carelessly dressed as ever, only in shorts and shades which I've never seen before. And she is, as I saw when she walked towards me out of the distance before I knew it was her, a women of true elegance and beauty and strength that will shine through any garment she might choose to wear.

And later, sitting together in the bar, we don't talk much, because we've discovered the wordless pleasure of touching hands secretly, of sitting side by side and just letting messages pass between us. Messages perhaps from that other planet.

We spend so long silently communicating that, by the time we get back to her room, just around the corner, we don't bother with any smooching, we just get straight down to it on the futon. And that's when things begin to get really crazy. She suddenly gets shy and a bit awkward, and puts her hand between my legs roughly and casually, and the shock of pleasure transfixes my whole body and makes me squeal with joy. It's the fastest orgasm I've ever had, but I'm still hot and wet with desire. My womb feels as if it's on fire. Every time she touches me, and sometimes just before, I come, and each time the pleasure is just as intense.

She's looking doubtfully at me, her brown eyes shadowy in the candlelight. "Is each one of those an orgasm?" she asks.

"Yes," I manage to gasp.

Slowly, her face lights up with joy and excitement. "Wow!" she says. Conversation may never be our strong point. But who cares? She touches me again. Helplessly, I come several more times. Her face is glowing now. "I have never, ever given so much pleasure to anyone," she says.

Later, after I have pulled myself together sufficiently to help her to a powerful, triumphant climax of her own (just the one, but it is a very good one), and she's drifting off to sleep with her cheek buried in my breast, a strange, shivery little thought pops up.

I have given pleasure like that. For months and years I have been giving what she's just given me. Could it be that now it's my turn? Is it some strange twist of that universal law – you get back what you give out?

She's gone out of my life, and even if she were still around I wouldn't be able to get a coherent answer out of her, but I've got a feeling Poppy could have something to do with it. A little thank-you-and-goodbye gift, perhaps?

A FEATHER

Susannah Marshall

A feather, scarce against my hand. Lois gave me it – speckled and pale. The feather – not Lois, though she is pale. Carries a weary tinge. Hollow eyes heavily hooded. She'd found it on her way over to see me. A friendly visit given purpose by the gift. Otherwise, empty hands could have proffered nothing. Not that they didn't want to give. They mimed over and over the motion of giving. Offering their touch to me.

In her dark room when alone, Lois practises this. She likes her room dark – the darkness cleaving to allow only the space of a candle flame. Teardrop-shaped, torn at the top – a jagged minaret.

She gives me her touches there freely. Her cupped hands pare round my empty shape. Hollowed out in the darkness; breasts, hips and thighs. Lois touches them in rehearsal.

The candle wavers inside my outline. Lois burns her finger

tips on the growing warmth. She blows on clawed fingers. Her breath is half felt like shivers through skin.

Her touches I can feel fully, though they are imaginary. Sitting in the chair, she does not stir while we talk, but I watch her stand and walk over to me. She presses her hands to my face and draws me into her kiss, her lips a slight presence.

She sits in her chair talking of something but all the time watches me. Her desire pushes me against the wall. Almost-fingers unbutton my shirt. Her mouth is wet against my stomach.

I sit on the floor facing her, back against my wardrobe, legs crossed. I hold the point of the feather in my left hand and run the slight tip across the palm of my right.

We like to talk of nothing. It interests us to build a night's conversation from a for instance. Solving rarely questions of our own manufacture. We pass nights like this. Building something together with hypothetical words.

I build a bird for my feather. A plumed singer which glides through windy skies. It battles against the gusts bravely but cannot maintain the struggle and sinks wearily to the earth.

It roosts in a tree. An outline tree which is drawn on Lois' window. In her ill-lit room, its shape is traced on the glass like darkness cracking.

The bird roosts in its branches one afternoon. Lois doesn't hear its call. She lies on her bed, possessed by the noise of a full-volumed radio.

She stretches her arms out before her. Her hands search the air: discern first the shapes of a song. A pocked beat. She pokes her finger tips in the hollows of the notes. Then, as the music fills out, her movements become bolder. The shapes she looks for in the air, more vital. My shape. She builds it and doesn't have to stop herself, alone in her room with no one to see her.

She's sketched me. I hang above her. She can gaze with a stare which pin-ups me to the ceiling.

But it's not enough to have an air-filled lover. She wishes she felt the weight of me on top of her and that our touches were real.

We cannot deny the attraction between us. Cannot deny it, but do our best to. It comes with us when we go out and sits like a gooseberry in between. It nags with monotone voice, reminding us not to touch. It tells me to think of something horrible when I look at Lois and want her.

I look at the way her blonde hair turns to dark wisps at the nape of her neck and think how they would tickle my lips, then think of her lips outstretched at some joke. I could suck them back into shape with a kiss – but I don't want her. Honest.

Lois swings her legs off her bed and pulls on her coat. She'll come and see me. She rips my image from the ceiling, ashamed at her thoughts. Friends only. She folds it up carefully, ready for the next time.

Once out of the building, the wind barges against her and blows the frustration from her thoughts. She remembers flying a kite on a similarly windy day. A luminous kite. It hung in the sky like an aura expelled along the string from her breezy heart.

As she passes a tree flimsy in the gusts, a feather tumbles at her shoes. She plucks it with cold fingers. She'll bring it to me and give it because she's able.

In pinched fingers, it shies from the wind and cleaves to the back of Lois' hand. Splayed there, her hand wears it as a curious birth-mark rippled by browns and greys. The mottled veins shoot up her arm, etch her fingers so they look like they're bound with fine thread. A tourniquet tightening – forcing blood from her fingers, out of her arm dabbed with feathers. A concentrate of blood rushes to her heart. Her heart pulses at speed. You can see it beat through her chest.

I found a scrabble of feathers once and picked it up in curved hands and warmed it with my curiosity. I could feel a small-bird heart beating against my skin. The creature pressed to my warmth, weighty with fear. The intermittent pulses panicked against the heel of my hand so it felt like the throb of my own blood through over-wrought veins. I cupped the bird carefully, trying hard to warm it. Its heart beat too fast in its paper body. I grasped a handful of fear and empty feathers.

The wind wants my feather but Lois won't give it. It slithers round her arm. The point pierces her hand. Her blood beats against the wind which shakes shivers from her. She'll give it up only for me.

At least she can give me this. A feather. An almost thing. Almost pretty but not through browns and greys. Almost useful but away from the bird it's redundant. Almost her touch.

She knocks on my door. I'm pleased to see her. I always am. But I'm irritated sometimes. It's not enough just to say "hello" and offer her a drink. I hate her because she knows this but we're both inert with inappropriate feeling. She grins at me, her arm behind her back. She stretches it round. I'm perplexed by her action. She gives me something. A feather. She holds it to me. I laugh. A wonderful gift. I like feathers.

She sits in a chair and tells me about the wind; how it nearly blew the feather away. I see it carried on the currents. A remnant of a bird, flying effortlessly. Enjoying the turbulence.

We wonder where birds go to die. You see some lying dead, but not many. Cats kill some, cold others. I found one in a garden, once, hardly alive. I picked it up but the shock finished it off. Perhaps they die in woods and fields. I see feathers at the base of trees at times. Clotted together and scrambling apart. Killed by a predator, I assume; but perhaps they are a soulless bird – all that remains after death. A heap of feathers.

Lois laughs at me while I talk. I talk a load of rubbish but we like talking about nothings.

But we never talk about the nothings of our touches; the

caresses that never happen. I run the feather across my fingers, tickled by its shadow. It thrills me with its nothingness as it barely touches.

I get up and walk over to Lois. I stand in front of her and reach out with the feather. She says nothing but watches me, her lips parted in doubt. I drag the feather across her lips – the opposite way to the lie of the barbs. They unzip their separate strands of translucent colour. Fine hairs caught against Lois' mouth, should she kiss the top of my head. I pull away and push the feather into her mouth. Wettened, the barbs blend together. Their colours darken. I draw it across Lois' cheek, leaving a trail of her own saliva, like my mouth would if I pressed it against her face.

Though frail, she can't ignore its touch. Her hooded eyes close. She breathes hard, longing for impossible touches to follow the traces of a feather.

VIRTUAL FEMME

Urszula Dawkins

You're under my skin like a layer of wire mesh, under my skin like veins, subcutaneous. Only the texture of you woven into my flesh matters to me at this point, where my blood is all over the sheets and the smell of your fingers is in my mouth and the satin lining rubs my skin from inside. I can't let you in without leaving you a way to get out, and I can't leave you a way to get out without a hole gaping somewhere on my surface.

I can feel you turning my catgut stomach into a bow and playing me like cello. I can feel myself with long hair held up in your hands so you can get to my neck to bite me. I've counted fourteen bites on our bodies, starting at my neck and finishing on your thighs, along with the bruises of my hands and the mark of my claws on you. And heaven knows the damage on the inside, where the flesh is even softer and the blood so much closer to the surface. All four limbs are ready for you; my mouth is open.

Independence

I cook for myself. I pay someone to clean my house. I drive my own car and know how to change a tyre, possibly even a tap washer. When I lost a ring down the shower plug, I had no need of a plumber.

These things are important, part of me and my lust for you as I lie on the banana lounge in your unfamiliar backyard, basking in the sunshine. You ask if I need a pillow and I leap to my feet, scattering the *Saturday Extra* in a flurry of dog paws.

"Stay there," you say, and I protest, and we teeter, a seesaw of generous insistence and firm refusal. Finally, I acquiesce. "Stay there," you say.

Indignant, I sit on the edge of the Lilo and await your return. I feel myself held back by your desire to serve me. Your dog puts his head in my lap. While I wait, I begin to give way, begin to feel restraint prickling through my fur like a set of long fingers. Sometimes when we fuck, you tell me not to move.

I remember you telling me to be still while you raised your head from my flesh like an animal listening for danger, sharp-eared, sharp-toothed, then lowered your bloodied jaws to feed on me again. I trembled under you and tried to move, just to hear you tell me again.

I bite the back of your neck and remember the lamb shank on my mother's roasts. There's gristle in my teeth and I keep biting till the oils are dripping off you. Fresh out of the pan, you're glistening. I take a baked potato into my mouth and burn my tongue, biting through the jacket too quickly. Your gravy is thick and smooth, better than any my mother made, and my mouth is full of boiled peas: scented with mint, crushed on my palate.

* * *

We go through the push-pull of lust, anger and jealousy, hunger and thirst. I punish myself for wanting you, like a ranging wolf imagining you putting your dick where it doesn't belong. I hunger like a dog does, I wait at the back door, I'm all over you with my rough claws recognizing the sheer naturalness of possession – you pat the cat while the dog tries to get into your lap; you feed one and the other's jaws are grinding.

I'm immersed in your black waters, shining in your sun, your smile, your bare head, your jewels flashing. The deep desires, the fears, necessity's bodily fluids, the imperfections, the animal irrational parts of you; I want to be thrown against the wall by your inexplicable wants and needs, your inconsistencies and silences. I want to run like a lamb by your side, be sugar and spice, frolic in a frock, fuck you like an animal, be there when you die – can't get enough, can never get enough of you. You part me with the shifting weight of curtains letting in the sun, dusty rays scattering; letting in the night, the starry scary totality of full moon, sliver or shard; searing sun on the back of my neck.

I can't get enough; I gravitate to the food bowl.

Animals have no shame: accepting domestication, they lie their troubled noses in their paws. Hunger and lust and all the rest. Keep your dirty paws away from her, I say, give me some respect. Feed me more, feed me and keep me on a satin pillow, leashed or leashing, let my scratchy tongue lash you with my criticisms and let it drink you in backward curls, milky and destructive, paws in the bowl tipping fluid everywhere. Pussy milk, you feed me your titbits and I spill myself, regurgitate wild things, feathers and the spoils of war, little brittle bones, things that used to fly. I mark you with pawprints and puncture-wounds; you tie me up in the backyard and refuse to walk me. I feed, I feed, I shit on the kitchen floor when you leave me alone too long, I leave my hairs on all your clothing.

You tell me to lie there while you leave the room. I stay. I stay and wait for you.

You're a girl/you're a boy. You do things for me, to me, in me. You kick at the sides like a drowning man. And you take BC and AD and suture them, bring all of me together again. No longer a straight girl and not just a dyke, I play out my girl stuff while I take a mouthful of your fingers; you smell of perfume and leather, smoke and drink and pussy.

You tolerate everything. You watch television while I clatter old bones between my teeth and drag them round your clean floor. It rarely irritates you and when it does I cower. Lust holds my attention like a cat on a fence. Dogs have only two barks: "come here" and "go away". I bark "come here".

Frustrated, I can see the innocence of my anger and I'm hungry again. No shame – in the end, I'll spill my catgut contents out for you to clean up and you'll do it every time.

You've never been a woman and I've always been a woman. I've always walked the way I walk – fucked with boys and longed for girls while you prowled dangerously uncomfortable between sexes – I left the boys and men one day and lost myself in cunt and clit while still you prowled your cage, pawing at a breach in the wire and waiting, waiting for the structure to weaken. You slipped your muscled forequarter through the gap to swipe at me and I was taken, taken in by your boy-power, and I knew how to handle a creature of your size and weight – no longer split between girl and dyke, I apply my knowledge to you fervently.

You make me feel like a woman again.

* * *

I knew a girl who caught a cricket in her hand. She held it in her fist, very quietly and for a long time, until it began to sing again.

Is there anything for you in this arrangement where I sit pretty while you serve me, does it strengthen you to be at my beck and call? I want to cry when I see the struggle you face with it all locked away, the constant dragging of it out of you with my manicured fingers scratching, scrabbling for you. I want to write four pages that give off the scent of your piss.

When you arrive home, I am waiting for you dressed like a woman. I am in black, elegant bare shoulders, breasts peeping up from a rich velvet decolletage. The sleeves of my dress are long and my small hands are decorated with rings. I take the rings off and put them on the mantelpiece – one by one. I notice you looking at my hands. I don't walk towards you. I wait for your approach.

Before you reach me, I turn my back and ask you to zip my dress. You can see the back of my bra, which laces up and might be made of soft leather. Obediently, you close me up in my dress; now I am velvet from thigh to wrist, radiating white skin.

Then I say to you, "bite me", and you've put your briefcase down and I feel both hands spreading a heat over my shoulders and back as you push me forward against the wall, sink your teeth in until I turn again to you, composed, and offer you a double malt.

You are a little confused, having engaged me only to clean your house.

Your cunt is frilled like Chinese mushrooms and wet like pitta bread soaked in olive oil. I suck the oil from your hair and I suck the hair under your arms. I feel your long forearms and hands laid out across my body. I watch you sleep with your mouth fallen open. Your smell is heavy like your kiss. Your scent is heavy and stays with me for days.

VANILLA

Maisie Langridge

My Vanilla sits and from the bed I watch as the sunlit window frames her, and the last late afternoon light kisses her neck and shoulders.

Vanilla knows that from the bed I am watching, but she is absorbed in her mirror. The mirror that she has taken to her window table to catch the last of the late afternoon light.

Vanilla is making up.

Primping and preening.

Me and my Vanilla are going out. Later we'll be eating. The table's booked. Bread breaking. Rich red wine drinking. Body and blood. Me and my Vanilla love food. Hearty appetites. Later I'll watch as Vanilla's mouth enfolds, closes over, bursts the flavours on her tongue. I'll watch her lips, wine-moistened, part into her smile. And Vanilla, I know, will watch me. But for now I must watch and wait because Vanilla is not yet ready and is sitting, in her lingerie, in the last late afternoon light.

Vanilla has showered and the room is lingeringly scented, softly soaped and warmed by her still slightly damp body.

Vanilla has showered and, I remember how earlier, I watched her, towelled and wet, stand dripping onto her brightly coloured bought-new-from-the-market woollen rug. The drops fell in a ring around her, marking the upright outline of her body. At first the drops had settled on the surface of Vanilla's rug and had danced, quivered, just touching the fibres' surface. And then one by one they surrendered, became absorbed, into the carpet's colourful pattern. Vanilla's wet drops had caused the colours of the rug to change. Its bright colours, its reds, were deeper, much deeper – the colour of blood – where she had made the carpet wet.

Vanilla shook her hair loose. It fell just to her shoulders, her dark curls kissing her upper back. Watching, I could feel the fine spray of droplets cool my face, and Vanilla dropped her towel and I watched as she stood in the centre of the room.

Naked.

I have seen my Vanilla naked many times before but each time is new, and I moved forward to be more comfortable on the bed.

Vanilla has showered and, I remember how earlier, I watched as my Vanilla reached for a bottle from her window table and began rubbing a sweet scented lotion into her arms.

Vanilla.

The room was perfumed with the sweet scent of Vanilla. Vanilla on warm skin.

I watched as she raised her arms and stroked the scented lotion into her forearms, upper arms, shoulders. The fine strong curve of her shoulders. The skin gave under Vanilla's firm strokes. The creamy lotion disappeared, absorbed, into her downy arms.

The scent of Vanilla on warm skin.

I watched as she worked down her body cupping and warming the lotion in her palms and smoothing her Vanilla hands across her breasts, her waist, her stomach. Across Vanilla's stomach. She lingered there. Her fingers, her palms, working the slippy lotion deep into her skin and my Vanilla raised her head to catch me looking from the bed in the late afternoon light, and held me for a moment, and smiled.

I watched and Vanilla reached for more lotion. Warmed the fresh sweet scented thick liquid in her palms and spread it smoothly, deliberately, along her thighs, her calves. I watched her, absorbed, and saw her muscles tense and watched as she moved her lotioned hands along, around, her buttocks. Saw her play her scented fingers around her inner thighs.

Vanilla looked at me and knew that she had made me shudder. Vanilla has a beautiful body but tonight the table is booked and we are going out.

But Vanilla is not yet ready and sits now, and I move to catch her Vanilla scent afresh and Vanilla, sitting, feels me and shifts her sitting weight and tries again to concentrate on making-up, to concentrate on her mirror.

My Vanilla sits. And I watch. And she is wearing her new lingerie. She has been waiting for an occasion and tonight the table is booked and we are going out.

Vanilla has chosen carefully what touches her body, what lies next to her skin. She sits fine and densely laced in ivory-yellow. A two-piece ivory-yellow bodice set. Its patterns are delicate and dense. Deep heavy lace with satin borders. I can see her skin through the intricate lace patterns. Through her lace her skin is barely present, barely traceable.

Vanilla's satin-bordered lace bodice follows snugly the curve of her high breasts: caresses the line of her sides, and her broad, fine, straight back, down to her waist.

I watch the lace bodice rise as Vanilla breathes. Her lower legs are gently crossed and Vanilla rests on the toes of her slightly pointed feet. Her thighs are long against the seat of the chair. The skin of her smooth upper thighs broken by the smooth ivory-yellow satin and lace of her underwear. Her ivory-yellow two-piece underwear that fits snugly high on her waist and hips. I can see the lace slightly taut across her stomach. I watch her breathe.

My Vanilla sits and the late afternoon light is turning into the deeper blue-red of her early evening and from the bed I watch Vanilla making up.

Me and my Vanilla have joked many times about my knowing nothing of making up. Of the absence in my girlhood and adolescence. Of my awkwardness around the colourful make-up counter. She has many times lover-threatened to make me up and, secretly, I want her to. But although I have never worn make-up and know nothing, I am fascinated by her ritual of foundations and powder, eye-shadows and liners. Mascara. Lipstick. Vanilla knows how to make up. Never overdoes it. Knows what suits her.

Vanilla brings her face closer to her mirror.

She has applied her base.

I watch her choose her eye-shadow colour. Vanilla can be Bright-Baby-Blue-Colour (playful) to Tone-Down-Autumnal-Shades (sophisticated). My Vanilla can play the spectrum from Young to Mature. Tonight the table is booked and we are going out and Vanilla has chosen: sophisticated.

Vanilla is applying mascara. I watch as her mouth opens in make-up reflex. Vanilla is concentrated. Absorbed. Her skin is stretched taut over her cheeks. Vanilla has a beautiful face. Real. Real and beautiful. Handsome. Statuesque. My Vanilla is not blank-canvas model looks – but she turns heads. I like that. She turned mine.

Vanilla sits and from the bed I watch her breathe and see the lace stretched taut across her stomach. From the bed I can glimpse Vanilla's skin through her ivory-yellow lace. I trace down her stomach and can just see the dark shadow of her pubic line. But she sits side-on and, tracing down my Vanilla, my gaze rests on her side-sitting upper thighs.

The room is warm now and Vanilla moves to open her window. Let in the glow-red evening light. She stands and stretches across her table, her mirror table, for the window clasp. I watch her front body, her breasts, rise high, her thighs lengthen, her back slightly arch, her muscles tense. I see her stomach, her buttocks. The flesh beneath the lace. The evening breeze kisses her face and hair, her chest. Vanilla's breasts tighten with the cooling chill of the breeze. I watch her nipples harden. Mine harden too as I watch my beautiful Vanilla.

Vanilla knows that from the bed I watch her, and knows I see her smile a not-so-secret smile into her mirror as she sits to choose her lipstick.

I like to watch Vanilla apply her lipstick and tonight Vanilla wants just the right shade, just the right amount, because tonight the table is booked and we are going out.

Vanilla teases out the lipstick from its tube. I see the shiny deep red-brown lipstick tip. The teased-out Vanilla lipstick tip.

To make-up her lips Vanilla needs to be closer to her mirror. From the bed I watch my Vanilla and my Vanilla knows I'm watching. Vanilla parts her thighs. Vanilla's legs open and she wraps them around the sides of her chair. Vanilla hooks her ankles around the front legs and rests her toes on the inside edge of her chair.

Vanilla moves forward. A little forward. Pushes forward. Vanilla's hips move forward on the chair. I watch as she presses down into the chair seat. I know Vanilla is swelling. I can feel the rush of blood. The blue-red blood rush of the early evening.

Vanilla is swelling and I rise slightly on the bed, shift slightly, to better support my own swelling weight. Vanilla knows I'm watching as she slowly parts her lips and brings her deliberate lipstick to her mouth.

Vanilla's lips are full and taut. Swelling. I watch as the lipstick tip pushes slowly, gently against Vanilla's mouth. Vanilla's mouth is open and ready. Vanilla spreads her lipstick. The tiny muscles of her lips are supple and taut. Vanilla is ready for her lipstick. Vanilla is open. I watch the shiny tip colour and moisten Vanilla's already red mouth. A subtle shade. But then tonight Vanilla has chosen: sophisticated. The table's booked and me and my Vanilla are going out.

Vanilla lingers over her lipstick. She likes the delicate tension and the slight resistance of her lipstick tip against her moistening skin. Her open mouth.

She's subtle, my Vanilla.

Vanilla knows I'm watching from the bed and pauses.

"Time to go, soon," says my Vanilla.

"Yep," I reply, "Time to go . . . soon."

In the blood-red-blue evening glow my Vanilla sits and from the bed I know she knows I'm watching and I see my lotioned, my finely laced, my satin-lipped, Vanilla turn from side-sitting to look at me. Looking.

It is warm, warm in this breeze-kissed warm room, and my Vanilla faces me, smiling, and she rises. Vanilla is nearly ready, now – nearly ready – and from the bed I see my beautiful Vanilla walk slowly through the wine-red evening glow. I watch as my Vanilla, looking, traces down my warm supine body. I shudder and I see she smiles.

Vanilla stands quite close to the bed now and, through her densely and delicately laced ivory-yellow underwear, I can trace the fullness of her beautiful swollen cunt.

Vanilla is looking and knows I know she's wet.

From the bed, I lie watching and can feel the heat of my Vanilla. Feel her blood-sweet body-bulk almost next to me. She is on the bed now. Vanilla is on the bed and I feel the warm full press of her breasts on mine. Her hardened nipples push and I am giving. Vanilla shifts her stomach closer. I can feel her taut wanting. I can feel Vanilla's breath. Vanilla's warm skin. The sweet sweet scent of Vanilla.

I can see my moist Vanilla's mouth. My open, ready, swollen Vanilla.

Vanilla.

The scent of Vanilla. The sweet scent of Vanilla. Vanilla on warm skin. And in the room's warm red early evening glow from where we lie – looking – it seems that although the table's booked me and my Vanilla will not be going out.

A PLACE FOR US

Karen X Tulchinsky

The first time I saw her was from behind a large paper sack full of groceries. She was stepping out of Mr Wong's variety store. The bag was almost bigger than she was. I could see her long black hair on her shoulders and, from the side of the bag, part of her face. She was concentrating hard on walking. It was a rainy fall day in Vancouver. The steps were slick with rain-water. It happened fast. She slipped. The bag was thrown from her arms, as she went down. A bottle of soy sauce flew through the air, then crashed beside her, spilling brown-black onto the sidewalk. Vegetables and fruit splattered on the pavement and pummeled her little body. A glass bottle of milk rolled down the cement steps. She had one hand over her head as the groceries fell all around her. Her little pink skirt was wet from the puddle on the sidewalk. She was wearing a white leotard and black leather shoes with a thin strap. I was twelve years old. She was a couple of years younger. Eight, maybe nine years old.

I rushed over. Bent down.

"Hey. Are you all right? Are you hurt?"

"Oh . . ." she said. She looked stunned. I wondered if she'd hurt her head.

"Where do you live? Should I get your mother?"

"Oh." She sat up. "I'm OK." She looked around. Saw the groceries on the ground. Wrecked. "Oh, no."

"It's OK. I'll help you." I retrieved the milk bottle, which was miraculously unbroken. The vegetables and fruit were all right, maybe a little bruised. There was a bag of rice. I gathered them all together.

"Wait here," I said, then ran inside the store to get a fresh bag. I put everything into the bag. "Where do you live? I'll help you home." She looked kind of scared, so I said, "Oh, my name's Roberta, but, you know, everyone calls me Robbie."

For the first time she smiled. In a soft voice, so quiet I barely heard, she said, "I know."

I had never noticed her before, but I was three years older. And when you're a kid, you never notice the younger kids. When we got to her house, I saw her mother peeking out from behind the living room drapes. She waved goodbye and started up the driveway.

"You should put something on that knee," I said.

She smiled again, and it was the most beautiful thing I'd ever seen. I started back down the street, then turned around. "Hey, what's your name, anyway?"

She bit her bottom lip nervously, and kind of glanced over her shoulder in the direction of her mother. "Akemi, but everyone calls me Kim."

"Akemi." I repeated. A Japanese name. It was beautiful. She

had two names, just like me. I had a Hebrew name – Rochel – and an English name, Roberta. "Akemi," I repeated.

"Kim," she said.

"Yeah. OK. Kim. Well . . ." I didn't know what else to say. "See you around . . . Kim."

After that day, I'd run into Kim at school sometimes and I'd watch out for her. But we didn't actually become friends until four years later. I was sixteen and she was thirteen. I didn't have a lot of friends my own age. The girls were all into clothes and make-up, things which had no interest for me. And the boys wouldn't let me play kickball or baseball with them any more. I saw Kim walking out of the corner store by the school, with a paper sack full of groceries. She looked so beautiful. Her long black hair was loose, bouncing against her shoulders as she walked. Her big brown eyes sparkled. There was a soft sweet energy about her, a kindness that reached out and penetrated my heart. Like Cupid's arrow hitting its mark. I felt weak from the impact. But I recovered, and ran to catch up with her. When I was almost upon her she swiveled around abruptly, a look of fear on her face.

"Hey, it's OK. It's me, Robbie. Remember?"

She smiled. "I remember."

I walked along beside her. "Can I help you? Can I carry your bag?"

She smiled again, stopped. "OK." She handed the bag to me. It was the most incredible thing in the world. It was an invitation. I took the bag in my arms. We walked on. We talked. About school, the other kids. She didn't have a lot of friends, either. She did well in school and the other kids didn't like that. She was lonely. I could tell. She didn't seem three years younger. We talked easily about everything as I walked her home. We arrived outside her house. She stopped.

"I better take that, now," she said, holding out her arms.

I handed over the groceries. Turned to leave. "Hey," I said on impulse. "What're ya doing on Saturday? I mean, do you want to go to the movies with me?"

She blushed. "I can't."

"Oh." I felt rejected.

"I have to help my mom on Saturdays."

"Oh."

"But see you around. OK?"

"OK."

After that, I'd wait for Kim outside school to walk her home. Her mother didn't approve of our friendship, at first. She thought Kim should have friends her own age. But eventually she warmed to me. Kim seemed so happy when I was around. My parents were wary at first, too, but they knew I had few friends and my mother was happy because Kim was so feminine. Maybe it would rub off on me. Maybe I would start wearing make-up and dresses, too.

One Saturday evening, a few months later, Kim was at my house. My parents and my brother Michael were out for the evening. Kim and I were alone in the house. We were sitting in the living room, on the couch, eating popcorn, watching a movie. It was a sad movie, about a woman whose lover died in the war. At the really heartbreaking part, Kim snuggled against my arm. She was crying softly. I put my arm around her and pulled her close. It felt so natural. I had a shaky feeling in my belly, but it was a feeling I liked. I held her for the rest of the evening, until we heard my parents' car pull up. Without speaking, we both knew enough to sit up and move to opposite ends of the couch.

We began to hang out every weekend, and whenever no one else was around, we'd cuddle up together. We'd never do anything more, but just holding her was exquisite. We carried on like this for most of the school year. Spending weekends together. Not ever talking about it, but holding hands and touching as much as possible.

All hell broke loose early in March. We were at Kim's, in the basement rec room. Her mother was upstairs, but we were sure we would hear her if she came down the uncarpeted basement stairway. So I threw my arm around Kim and we flipped through the channels looking for a good movie. We found a romantic comedy. Toward the end of the movie, the leading man looked deeply into the leading woman's eyes, and slowly they moved toward each other and kissed. It was turning me on, but I kept my feelings to myself. Then Kim turned to me on the couch. I looked at her. She said nothing. We looked deeply into each other's eyes for a long time. Then, just as the actors in the movie had done, we moved slowly closer until her lips were on mine. We kissed. It was like a dam bursting. All the months of holding hands and cuddling on the couch exploded in that one kiss. Kim leaned back so that she was lying on the sofa. I lay down on top of her. We didn't think about what we were doing. We just kissed wildly, arms everywhere. We didn't hear her mother come down the stairs. We didn't hear anything but the sound of our own breathing.

Suddenly, I felt Kim stiffen. She pushed at me to get off. I opened my eyes. Her mother was standing over us. I jumped back to the opposite side of the couch, straightened my clothes. Kim and her mother just stared at each other silently. I could see anger, shame and guilt in her mother's steely gaze. Kim's eyes were huge. It was like she was receiving all of the feeling through the silence. It was worse than yelling. The air seethed with tension. When the silence was beyond unbearable, Kim's mother broke away and quietly went back upstairs. Kim slumped forward over her knees, head in her hands. Cautious, I moved near her, stroked her back gently. She was crying.

"You better go home," she said.

"Listen . . ." I wanted to ask her to run away with me. She could stay in school. I would find a job. I was sixteen. I could take care of us. We'd make it. I knew we would. This was true love. I was sure of it. We had nothing to be ashamed of. We were Romeo and Juliet. Our love was meant to be. No one could tear us apart. I bent over and tried to look into Kim's eyes. Her misery was so complete, it broke my heart.

"I'll call you later," I said as I stood.

She shook her head. Said nothing. And, though I longed to hold her in my arms, I left.

By the time I got home, Kim's mother had already phoned my parents. They were furious. I was sent to my room until dinner. We ate in stony silence. Then my father sent my brother to his room.

"Your mother and I have made our decision, Roberta. You'll be leaving tomorrow for Toronto. I've already spoken with your Uncle Phil and Aunt Gloria. They're willing to take you in. You'll finish your last two years of high school out there. You'll be sharing a room with your cousin Naomi. I expect you to be helpful around the house. Your uncle and aunt are doing me a big favour."

"What? I don't want to move to Toronto. I want to stay here. Please."

My father slammed his fist down hard on the kitchen table. "What's the matter with you, Roberta? How could you do such a thing? It's not right. You're not normal."

"Dad, please. Don't make me go. I want to stay here."

His eyes were hard, hateful. "Don't you understand, Roberta? Her parents could press charges. You're sixteen, for God's sake. She's only thirteen. I gave them my word. They want this kept quiet, too. Now go to your room and start packing a suitcase with your clothes and school things."

"Dad. Please, there must be another way."

He leaned back in his chair and folded his arms. "I've made my decision, Roberta."

I went upstairs and crept into my parents' room, where quietly I dialed Kim's phone number. I tried to disguise my voice.

There was silence on the other end. Then her father said, "You are not to call here again, Roberta. Kim doesn't want to speak with you." And then, the phone went dead. It was the moment a large piece of my heart broke off. A piece I knew would never return. The wound was so deep and so wide, it would never completely heal. There would always be a large jagged scar to remind me of my loss. My guilt. And my shame. Kim and I never got to say goodbye.

The next morning I was on a bus heading east. Three thousand miles away.

Ten years later, I moved back to Vancouver. At first, I thought of her all the time. If only I could have spoken with her myself, just once, before I left. Just to see if she was OK. To tell her I'd come back, to ask her to write. Maybe things would have been different. Maybe my time in Toronto would not have been as desolate. But there was no way. I was banished. Sent away like a criminal. Guilty until proven innocent. I finished high school in Toronto, staying in the home of my aunt and uncle. I was a complete loner. Didn't even try to make friends. What for? It hurt too much to have friends. Better to be alone. Where it's safe. I wrapped a tight bandage around my shattered heart and each year I added a layer of gauze. I wanted to be sure no one could ever reach in as deep and hurt me so completely ever again.

I left my aunt and uncle's house and moved out on my own one month after graduation, got a job waiting on tables in a big new pasta restaurant downtown. Lied on my application. Said

I'd worked summers as a waitress at The White Spot in Vancouver. I never even went to Vancouver in the summers.

My family came out to Toronto, the first summer, to see me, but I wasn't allowed back. I was a criminal. I learned to keep my eyes down in shame. I half expected to see my face on a wanted poster in the post office.

I came out shortly after moving out on my own and finding Toronto's dyke bars. I only thought of Kim sometimes. Late at night when loneliness washed over me. Early in the mornings when I first awoke and memory flooded my senses. I wondered if I'd ever see her again, but figured she'd grow up, get married, have a family and forget all about me.

Ten years after I was sent away, I moved back. I couldn't stand the thought of one more long cold winter back east and I longed for the scent of the ocean, the comfort of mountains in the distance, the green green wet rainy winters. My family seemed happy when I told them. I guess my crimes were all water under the bridge, by then. Seven years is the statute of limitations and I had stayed away three years longer than that.

It didn't take me long to find the local dyke bar. The Lotus. Not much different from the bars in Toronto. I started going for a drink, hoping to meet other women. I'd been back in town for six months. It was a Friday night. I liked to go to the bar early, before the crowds arrived, so I could get a good table, and soak in the atmosphere before it got too loud, too dark. I was with my friend Ali. She was trying to get me to join her baseball team. I was telling her that I hate sports. That I'm not that kind of butch. That I'd drop the ball and fall over my own feet trying to run to a base. I was gesturing wildly with my body to convince her; she was laughing.

Something. Some invisible force lured me to glance toward the bar. I froze. My mouth must have been hanging open. Ali was staring at me.

"Robbie?" she said.

Kim didn't see me. She was with someone. A butch. Her lover? I watched as she stood in line at the bar, ordered a drink and then began walking in my direction. She was two feet from me when she looked over and caught my eye. Her eyes widened. I don't know for how long we stood there, staring at each other, suspended in space, in time.

"Robbie," she whispered.

My eyes filled with tears.

She raised her arm just a little, like she was going to touch my face, then she caught herself.

"Uh, Robbie, this is Jan. Jan, this is an old friend, Robbie. We went to school together."

I brushed the tear out of my eye roughly with the back of my hand, nodded hello. "Excuse me," I said, and I fled. Ran to the door, abandoning Ali at our table. I ran for five blocks until I was winded. Then I stopped and slumped against the brick wall of a building. Her lover. She has a lover. Damn. I punched the wall, hurt my hand. What did I expect? It's been ten years. Did I think she'd be sitting at home, just waiting for me to return? Course not. A beautiful woman like Kim probably had half the women in town chasing her. Anyway, I should have called her. Tried to look for her. I could have called her mother's place, but I was scared. And she wasn't listed in the phone book.

I supposed it was good news that she was out too, that she had a lover, and was out at the dyke bar. Could have been worse, I guess. She could have been married to a man with a brood of kids. Still, my heart broke all over again. I felt as raw as I did the day I first left Vancouver, banished with a scarlet letter across my forehead, a huge scarlet L for Lesbian. I took the bus home and, in my torturous state, I drank the rest of a bottle of rum I had in the cupboard.

Next morning, my head was pounding with a hangover. The

phone was ringing. I was lying on my sofa, fully dressed. I'd forgotten to turn on my answering machine, so the phone kept ringing. To shut it up, I picked up the receiver.

"Yeah?" I barked.

"Oops. Did I wake you?" It was Kim.

I sat up. My head pounded more. "Oh, yeah. Sorry I yelled."

"Should I call back later?"

"No. No, it's OK. How did you get my number?"

"Your friend, Ali."

I vowed to kill Ali later. Although really I wanted to kiss her. "Oh."

"When did you get back?"

"To Vancouver, you mean?"

"You know what I mean."

I paused. Same Kim. She could still read my mind. We were like two parts of the same person. Why hadn't she waited for me? "Couple months ago."

Silence.

"Why didn't you call?"

"I don't know."

"Robbie, come on. Tell me why you didn't call."

I sighed. Searched the table for the rum bottle. There was still one shot left. I tipped the bottle, drank it. "I thought maybe you'd be married with a bunch of kids by now. Anyway, I thought about it, but you're not in the book, and I didn't think calling your mother would be a good idea."

"She's dead."

"What?"

"My mother. She died two years ago."

"Oh. I'm sorry."

"I live in her house."

"You do? What about your father?"

"They divorced about a year after you left. He lives in

California, now. With his brother, at first. Now he's married. A younger woman. She's only five years older than me. Can you believe that?"

"So you got the house?"

"Yeah."

"What about your sister and brother?"

"Both married. Liana is a lawyer, married to a computer programmer; they live in a huge house in West Vancouver. And Wayne is in medical school in Toronto. His final year. His wife is from a rich family. So I got the house."

"Wow."

"Robbie. Why don't you come over later? I want to see you."

"What about what's her name?"

"Who? Oh, Jan. She doesn't live with me."

"But you're together . . ."

Pause. "Yes."

"Then I don't think it's a good idea."

"Why not?"

"You know why."

"Please, Robbie, just to talk."

Pause. "I can't, Kim. I can't just talk to you. I'm sorry." Reluctantly, I hung up the phone. So she wouldn't call back, I took it off the hook and buried my head under the pillow.

I managed to get through most of the year without obsessing on Kim. I even dated a couple of women during that time: no one special, but I went out on dates. The next time I saw Kim was in the middle of the Gay Pride Parade, that summer. It was a hot sunny day. People were stripped right down to shorts and tank tops. Most of the men were shirtless and some of the women, too. I was hanging with Ali. We were standing on the sidelines watching the parade go by. We had planned to join in when

Ali's baseball team walked by. I felt Kim's presence before she called my name. I turned around. Standing behind me, alone, looking as beautiful as ever, in a tight red dress, was Kim. She smiled. I smiled. All my desire for her washed over me. My nipples became instantly erect, my knees were jelly.

She walked over to me. Stood on her toes, kissed me on the cheek. Her scent surrounded me. She wore the same perfume she used to wear when we were kids. I was taken right back to that time, to the days of cuddling on the couch. My one true love.

"Can I join you?" she asked.

I gestured to Ali. "Well, I'm here with Ali."

Ali turned around. "Hey, Kim. Come on, join us. Plenty of room."

Kim moved forward and stood beside me. We watched the parade for a while. I was happy and sad at the same time. I knew I would never love anyone the way I loved Kim, my childhood sweetheart, and here she was and I couldn't have her. I wanted to run away again, but I didn't want to give up this precious time with her, either.

"So? Ask me what's new," she said, facing forward, watching the English Bay Men's Swim Team walk by, in matching swim trunks and fancy pink bathing caps, dancing to a hit disco song as they marched by.

"OK. What's new?" I turned and eyed her suspiciously.

"Me and Jan broke up." She said it casually, the way you'd say, "It's supposed to rain later today."

It took a moment to register in my brain. She's single. Single. She's here and she's single. Single. Single. Single. I moved in front of her. "You mean . . ."

"That's right."

I didn't know what to do. I wanted to throw my arms around her and kiss her. I wanted to pick her up and carry her home like a cave man, throw her down on the floor and make mad passionate love for days, stopping only to eat, drink and occasionally breathe. But I felt immobilized, like it was too good to be true. I stood by the side of the road, gaping.

"So kiss me, stupid." Kim said, her gorgeous brown eyes wrapping their magic around my heart.

"Oh." I inched forward, tentatively placed my hands on her waist. She threw her arms around my neck and looked at me intensely. Slowly, silently, just like we had done ten years before on her mother's rec room couch, we inched our lips toward each other. When they connected, it was like the beginning and the end of the world at once. I would swear later that fireworks erupted. It was the most exquisite kiss of my life. It was the moment I had dreamed about for ten years. Not once, during my exile in Toronto, had I given up the dream that one day we would be reunited. Only these last few months since I had returned and found out she had a lover had I felt any sense of despondency. Her tongue was in my mouth. I pulled her tighter to me, felt her hard nipples pushing against mine. Time was suspended. I forgot where we were. We were back on her mother's couch, two scared, anxious kids, totally in our bodies, our desire flowing. Impulsive. Spontaneous. Frantic with lust. We must have been creating quite a scene because, the next thing I knew, I felt someone tapping my shoulder and I heard Ali say, "Hey, you guys. Why don't you rent a room or something?"

We pulled apart. I looked into Kim's face. She looked as happy as I felt and my heart was bursting with joy.

"Oh, God," she said, "do you know how long I've been waiting to do just that?"

"Ten years?"

"Come on." She took my hand, and led me through the crowd. Neither of us had a car, so we waited for a bus and tried to remember we were in public. We held hands and kissed at the bus stop. We touched and stroked, groped and petted. Luckily it was Gay Pride Day and most of the other people waiting for the bus were also queers who were heading home from the parade. On the bus, I thought I'd die in anticipation. All of my desire was in the hand that held hers. It was the most erotic bus ride of my life. I thought we'd both slide right off our seats. We went to Kim's house. I hesitated on the porch. Wasn't sure I could go inside. Couldn't believe her mother had actually died. She was a tiny woman but forceful. As a kid, I had been scared of her.

"It's OK," Kim reassured, "she's gone. I promise."

I followed her inside. She led me downstairs to the rec room, the scene of our crime. The same worn sofa was against the wall in front of the TV. Kim sat down and patted the seat beside her. I sat. She threw herself back into my arms. We kissed. It was better than *déjà vu*. We weren't just imagining we had been there before. We had been and now we were doing it all over again. Only, this time, we were adults and there were no parents to break us up and send me away.

"Unzip my dress." She presented her back to me.

Slowly, I lowered the zipper. She wore nothing underneath. She turned to face me again. I couldn't stop kissing her. I wanted to kiss her everywhere. Her skin was fine silk. She tasted like heaven. She tore off my T-shirt and struggled with my belt. My hands were all over her breasts, which were much larger than the last time I'd seen them. Her body had filled out into womanhood in the most beautiful way. Her nipples were hard under my fingers.

"Oh, Robbie," she moaned.

I ran my tongue along the contours of her neck. She was salty with sweat. It was the best taste in the world. Better than in my wildest dreams.

"Get undressed," she ordered, still struggling with the buttons on my 501s.

I unbuttoned my shorts, stood and let them drop to the floor. She lay back on the couch. I laid down on top of her. Naked, we were skin to skin. Our bodies fit together like they were meant for each other. I knew I could die right then. And I would have been happy and fulfilled. It would have all been worth it. Her hands were all over my body. I gasped with pleasure. I could feel her wetness on my leg. I reached for her and plunged two fingers inside. She moaned. She begged for more. She writhed underneath me, as I fucked her with my fingers, my thumb circling her clit, which was swollen with desire. She reached for me, and it was magical. I didn't have to say a word. She knew just what to do to pleasure me. We yelled out together as we came. And then we fucked some more. For the rest of the afternoon we made love all over Kim's house. Her mother's house, exorcising the ghosts of our tortured teenage romance. In the rec room, the kitchen. Bathroom. In the tub. Living room. Dining room. Front hall.

After, we lay in Kim's bed together, exhausted, my arms wrapped around her, we sipped red wine, and ate fresh strawberries from each other's fingers, basking in the afterglow. It was a dream come true. A gift from the universe. She was my one true love and we were back together again. All of the anguish of leaving, the shame and the guilt melted away, in the safety of her arms.

We had come full circle. Neither of us knew what would happen next. But it didn't matter. We were young. But we were old enough to know how precious a love like this truly was. I held her hand tightly in mine, brought it to my lips, kissed each finger, one at a time. Her eyes were closed. She was falling asleep. I watched her for a while. Amazed that something so good could happen to me. After everything I'd been through.

I took a deep breath and for the first time in years, I felt the tightness in my chest loosening. The lock around my heart coming unhinged. I pulled the covers up around us and snuggled into Kim's warmth. And I fell asleep beside her. Into a deep untroubled sleep. For the first time in ten years.

SWEET VIOLET

Ruby Vise

Violet looked at herself in the mirror. "Sweet violet," her mother used to sing to her. "Sweeter than the roses." Violet smiled at her reflection; if only her mother knew. In her new blue jeans and her brother's shirt, she looked anything but sweet. The shirt smelt a bit, of boy's sweat, but she quite liked that. In fact, if it weren't for her breasts pushing through the shirt, she looked just like her brother, and all the girls thought he was dishy.

She looked at her watch; it was five o'clock. Katherine said to come around at five thirty. It would take fifteen minutes to walk there. Violet had timed it earlier. Katherine's mother was going out for the night, all night.

Violet sat down on the bed and then stood up again. Even if it was too early, she was going, she needed to be moving.

"I'm off," she called to her parents as she left. They were

watching the Test Match on TV, New Zealand versus Australia. New Zealand were 108 for 9; they were going to lose. Violet had told her mother that Katherine was having a sleep-over party and that all the girls from swimming would be there, the sixth-formers anyway. Her mother never came down to swimming so she'd never find out.

"Have a nice time," her father called, not taking his eyes off the TV. New Zealand had scored one run in the past ten minutes; he didn't want to miss anything. Her mother was in the kitchen, getting their tea, and Violet was pleased to have avoided her.

Violet set off walking, very slowly; she wondered if she should have bought some flowers or chocolates, like people on TV did. She tried to imagine herself presenting them to Katherine. She couldn't really see it. Katherine didn't look the least bit like the woman off the Milk Tray ad.

It was a nice evening, but most people were inside, watching the match or having their tea. There were some boys playing cricket in one of the gardens she passed.

Violet forgot she was supposed to be walking slowly, and it was only twenty past when she arrived at Katherine's place, so she walked round the block again. One of the gardens had a rosebush by the fence. Several of its pink flowers hung right over the footpath. Violet had a quick look around; no one seemed to be about. She grabbed one of the roses and bent its stem. It broke, but wouldn't come off. She had to bend it back and forwards, and then twist it around to get it off. She quickly walked away with it. It wasn't until she was nearly back at Katherine's that she noticed it was crawling with aphids. She dropped it onto the road.

She looked at her watch again: five to. She was back on Katherine's road. All the houses had neat low fences, recently mown lawns and carefully tended flower gardens. All except

Katherine's. It had several large trees overshadowing a gravel drive and a tangle of long grass that might have once been a lawn. There was a verandah around the house, its paint peeling, and a plant growing all over it with droopy, purple flowers.

Violet's mother tutted whenever they drove past it, and her father sucked the air through his teeth at the sight of the exposed weatherboard. Violet quite liked it, though; even before she knew Katherine lived there, she thought it looked mysterious. Like interesting things went on inside. Violet hoped so, anyway.

She pushed open the gate, which swung off its hinges. She had to lift it back on to close it again. Violet's footsteps crunched loudly on the gravel; she made her way to the veranda, which creaked as she stepped onto it. She knocked on the front door and noticed her hands were shaking. She tried whistling to calm herself, and then stopped; she sounded like her father. She straightened her shirt and knocked again. Through the stained glass of the door, she saw a figure coming towards her. She ran her hands through her hair, then clasped them behind her back so Katherine wouldn't see they were shaking.

Katherine opened the front door; she looked hot and a little bothered. She smiled at Violet. She was wearing her usual old jeans and a white T-shirt. Her hair was curlier than usual and that seemed to make her eyes look bluer. She took Violet's arm and pulled her into the house, then led her down the hall. There was no carpet on the floor, and no wallpaper on the walls: just white paint. Violet hadn't realized they were that poor. There were photos on the wall – not pictures of people, like Violet's family had on the sideboard, but pictures of places. Funny-looking places, obviously foreign.

Violet followed Katherine into the kitchen at the back of the house. It had a big wooden table in the middle, and an old-fashioned stove. Katherine went to the stove and looked in it.

"I'm not sure the garlic bread is cooked."

Violet had never had garlic before; she thought it was for keeping vampires off.

The table was covered in bowls and plates with different food on them. Some of it Violet recognized.

"Mum helped me," Katherine said, standing up again and waving her hand over the plates. "That's tabbouleh, it's from the Middle East, and falafels. That's just a normal salad; that's a Caesar salad – only without anchovies. I hate anchovies."

Nothing looked particularly "normal" to Violet. The salad was just a mess of leaves with the odd tomato, tiny little things. No grated cheese or carrot like her mother made.

"There's pizza in the oven, too." Katherine smiled.

"Great." Something she had eaten before. Violet tried to smile back.

"What's wrong?"

Violet didn't say anything.

"Don't you like the food?"

"I don't know, yet," Violet said. "I haven't heard of half of it."

"Mum said it was too fancy."

"Not too fancy." Violet took Katherine's hand and squeezed it. "Just different."

"Come on." Katherine led Violet out into the back garden. It was even more overgrown than the front; you could have been in the bush, miles from anywhere.

"I thought we could eat out here." There was a rug on the ground and a bottle of wine. "Mum said we could have it. She opened it for me."

Violet had never had wine before. Her father sometimes let her taste his beer, and her brother once had some cider.

Katherine poured two glasses and handed one to Violet. "Cheers."

Violet took a mouthful and nearly spat it out again; it was horrible.

Katherine took a sip of hers and pulled a face. She laughed. "It's disgusting." She threw the contents of her glass over a small bush, and Violet did the same.

"We've probably killed it." Katherine giggled and sat down on the rug. Violet sat down, too; she leaned in close to Katherine and kissed her on the lips. Katherine giggled again, and Violet sat back. Katherine put her arm around Violet's neck and pulled her close again.

They had kissed before, behind the swimming pool, but this felt different. Safer and more dangerous at the same time. Safer, because no one was going to come and stop them: more dangerous, for that same reason.

Violet ran her tongue along Katherine's lips. Katherine opened her mouth a little, and Violet pushed her tongue in and found Katherine's. The feel of their tongues touching sent shivers down Violet's spine. She put her hand up and felt Katherine's cheek; her skin was so smooth. Violet slid her hand down Katherine's neck and over her T-shirt till she had it on Katherine's breast. She could feel through the T-shirt that Katherine wasn't wearing a bra. When she brushed against the nipple, it got smaller.

She pulled Katherine closer; she wanted to be touching as much of Katherine's body with hers as she could. She stretched out on the rug and pulled Katherine on top of her. She could feel their stomachs touching, their knees, their thighs. She slipped her hand under Katherine's T-shirt, and ran it across her smooth back and up to her shoulderblades. She could feel Katherine's ribs. She hugged her tighter and felt their breasts squash together.

Violet rolled Katherine over so she was on the top now. They were still kissing, their tongues sliding together. Violet pushed up Katherine's T-shirt until she was touching Katherine's breast. Once, a long time ago, a girl had let her suck her breasts. Patricia Masters, it was. Patricia had told her mother and Violet had got into all sorts of trouble, but it had felt so wonderful. Violet was ready to risk it again.

She ran her hands over Katherine's body, lightly at first, feeling even the fine hairs on her skin. Katherine moved her body slightly, stretching and arching up towards Violet's touch. Violet started kissing Katherine on the neck; her thumbs found Katherine's nipples under the T-shirt and she circled them around them. Katherine sighed.

Violet pushed Katherine's T-shirt right up to her neck and sat back a moment to look at Katherine's breasts. They were beautiful, small and round with dark nipples. Violet had seen then outlined through Katherine's swimsuit at training, but to see them naked was like magic.

Violet bent down and very gently she kissed one and then the other. Katherine sighed again. Violet put her lips right over one and sucked it into her mouth. Katherine gave a little gasp. Violet looked up at her friend's face; Katherine's eyes were closed and her head was thrown back slightly. Violet decided to carry on. She ran her tongue around the nipple, feeling its little ridges. Katherine arched her back and pushed the breast further into Violet's mouth. Violet sucked harder and flicked her tongue against the nipple, this made Katherine arch her back even more.

Violet moved to the other breast, cradling the first in her hand so it didn't get too cold. She checked Katherine's face again; she had a look of deep concentration, like she was trying to work out a difficult maths problem. Violet wasn't sure if that was a good thing or not.

Violet ran her hands down over Katherine's stomach and along the waist band of her trousers. This was the furthest she had ever been. She undid the top button and looked back up at Katherine's face. Her eyes were still closed, but she did look a little worried. Violet carried on; Katherine could stop her if she went too far.

Under her jeans, Katherine was wearing white knickers with little flowers on them. Violet was a bit disappointed. She had expected black, possibly with some lace. She wasn't sure what to do next. She ran her cheek over Katherine's stomach and felt the smooth skin against smooth skin. Katherine's skin smelt faintly of chlorine, and something warmer, deeper.

Katherine arched her back enough to let Violet pull her jeans down and there was Katherine's body laid out before her, naked except for the flowery knickers. Violet ran her hands down Katherine's body from her breasts to the top of her knickers. She slipped her hand into the knickers and felt the roughness of her pubic hair.

Katherine's eyes were open now, watching Violet. Violet lay down beside her. "You OK?"

Katherine nodded, but she looked a bit uncertain.

Violet ran her fingers through Katherine's pubic hair; Katherine closed her eyes again. Violet kissed her on the lips. She slid her fingers up and down, a little deeper each time until they found a soft wet patch.

"Oh, God." Katherine tried to sit up, and then lay down again. Violet circled her finger around very gently. Katherine's breathing had got faster. Violet noticed her own breathing was faster, too. She could feel, whatever it was she was touching, expand under her finger and get wetter.

"Oh, God," Katherine said again, but didn't try to sit up. She pushed her hips up so that Violet's fingers went deeper inside her. Violet kept moving her fingers and her thumb, which was now on the soft place. Katherine's breathing was now so short that Violet thought she was going to hyperventilate. She was moving her hips, rocking them against Violet's hand. Violet increased the speed of her rubbing. Katherine's skin was shiny with sweat and her face was red. Violet was pretty sweaty herself, too. The way Katherine was moving her body and the feel of her under her thumb made Violet feel very hot.

Violet was moving her thumb and fingers as fast as she could; they were beginning to ache. Suddenly Katherine put her hand on Violet's and Violet stopped moving it. Katherine went completely stiff, then shuddered. The shudder started somewhere under Violet's fingers and seemed to radiate through Katherine's entire body. Twice it went through her and then her body went limp.

Violet wrapped her arms around Katherine, terrified that she had done something terribly wrong

"Katherine?" Violet asked after a moment. "You OK?"

Katherine let out a long drawn out sigh. "Oh, yes," she said and smiled. "Very OK."

Violet pulled Katherine's t-shirt back down and put her jeans over her legs. Katherine curled up in her lap.

"God, Violet, that was . . ." She sighed again. "So good."

Violet stroked Katherine's hair. She put her own hand to her mouth, and there on her fingers was the smell of Katherine. She closed her eyes and for a moment she thought she was going to cry. She must have fallen asleep, because when she opened her eyes again, it was darker and she was cold, and there was a distinct smell of burning in the air.

Katherine woke at the same moment. "The pizzas." She jumped up and ran inside, holding her jeans; Violet followed her. The pizzas were a blackened mess, and the garlic bread had shrivelled to almost nothing.

Katherine was almost in tears. "It had courgettes and peppers and mozzarella cheese." More things Violet had never heard of. Her mother put mincemeat and tinned spaghetti on theirs.

Violet smiled. "I didn't come round for the food."

"I wanted everything to be perfect."

"Everything was perfect." Violet put her arms around Katherine; Katherine leaned her head on Violet's shoulder.

"I wanted to impress you."

"You did that." Violet laughed and Katherine did, too. They kissed again, standing up in the kitchen, tongues touching, breasts touching, toes touching. Violet thought it was the happiest she had ever been.

Katherine started to shiver; she pulled away from Violet. "I've got to get a jumper." Violet let go of her reluctantly. Violet looked at all the bowls on the table; it looked more like a meal for twenty, not for two. She went into the garden and looked at the rug, the two wine glasses and the bottle. She stared at them, wanting to imprint them in her mind, fix them there. She wanted to remember what it was like forever. Then she picked up the rug and pressed her face into it. Very faintly, she could smell Katherine on it.

"What are you doing?" Katherine was at the back door. Violet tucked the rug under her arm.

"Just bringing these in." She picked up the glasses and the bottle.

"You're so sweet." Katherine kissed her on the cheek. "Sweet Violet."

VISITING

Susan Stinson

I was washing potatoes in my aunt Frankie's kitchen sink when, suddenly, it was obvious: Frankie and Ida had been lovers. I shut off the faucet, but kept pushing the scruffy against the potato's disappearing skin. I should have seen.

I finished scrubbing the potatoes, and filled a pot with water, but I didn't set it on the stove. Instead, feeling nostalgic and aggrieved, I stored the potatoes in a giant Ziploc bag, and left the diligent air-conditioning to go find Frankie.

She was on the tractor in sunglasses and a bandanna, mowing the grass on the edge of the white dirt lane. The wide seat on the old, big-knobbed John Deere held her high above the ground, massed like a cumulus cloud in her blue polyester pantsuit. She did a smooth turn at the bottom of the lane and headed back towards me. The sunlight quivered around her. The motor roared.

As I walked down the lane, she shut off the blade and cut the engine. I stood next to the enormous tire, and called up to her. "Frankie."

She took off her sunglasses and squinted at me. She seemed serious, maybe a little dazed from the noise, the fumes and the heat. "Carline."

I held up a jar of cold water. As she reached for it, I touched her wrist. "I want to talk to you. When you're done."

She took a deep drink. I looked up at her thick thighs and hips, her sunburn and strong hands as if everything had new meaning, as if it were all a code. I knew the bandanna meant that she was trying to protect her hairdo, which wouldn't fare well under a feed cap.

She screwed the lid back on the jar, handed it down to me, then said, "I'm going to mow a path to the tank. I'll meet you at the water."

I went back to the house and finished making the potato salad. I recognized the pink label on the mayonnaise jar from childhood with embarrassing pleasure. As a home economist, I was very aware of how often thrift was undermined by brand allegiance.

I didn't want to walk through the field in a housedress with my bare ankles hanging just above the snakes, so I found some boots, jeans and a clean shirt in Frankie's closet. The waist of her jeans was a little loose on me, but we had the same basic build.

Frankie was climbing down from the tractor when I reached the tank. She moved slowly, and winced. The tank was a small pond, dug to give livestock a place to drink. Frankie didn't raise cattle any more, but I could remember her herd sleeping off the day's sun there. Now, the water was green, and there was a ring of cracked mud extending its bank.

"It's low," I said, eyeing Frankie as she leaned against a

tractor tire. I worried about the back of her pantsuit. Machinery stains were among the most difficult to remove, right up there with mustard and blood. Still, Frankie knew her way around stains.

"We need rain." Frankie glanced at the hazy sky. The smell of cut grass was thick as steam. Tartar, her border collie, stretched out in the shade of the tire, panting.

I spotted the hulk of the old row boat beneath a tarp. Frankie groaned, but squatted down with me to lift it off the blocks. We dragged it into shallow water. I knocked the mud dauber nests from the oars, took off my boots, rolled up my jeans, and gave Frankie my hand to help her into the boat. She moved with deliberate vigor. Tartar jumped into the prow and put her nose in the air. I pushed the boat into deeper water, then clambered in.

We floated low but well balanced. I was clumsy at the oars. Tartar stared into the water. Frankie untied her bandanna and dunked it over the side, then closed her eyes and draped it across her face. Rivulets ran down her neck. When we got to the middle, I pulled in the oars and let us drift.

I leaned forward and lifted the bandanna away from Frankie's eyes. "Tell me about Ida," I said.

She didn't say anything. Tartar, scratching, rocked the boat. I moved the bandanna away from Frankie's mouth, too, so it hung damply across the bridge of her nose. She swatted at my hand without opening her eyes. "I've always preferred discretion."

That irritated me. "I've been out to you for years." Something throbbed in my palm. "I think I got a splinter from the oars."

Frankie opened her eyes and reached into her pocket for her knife. The bandanna fell into her lap. She traced the closed edge of the blade with her thumb. "Give me your hand."

In a tribute to childhood, I sucked it. "I don't want you to try to get it out. Not in a boat."

She shrugged and opened the blade. "Have you got a match?"

In my purse, which was on the bed table in the guest room back at the house, I had a book of matches from the Blue Haven Motel. I reached in the pocket of Frankie's jeans and found a cheap lighter. I handed it over.

Frankie clicked the lighter on and held it to the blade. I bent forward to see. The boat rocked, and Tartar looked back at us.

"Stay there, girl," said Frankie. "It's OK." We both stared at the metal, waiting for it to turn black under the flame. Frankie had taught me as a girl to sterilize a needle by burning it before breaking skin. Still watching, she said, "We used to go on long drives in the Mercury, looking at crops and making plans. Ida had a family at home, but she was reckless in that car."

I wondered if she meant reckless like a drunk driver or reckless like a teenage couple at a drive in. Trying to think of a tactful way to phrase the question, I reached for the knife.

She gave it to me and let the lighter go out. "Ida loved to drive, and she loved to dance."

I stroked the blade across my palm, pressing near the splinter to try to get the end to pop out. It was tender, but I could feel it shifting.

Frankie reached out of the boat, and drew circles in the water with her fingers. "One morning when we were putting up peaches in freezer boxes, we started dancing in the kitchen to the radio. Patsy Cline. I wedged my fingers in the knot where Ida's apron was tied low on her hips."

I could see Ida in a yellow apron. I remembered slicing scores of peaches with sticky fingers. Now I spotted the end of the splinter. When I touched it with the knife, it sank deeper into my hand. Wincing, I squeezed the skin, then caught the sliver with the tip of the knife and pulled it free. "Got it."

Frankie looked at me, then back at the water. As she stared at the rippling surface, she reminded me of a movie starlet gazing into a wading pool while she sang the theme song of *Tammy's in Love*. Frankie was forty years older and maybe a hundred and fifty pounds heavier than the Hollywood version, but the essential yearning was the same. I flicked the tiny hair of wood over the side, and asked, "Did people know?"

She pulled her hand out of the water and shook her head. "I remember private things." She dried her fingers on her pants. "Gathering Ida's skirts against the back of her legs."

I took my turn staring at the water. It was opaque. The boat cut and muddied the reflections of the trees. I was disturbed to find that I had come all this way to hear the kind of romantic details I was used to getting from my friends back East, except that Ida was dead and I had always imagined Frankie to be in love with the white rock, the tractor, the grasses and the kitchen cabinets, not reaching for the edges of her friend's clothes.

I pushed my memory for images of Ida that were different from this new one of Frankie's fingers on her legs. A long braid and a corded neck. She squeezed the tops of my arms in greeting, making jokes about butter and pies. She sewed and had driven Frankie and me in the Mercury down some dark curving road to a county talent night, where she played the banjo.

Once, Frankie and Ida had gone to Padre Island for the weekend when the husband was away on business. I baby-sat. All I remembered were those skinny boys staring at me across a pan full of frozen fish sticks. I couldn't get the oven to light. We ate peanut butter, instead.

A frog jumped with a dense splash like a stone. Tartar started and shook, wanting to chase it, but stayed in the boat.

"Lilian ate frog legs once. They tasted like chicken." It felt right to find a reason to say my lover's name. Lilian was a vegetarian, but she had a past. I missed her.

Frankie reached for the oars and handed them to me. "I've got to get changed before the Library Guild shows up." Her tone was definite, but her face sagged. The tag was sticking out of the neck of her tunic top. I leaned across to tuck it in. She put her hand on my collar and pulled me in so she could kiss my cheek. "Thanks for coming to see me," she said.

I kissed her back, feeling both joined and far from her. Tartar – a little jealous – tried to stand on my shoulders with her sharp claws. I shrugged her off. She sulked in the bottom of the boat until a trout broke out of the water just as we reached the edge of the tank. Then she barked.

That night, while Frankie was drinking a malt and watching wrestling, I went out to the shed to call Lilian. I didn't want to worry about being overheard. Frankie had an extension out there so she wouldn't miss calls while she was working on the tractor. I flipped the switch to turn on the light bulb, took a deep breath, and dialed.

It was a rotary phone. My fingers recognized the hard dial, with its clicks and spins. The ring at the other end sounded distant. Lilian picked up. "Hello."

Her voice was warm and faintly businesslike. I wanted to stroke her belly and tell her everything. It was overwhelming. "Hi, Lilian."

"Oh, Carline." She faded, very angry. "How have you been?"

I picked up Frankie's broom and leaned my chin on the wooden end. "Lilian, I miss you."

We both waited for the next thing to say. She came up with it. "Are you at Frankie's? How is she?"

I told her. I spoke about Ida dead, Frankie wanting to mourn her as a lover, and the memorial service to plan. I told her about the men on the bus. I told her the sky was looking big. I told her I would be gone at least two or three more weeks. I said I was sorry I left our home for this visit the way I did: abruptly, without showing her the right attentiveness. I talked until my ear was sore and my tongue was dry. When I propped the broom back against the wall, there was a round red mark on my chin.

Lilian told me nothing, but she listened. I didn't press her to talk, both because I was selfish and because I was scared. In the end, when I said, "I love you," she said, "I love you too."

Lilian seemed more present to me after we hung up. I wasn't sure what she was feeling, but I had a sense of her near me as I looked around the shed. The bulb was generous with its harsh light. There was a lot of dust. The floor itself was dirt, and the shed was open on two sides. Dust coated the tractor, the Mercury, the trailer, and Frankie's pickup. I found it restful rather than disturbing; this was dirt that belonged. I had on a stain-resistant skirt from my suitcase. It was good to feel familiar to myself. I sat down on a wooden bench. The night was warm.

I caught the end of the rope I used to swing on. It was frayed below the knot. The bench made my back ache. I needed support, and I was restless. I dropped the rope, got up and switched off the bulb.

Low, long and wide, the Mercury shone in the angled moonlight. I could see the coat of arms on the headlight covers: a cross surrounded by flames. "Mercury" was written in silver cursive above the right headlight. The bars of the grille shimmered above the big front bumper. I walked over to it, wondering why Frankie got to keep Ida's car. Did Ida leave it to her in a will, or did Ida's husband feel that it belonged in Frankie's shed?

I stood in front of it and saw a shadowy reflection in that

great creased lake of a hood. Something skittered along the tin wall of the shed. I got spooked. If Ida had a ghost, I imagined that this was where she would be.

I tried to hop onto the hood, but didn't make it. I brought the bench over, and used it to step up. The whole car bounced a little, but the body held firm. It would be a considerable pity to dent Ida's car. I stretched across the hood, and leaned against the windshield. The dust made me sneeze.

I probably should have gone into the house, where Frankie had cool air, good lighting, and plenty of strong, wide chairs. Or I could have slid off the hood and opened the door of the Mercury. I could have sat down in the roomy passenger seat, lifted a lever to recline, and visited more deeply with the surfaces of Frankie's old passion and Ida's ghost. If I remembered correctly, it was well-upholstered in there.

What I did, though, was kick off my shoes. In brief socks with fluffy balls on the back like winged sandals, I gathered my feet beneath me, rested one hand on the roof of the car, and stood up on the hood. Slowly, I let go of the roof, then leaned out over the hard ground to grab the rope.

I teetered, but finally hauled it in. Holding it under one arm, I found my balance again. I felt clumsy, but steadied by bodily memories. I had already been a fat girl the first time I played on the rope. Now I took a firm grip, tucked it between my thighs, and jumped.

It was a short drop. The rope held, but I just hung, without the thrill I remembered. I kicked at the bench, knocking it over, then got my feet flat against the door of the Mercury, and pushed off hard.

This time, I felt the thrill. I worked my body in the air, urging it higher. Finding a rhythm, I swung back towards the car, pushed off again, then arched into a dizzy circle above the ground.

The rope was rough and bristly. My skirt bunched. My arms were already tired. I lurched sideways into a post, then pushed off with one hand, leaning back. It was too dark above me to see where the rope was tied in the rafters.

Sweating with effort, I twisted the rope tighter to my leg. I wasn't very high, but there was intensity in the rushes of air and the chafing rope. I kept bumping against the car and the post. My feet rested on the knot. It was so good to be out of contact with the ground.

As I finally slowed to dangling, I knew I wasn't a child any more. I slid down the rope to the ground. My hands burned. I set the bench upright and found my shoes. I knew that Ida's big Mercury was both excessive and beautiful to me. Sitting on the bench and leaning against the fender, I peeled off the little socks to save myself from hobbling back to the house on a layer of dirt. As I slipped my bare feet into my shoes, I knew for certain that I wasn't leaving Lilian.

I walked to the house. At the front steps, I stopped to look up. The moon's swelling light sent shivers through the undistinguished dark. It made my body throb.

The front door opened, spilling glare. Frankie came out, groping in her purse. She crossed the porch and leaned down, holding out a roll of candy. "Want a wintergreen?"

I sliced the wrapper with my fingernail, and lifted a lifesaver off the roll. The sharp flavor filled my mouth. I went inside with Frankie, sucking hard.

HAVING YOUR CAKE AND EATING IT

Amazon

Gail has a body to die for, Abena has a body to kill for, and I'm the living embodiment of the seven deadly sins and I'm just about to blow out the candles. Egotistically rich but economically challenged, I wish for a night of Abena's lush kisses inhabiting Gail's mesomorphic frame. And I'm pissed off that laziness alone prevents me from fulfilling my desire.

I fill my lungs and the flames dance in synchronized panic as I extinguish them one by one and inhale the silvery sinewy smoke and everyone cheers and someone somewhere releases the pressure from a bottle of pink champagne. And I close my eyes and I wish. I wish that wish as if my life depends on it, squeezing my eyes tight like fists each concealing a sumptuous treat. Which hand? You've got to have one you can't have both, which hand? Because you only get one thirtieth birthday, one chance to blow out all the candles and one wish.

"Penny for your thoughts, Dana."

"Sorry, my thoughts don't come that cheap."

I regret it as soon as I've said it. If only we could rewind, sixty seconds . . . sixty months. Oh, to be twenty-five again and to not have said what I just said to Sarah. But as she turns to conceal her humiliation, I remember my quarter-of-a-century drunken orgy and decide that perhaps the here-and-now is preferable.

"Anyone for some cake?"

Cake is an absolute must at any serious gathering. It enhances conversation, heightens the senses and turns even the most disgruntled of dykes into a satisfied punter. Especially when it happens to be a layer of chocolate, a layer of coffee and a layer of vanilla with chocolate butter icing that oozes out of the sides as you cut it. Even the most lipstick of lesbians cannot resist the licking of lips, the bulging of the belly but the need, the insatiable need, for a little more pleasure, a mere sliver, a mouthful, a morsel, more.

I cut and they queue and suddenly Sarah is by my side again but I'm admiring Abena who's wearing a dress and I love a woman who can wear a dress well, who can wear a well-cut dress with style. It's a forties original, cut from rationed cloth, tailored, tight. And underneath it, silk nylons with a seam that goes from her ankles to her armpits. And she's been blessed with the high cheekbones and noble mien of a West African Princess, the gap-toothed smile of a Ghanaian goddess. Everyone else is in the latest trousers and the latest trainers or the latest trouser suit or the latest latex. But Abena's the most post-modern of them all, anarchic, anachronistic.

And behind her, her partner, Gail, good-looking and a good

two inches taller than me. And if I could only dislike her, my jealousy would be absolute. She sees me looking and winks jet-black mascara which contrasts heavily with her freckles. She's beautiful and desirable and I want to *be* her. Great body, stunning black girlfriend, what more could a girl want? And impossible to dislike as I find myself cocking my head to one side, winking back.

I cut the cake, one layer for each decadent decade, and we bite into the chocolate butter icing that sticks to the roof of the mouth and the sweet, moist crumbs of sponge. Occasionally someone surreptitiously licks her lips and emits a sigh of pure gastronomical pleasure. Soon, the cake begins to take effect. Jane opens another bottle of pink champagne and they make a toast: "To Dana," followed by cries of "Speech! Speech!"

"OK, you ravenous, ravishing sex goddesses. But I'll keep it short." I stare round at the masticating crowd and take a large gulp of the heavenly bubbly. "First, I'd like everyone to give a huge cheer to Flor who made this mouth-watering birthday cake."

Flor appears from the huddle in the corner and takes a bow so low that her hair touches the carpet. There are whoops and excited applause. Flor makes an impression in more ways than one.

"Secondly, big thanks to Elizabeth and Rebecca for letting me use their beautiful house for this party, especially as they're leaving the country a week on Tuesday. Can I be your tenant? I promise to pay the rent on time."

Many glasses and a few eyebrows are raised. The couple have kept their departure date close to their chests. I hadn't intended to let the cat out of the bag but I catch Becky's eye and she seems relieved. Thank God. It could have been a real *faux pas*.

"Finally, please raise your glasses to yourselves for being such special friends, seeing me through thick and thin: mainly thick." Everyone laughs at the reference to my expanding waistline. Only my best mates could get away with that. "And for supporting my hair-brained schemes and recommending me the best therapists in the country."

"Yeah, but did you take our advice?" It's Sarah, trying to be witty. She's a wonderful, caring woman but she doesn't know when to give someone space. *I'm* the one who's thirty. This is *my* speech. No hecklers allowed.

"No, but did you *give* it?"

That shuts her up long enough for the crowd to drag me into the lounge to open the Mount Everest of presents awaiting me. I tear at the dark shiny foil, pastel crêpe and patterned tissue paper revealing black satin three-quarter length gloves, a royal blue-and-gold smoking jacket, a china tea-set, a reversible rug, a Nina Simone box set, an obscene selection of milk and plain chocolate, a mirror ball the size of a football, a vibrator the size of a truncheon and various books, including *The Mammoth Book Of Lesbian Erotica.*

I kiss everyone as if it's New Year's Eve 1999 and for a few moments I'm blissfully happy, chatting to the accompaniment of Nina Simone and the low hum of the vibrator which is causing some hilarity on the sofa. But after a while I experience that first of January anticlimax and I sit watching my friends cruising each other, teasing each other and, try as I might, I can't relax. And I know that no amount of champagne will do the trick. I feel edgy, almost angry with everyone for being in my space, then I realise it's not even my space and I feel inadequate that my flat's too small to entertain more than three friends at a time.

Now, If I'd done the therapy as Karen and Claire and Tania and Sharon suggested, I might be able to access and overcome my negativity. But I haven't and I can't. I *should* be enjoying myself, so I can't. New Year's Eve in the middle of June. It's that weird sensation of not enjoying your own meal because you prepared it. Everyone else is complimenting you on your culinary expertise and you're eating mechanically, knowing it tastes good but knowing too much about the preparation to be able to dissociate from the hard work and just enjoy.

I find myself sitting on the toilet, head in hands, thinking, "Well, the party's a success, I've got some gorgeous presents but I feel really, really distanced from it all."

I zip up my trousers, flush the chain, wash my hands, splash my face with cold water, apply another coat of lipstick, and open the door.

"Thought you'd drowned in there."

It's Gail, Aberdonian, playful, coral red lipstick, jet-black mascara: Gail. She has the ability to outstare a cat. I blink and she laughs triumphantly.

"Is everything OK?"

"Yeah. I'm just having a dose of it's-my-party syndrome. It'll pass."

"And is there a known cure for this illness?"

"Yes. No. I don't know. I've never been thirty before. I feel really weird. I mean, I'm not connecting with people. It almost feels like I've gatecrashed someone else's celebration. I'm probably just drunk."

"No, you're just stressed, Dana." She puts a hand on my shoulder. "You're really tense. Jesus, it's like you've got an iron girder across your back."

So she's massaging my shoulders, pummelling them into compliancy. And it's so painful and it's so perfect and I'm plasticine, elastic, fluid. She's moving her hands down my back and gently guiding me into the back bedroom. I hear the door click shut and the light click off and we're playing see-saw, tug-o-war with our tongues. I should be thinking "oh my God this is wrong, this is bad, this is wicked". But I'm not . . . I'm not thinking at all because my brain has melted like my limbs and I'm pure liquid ecstasy. Gail's eating me. She's devouring me whole and I'm surrendering. I don't know whether she's swallowing me or I'm diving into her, I don't know where I end and she begins, but I'm entering her every crevice, freer than water. I flow with every spasm of her fingertip and sweat through every pore of her body until we convulse in exquisite symbiosis. I am inside her. I have *become* her. And checking myself out in the mirror, pecs, lats, waist, honed hips and legs so long I almost get vertigo, I decide that she definitely becomes *me*.

I explore my new body, gingerly at first, then begin to stroke myself to a rich moistness. I'm well on the way to paradise when there is a subtle knock on the door. I momentarily freeze. But it's Abena who gently pushes it open, clicks it shut and slowly turns the key. I find myself saying, "I've been expecting you, babe," and smile a black-lashed, coral-lipped smile of anticipation.

Abena leads me by the hand to the bed which is covered with deep purple fake-fur. She doesn't seem to realise that her girlfriend has been possessed by the spirit of three decades of debauchery. But why should she? To all intents and purposes I *am* her partner. I look the same, sound the same, perhaps even smell, taste and touch the same. I lay on my back, tortured by a cocktail of lust and fear.

She tells me to lie still, which is difficult since the fur is ticklish and my skin is sensitive, and begins to undress. I watch her unzip her dress from the side and pull the yellow crepe material over her head. I try to remain relaxed but my breathing has doubled in speed and volume. Underneath the dress, Abena's wearing a cream satin corset with suspenders that hold up her nylons, and matching cream briefs. She watches me watching and holds her index finger to her lips. Her body is lush, full, strong, blue-black. I very badly want to know what is feels, smells like.

Once she's comfortable, she begins hunting for something in the chest of drawers and emerges with several silk scarves. She approaches the bed and begins to tie my wrists and ankles with them. She doesn't say a word but I can smell the faint scent of roses about her skin and I'm giddy with pleasure. When she's finished, she strikes a match and begins to light the plump, white candles adorning every surface of the room until they form a resplendent choir. It's then that I realize, as she lights the thirtieth wick and turns to face me, that she knows the score.

But I'm scared. Wondering what Gail and Abena do behind closed doors and now understanding that I'm soon to experience it in the full, uncensored version. The Director's Cut. And she's humming and singing in a language I don't understand as she holds the first candle above my naked torso and lets the wax drip fat molten heat onto my taut body. I tense, anticipating pain, but the sensation is deep heat without the smell of menthol. Just the subtle aroma of roses and the stronger smell of frankincense that emanates from the far corner of the room.

Still singing, Abena anoints me with several more candles. And I'm relaxing, beginning to really enjoy this new sensation and the thrill of the ritual. Then, abruptly, she stops. I turn my head from side to side, realizing I've had my eyes closed for the past minute. She seems to have left the room. I hear murmuring outside the door and hold my breath to hear what's going on but all I can make out is the low hum of hushed voices. I burn with humiliation. Then the door opens again and Abena enters the room, this time in a red silk gown.

"Gail," she commands, and her voice startles me, reminds me who I am and whom I must obey. "I want you to close your eyes. I'm going to blindfold you. You mustn't say a word. If you do, I'll have to gag you. And I don't want to do that. Yet."

There's something charged about silence. You instantly feel embarrassed, nervous, wanting to fill it up with inane chatter or music. But you simultaneously love the power of absence, the electricity, the heightening of the senses. Deprived of one faculty, the rest work twice as hard to compensate. As I feel the silk wrap its way around my head, I become acutely aware of the salt caking my lips like a glass prepared for tequila, the sweet smell of candle smoke, and minutes later, the cold, wet shock of something that smells suspiciously like chocolate icing, hitting my belly.

"This wasn't in the script," I hear myself saying.

Me and my big mouth. The third time today it's let me down. There is a terrible pause then footsteps, the rummaging in the drawer and the firm punishment of silk smudging my lipstick. Abena coats me with a thick layer of icing. She works in silence, covering all the erogenous zones, including my earlobes. I'm aware of the contrast of the sticky icing and the globules of wax solidifying on my body. I lay perfectly still, knowing that the intense heat of my body will soon make the icing run in rivulets, like molten lust, and Abena will have to lick it off my skin. She may be from West Africa, where "sweet" means fine-tasting rather than simply sugary, but she enjoys a good nectareous high like the rest of us.

When she first begins to lick me, I writhe all over the bed, forgetting the restraints and the tension mounts, deep in my solar plexus, at each silk-straining limb, and as she sucks me I want to come immediately, violently, shouting and thrashing. But she's listening to my breathing and she won't let me. And this is torture, pure unadulterated torture because I want to drown in her bed of roses and feel her fingernails clawing at my back as she comes with me. I want to *see* her. I can feel her swollen nipples through the satin and I can hear her sucking me and licking me and kissing me, feel her kissing me. I imagine her dipping her finger in the bowl of cake mixture and licking her lips when mummy isn't looking. I picture her running her finger round the inside of the bowl when there's still enough to make another butterfly cake, and I picture her putting her whole head into the bowl and licking, licking hard, licking the bowl clean. And I implode.

And I'm all body. My brain has melted like my limbs and I'm pure liquid ecstasy, overflowing and effervescent as someone somewhere releases the pressure from a bottle of pink champagne. And someone cannot resist the licking of lips, the bulging of the belly and the need, the insatiable need, for a little more pleasure, a mere sliver, a mouthful, a morsel, more.

THE CAKE MAKER

Stella Duffy

Natsuki awakes from a fitful sleep and rises an hour before dawn. Lies silent for a moment, then blesses the new hours, sighs into breath months of anticipation and begins. She stands on thin feet, walks reflective naked to the door across the smooth scrubbed floor and washes in almost dawnlight. On the step of her hut she cleanses sleep from her flesh with water that is mountain pure, ice crystals scraped from the edge of the wooden bowl to scour her already satin skin to a still finer silk. There is a final star waiting to reward her care and she will be meticulous in every action today, each gesture and moment is vital. Because the warrior will come today. Her warrior. Natsuki has twelve hours, thirteen at the most, to ready herself. There is not enough time and there are also far too many hours to endure. When the day comes that has been so long awaited, there is both pleasure and pain in the anticipation. Natsuki understands each to be of equal value, the one enhancing and making still greater the intense joy of the other. She knows how to wait, calmly holds time within where the smile is hidden.

Inside an isolated mountain hut with a burnt-out fire and one bare window, she begins to pray. Earnest pleas for the warrior's safe arrival, for what she would wish to be. She knows better than this. Knows that what is to come will happen in the fullness of its own time, that her wishes will have no effect if they are not in tune with what is already meant. Knows this but prays anyway.

There has been a perfect melancholy to her waiting. It has been many months since the last visit. Natsuki has simply waited, knowing that their time would eventually come. She understands the need for proper order. The cherry tree is bare through the long dark winter and sits out its time of darkness in a shell of dead wood, holding inside the potential for spring life. New life that comes not easily, but always. Buds rip themselves from inside the branches, splitting hardened bark, spewing acid sap and forcing through to the elements, presenting an expectation of blossom to the old world. There are things which are ordered and meant. The heron always returns. The journey from Kamakura to Kyoto takes twelve days. There is no way to speed either the return home or the journey onwards. And no need. So Natsuki has waited. Knowing autumn would pass, giving herself up to spend the winter alone in dark and cold quiet and knowing that with the first of the cherry blossom the warrior would come to her come for her, be the coming spring. Because Natsuki must wait, then she welcomes the waiting. She is neither the arbiter of seasons, nor of her own desires. Time has made her ready. The season is come.

Yesterday Natsuki walked down to the village. It was a long journey, three hours there and a longer four hours back. Laden with provisions and expectation, the trek home was protracted and tiring. It was also more joyful. To return home was to escape the fuss of people, the harsh noise of light, to go back to her silent life and dark room for another night alone. The last without the scent of new flesh, fresh blood, in her home, in her hair, on her skin. In her. The village is a small fishing settlement; it has clung to the side of a hill for over five hundred years and will no doubt stay there for five hundred more. The sea is its reason to exist and the Pacific is not going anywhere soon. Between the new green of the almost spring land and the dark blue of the constant waves lies the village of her birth, the only settlement Natsuki has ever known. She will greet but a handful of people, mostly in silence with a nod or shake of her head. She will visit her grandfather to kneel before him and kiss his hand. Leaving behind her gifts and food, she will not speak. She will pray at her mother's graveside with silent tears. She will barter at traders' stalls with as few words as possible, collect her precious goods and travel on again. She will not eat or drink in the village. She will leave none of herself behind. Natsuki walked away from the village on the day of her twelfth birthday, the morning after her mother was buried. She has lived alone and often silent for almost seven years. The necessary visits to the village are difficult for one who so enjoys the privacy of her own mind and in the past few years they have become so rare that now her presence in the market is welcomed as a sign of good luck by superstitious traders and sceptical housewives alike. Following her fleeting and always unexpected excursions among the people, harvests are larger, children sweeter behaved and fish swim into rather than away from the nets. There is no empirical data for these facts, only belief and the soft proof of a gentler breeze. The old men say it is her purity that brings them grace; the young women believe it is her beauty. Natsuki knows it is her silence. In a village stuffed full with cries and laughter and the thundering beat of skin against skin, the soft walk of a silent woman breeds a spreading wave of peace. Natsuki is careful when she speaks, still more careful with whom she shares herself.

Yesterday Natsuki journeyed to the market in patient and rhythmic steps. She made her purchases with calculated bartering, counted out the prized currency it had taken her months to save and, having ensured her grandfather's safety and comfort, spent all the remaining money on provisions for her visitor. She will feed and water the guest with six months of her stockpiled life. Neither gratitude nor awareness of her sacrifice is necessary. Natsuki has made her plans and acknowledged her desire. She will bow herself down, happily submitting to her own will. There is nothing else she can do. There is nothing else she would do. The journey home is long and tiring, the rivers full swollen with early spring rains and the steep uphill paths muddy and precarious. The journey is also very, very easy. Each step takes her closer to the when.

Natsuki has prepared long for this day. Sitting proud in the centre of her small room is the flour with which she will bake her cake, just one, a single cake for the warrior alone. She purchased the rice on another soul-giving journey and returned to the silence of her home with the precious base material. She ground just a tiny handful of grains each day. Three grains first and each ground separate – one for her guest, one for herself and one for this day. Each one carefully cracked open, gently beaten to free the soft powder, the dust of three grains then fusing together. Every day a new mingling, every day adding fresh flour to the covered earthenware bowl, placed with infinite care on the dry shelf above her hearth, and when there was not wood to burn the fire she slept quiet with her small body folded around the bowl to protect the flour from the cold. With each new cracked grain she silently begged that this longed-for return might be allowed. Begged but did not expect, knew better than to tempt her own fate with petitions of personal desires. She will accept what comes. Natsuki has no choice; she is given to this moment by her own hand. Yesterday the first bud on the tree outside was ready to burst and this morning the shaft of blossom blessed her with its pale pink. She knows and yet cannot know for certain that the warrior will come today. But her skin reaches toward the road, her body turns involuntarily to the west, urging the sun to set, deep within her flesh she feels the journey begin.

The cake she will make today is not the traditional cake cooked in every home across the land. Not for this warrior the ordinary cake from glutinous rice, eaten by anyone. Natsuki will do far better than expected. This guest is a traveller as well as a warrior. Natsuki has heard tales of the journeys, listened both in reality and in her dreams. Knows of the sweet, soft almond cake that was given in love in Italy, remembers in her own mouth the melting on the tongue of the rich cream pastry fed slowly in Germany. Natsuki understands the desire for light and sweet. It has been winter for many months; the blossom brings spring and, like the body, senses turn from the dark, reach instead for soft and gentle bright. Natsuki has travelled nowhere beyond her village and even that is too far for her, but with knowledge of desire she will bake this cake. Her yearning is all the recipe she needs.

In the year Natsuki was born, Izu Peninsula was rocked by the severest weather the old women could remember. While her mother cried out in the red blood of labour, dark tides lashed the shoreline of the little fishing village and many lives found their end in salt and grinding sand. The next day, as the fishing population counted their dead swimming home to them on swollen tides, the farmers watched their cultivated hills, attacked by torrential rain and the indifferent grasp of gravity, slide downwards. At the waters' edge, earth and ocean congratulated themselves on another display of natural strength over human will. And while the people gathered their broken belongings together and began again, Natsuki's mother prayed over the new girl child, born in a storm and quiet as the after-rain and held her baby up to the cool moon for blessing. The baby grew into speech and song, learning resignation from her mother and acceptance from her grandfather and, tending her father's sea grave, chose the path that allowed her face to smile as well as endure. She elected a mask that granted her the blessing of silence. When her mother died and the child Natsuki left the village, she took with her nothing but knowledge. And just a little hidden need. With time she became like the still pool in her nature-planted yard, only the softest of ripples crossing her face to indicate fiercest of storms. Eventually the warrior came, as Natsuki had known she would, passing the hut and stopping to drink from the cool pool. And though the guest thought she was lost, Natsuki understood why she had come, and with knowledge came remembrance of desire.

Natsuki has dug a small pit in her yard. It is exactly one foot deep and another wide. In the bottom of the dark hole she places four round flat stones, fitting them close to the earth and to each other. Over the stones she lays out crisp dry twigs and grasses, adding in thin branches of dried herbs. She has collected these for weeks and carefully dried them in the hut. They burn easily even in the cool air, catching quickly and bringing a warm amber light to Natsuki's face. On top of the young fire she lays pieces of wood one by one, cut from a living cherry tree, edge of a branch here, surface breaking root there. She has cut and dried this wood, each chunk the size of her tight closed fist, small hands. She adds one piece of wood at a time, eventually the hole is filled with bright fire. Now she has a little over an hour until it will burn down. Time here is precious.

In her hut she takes two fresh eggs carefully lifted from an untended nest a day ago. She breaks the eggs over a bowl, separates the yolk and white with her hands, letting the translucent white wash and spill through her fingers, cradling the yellow in her palm. Over a stone bowl, she blends the two yolks in her right hand with the fistful of honey she holds in her left, creaming the two together with her hands, scooping up and combining what falls to the bowl until her hands run with the sweet creamy mixture. She places the honey and yolks to one side. Holding the other bowl in the crook of her right arm, she then whisks the egg whites, the narrow fingers of her left hand dancing air into the mixture. When both sets of eggs are combined she reaches for her precious store of flour, lifts the three fine handfuls of dry white matter and sifts it into the eggs and honey with her own breath, dropping just a little at a time, breathing gently across the flour as it falls. She swirls the flour into the creamy mixture, tipping the bowl and letting the ingredients run together; she will not use a heavy hand this time, searching for the effect of light. The warrior told her she had seen this made in Italy. She told her once, in the middle of the night, many months ago. A story of a delicious Italian cook, a wide woman of sun-leathered skin and lush flesh, hard-worked body tempered and enriched by hands of bird-bone fineness. Natsuki has waited until this moment to test her memory. There has been no rehearsal. She leaves the mixture in her hut, covered with a narrow piece of thin white silk and returns to the fire which is now completely burnt down. With a split stick she stirs the remaining embers in the pit oven, pushing them to the sides, uncovering the burning hot rocks. She places one hand on the cool earth and with prayer and concentration moves the rocks just a little with her other hand. She would have the base be perfect flat. She removes her hand from the outdoor oven and plunges it deep into her cool mouth. When her flowing saliva has cooled the heat she looks at her fingers: they are red but not burnt, hot but not blistered. The cold earth connection has protected her as she prayed it would. She lays heavy rice leaves on top of the embers to hold them down so they will not pollute her cake mixture. Rice leaves too, line the small tatami basket, soaked overnight in rain water to be the container for her cake. This way it will dry out in the oven, drying as the cake cooks. In the darker light of the hut, Natsuki slowly pours the mixture into the basket, and carries it carefully outside. She kneels before the fire and bends to place her offering into the ground oven. A little of the mixture seeps through the basket and spills on to her thigh. She licks at the sweet cream and remembers the story of the Italian cook, the story of the mouth of the Italian cook. Natsuki prays for warmth and honeyed lightness and sets the basket on the hot stones. She covers the whole with more leaves and then sits, waiting for her cake to cook in the warmth of the earth. The ground she sits on is cold, but Natsuki who knows and waits is not. She has the heat of anticipation to keep her warm.

Time passes with the light, Natsuki finally moves. Her seat on the earth is cold but she is not. Natsuki is warmed by the passion-heat of her still dance. She knows the cake is ready. Carefully she lifts each fine layer of delicate cover from the earth pit. Too fast a shot of cold air will kill the airy warmth of her creation, too long in the heat will injure just the same. Natsuki does not know this from experience. She knows because she listened to the warrior's story. Understood the explanation of bakers and ovens and timings half a world away and centuries distant. She waits a long prayer of bidding between each uncovering. She is perfect because she must be; there is no other option. Natsuki hears and sees nothing but the necessity of this moment. Like the cloth dyed a fifth time in indigo, her concentration grows ever deeper each time she dips her hand into the still hot embers. She cannot be burnt, the ashes are blood warm, her temperature has risen to meet them, her skin is a translucent carapace, there is nothing to burn. In this moment Natsuki is pure wanting, no flesh. Finally the last leaf. Natsuki's hands are soft ash grey. She washes them clean with the brimming flood falling from her eyes. The sweet cake is revealed, mellow-lit by the glow that comes from her face. Small and perfect, maybe three willing mouthfuls to feed a hungry travelling warrior woman. It is covered and laid aside.

Natsuki readies herself. From a deep sandalwood chest that has not been opened in seven years she takes a long gown of silk. The cloth is dark green, shot through with purple and blue glimmers of unimpeded light. The cloth was given to her mother on her wedding day. Dyed by hand in the dammed stream pool of the yard where Natsuki's father played as a child, the chosen only son in a wide family of women. The cloth was woven by Natsuki's paternal grandmother, a wedding present for her new daughter-in-law. A year after the two young people married, Natsuki's grandmother died in her sleep; old before her time with worry and work, she nonetheless lived long enough to see her last grandchild born. She blessed the baby Natsuki with arthritic hands and sang to her in the quavering voice of age. After her death, the young family of three travelled to the shore in search of a better life. In the large chest that held all her mother's world, the toddler Natsuki saw the cloth laid down, a relic of a time when beauty had been a permissible dream. As a fisherman's wife, there would be no room for silk. But still the cloth was not sold; though there were many times when the men returned with empty nets, Natsuki's father insisted that one day his wife would wear a gown of the silk his mother had hoarded throughout his young life. The wife never did wear the cloth for the man who drowned in a dark green sea, shot through with the cries of his dying friends, but before she died Natsuki's mother cut and sewed it into a gown for her young daughter, the silent child who seemed unlikely ever to need a bridal gift. Natsuki's mother fashioned the cloth into a gown, shaping it with possibility for her template. She cut the material on the body of an eleven year old child and fitted it to be worn by that eleven year old when she would be a woman of eighteen.

Natsuki removes the gown from the chest, carefully unfolds it and allows it to fall on to her thin flesh. It is a perfect fit and the seven-year creases drop fast from the cloth with the warmth of her willing body. Having tried the gown on, Natsuki removes it again, laying it across her sleeping mat. Beside it she lays out another gown from the chest. This one is soft white and older still. It was her grandfather's and will be an accurate fit for the warrior, a woman stronger and wider and taller by a hand's breadth than Natsuki. The two gowns lie side by side on the bed, warm silks spilling into each other, running across the floor. She covers her body with a cotton shift. There is still time.

Natsuki stands beside the thin cherry tree; she plucks a fresh fist of blossom from a branch. Holds in her hand the six points of soft pink. The petal is tinted rose as when blood runs under fine skin. Natsuki holds the blossom to her open mouth, smells the taste of flowers on her tongue, the bitterness of pale yellow stamen, the sour of thin green stem. She caresses her face with the flowers, coaxing her skin awake. Natsuki's knees bend and pull her to the ground; her narrow back lays her out beneath the trees, her hands pause fingertip-touching beneath her breasts, the blossom falls across her heart, rests on a hollow of indented ribcage. She looks up and watches the deep red of sunset breaking against pine needles, burnt amber falling over the blue-green, mixing it into the dark of the sky. Her eyes shut against falling night: the waiting is done.

The warrior's footstep comes first. Leading her tired horse through the narrow pathway, overhanging trees grown too long for her to ride in comfort. Natsuki's breath catches, waiting. Her body, her limbs, are at once both still and ready to spring. There are five minutes or more until the warrior woman is close. When her feet finally rest, Natsuki opens her dark eyes. From the perspective of the ground, the woman is taller than the pines, silhouetted against the dark sky, blossom reflected light glinting off her armour, held into place with thick embroidery. The woman holds out a callused hand to Natsuki, who takes it, guiding the guest's hand to her mouth, just brushing her fingers with a silent touch of wanting breath. She stands and leads the woman to water. There are no words.

The woman deals with the horse; Natsuki deals with the woman. The warrior takes off the heavy saddle, removes the heavier blanket. Natsuki lifts away her visitor's outer coat, the layers of thick material, lays down the offered sword. When the horse has been stripped and the woman is light again, dressed only in the woven layers next to her skin, Natsuki takes the woman and the horse to water. The horse drinks long, the woman reaches to wash her face, Natsuki takes her hands and washes them for her. Cups cold water into herself and smoothes the warrior's face with it. Rinses her neck and arms with the cool, pours water across her back, warmed as it comes from Natsuki's desire-heated hands. Natsuki washes the woman's feet, the length of her legs. They do not speak to each other. When the woman is clean and cool, Natsuki is drenched, soaked with the water running from the woman. She takes the woman into her hut, for a moment in the dark of no starlight, they are naked, blossom distance apart, until she covers the woman's skin and her own with the waiting gowns. Dressed again, she lights a single candle, gives her guest a cushion to lean on and leans her head in close, offering her hair to stroke.

Soon the woman will tell her the story of where she has been and why, will explain about the world and its people. For now, there is silence and time enough to be still.

The woman's stories are not long, but they are full. Natsuki travels half the known globe, the world that is still no globe, in an hour before the bright fire. When she has finished the telling the woman is hungry, thirsty. Natsuki brews tea, slowly allowing the bubbling water to filter through the fine dried leaves. Pours for her guest, hands the warrior the single porcelain bowl, a gift from the woman, returned still more full. She waits while her guest drinks. The warrior who is no warrior without armour takes in the tea with care and great joy. This drink is from her homeland, the stores are from her past. With the tea from Natsuki's hands she is returned to this moment, the reason for her coming. When she has finished a full mouthful from the second bowl, Natsuki rises from her side, reaches up into a dark shelf and brings out the cake. It rests small and perfect, covered with fine silk. Silk the woman left with her on the last visit. Natsuki is returning the woman to herself.

She uncovers the plate, keeping herself hidden in the shadow cast by the woman's body. She would not have the guest see her own desire. The woman smiles, surprised. Natsuki has recreated her favourite story, made it out of thin air and old tales. She had given away the entire story to this young girl, and now Natsuki knows exactly what to do. The woman closes her eyes. Natsuki lays the plate on the ground, between her own thighs. Her legs encompass the woman; their skin does not touch. She holds the cake in her left hand, holds it close to her guest's nose. The woman smells the scent of past and present and denies herself thought of the future, the next moment. She would be only here and all her skills of war and passion are brought into play to bring her home to this time. Natsuki replaces the cake on the plate, breaks a tiny bite from it. The bite is less than small, but in it are all the flavours of the cake. She holds the cake to the woman's mouth. The warrior's eyes remain closed. Natsuki tightens her legs around the woman, inner thighs just touching the other's cross-legged knees. Natsuki's gown has fallen back a little and she touches the silk of her guest's gown with her bare flesh. The silk is cold against Natsuki's skin. The woman's eyes remain closed. She opens her mouth and takes in the taste of the cake. It is there before the meat of the food: there is the scent that arouses her desire, the smell of fresh matter, the flavour of Natsuki's hand. The young woman lays the piece of cake on the warrior's tongue; the airy stuff melts there, and she catches a touch of Natsuki's fingernail against the side of her lip, closing her mouth too soon and with perfect timing. Natsuki feeds the small cake to the woman, each tiny morsel delivered mouth to hand. The woman does not open her eyes. The travelling warrior adventures through all lands with her eyes wide open, her ears alert for the next sound, her flesh yearning for new feasts. Here she does not need any senses; Natsuki will be all senses for both of them. The warrior is surrendered hunger and Natsuki is satisfaction.

Then the cake is finished. There are crumbs on the plate. Natsuki lifts each one, lays them on her guest's willing tongue, closes her lips around the taste of completion. She sits back, empty plate in her hands. She rests, places the plate on the ground beside her. The woman's eyes are still closed. Natsuki lifts her hand to the warrior's lips. Rests a fingertip there, closes her own eyes, feels the narrow, worn face with closed eye hands. Takes in every inch of the guest's face, the contours and lines, each deep defined scar. She knows the stories of the scars, knows where they were fought for, how hard-won. Natsuki's hands run from the woman's face to her neck and shoulders.

She bends in closer to her guest, the crown of her head touching her chest – now unbound – now her breast. Natsuki reaches around the woman to her strong back, hands climb the ladder of her spine back to the warrior's hair. Pulls it from the binding and they are two women covered in a gown of their own growing. Natsuki rests there, her head against the older woman's breast. The drum of the warrior's heart asks Natsuki to wait and for a time they breathe together in unison. Natsuki's cheek is warm against her breast; she soothes and invigorates the woman. The warrior has rested with her. Natsuki sits back. The woman has had her fill.

She opens her eyes. Natsuki is before her. Looks at the young woman for a single moment, eyes met and ready. Then Natsuki lowers her eyes, moves her gaze from too close to the soul, closes fine eyelids against the dim firelight of her room. The warrior woman looks at this girl who has fed her. Looks at Natsuki in gratitude and awe. She is perfect. Not merely in her clear beauty, nor is her perfection in her ready willingness to serve. While the warrior has enjoyed the offered gifts, she has not fooled herself that this was not also Natsuki's own gift to herself. There was interaction here, desire and accomplishment for both. Natsuki has served the woman and herself. She had not requested the cake but received willingly. Just as Natsuki had not asked for her stories but her ears were open and ready to take them in. The warrior feels the pressure of Natsuki's flesh against her legs, the warmth of their breath in the cooling room. The fire is dying, the horse is rested: it is time. The warrior half rises, leans to the small woman before her. Natsuki is ready, lifts her open face and as she does so the warrior catches the whole hank of hair falling down Natsuki's exposed back. The woman holds the heavy silk of her lover and kisses it softly. Natsuki feels the warm touch through the dead matter of her hair, feels her breath through the night in the room. She touches the warrior's hand with her own. There is skin and wonder.

Then the woman rises. She dresses and moves away. Natsuki listens as the woman buckles on her own armour, walks outside, saddles the horse. She hears the animal in the dark distance, travelling away from her and remains seated. Natsuki sits through the silence until morning, holds the woman in her stillness.

Natsuki moves from her place on the floor as the last star burns out its light in the hour before dawn. Her skin is cold, but from deep within she radiates a fierce heat of pleasure fulfilled and joy realized. She knows the woman left her presence eased and calm, knows she will arrive at her own home later today with the mark of Natsuki's breath on her skin, the taste of Natsuki in the sweetness of the cake as it melts on her tongue. Now she too will become one of the warrior's stories. The best of her tales.

DIESEL DONUTS

Isle Jule

As Lu and Dee peered at the huge selection of donuts, Dee leaned back, resting most of her weight into the heel of her boot, playfully crushing Lu's toes. "Oh, ouch, you're killing me," Lu deadpanned. "Don't the donuts look glamorous? I always thought fluorescent lighting made things look dead. Those donuts could come to life and hurt me."

Dee turned so that her cheek brushed Lu's and said, "There are so many of them, I can't decide which one I want."

Lu leaned hard into Dee and draped her arms over Dee's shoulders. She pointed at the donuts and said, "That cruller looks good."

Dee thought it was odd to see Lu's fingers instead of feeling them inside her. She gazed at the hand hungrily and thought perhaps they should have stayed in bed.

Lu added, "Looks good enough to stick in your ear."

Dee replied dreamily, her hair against Lu's face, "I suppose the only way to find out is to buy it and . . ."

Lu cut the sentence short by rubbing her fingertip first along Dee's lower lip and then inserting it into Dee's mouth and stroking her tongue.

Dee bit down on the finger and Lu felt herself get a hard-on instantly. Lu wondered if the donut thing was going to work out. We probably should have just stayed in bed. Getting dressed is such a hassle. Of course, there is the inevitable undressing to look forward to.

They were in the donut shop at Dee's insistence. Lu, being a gentleman, allowed breaks for meals, although she herself would never let anything like hunger get in the way of fucking. Lu predicted that the remark about the ear would get to Dee. It referred to their first night together, some weeks ago, when Dee still had a boyfriend. Lu had never fucked anybody in the ear before, but their first time together required all the resourcefulness Lu had acquired through decades of pleasing women.

They ended up on Dee's couch which, as luck would have it, converted into a bed – and wasn't the only thing that was converted that night. Lu was propped up on her elbows, lying on top of Dee. They were giving each other small kisses, wondering what it was the other might like. The lights were off.

Lu had felt Dee tense up when she reached over her to tug the little pull-chain, turning off the lamp.

"Are you OK?" Lu asked.

"Umm, not really," Dee said, biting her lower lip.

"Do you want me to turn the light back on?" She watched Dee's expression in the fluorescent glow from the street light.

Lu thought to herself, it's that damn boyfriend getting in the way. How serious can she be about a guy she won't live with, anyway?

Lu felt responsible for the outcome of their first date, since it was Lu's experience that Dee was counting on. Even though Dee had been the one to devise the evening. After months of flirting on the phone, she invited Lu over when her roommate went away for the weekend.

Lu ached to fuck Dee. She moved so that they weren't so mashed up into one another. "What's up?" asked Lu, not ready to give up on this mission.

"I'm just way past bending the rules," Dee said forlornly, invoking his presence with the small sentence. Lu had assumed they were past bending the rules when Dee had lifted up Lu's shirt and started kissing her breasts.

That was all the way back in the sitting position.

"Look, I'm not going to fuck you, so don't worry about it," Lu said firmly.

This seemed to be what Dee wanted to hear. She relaxed, reached up and pulled Lu's face back down to hers. Lu was kissing her and contemplating the fucking-while-not-fucking angle. The dyke in her knew it could be done.

She undid Dee's bra one-handed and Dee remarked, "You're very good at that."

Lu laughed, pressing her face between Dee's shoulder and neck. With a mouth full of shirt, she muttered something about "years of practice" and Dee laughed also. Lu looked up to catch her smiling and saw the light reflect off the small even teeth.

In the weeks that led up to that first night, Dee had expressed discord around having a boyfriend. She said she yearned for a girlfriend but wasn't sure how to go about getting one. Lu knew that Dee meant "female lover", not "girlfriend". She and Dee would have a short-lived, fierce sex life and Lu would have to leave, as her cultivated dyke desires could not be wholly satisfied by Dee's eager, but inexperienced, new-found lesbian identity.

This did not discourage Lu from kissing her, Dee's mouth becoming softer with each kiss.

Dee pulled Lu into the fullness of her breasts. "Your skin is so soft," said Dee, a note of surprise in her voice as she ran a hand along Lu's back. "Softer than mine."

Lu's hands caressed Dee's waist and eagerly awaited a visa for down there.

Lu was chewing on her neck when Dee pulled away saying softly, "Don't mark me."

Lu looked her in the eye and, pressing her pelvis down with force into Dee's, she reassured her, "I won't fuck you and I won't mark you. But you can mark me."

Lu felt her nipples get hard as Dee lifted her head from the cushion and bit into her. She sucked harder and Lu was glad to be the first, and not the last, woman Dee would leave a mark on. Lu nibbled Dee's lips kindly and then ran her tongue in a sloppy fashion across Dee's lips. She pinched Dee's nipples and wondered what color they would be in daylight. She continued to ponder the fucking while not fucking. Lu ran the tip of her tongue along Dee's ear. Then jabbed her tongue inside the ear and tasted the bitter wax. Dee drew her breath in sharply.

Lu realized that she could fuck Dee without actually fucking her. She pressed the tip of her index finger into the opening of the ear canal. As Dee's breathing got heavier, Lu noticed that he was no longer in the room.

There hadn't been enough room for the three of them on that small couch. As she pressed her fingertip into Dee's ear, she whispered into the other one, "I'm not going to fuck you."

Dee lifted her pelvis and groaned. She grabbed Lu's hands, pulled them to her waist and guided them down her stomach and inside her pants. Lu resisted the urge to put her hands down there as she felt Dee's soft stomach.

Her fingertips hazarded the elastic waistband of Dee's bikini underwear.

While it is true that the pussy is generally located below the waist, Lu knew that it could be found in other places. She had once located it in the fold of skin below the armpit.

Dee started moaning softly and Lu knew that Dee knew that when Lu said, "I'm not going to fuck you," she was playing a game that all schoolchildren play called "Opposites". Dee's back started to arch and she was grinding her pelvis into Lu's. Dee rubbed the tip of her index finger back and forth along the short hair at the base of Lu's neck. Where the electric razor of the barber scolded bi-weekly, Dee's touch now assuaged any hard feelings.

Lu thrust her pelvis into Dee's, returned her fingertip to Dee's ear canal and cleared her mind of all thought. With her free hand, she grabbed the frame of the couch, sandwiching Dee between her and the cushions. Their hips moved together and they had a small, joint, celebration normally called an orgasm.

When one considers that months of flirting over the phone and being attracted to someone does not guarantee against disaster or disappointment, one small orgasm can be classified as quite an achievement.

Lu opened her eyes, her heart racing, and Dee said, "Did you know this couch turns into a bed?"

Lu laughed, stood up, put her hands out to Dee, pulled her to her feet then stated, "I think it's time we got in bed."

It became clear to both women that the boyfriend's tenure was up and Lu's time had just begun.

That big ole butch Lu wants you to think she's clever, that we ended up on my couch and then in my bed and that this was all her doing. As if.

It's true that those huge hands reshaped my way of thinking. While she was caressing me, a portion of the credo of the arts and crafts movement of the Nineteenth century I had memorized for an art history class popped into my mind. "A handcrafted object is inherently more desirable, beautiful and worthy of human endeavor than anything made by machine."

I had seen objects made by hand and by machine and could tell they were different, but I had never known quite what the difference was. I realized through my experiences with Lu that the hand imparts an ineffable quality. I wanted her to mold me. I am not sure if this means that lesbianism rather than art history needs to be added to curricula.

Lu left out the part she doesn't know about. The part where I was riding the bus to go window-shopping downtown, then I saw her and decided that a wardrobe I couldn't afford anyway could wait. Sure, she got me into the sack, but she didn't do it with a phrase or a touch: she did it on the bus, just by the way she was standing there. The way the back of her neck, fresh from the barber's, presented itself like an engraved invitation cordially requesting my presence at a gala event. Her neck was graceful, in contrast to the rest of her which was hard.

I was struck by a Sapphic thunderbolt. I am not the only one who experiences this upon seeing her. She stirs desire in people. I have noticed that men take a liking to her. That's a waste of their time. She's just a closed-minded butch. Not that she doesn't have good reason to be closed-minded.

For me, I prefer open-mindedness. If I didn't have a sense of options, I never would have annoyed the bus driver as I jumped through the closing doors.

He barked at me, "Lady, ya tryin' ta get yasself killed or what?"

I laughed and fell a few paces behind her. I watched her feet, big in men's shoes, looking just like men's feet as they owned the pavement they walked on. I liked how she filled the shape of her overcoat. I thought it was a joke, that a woman looked handsome.

I noticed her hands as she pulled out a shopping cart. They were enormous.

I was glad that she didn't look around, seemed caught up in her own sense of being. She didn't need me. Yet.

I grabbed one of those blue plastic baskets and wondered if I could play a woman the way I could a man. I stepped near her in aisle five, reached right in front of her and grabbed a jar of spaghetti sauce. She looked up, disregarded me, and moved along.

I came close to frisking her. I wanted to pick-pocket her, to glean personal details: where did she live? Whose photo did she carry? Was she into herbal tea and cats? Black coffee and a dog? Or ginseng tonic and a bird?

She continued to walk the aisles, brooding, with a tendency to bump into the carts of others. She was completely oblivious to small children. She seemed to have the standard bachelor diet: frozen entrees and a thirst for sports drinks. It wasn't until we passed the pastries and she selected a box of chocolate eclairs that it occurred to me she might have a girlfriend.

I was determined, even though she might be married, to at least speak to her. She was heading to the check-out and I knew that if I didn't act fast I would lose my nerve. I grabbed for something, anything, and when I reached her I said, "Excuse me, sir, I think you dropped this."

She looked at me, figured out I was the woman in the spaghetti aisle, and asked churlishly, "What?"

I raised my hand, and laughed when I noticed I was holding a box of maxi pads. At this she started to smile and then laughed.

When she smiled, she didn't look like a man at all. She had pretty teeth and the shape of her eyes changed. She appeared powerful in a way that she would use to make you feel happy, not sad.

Once the thrill of the maxi-pads dimmed, I asked her for her phone number.

She said, "You can call me at work," and handed me her card.

A few weeks later I felt the scratchy wool cuff of her overcoat as we stood next to each other. We had decided to go to the only store open this late on a Sunday night, the 24-hour bakery that was a short bus ride from bed.

Lu was standing behind me, leaning into me. I liked when for no reason we both agreed that holding hands was just too conventional and so we'd stand close, pressed into each other. I like that men and women want her. I want to laugh at the men who smile at me when she and I walk down the street as a couple. As if I would ever consider their brief proposals. If they could feel her lips (and no man ever has or will), they would know in an instant just how stupid the idea that I would ever let them touch me was. Her kisses have the feel of a nice afternoon you had in grade school. I like that she has the heart of a woman and the body of a man (sort of). Her knees get pink during sex. Afterwards, I rub lotion into the abraded skin. Who knew cotton sheets could be so brutal?

As we stood at the counter I looked out the window and a bus went past, sending snow flakes from a drift into the street, like a small ghost. I cleared my throat and said loudly, "Excuse me," in the direction of the counterwoman who continued to ignore us. Lu took a napkin off the counter, crumpled it up and threw it towards the woman. It wasn't supposed to hit her, but it bounced off the hot chocolate machine and landed in the fold of the newspaper she was reading. She looked up and glared. We both suppressed a laugh.

She walked up to us. "Yeah, what do you want?"

In a friendly voice, Lu said, "We'll take two of the chocolate creme donuts please."

The counterwoman looked puzzled and said, "You're a woman?"

"Kind of," answered Lu.

The counterwoman looked to me for help and then at Lu, as if she were carrying a virus.

Lu and Dee waited in the bus shelter, Lu holding Dee and the bag of donuts.

Lu, who is in the habit of horsing around in public, of speaking her opinions loudly, and not caring what others think of her persona, started jostling Dee. Dee laughed it off and then, as Lu pushed with more force, Dee implored, "Baby, please stop. That man just mouthed, 'Are you all right?' to me."

Lu stopped messing around. There was something in Dee's tone that Lu had not heard before. Something in her tone that hinted at endings and conclusions.

Lu contented herself with placing her arm around Dee's shoulders. She liked the way Dee's neck fit perfectly in the crook of her elbow. As if Lu were meant to hold her there in that way. Not like a headlock from one butch to another, but with a sense of comfort and security. Lu pulled Dee close and sniffed her sweet hairline.

When they got back to Dee's, as soon as they were in the door, the cool night air still fresh on their clothes, Dee turned and, with a bright look in her eye and a sharpness in her voice, commanded, "Don't you ever shove me in public again."

Lu felt sucker-punched. She resisted an urge to shout back.

Instead she stood frozen, as if her feet weighed thirty pounds each. She was puzzled as to why Dee had waited so long to reprimand her. And why was it that she felt she needed to reprimand her? Couldn't she just as easily have asked her not to do something? Lu was unable to gauge how much of a threat the words posed. And did it mean that Lu was free to hit Dee in the privacy of her home?

"I'm sorry," Lu said, clearly not used to taking orders.

Dee sensed that the way in which she spoke had carried more meaning than the words. She said quietly, dropping her coat onto the couch, "I just don't want people to think it's OK for a man to hit a woman. That's all."

Lu stood in place and felt as if her heart had stopped and then said defensively, "Oh, right, I forgot I'm a man."

"People think you are. You owe it to yourself as a person, and to other women as a lesbian, to be the one man who sets an example of decency."

"I was just horsing around; I didn't mean anything by it."

Dee raised her arms and said, "Baby." As soon as Lu was in Dee's embrace, the tiff passed and the fear that had bristled in Lu subsided.

They slowly fell to the couch. Dee took one of Lu's fingers and started to suck on it, pushing it slowly in and out of her mouth. "I know you're a woman; that's why I love you. It's just hard for me, sometimes."

Lu kept her head in Dee's lap while Dee continued to suck on her finger, Dee's mouth feeling more like a pussy. "Why is it I can't be an unconventional woman?"

Dee lifted Lu's head out of her lap, stood up, dropped her pants and then straddled Lu. "You cannot be an unconventional woman, my dear, as long as you remain a conventional man," said Dee.

Lu laughed out loud. "Now, there's some logic for you."

Dee then took Lu's face in her hands, gently rocking her hips, and started to kiss Lu all over the face with tiny passionate kisses.

"I thought you were hungry," Lu said, ignoring the effect the kisses were having on her. Lu reached over and pulled one of the donuts out and licked some of the chocolate filling off.

"Baby, please," begged Dee, pressing into Lu, feeling the wool pants against the inside of her bare thighs. Dee reached to take the donut from her.

Lu swung her arm away and held the donut out of reach. "Honey, I really think you should eat. You're going to need all your strength," said Lu, who then took a big bite out of the donut.

"I don't want to eat, right now," sulked Dee.

With Dee still sitting on her lap, Lu continued to eat the donut. "This is a really tasty donut," said Lu.

"I can think of something else that's tasty," said Dee.

"Really?" said Lu.

"Yeah, and it also starts with the letter D."

"Hmmm." Lu closed her eyes, chewed, then swallowed. "Let's see: pussy doesn't start with the letter D, nor does finger nor fist."

Dee slapped Lu's face. Lu smiled.

"Aren't you going to eat your donut?" asked Lu, her hand loudly rummaging in the bag.

"I don't give a fuck what happens to that donut," said Dee, who moved to stand.

Lu encircled Dee's waist with her free arm and pulled her back down to Lu's lap.

They didn't speak and Lu started to eat the second donut. Dee looked out the window, with Lu in her peripheral vision.

After finishing the last bite, Lu smacked her lips loudly. She then licked her fingers in an exaggerated fashion. Knowing that Dee could see her every move, she shoved three fingers into her mouth. She took her time in pulling them back out. "Mmmm."

While Dee continued to look out the window, Lu lifted Dee's ass slightly with one hand and, with the fingers that had been in her mouth, she pushed past the underwear and buried two fingers into Dee's wet pussy.

Dee closed her eyes, drew in her breath, and Lu said, "Tasty."

"Indeed," said Dee and adjusted her hips so that Lu's fingers were at home.

"You know, there's something I never told you," said Dee.

"I'm sure there are lots of things you haven't told me," replied Lu.

Dee opened her eyes. "I'm being serious."

Lu: "Oh, right." She made a serious face and asked, "What is it?"

"You remember that first night we were here?"

"Uh huh," said Lu.

"Well, I was worried that if we fucked in my bed, Don would smell it. I figured two women being together would smell a lot different than when a man and a woman are together."

"Fortunately, I am not familiar with the difference," Lu said smugly.

"Anyway," Dee continued, "after you left, your scent was on the cushions. I flipped them over when I put them back. One night, when I was missing you, I went and got one of them and took it to bed with me. The smell of your pomade made me feel close to you."

"Mmm," Lu said, considering the turn of events in her favor. "Now you get to take me to bed," she said.

Dee lifted her shirt, stretched out her arms and pressed her hands against the wall behind Lu, her bare stomach close to

Lu's face. Lu reached over and pulled the chain on the lamp and, as the light went out, she felt Dee begin to melt.

Now in the dark, whether they are in bed or on the couch, they know exactly how to find each other.

TEA AND SYMPATHY

Stephanie Sellier

Whenever I try to seduce a woman, I always make some mistake. Once, I tried to impress the object of my desire with my newly acquired knowledge of Dostojewskij studies. It was absolutely lethal. She was indeed impressed, but completely turned off, of course. Honestly – who'd want a woman who gets turned on by such a topic? Yes, there's the rub: I don't want a woman who is as crazy as I am, I want somebody sane, and the sane women of this world don't want me.

But I wasn't responsible for the episode that happened to me recently. You see, there was this incredibly cute shop assistant in my local speciality tea shop that's owned by two gay guys. She must have been just over twenty, and she looked like Tippi Hedren, a fact that was emphasised by the current sixties retro fashion. Perhaps you remember: Tippi Hedren is the blonde bombshell in Hitchcock films, *The Birds* and *Marnie*, and, to the chagrin of those who are with her, she attracts evil like gold dust. And I do like dangerous women.

Well, the shop assistant wore her bleached hair shoulder-length and tucked behind her ears with hairpins, so that she looked like a naughty schoolgirl. Her eyelashes were long and so heavily mascara'd that you could have easily hung your washing on them; and she wore some kind of shaggy woollen coat and a ring pierced through her left eyebrow. What is more, she had personality. She really was racy. In five years' time, she would be stunning. I adored her already.

I hadn't drunk as much tea in my entire life as during the time since I first saw her standing there. Even now, the bags of Earl Grey, Christmas Blend and green tea are stacked high on my kitchen shelves. Most of all I liked to buy exotic herbal teas, because it was such a delight to say to her with a buttery-smooth voice, "I'd like four ounces of Magic Fire, please." She never said no. Thanks to my staggering tea consumption, we soon started to chat. I always got great music recommendations from her. Sometimes, when there were no other customers in the shop, she played something for me. I never found it difficult to get into a mood that was sufficiently melancholy so that I could enjoy the thumping bass notes.

For two weeks I just had a mild crush on her, but then I had a fit of the doldrums, and I was bored. These are the times when those crazy ideas get you. It got worse. I already had two tattoos, but I started wearing the same corpselike makeup she wore, bought one of those shapeless woolly hats that always slip over your eyes, a pair of Doc Martens with steel toecaps and a stack of aching nineties music, the kind where young women sing in a voice like twitching, raw meat, screechy with rage. When, one afternoon, I went into the Cap Horn bar for a coffee, Annemarie began to hoot.

"How old are you, Suse – sixteen? You look like a Russian peasant after a hard day's work!"

"But Annemarie! She's so cute!"

"OK, tell me. Want a cappuccino?"

"Yes, please."

"Now, who's cute, cradle-snatcher? According to your outfit, she must be just about eighteen."

"I'm only just twenty-eight myself!" I screamed in protest. "It's the woman in Jochen's and Werner's tea shop."

Annemarie grinned. "Twenty-eight means you're comatose, my dear." She poured foamy milk into the cup, sprinkled a bit of cinnamon on top and placed it in front of me. "Ah, that Katharina? She's a piece of work. Looks like an angel, but has a tongue like a razor. I don't even know if she's a dyke, and I think she doesn't know herself. Really, forget it, Suse."

I tried. I tackled my hoard of tea. I exchanged the steel-toed boots I could barely lift off the ground and which bruised my toes for the usual black cowboy boots and put k.d. on the CD player. To no avail. Nevertheless, I could smell disaster. If only I hadn't relapsed and spontaneously invited the woman to my place – she'd still talk to me.

She must have lived in the south of Cologne as well, because I sometimes ran into her in the streets, and we waved at each other. One Saturday afternoon, I met her at the supermarket. My heart throbbing, I snatched at the opportunity and asked her if she would like to watch the video recording of an Alanis Morrissette concert I just got from a friend in Canada.

"Yes. Wow!"

"I live just across the road."

Perhaps Annemarie was right when she called me a cradle-snatcher, I thought guiltily, but then I was carried away by my success.

Even when I opened the door to my flat, I felt that something was odd, but what was it?

"Nice flat", Katharina said, looking around. "You live here alone?"

"No, I've got a flatmate."

We went down the long corridor to my room. I left the door open so that she could feel safe. We only knew each other from the shop, and that was a somewhat formal affair. We chatted for a while, sitting on the sofa, and not before long it started raining outside. Well, that's what I thought, until I looked out of the window and saw that the ground was bone dry.

Katharina, noticing my irritated look, looked out of the window, too, and said, surprised: "That's funny, it doesn't rain at all! What's this noise, then?"

I listened more closely and heard that the sounds came from Christina's room. I had a sinking feeling. This wasn't rain, it was the swishing of a whip! Once I got my hands on that woman, she'd get an extra spanking from me. When I had moved in, I had told her in no uncertain terms that she should conduct her silly SM scenes at night, when I was asleep, and now Katharina, of all people, was visiting me.

"Something, I dunno. Would you fancy a cup of tea?" I said, desperate to distract her from the swishing sounds.

"I'd love some", Katharina said amiably and winked at me.

How should I explain to a twenty-year-old that the world is full of perverts, and we are some of them? I shoved her in the direction of the kitchen, because it was farthest from Christina's room. We could have some tea. That's what I thought, until I had opened the door, and quickly closed it behind me, in the face of the perplexed Katharina.

"Won't be a minute!"

I hoped she hadn't seen anything. In the kitchen crouched Gesine Schäfer, whom I knew superficially from the Gay and Lesbian Centre's dance class, and she was chained to our fridge, clad only in a dog collar. Well, there was no ounce of flab on her, bless her. "Gesine," I hissed, flabbergasted. "What are you doing here? And where are the goddamn keys?"

"Christina has gone shopping, and she's punishing me by pretending to have forgotten about me. She has taken the keys. I'm really sorry, Suse." She shrugged helplessly.

I almost smacked her. "It's three in the afternoon, and I've got a visitor! This is no good, really! You must be off your rocker!" Cursing under my breath, I made the tea, because I didn't want to confuse Katharina any further. I had only briefly dunked the tea sieve into the water when I threw it into the sink. Carrying the heavy tray, I rushed back into my room, where I found Katharina.

She pushed back a blonde strand of hair with a thumb that was adorned with a fat silver ring and said, "Funny noise. It's not like rain at all. Sometimes it stops, and then it is stronger, then weaker. It sounds more like wet logs in the fireplace, but it can't be that."

"Really funny, indeed," I said, almost losing my nerve, and put down the tray. But if we stayed in my room and put on the video at last and turned up the volume, nothing really bad could happen.

Alanis Morissette's ghostly expressive face appeared on the screen. "Isn't it ironic," of course. Yeah, life's a joke and if you don't lose your sense of humour, you'll have great fun. Soon the swishing noise and Gesine were forgotten. I almost screamed with glee at "You Oughta Know," and Katharina spontaneously grasped my hand. The heat rose into my head. Her long lashes quivered with excitement. Then, somebody knocked on the door, and before I could shout, "No!" Beatrice, a friend of Christina's, stood wet-haired in the doorway and said: "You have some cigarettes at all?"

She must have had a shower. Katharina's eyes were wide with shock, and she dropped my hand. Only then I looked down on Beatrice and saw that she was in her underwear, leaving the traces of her recent scenes with what's-her-name for all to see. She looked as if she had just been hit by a bus: she was covered in multicoloured welts and bruises.

"So sorry, Susanne, but this is too much for me, really!" Katharina jumped to her feet, grabbed her jacket, and I could hear the door slam shut.

This was too much for me, as well; I was hopping mad, and two months later I had moved out of Christina's flat. And switched to coffee, for safety's sake. The woman at the coffee shop is absolutely straight and forty years old. Comatose, that is.

HUNGRY LOVE

Ava Hines

The rain pelted down. It was a bitterly cold and typical British winter. Why, oh why, did I not believe in umbrellas? My dreads were sodden. Shit, I thought, it's going to take two hours of washing and conditioning to get them back into proper shape. I always had been one to exaggerate.

The main reason I had come out on this foul night was to attend the final meeting before the Cultural Evening in two days' time; to work out the running order for the night. I was one of the co-ordinators and was also the resident singing sensation and passionate poet on Campus, so there was no way I could bow out. Not that I really wanted to: this was the only real Black cultural event that took place all year. All the Black students were really involved, letting their work slide as a result.

The other reason I didn't really mind going out was that I felt myself succumbing to morbid introspection – never a good idea, in my case. My last relationship had turned out to be a real dud.

Sarah had demanded my time, my money and my heart. The first two I gave willingly, being a giving type of gal, but the last, even I could not pretend to give. It wasn't because she was white that I had a problem: more that she was as far from my perception of my ideal woman as one could hope to get. She was materialistic and socially and politically unaware and, quite frankly, I just didn't feel the sparks fly. So I'd been pondering long and hard on my choice of partners and had severe doubts about my ability to judge people. I wanted to steer clear of all future relationships, until I had restored faith in myself.

As I neared the meeting hall, I heard the buzz of voices. I knew I was late, but wasn't prepared for the looks of resentment and hostility from some of the other performers. As if to say: "Who the hell do you think you are?" I felt like saying, "The star, actually." But of course I didn't, both because it wasn't true and also I wasn't that sort of person. Ah, Black solidarity – I love it.

We quickly went through the routines and sorted out the clothes for the fashion show and I laughed inwardly at the clichés. The garments were beautiful, there was no doubt about it. They were on loan from an up-and-coming Black fashion designer, but the African-styled garbs were so far removed from what these people wore everyday as to be laughable. The choice of models was no surprise, either. The lighter-skinned girls and women with the slimmest noses and straightest hair modelled most of the really sexy garments; while the darker-skinned African-looking types like myself were given the cast-offs. Of course, this wasn't a conscious decision by the organisers, just the norm. I had already brought up this issue at countless meetings of the Afro-Caribbean society, and I wasn't about to face any more hostility by bringing it up again.

The meeting went fairly smoothly, as they had obviously sorted out most of the problems before I'd got there, so I just did my pieces to the usual muted applause and everyone started packing up.

I was the last to leave, as I thought I'd score some points after arriving late. As I was putting away the final piece of furniture, I heard the door open and a vision strode towards me. Her self-assurance was evident in her walk. Her hair was cut close to her scalp and emphasized a strong jaw line and huge dark brown, almost black, eyes. Her dark skin had the most amazing sheen to it, with red and gold undertones. Her purple-brown lips were firm, seductive and soft. I, for no reason I could rationalize, wanted to pull them down towards mine and feel the contours of that beautiful mouth, lick every perfect, minuscule line until her lips stung and were ripe with the force of my hungry lips.

She was simply beautiful, with eyes that had such depth that they seemed to reflect and contain a lifetime of beauty and pain. Is this what heaven looks like? Yes, my mind waxed lyrical at the sight of her. Wake up call, she'll think you're crazy if you keep staring at her like that. I smiled instead.

"Hello," she said. Deep brown, rich bass, sexy, round voice. I felt such a feeling of lust flow through me that I gripped the chair and sat down without taking my eyes off of her. She knew I wanted her and smiled, not at all intimidated.

"Hello," I replied, "are you looking for anyone in particular?" God, why did I sound so lecherous?

"No, not really, I'm actually looking for the Black students' meeting, but it seems I missed it."

Their loss, my gain, I thought. "I'm afraid you've just missed it," I managed to get out.

"Forgive my manners. I'm Sophie," she said and held out a hand with the most sensuous fingers that I'd ever seen.

I tried not to let my mind drift away again. "Hi, I'm Ava,

pleased to meet you." I tried to sound self-assured but couldn't quite mask the huskiness in my voice. "Are you new here? It's just that I haven't seen you around."

"Yeah, I only started here at the beginning of this term. I couldn't change courses at my last place and decided to take up the place I was offered here, though I've been ill these last few weeks and haven't been able to make any classes."

That explained it; there was no way I could have missed her around campus, though I was surprised that I hadn't heard a buzz on the University grapevine.

"Crap weather for you to be coming out in when you're ill; especially as you've missed the meeting." I hoped I didn't sound trite.

"Oh, no, I'm much better now and besides, I knew it was the last meeting before the show and I wanted to see if I could offer any help."

"Well, just so your outing wasn't completely wasted, why don't I invite you round to my place for a cup of tea or coffee, if you'd prefer? I don't live on campus any more, as this is my final year, but I managed to find a place just around the corner, so you're quite welcome." I couldn't believe my composure. I wondered if Sophie knew the effect she was having on me. The playful look in her eyes told me she did. She hesitated for a brief moment, then smiled gratefully and accepted.

I don't remember much of what was said over coffee that night; all I remember is staring, wanting and smiling. Warmth and Sophie. I knew she liked me. She was not hesitant about showing that, yet no specific words had been spoken. We hadn't even specifically talked about women loving women. Yet the hungry look in my eyes told her all she needed to know and, far from appearing wary of my obviously repressed passion, she seemed to invite it. Maybe I didn't ask because I didn't want to deal with her not wanting me in that way.

We met regularly after that, but neither of us wanted to make any overt sexual moves. Well, I didn't, at any rate. We attended the show together, with Sophie being suitably impressed by my many talents and I being suitably flattered by her compliments. In fact, they meant the world to me; I needed to feel worthy of this wonderful woman.

After all the hubbub of the evening had died down, we continued to go to meetings and meet up after classes or accidentally at parties and very occasionally at each others' homes. Sophie, I'd discovered, went with the flow and she wasn't likely to instigate a situation herself. I phoned her at home and asked her to come round to my place at around 8:30 that night. Thankfully, she agreed – if she had cried off, I would have screamed, I was so wound up.

I spent the rest of the afternoon clearing away a week's worth of debris that I had allowed to gather whilst plucking up the courage for this night. I bathed and pampered myself to full beauty; my locks looked shiny, black and thick. My ebony skin seemed to give off a deep glow; I appeared outwardly serene, yet the throbbing sensation between my legs was a constant reminder of my wicked imagination.

My muscular yet womanly frame looked good in the pale green silk shirt and tailored trousers; my eyes shone and my heart pounded. "Woman, you look good, if I say so myself."

I prepared the tapes and lit the candles and placed some food on the long low table in front of the fire. I made myself a spliff; Sophie probably wouldn't be here for twenty minutes or so and I needed to calm my nerves. I checked the chicken warming in the oven and tried not let my mind run wild, but I knew ultimately "it" was going to be tonight or not at all; then the doorbell rang.

Slowly, I got up to answer the door, hesitating a moment

before I opened it so I could wipe the sweat on my hands onto the back of my trousers.

"Hello, you," she said.

"Hello, you," I answered. "Come on in."

As I took her coat, I smiled in appreciation at her choice of clothes. "You've got real style."

She smiled. "You're looking pretty good, yourself."

I smiled. The off-the-shoulder black jersey was complemented by the pale lilac silk top underneath and the way she looked in those leather trousers, well. Her outfit was completed by heavy sculptured earrings, which swung in rhythm with her body movements.

"You open the wine while I get the serviettes. It's purely finger-licking, tonight: less washing-up." God, that sounded like a come-on.

"Sounds good to me," Sophie agreed.

I nearly blew it right there and then by jumping on her, but managed to control myself; instead, I suggested we sit on the cushions by the table and help ourselves to food and wine. The baked chicken tasted just like my mum used to make. The crisp rolls and corn on the cob made a delicious mess. I wanted to reach over and brush the crumbs from her lips, but I hesitated too long. The wine was plentiful, the food delicious and Sophie . . . Sophie was watching me. We sat in silence and drank and ate and listened to the music; Dionne Farris was doing her thing and I just tingled.

I got up to clear away the plates and lower the volume on the stereo. Then we sat side by side, talking until I could take no more unnecessary small talk. "Sophie, I want you. I need to hold you, feel you, caress you and make sure that you're real and that these feelings I have for you are real. Though if you don't feel the same way, I'll understand."

Whew! What a relief to have said it.

In response, Sophie leaned over and undid the braid holding my locks in place, letting them fall free. I shook my head to let them fall into place, then I felt both of her cool yet electric hands on my face, drawing me closer.

Closer to those lips I had waited to taste for so long. As her lips touched mine, I felt a searing chemical reaction shudder throughout the length of my body. I looked into her eyes and suddenly I was on fire. My tongue whip-lashed the inside of her mouth. Exploring, tasting, savouring. A quick suck of those wicked lips, first top, then bottom. I tried to take both of them together, but they were much too full for my crazy passion.

Sophie laughed her husky laugh and leaned back under the weight of my urgency, her hand falling back to support her. "Wait," she said and slowly pulled her sweater up and finally off, but left her lilac T-shirt intact. It truly looked beautiful against her mahogany skin and sculptured shoulders.

I nuzzled her from her neck to the oh-so-inviting valley between her breasts. I had waited long enough. I lifted that frustrating yet complementary garment above her breasts as slowly as I could. I wondered at the smoothness, the fullness and heaviness that had given her a true passport to womanhood. Not for me those pre-pubescent breasts others seemed so into. The wide, dark, and tender areolae, with equally large nipples, seemed to beg for attention. I sighed, and bent over to kiss first one then the other, slurping both nipples in and out of my mouth. Nibbling, twisting with my tongue, burying my nose under the rich, firm underside of her breasts, breathing her in.

I stopped for a moment to remove my shirt, the better to feel the texture of her satiny skin, then loosened my trousers and started to take them off, but impatience overwhelmed me and I again buried my face in her voluptuousness.

The way Sophie looked at me, the soft moans that were

escaping from her, made me melt inside and I shivered as she pushed me slightly away from her and said, "Let me look at you."

I stood her gaze for as long as I could, then leaned over her again as she lay back full length on the floor, allowing me to raise her hands above her head, holding them in place whilst we kissed. She moaned my name over and over and I begged her to let me worship her beauty, those lips so sweet and fiery. Her arms broke free and were everywhere, in my hair, on my breasts, my ass, then grazing against my burning cunt.

I stopped her. "No, me first . . . please. Do you understand: I need you." She nodded, for a moment looking shy.

Sophie. Kneading and sucking her breasts, while she directed me with pressure on my head. I fumbled to get a sight of her beautiful body entirely exposed; sensing my urgency, she pushed me away and slowly stood and removed the hot leather trousers, all the time staring directly into my eyes as she let them drop to the floor. I kneeled beneath her gaze, breathing her in, and was instantly bewitched. Potent, intoxicating, with a burning heat emanating from that thick, coarse triangle that would be the source of my pleasure.

I gently pulled her closer to my mouth, spreading her legs with the same gentle action and stared at the awe-inspiring sight of her deep-pink and swollen vulva. Glistening with warmth and wetness and frustration. I opened her legs still wider. She watched and did not blush; she had no need, for she knew she was all I'd ever wanted.

Bending her knees, she slowly lowered her beautiful pussy onto my face. My hands reached up to part her lips and inhale her one more time before she made contact with my hungry mouth. She teased, hovering just above my face.

I let my tongue slowly tease its way between her inner and outer lips, using my fingers as a guide. I slid them agonizingly up and down the sides of her pussy; she groaned long and deep. I felt her legs tightening slightly around my head, winding her hips gently over my face as my tongue searched out the hooded fold at the top of her succulent lips. Drawing her pearl into my mouth, I sucked on her gently, sideways, head-on, underneath. Burying my nose into every crevice.

Sophie clenched tighter with her sculptured thighs, which were moistened by her natural flow and the volcanic heat we were creating between us. Lava flowed onto my tongue; I twisted slightly to enable me to crawl between her legs till I was as close to her magnificent ass as anyone was likely to get. I let my fingers trail from her clitoris to her ass and back again. Sophie leaned forwards onto the low table, opening her legs wider still, pushing out her ass in anticipation. The roundness of her silky-smooth cheeks, drawing me like a magnet. I spread them and sniffed her deeply. She nuzzled her ass deeper onto my face, moaning and letting out a deep sigh when I made contact. My tongue hungrily searched for the source of her pleasure. Licking, stretching, circling and finally penetrating with my tongue; Sophie had now reached almost crab position in her excitement and I turned onto my back underneath her to better accommodate her increasingly frenzied movements. I knew I was going to suck and fuck her ass and pussy all night long and I knew she wouldn't stop until I had.

Pulling her down over my frenzied tongue, I wormed my way into the glorious wetness that was Sophie, opening her up with two fingers while I kissed the length of her beautiful pussy. I allowed my saturated fingers to ease their way into her back passage, gently at first and then with firmer and firmer strokes and she responded with guttural yells. I wanted to hurt her and caress her at the same time.

"Sophie, turn around. I need to see your face."

She turned and fell backwards and I cradled her body with

one hand while I finger-fucked her pussy furiously, with each stroke letting another finger find its way in as she spread her legs as far as they would go.

"More, please; more, more, more," she screamed.

Her beautiful mahogany form writhed and gasped with abandon.

I felt my fourth finger begin to slide its way in. I stopped for a moment thinking I should calm down, this amazing woman was making me crazy; but Sophie groaned even louder and I could not resist giving in to my passion. I eased my final finger in and let it rest. We looked at each other long and hard. Something in Sophie completely gave way; I felt her relax completely around my hand. I knew I had been given the very special gift of trust. My heart was ready to burst with the emotion this siren inspired in me. Slowly I opened and closed my fingers inside her; her nipples were no longer hard, they were huge and deep purple, soft and pliable. I needed them.

Ravenously, I gorged myself on them, pulled and twisted and sucked them until her pussy was so wet that I could move in and out of her with relative ease. I was about ready to faint from the intensity of it all. I guessed Sophie was feeling the same.

"Sophie, I love you. I cannot live without you, without this: you're driving me crazy."

As I said this, I applied pressure to her neck with my other hand so that her breathing was hampered just a little and I pushed out my tongue for her to suck. She pulled my head down to her mouth and sucked hungrily. I was twisting and turning my hand in and out of her pussy.

Suddenly she tore her mouth away and screamed: "Fuck me. Don't ever stop fucking me: you are mine, all mine, now." She came loudly.

I lowered my face to her breasts again, partly because I couldn't get enough and partly to hide the tears streaming down my face. I eased my hand gently out of her, thinking we needed to rest, but Sophie pushed my face downwards, clamping me between her legs; *she* couldn't get enough. My tears combined with the spicy taste of her, intoxication, and I bit and pulled and stroked and licked her pussy raw, spreading her wider, while her juices poured in continuous mind-blowing streams.

"Sophie, you're all I ever hoped you'd be and more."

"Yes, baby," she gasped, "but you, Ava, are a dream. Please don't stop now; I love you." With that, she rolled me over and fucked herself on my face, bucking and shouting, looking down at me in wonderment as another orgasm started to shudder through her.

I could not believe the passion and beauty of this woman. I thrust two fingers into her ass as she came, but the force of her contractions immediately started to push them out. My own pussy screamed out, though there was no direct stimulation and I was not surprised when I came just by looking at the mystical expression on her face.

She slowly opened her eyes and smiled down at me, stroking the tears off my cheeks. "I know I'm greedy but I hope you're not too tired, because I'm about to . . ." And with that, she eased herself off me and stretched out beside me, bending her mouth towards my aching breasts.

STILL

Mary-Kate Kelly

She always had such a grace to her, like someone who knows they're being watched. Her movements were so unforced and make me smile even now. I can hardly believe there was a time I did not know her.

"Here's your change." I noticed the girl blushed as she gave the money and looked you straight in the eye. All I could see was the back of your head, and the dark brown curls lying on your neck. I was rushed and stressed and tired, with too much work and not enough time and wanted to get my sandwich and eat it, thank you very much; so all I felt was impatience at this delay.

I must have sighed or something because you turned around, looked at me, and said, "Having a tough day?"

I forgot to answer when you smiled. Your eyebrows reminded me I needed to speak and I came out with "Yeah, pretty much." Pretty much? Was that all I could say? Already you were making your way to a corner table with your tray and the blushing girl was still looking after you. I'm sure if you had turned around at that point, there would have been a whole row of red faces pointed your way.

I paid £5.40 for my lunch that day as I suddenly decided to stay. The counter girl gave me a tray and I piled on a coffee and chocolate bar as well as my sandwich. I could see a table next to you was empty and breathed deeply as I started to walk towards it. As I sat down, you looked up and smiled again. I smiled back and concentrated on not blushing like the girl again.

"Some light reading?" You nodded to the load of books I had set down on the table.

"You could say that," I said, rolling my eyes and feeling sick with nerves. Thank God this was a Gay café or I would never have attempted this. This? What was I attempting, anyway? A pick-up? A chat-up? A love-at-first-sight-please-stay-with-me-forever moment?

You were reading your newspaper and I was pretending to look around the café while secretly taking you in.

Your neck, your hair, your nose, your hands, your jaw, your lips. I was feeling all hot and bothered again and tried to start my sandwich. Instead of tasting bread, I was brushing your skin with my mouth. Instead of swallowing cheese, I was inhaling your smell and eating you whole. Instead of tasting the burning coffee, I was gritting my teeth and looking at your neck.

And then you looked up and into my eyes.

And my whole body was alive and the winter air was warm. Your cheeks began to flush ever so slightly as you held my stare with your ice blue eyes. I felt you glide all over me with the softest touch. And then you pulled back and looked wistful and wondering. And closed your eyes before looking away.

I felt tears burn at the back of my eyes as I watched the world through the window. Slowly I brought my heated breathing under control and tried to sip easily at my lukewarm coffee.

Your girlfriend kissed your flushed cheek as she sat down and looked so at home sitting beside you. It takes years to get that comfortable, and a lot of love. I felt a loss for what would never happen between us. The passion we would never push into each other's bodies. The sweat I would never taste and the smile I would never see. The breath I would never feel.

I took my own deep breath and held it in gently, I stayed still, and then let it out. I would not cry from the loneliness I felt right now. I would wait until I was home and had a cushion and darkness to comfort me. Maybe I would have a bath to warm my freezing body. And some friends to catch my salty tears.

I see you from time to time and still clench my stomach and suddenly hear my own heart beat. You still meet your girlfriend here for lunch and look for all the world the happy couple. I still sit in whenever I see you are there and exchange glances if I am feeling brave. I know you recognize me and am glad when you speak to me in passing.

One day we may share a table and one day your girlfriend may not turn up – too much on at work; go on without me – and one day we might just dive in to the deep waters that lie between us.

THE WET ROOM

Rosa Riley

I am poised to flee. Will she say, as usual, "Can I have a hug?" She knows I can't say it She makes me wait; I suppose she must have some entertainment, though she's not supposed to play games with me. She is congruent. I don't want congruent, I want ordinary. I can go on wanting.

For a moment, she sits watching me, a smile on her plain, radiant face. The low armchair supports her. When I leave, I always wedge the door open for her with the little pumice-coloured mouse shape. It's the only thing I can do for her. The one, single thing in all the world. Her other chair is always across the room; how she gets to it, I've no idea. I've never seen her do it. I hope it's not on her knees. Once she came to me when I was crying to "give me a hug", kneeing her way across the rough wall-to-wall. When I'm on my knees, it's either cleaning the floor or having sex. But I have more use of my legs than she does. Her other chair is all black. It has a name stamped on it. The Quickie. No comment.

Finally, she arranges her legs with her hands; she has boots like teapots with Caterpillar on them. I remember caterpillars, how they lie back, green, and writhe in a dislocated abandon that might be agony or ecstasy. She heaves herself up out of the chair on her arms and, balancing, stands holding them out to me. I move into them. I wonder how strong they are. Each time we do this, I promise myself that I will touch them as I enter or leave that brief unsatisfactory embrace. I will let my fingers steal the strength of the power that must be there. I've seen her in that chair move like greased lightening, arms like pistons on the wheels, in a rush to be on time. Those arms must be strong. I think about her muscles. And her hands: large, white as porcelain. I think of their coolness on me and know I'm being inappropriate.

In the weekly farewell embrace, we are two beams of an A-frame. Locked and secure at the apex, distant and impartial at the base. Breasts together, OK. Hips not. Hips are pelvis, mean genitals, like dance, grind a little, fuck me. Not allowed. So I make do with tracing what part of her skinny little body I do have access to. Her hard bony shoulders and slight back. I feel her bra strap and immediately I am inappropriate once more. Dare not touch her shaved nape. It's only a little way from there to holding her face and falling on her marvellous mouth. Sometimes we embrace, me kneeling before her as if I am praying with my arms round the neck of my saint. I love this; it's the nearest I get to lying down with her. And it feels as if I am her child. When we do it this way, she doesn't have to strain up to me, so she thinks I'm being considerate or congruent or some other damn C word. I can sure think of one or two. Once in a while, her soft face touches mine, cool and warm, smooth and almost too intimately real to bear. I sense the exquisiteness of this reality; frail, as weak as I am. Insubstantial, perilous. All the time I am controlling those moans and groans that spring authentically from the lips when you hold the one person in the world who at this very moment could salve all wounds.

But we move away from each other and I hold her hands as I have learned to and let her use my standing weight to lower herself back down. She has never told me how to do this and I feel very clever having worked it out for myself. We eyeball each other and smile. She knows how I feel. Our smiles are so different that there are no words for them. I do the wedge thing and leave.

Another seven days to go. But she comes with me wherever I am. Especially to those hidden places where I don't go. Where I couldn't go with her. Anywhere that I may be in close proximity with her. Anywhere where we might be alone or naked, or just alone. A train, a park, a room. In the steam baths, the screening mist of evaporating water hides my shame and the scalding drops fall on our naked bodies like warning from heaven and we touch each other with fingers stinging from eucalyptus. And the heat is within and without.

I must have wished so hard that some deity took pity at last and helped me out. One day I had come to her straight from the swimming baths. My hair was wet and she said she loved to swim, too. I wondered if she meant now or before. I couldn't imagine how she would get into the water – short of the humiliation of being carried. And she turned to her chairside table and I saw a shell there that I'd never noticed before. A cowrie but such as you couldn't imagine. Not like those that black women often wear round their neck. Or that you might slip in your purse for luck. No, this was huge. As big as a fist. White, touched with apricot, its toothed mouth like a brown knowing smile.

"Listen to the sea," she said and handed it to me.

I lifted its heaviness to my ear and there it was, the rush and shush of ever-repeating waves. I didn't want ever to stop listening to that hypnotic song but she was holding out her hand for it and we had to get on. But before I could put it safely in her hand it rolled from our fingers and fell onto the carpet with a soft thud. She gasped and clutched the arms of her chair. No real harm done, I thought, until as I bent to rescue the thing I saw a little thread of water slip from its serrated edge. "Hold on tight," she said, smiling strangely at me, and as she held out her hand to me a spout of water gushed from the shell. Swiftly a flood swelled in that tiny room and lifted us. Pointing one long finger at the window, the glass dissolved, and she floated out, trailing a hand behind for me.

But the flood surged and we were swept apart by an engulfing, obliterating wave and I found myself in deep, very deep water. She had obviously known what to do for, in between the rocking and rolling and heaving of this mighty sea, I glimpsed her afar safe on a sandy strand in her trusty Quickie. Fear swept through me for I am only a calm water swimming bath type of a person, and here I was, ready to drown in salt water. But as well as terror and wet water and watching the tiny dot that was her, I realized that other strange things had occurred. For example, I seemed to be staying afloat more easily than I would have thought. Afloat, abreast. But I can no longer feel my legs. They seem to be frozen, though I am moving something beneath me in my efforts to manipulate myself in this environment. As I wonder what has happened, a great gleaming tail like a snake, all scales and flickering muscle, undulates and revolves around me, beautiful under the pale water. Suddenly it flips up, fluke like a flag, and propels me through the waves. I believe it belongs to me. I believe I am now very different.

I have a conch which I blow loudly across the cold empty beach and that tiny dot becomes bigger and bigger as she races across hard packed sand. Pausing at the tide's edge she watches me, novice diver in deep water, practise skills I've never even heard of. I rise up, blowing the conch shell more gently now. I am very beautiful. The sea lifts me and pulls me back; lifts me and throws me towards her. My skin shimmers faintly green but my breasts are burning hot. Sea water burns me and she knows it: I can tell from her face, even from this distance. I flaunt my new shape; I glisten at her, rolling and rippling for her. Before, I would be experiencing sensations of enlarging, expanding, my legs falling open; but now it's different in a similar way. Now I feel an urge to coil, to wrap, to engulf, to grip with this tail, to use it like hands. Beneath the waves I beat my new tail impatiently, lashing the water to hot froth.

Already she has wheeled herself into the shallows. Is she getting the idea or does she just want to save me? Waves throw themselves at her; her legs are wet. Soon she will be sitting in water. But it is no use waiting for the tide to rise. You can be sitting there all day, as if you were bird-watching. I call her again and again, letting the heaving quilt of this wet bed support me. I hold out my arms to her, the water streaming off me. I shine, I gleam. A strand of Bladder Wrack fastens itself around one of the wheels of her chair. I seize it and pull but I am lightweight; the chair holds fast and I only succeed in stranding myself on the sand. So I remember my previous form and try to move myself as I once would. But I heave and hump like a walrus. Each time my poor tail flexes and thrashes against the gritty sand, I move but a few inches. As I crawl on my elbows, broken shell pieces slice my water-soft skin, reddening the sand. My tail weighs heavy; I cannot drag it. I cannot move in this place as I used to. Face on the sand, red suffusing green; I am bruised both in and out. I have lost the grace I once had. My light dies, my tail fades. I remember how I used it to flirt with her. What must she think of me; I want only her good opinion. I pray for a pitying wave to bring me back home and, as one comes, I roll into it and return to my deep safety.

Water always rises before it falls and she waits until it comes to her knees. Then, with a sigh and a push, she lets herself go and falls towards me. I catch her and wrap myself around her.

When I am human, I dream all the day long of being in her arms. Now she is in my world and I am holding her in the infinity of this private gloaming. We sink, green hair electric, pale as mooli, into the deep abyss of silence, only the pulsing bell of heart's blood roaring in our ears. There is a moment of painful bliss when our lungs learn to breathe water and our eyes see past salt: then she is mine. We tumble *fischlein*, lifted all the time by a thousand different currents. Weightless, directionless, fetterless. Above was only fear.

Here below, all is possible. She is laughing as my body guides hers in this new dimension. In my human form I would pull her to a bed, in my need for the horizontal. Here, there is no horizontal. We are fused together by briny forces. Wet meets wet. My tail, its thick muscles supporting her, coiling around and around her. Her feet on my fluke tremble. My scales like glass flash, dazzling, in her eyes; we hold fast. My sea hands are strong as hers now. In this tremulous light beneath the surface, she glimmers like a ghost; her small breasts are pearls. The fins on my back erect with desire, my gills opening and closing fast in time to my beating heart. And the unseen fissure in my body where flesh becomes scale, that hidden mouth, the one that sailors dream and lie about, now gapes and pants. Swollen like a sea fruit, it unwraps, uncurling, releasing such a hunger in me. My eyelids droop in a half fainting languor; I nearly lose my hold on her.

She is a fish slipping in and out, again and again she comes and goes between my legs, weaving through their strong arch as I swim, swim for the shore. Again she rescues me, hands supporting and caressing, my name bubbling from her mouth. Then she too surrenders and her lithe body opens like a starfish waiting for food. I offer myself.

Spring tides rise dangerously fast, changing landscapes and lives. As swiftly as we had been swept there, we were swept back. The current sucked back, reversing into its shell. We with it. I sat dazed in silence; what could I say? She was, as ever, self contained. Not a hair out of place, dry as a bone. Water was dripping from my hair onto the carpet. The room hollow as laughter.

Soon after that, I refused to come to the little room any more. I'd had enough. She agreed: she was congruent. It broke my heart. I did see her one more time, however, though she didn't see me. I was stuck in traffic in a car that stank of petrol with a woman who hated me. We waited and I wound down the window and breathed in more foul air. Suddenly, I heard a joyous noise of cheering and laughter, whistles and honking and, round a bend in the road behind us, came the cause of our stuckness. A procession of wheelchairs, banners and flags came down upon us like a hoard of stampeding animals. That's where I saw her, in the middle of that riotous assembly, the black bones of her chariot shining like the sinews of an exoskeleton. She passed quite close; still she didn't look at me, though above the stench of the traffic I caught a whiff of something salty and from one of the wheels of her chair I thought I saw a little piece of dried Bladder Wrack streaming behind her like a tail.

Deepest thanks to Maggie Murray and to K. for your critical help with this piece and for your loving ear and encouragement always.

FISKAR

Patience Agbabi

I'm having an aquamarine wet dream. We're far out at sea. She's got seaweed hair and I've got a tongue like an electric eel. As we French kiss, my whole body begins to spasm and I reach down to the lush fullness of her turquoise sequinned hips while she simultaneously runs one finger down my spine and another up my inside thigh. *The postwoman is approaching my letter box.* I'm making strange foreign sounds as she parts my lower lips, enters me and begins to fill me with her long, strong fingers. I begin to moan, high-pitched and rhythmic. *The postwoman eases the huge bundle of letters through my door.* Strange siren. Danger! Clear the beach!

Strange ringing bringing me back to earth. Coitus interruptus. The phone mixed in with the single dull thud of post coming through the front door. Sod's law. Resignedly, I press "talk".

"This is your reminder call. This is your reminder call . . ." says Ms BT and I leap into the hall like a hyperactive child on Christmas day, expecting a treat from the land of reindeers and sleighs. My enthusiasm soon dies when I catch sight of the BT envelope but I enjoy the barefoot luxury on the way, the urban equivalent of sand between the toes. My best mate Virgo Jo says it isn't real shagpile, but the guy on the doorstep was so sweet and on the dole with seven kids to feed, so I'd kind of taken pity on him.

Sipping a herb tea that could be anything from ginger to gunpowder, I open my letters leaving the bad news last. A phone bill the length of the complete works of Shakespeare. Finally, I leaf through the contents twice, avoiding the *£472.57 Total amount now due* on the front page. I'm more interested in the numerical diary of my life over the past quarter. The 00s and 001s of the overseas tour where I began drinking as soon as the plane was horizontal and returned with an air hostess in tow, and enough duty free to open a shebeen. But that's foreplay compared to the 0891s.

0891 on my touchdial phone is music to my ears. There's only one 0891: The Pink Paper Personals by Phone – Women. Actually, most of this bill is 0891 and it's only the dates that distinguish one call from another. Of course, if Jo walked through the door right now, I'd hide the evidence, cos she'd only lecture me on my excesses, beginning with the phone, then moving onto alcohol and ending with shagpile carpets. But even I'm a little shocked at the cost of those quiet evenings in and make a mental note to hang out on the scene a bit more, even though it makes me anxious, which makes me drink more, which spells trouble.

Like on 8 March, International Women's Day. 8 March is a mixture of Pride and Christmas. It was a Friday night and I'd started drinking early, enjoyed a mixed-media event near Brick

Lane, crashed a party in Brixton and been delivered by cab to North London in the early hours. Luckily, I live in North London, so I didn't have too far to walk when I disgraced myself on the back seat of the cab, convulsing with nausea and, hey presto, the entire evening regurgitated. Then apologizing profusely and parting with a fifty pound note. Then getting home by braille and jabbing with the key and laughing hysterically at my lack of success in opening the front door.

By the time I finally dived into my flat, the humour had dissolved into hangover. I needed a bath but had clothes soaking in it and the water was definitely on the turn. The flat looked like it had been broken into but the thieves had decided there wasn't anything worth taking. It wouldn't normally bother me but, once the violins are out, I drown in self-pity. Even the cab driver hadn't tried to chat me up. I slumped over the kitchen table, slurping a coffee strong enough to wake the dead. It seemed to have the desired effect cos, before I knew what was happening, I was eyeing up the curves of my cordless phone which beckoned like a multi-speed vibrator. I dialled those ten digits like a Girl Friday on heat.

When Jo's around, we read ads out loud in bad regional accents like Eurotrash and giggle like hysterical teens, then guilt-trip each other when we've sobered up: but when I'm on my own, I go with the flow. Earlier that evening, I'd picked up my Paper and squashed it into my bag, dreaming that this wild night out would end in romance. But now it was 3 a.m. and the familiar recorded message was telling me to press the star button on my phone twice now. I obeyed.

Instinctively, I went for bold: but in reality, it was the only print I could easily read in my confused state. So what if I wasn't tattooed and twenty or owned a villa in France? It could still work out. I'd been on the phone for about half an hour, listening to matching messages and forgetting I wasn't in the

Virgin megastore with my headphones on, swaying to the latest cheesy love song, when I came across:

SIZZLING SCORPION
seeks passionate Piscean.
If you fancy lobster bisque in
Heathrow, sushi in Schiphol
or caviar in Keflavik, don't delay.
London. ML47257.

Dehydrated though I was, my mouth watered. The ad had my name written all over it and, before I knew what was happening, I'd dialled those five digits.

"Hello, my name is Anna and I live in London. (Sounds like a Blind Date enthusiast). I would like my ad to read like this: 'Sizzling Scorpion seeks passionate Piscean. If you fancy lobster bisque in Heathrow, sushi in Schiphol or caviar in Keflavik, don't delay'."

Her accent was weird. There was definitely an American twang somewhere in the mix, so she'd probably spent some time in the States, but she rolled her r's like a Scot. I gave up on the guessing game and listened to the message again, for the sheer pleasure of it, then took a deep breath before launching into my reply.

"Hello, Anna. They call me Ms Pisces cos I'm a beach babe into sun, sea, seafood and champagne. (Obviously a Blind Date enthusiast!) I adore travel and romantic dinners.

"I've got short black hair and green eyes, I'm twenty-seven years old, medium build and athletic. I was in the rowing team at university but gave up cos I hated the six o'clock start. (The reality was they dropped me cos I turned up late once too often).

"I'm a late riser, especially on Sundays, when I like breakfast in bed, and trashy magazines. I'm an actress and I'm mad keen on soap operas."

Amazing how quickly I sobered up during the message, though I still found it hard to make the sentences flow. It was like doing an audition, with no script, no audience and no one to say, "Thank you, Ms Fisher. We'll be in touch. Next!" I listened to it, smiled and it was only when I pressed "talk" at the end of the call that I realised I hadn't left my name or telephone number. I rang a second time, jumping through all the 0891 hoops with my eyes closed. I was literally falling asleep. By then, the adrenalin rush had curled up in bed with a hot water bottle and a couple of nurofen extras. But I still fell asleep wondering about Anna. She certainly hadn't given much away.

I dreamt I was in my mother's womb, somersaulting in amniotic fluid with a twin sister, and woke drenched in sweat and dehydrated to the dulcet tones of the BT wake-up call which I'd forgotten to change for the weekend. Having silenced the call, and downed a pint of ice-cold water, I collapsed on the bed for the best part of Saturday.

Till the phone rang again. I rolled over in bed and picked it up.

"Hello?"

"Hello. Can I speak to Marina, please?"

"Yeah, that's me."

"Marina, it's Sara. We met last night at the party. You left me your number so I thought I'd give you a call."

Her voice was disjointed, as if she was on a mobile. Then I remembered that I'd requested Call Waiting, and the peculiar hiccups meant there was another caller trying to get through. I decided to ignore it, since I was particularly braindead that morning and hadn't worked out how to use it anyway.

"It's very early . . ." Dry and hoarse.

"You left last night without saying goodbye!"

I was racking my brains to put a face to the name that had just accused me of the cardinal sin of rudeness. In a split second, it all came flooding back. Sara was probably the psychiatric nurse who'd accosted me on the way out, trying to persuade me to stay another half hour. I must have given her my phone number so she'd leave me alone. Then I slipped out into the night. It was the usual story of a woman I didn't fancy at all ringing me at the first possible opportunity. Like nine in the morning on a Saturday.

"I'm sorry, Sara, but it's very early and I'm not feeling too good – . . ." (And I've got a feeling that there's a hot date on the other line.)

"That's OK. I can come round and cheer you up."

(Definitely on Prozac.) "Sara, I'll call you back some other time, yeah?" I lied, desperately wanting to get Sara off the phone but not wanting to give her a complex.

"OK!" Enthusiastic.

My heart sank. Now I'd have Sara on my conscience as well as a raging hangover that even codeine couldn't zap. I made a mental note to cut down on my drinking. It always got me into trouble.

"Bye, then."

"Hear from you soon!"

The other caller hadn't waited so I dialled 1471, only to discover that their number hadn't been recorded. Dejected, I snuggled back under the covers. But when the phone rang again that evening, I knew it was the same person. Something in my psyche told me it was Ms Scorpio.

"Hello, I would like to speak to Ms Pisces, if she's free."

(Wow!. She didn't even give me the chance to say hello and she'd called me!) "Yeah, that's me," I replied, casual.

"This is Anna. You replied to my ad. I like what you said. I think we're on the same wavelength."

Butterflies between my thighs. Whatever the accent was, it worked. "Did you ring this morning?"

"Yes. It was engaged and they played the Call Waiting message. I found it very frustrating and I had a plane to catch so, I decided to ring you later. Are you still in bed?"

"Yeah, I mean no. I'm making food. Where are you?" Not believing my bad luck. I made a mental note to learn to use Call Waiting.

"I'm phoning from abroad, so I'm afraid I can't speak for too long," she replied enigmatically. "I"m an air hostess and I'm having a week's holiday." (Another air hostess. It was unreal).

"When are you back in London?" Not wanting to sound too desperate.

"In ten days' time." (Ten days of torture!) "Would you like to go on a date with me?"

"Yeah, I'd love to," I whispered. No point in even trying to be cool. I could hardly breathe, let alone speak. Cymbals were drowning out the violins for sure.

"Are you free a week on Thursday in the day? Let's meet at the entrance of The Women's Pond on Hampstead Heath. We could even go swimming if it's raining; otherwise we can go for a drink in one of those old-fashioned bars."

I had a strong sense of déjà vu. "Swimming in the rain sounds great. Haven't done it for years. It's like getting into a warm bath, isn't it?"

"Yes, it's *very* good. But are you free?"

"Yeah, I'm free most of the time at the moment, cos I've just finished a tour. What time did you say?"

"I didn't say, but how about three-thirty? I mean, half past two?"

"OK."

"You must tell me what you look like, Marina, in case I go off with the wrong girl," she teased.

"I've got short black hair and green eyes."

"How tall are you?"

"About five six. But how will I recognize you? Will you wear a rose in your buttonhole?"

"I'm tall, dark and handsome." I sensed a smile creasing full lips. "I'm mixed race. I have long black hair, usually tied back. And I'm *very* fit."

I did thirty lengths of the pool that evening, instead of getting pissed in the pub, deciding it's better to swim like a fish than drink like one. So what if I can't do butterfly? I wanted those strong but lazy muscles a little more taut by Thursday week and I really adored being back in the water again. My Cancer ascendent rose to the occasion, telling me that this was the best catch I'd had in a long while, so I'd better impress my mysterious date; while my Piscean psyche was a little scared of getting swallowed up by this proud Scorpion.

Tuesday morning, the postwoman arrived with a recorded delivery envelope. I signed for it and ripped it open, assuming it was some kind of business letter. Inside was a single shiny faxed sheet dated Sunday 10 March.

Dear Marina

It was good speaking to you on Saturday, so good that I will find it impossible to wait nine days before we meet. I would like to meet you midweek, if you are free. You said you are not very busy, so I'm sure you will like to see me. I have arranged an air ticket which you can collect from Heathrow airport that morning. My colleague Helga will meet you . . .

[(Various technical details which I completely ignored in my excitement.)]

I'm very much looking forward to seeing you this Wednesday. I'm faxing this letter to Helga in London so you will receive it in time. It will be nice getting to know you intimately away from London. I work very hard and play very hard, and I'll give you a really good time. Everything is taken care of, the flight is paid for and no need to fret about money. And do not worry about the weather as you English do.

I must go now because I need to fax this letter in time. See you on Wednesday. Bon voyage.

Anna

(a single large kiss)

"Iceland!" shrieked Jo, halfway down the letter, "In March! She must be joking!" We were having a drink in the local that evening and Jo, usually mild-mannered and softly spoken, bombarded me with a barrage of exclamation marks. "And you must be mad, Marina, to even think about it!"

She launched into a long speech about psychopaths who lure gullible English girls abroad, cut them up into little pieces and send bits of them back to England by air. Typical Jo, sensible to the extreme.

"You're paranoid, Jo," I laughed, taking a gulp of piss-weak lager. "It's the most exciting offer I've ever had. I bet you'd go abroad if someone else was paying, especially on a hot date."

"Hot date? You'll freeze your tits off out there! Land of fire and ice? More like the North Pole!"

A dyke couple looked up from their beer at the mention of "tits" and eyed us with unconcealed curiosity. Jo looked embarrassed and I decided not to admit that I'd spent the entire day fantasizing about sun drenched beaches with sand dune curves.

"I'm sorry," she said. "It's just that you don't know anything about her. She's mixed race but you have no idea of her cultural background. How do you know you'll fancy her? How do you know she'll fancy you?"

I chose to ignore the latter statement. Jo was always a teeny weeny bit jealous of my lovers, potential or otherwise. We'd got it together a few times in the past but it hadn't worked out so we'd chosen friendship. Typical dyke scenario.

"Fire and ice, that's so romantic," I replied, sipping my whisky chaser and meaning it. I loved polar opposites; that's probably why I managed to stay friends with Jo for so long. And I did appreciate her concern.

"OK. They've got a few volcanoes that erupt now and then but the glaciers are there all year round."

"I've never seen a glacier before," I began, and then, sensing Jo's exasperation, added, "How about one for the road?" as if it really *was* our last drink.

The flight took about three hours but it seemed like forever. When the plane had left the safety of the runway, I'd been terrified that I was making a mistake but there was no turning back, and by the time it got horizontal I got philosophical. I realised my nerves were more to do with flying than Anna and that even though part of me loved the magic of it, the other half wanted to be on firm ground or, better still, water. Why couldn't I sail there? Because it would take weeks and weeks and I'd die if I had to wait that long.

Midflight, I spent the time admiring various cloud formations and a blonde-haired blue-eyed air hostess who was obviously straight but enjoyed the attention all the same. I doused myself with the Duty Free perfume I'd bought at Heathrow and fantasized about sex with Anna. After my first glass of wine, I declined all alcohol, enjoying the adrenalin buzz neat, for a change, and went to the loo about five times to masturbate myself back to normality and try to keep my nerves in check. It didn't work and by the time the plane made that characteristic thud on the runway, I was ready for anything.

Except the black crater landscape that spread out as far as the eye could see. It was like landing on the moon. I'd expected ice and snow, not barren lava fields, and I desperately craved BT's wake-up call to rescue me from this Dr Who nightmare. But before the violins were in full swing, I was collecting my duty free and hand luggage, striding through the airport to pick up my suitcase that Jo had insisted on packing so I was prepared for my arctic adventure, and walking through "Nothing to declare", the butterfly wings flapping violently in my belly signalling a change of weather in a few hours' time.

Ms Scorpio was waiting, the only brown face in a sea of pink. She was definitely handsome with the kind of face that changes with the weather so you never get bored looking. It was as if you could see her mother, her father and each of their parents, depending on her expression. She was wearing a tight cotton sweater and hipster leather trousers, which accentuated her full but firm hips. My mouth began to water as it always does when I fancy the pants off someone. I smiled shyly as she greeted me with a kiss on the lips. She had a way of gazing into my eyes as if asking a question.

"The flight was great," I responded. "And I bought as much duty free as I could carry."

She laughed. "I forgot to tell you you can buy it here at the airport. But you're the athletic type, so you probably enjoyed carrying it."

We both laughed nervously, holding the gaze.

"Do you fancy a snack and a drink for starters?" Heavy emphasis on the "k"s. Everything she said, even the most innocent of suggestions, sounded sexual.

"Are you trying to lead me astray?" I teased.

"I've already led you astray," she replied. "You got on the plane, didn't you?"

Sipping a glass of very good muscadet that was so expensive I could hear Jo's exclamation marks ringing in my ears, and nibbling a sandwich filled with some rather strange, delicious seafood, Anna sated some of my curiosity.

"My mother's Icelandic and my father's African-American. He was in the US military and they met over here, got it together and had me. It was hard for us, at first, cos there isn't much racial mixing here. During the US occupation in the war, they didn't even let black GIs into the country."

"So what's it like now?" I asked, scanning the bar for an obviously foreign face and seeing none.

"It's fine. People are cool. The capital's small so I know a lot of people." Confident. "We shouldn't have any problems. They don't give gays a hard time, either," she added, pre-empting my next question. "What about you, Marina?"

"Oh, I'm a Heinz 57, you know, I've got some Irish, Greek, English . . ."

"That sounds like a cocktail I would like to drink." Her dark eyes sparkled with fun. "Would you like another drink, Marina?"

"No, thanks." Alcohol was the last thing on my mind.

We shared a minute or so of silence which would normally embarrass me, but I enjoyed the flirting space. Then she leant over and kissed me very lightly on the lips. I smiled again and she raised her eyebrows.

"Are you into water sports?"

It took me a second or two to digest the question, since it was a little unexpected.

"What do you mean, deep-sea diving or golden showers?" What had she *really* meant by all those fish references? Even I felt out of my depth and I casually cast a glance at the departure board, remembering Jo's psycho speech.

"You English are so naughty; you always hear a *double entendre.* I mean, do you like swimming and diving, Ms Pisces? I know you used to row but you preferred your bed to the boat."

I loved the way she played with words and I'm sure she played on the fact that English was her third language, pleading innocence when really she was very much in control. She could wrap me round her little finger if she liked; I wasn't going to complain.

"I'm a water babe," I chuckled. "It goes back to the womb. I can't think of anything better than being inside a woman in water."

"When I was growing up here in Iceland, the Danes called me 'The Little Mermaid'. They have a statue in Copenhagen after the fairytale. I was always in water. Icelandic people like to swim but I was mad on the water. Why don't we go for a swim now, Marina? I will take you to a *very* special place."

"Is it better than The Women's Pond?"

"You bet."

The Blue Lagoon is paradise, even in March. So what if it's freezing outside? I expected it to be minus forty, the way Jo was creating. It doesn't even feel *that* cold. I tease Anna for wearing latex gloves.

"Are they to protect you from frostbite or to protect me from your unbridled lust?"

Anna remains silent, watching me pull the nylon/lycra Speedo up my muscular torso. She wraps her arms around me from behind and begins to nibble my earlobe. I take a sharp intake of breath.

We have to shower before going in, which gives us the chance for some serious French kissing in private. Most people swim before or after work, and the pool lies between the airport and the capital, so you have to make a bit of an effort to get there. No one else has made the effort today. I manage to put my training to good use by letting Anna feel just how firm my tits are, how strong my thighs are. But she's stronger, taller, liquid gold and the only swimming we do is part of the dyke flirting ritual, the "come and get me if you really want me" synchronized swimming. And the grins on our faces far outshine the entire US Olympic team.

The blue lagoon is a huge hot bath of strange, cloudy blue-grey water, thick with natural chemicals like exotic bath oils. Steam rises into the chill still air. Anna begins to kiss me, running a single finger down my spine till she reaches the crease in my behind. I gasp as she traces a spiral on each magnificent dome. Her touch is light but firm. Just how I like it. We join tongues, playful at first and build to a deep persistent rhythm, in, out, in, out, and my tongue begins to vibrate in her mouth and she's sucking my lips like she's deep down between my thighs. And she's sucking me, deep tongueing me, biting my lips. My whole body begins to spasm and I reach down to the lush fullness of her hips while she simultaneously runs one finger down my spine and another up my inside thigh *and I'll die if you don't fuck me now.* And I'm making strange foreign sounds as she parts my lower lips, enters me and begins to fill me with her long, strong fingers. I'm swollen with lust, *fuck me*, and my cunt begins to moan, high pitched and rhythmic, clawing at her liquid body. She responds by adding a finger and upping the intensity – *oh, Anna, make me come, babe.* And I'm cunt, all cunt, as she's vibrating my clit with her thumb and biting my lips and she's teasing me between the butt cheeks with her other hand and I'm talking in tongues and we're Siamese twins: same heart, same lungs, breathing heavy duty as she enters my behind, fills me, possesses me completely, and I cry out like I've just given birth, like I've just been born, like I just died.

Our twin bodies remain entwined for minutes, hours, oblivious to the arrival of other bathers and I think to myself, this is perfect.

"This is my favourite place in the world," whispers Anna, breaking the silence.

"Is this your ideal cruising ground, then?"

"That is between me and the lagoon."

A stray ripple of lust seizes my body again and I'm pure liquid lust. I've never met a woman so good with her hands.

"You never told me you had octopus tendencies, Ms Scorpio." She lifts her latex hands out of the water.

"Only eight fingers and two thumbs. Anyway, you never told me you had volcanic tendencies, Ms Pisces. You must have a fiery ascendent."

"No, I don't, but I bet *you* do!"

"You bet!" she says, tossing her long black mane. "But we must leave now, Marina. I can feel a change in the weather and I want to get you on dry land. We're both hungry and I think you'd appreciate an Icelandic dinner for two." I lick my lips in greedy anticipation.

"And what will that be, Ms Scorpio: seafood or freshwater fish?"

"*Definitely* the fish."

"Fried, baked or raw?"

"I'll leave that for *you* to decide, Ms Pisces."

TABLE MANNERS

Ros Marinus

You could have said any number of things. (Bearing in mind, of course, that it had to fit into 30 words or less.)

It must have been difficult, deciding what to say, what to tell everybody (after all, you're not good with words; that's what you told me).

You could have said: I breed parrots. I write poetry. I play chess. I play hard to get. (You didn't, of course, because you don't.)

Or you could have said: I'm a professional lesbian. Well, that *is* nearly what you said, but not quite like that. And I'm glad you didn't, because I wouldn't have been able to stop myself asking you how much your salary was; what you had to do to get promotion and what the perks were.

But you didn't, so I didn't get the chance.

*   *   *

You could have said what some of the others said:

Do you enjoy reading, then? (I'd said I was passionate about books.)

Well, actually, I live in North London, but I have been down there once or twice. It's quite nice, isn't it? (I'd specified that I wanted someone who lived in my area.)

Oh, a dog? Mmm . . . I've got two cats . . . (That one really was barking up the wrong tree.)

But what you actually said, was: I've got a car and a cat (in that order, please note); I go to the gym; I like going for walks by the sea.

And then you said: I'm looking for a woman with a definite female shape – that means good tits and bum.

Yes, that's what you actually said. It was on your message – you said it, you spoke that into the machine, onto the tape, for anyone to hear.

You were telling me what you wanted. Not what you thought I might want to hear, what was polite or correct or euphemistic. You wanted a woman who had curves, not one who was as flat as the proverbial. You wanted something – several things – someone you could feel and hold on to. I heard you say it – and it sounded like me.

You wanted someone who liked to feel spray on their face, who didn't mind that wetness on their face, or the taste of salt in the corners of their mouth.

My name means, "dew of the sea". Which is not quite the same as "good tits and bum". But you might like to say it, to whisper it in the dark some night, when we're too tired to sleep, too content to stay awake.

I'd like to hear you say that.

You said you like to walk by the sea, while the waves crash around you. (Perhaps we could watch *From Here To Eternity*, one evening? Maybe you've never seen it. I thought that was one everyone would have seen at least once, but that was before you told me you'd never seen *Mommie Dearest*.) I listened carefully to what you said, I wrote it all down, and then I clipped the piece of paper to your advert, so I didn't get you mixed up with anyone else.

There are plenty of pebbles on the beach.

I like to pick out the ones with holes through the middle. "Magic stones", I call them. They're not perfect, these stones. They've been worn away by every element that's come into contact with them: water, earth, air, fire. You can see everything that's happened to them, just by looking. If you pick up a shell and hold it to your ear, you can hear the sea. Or maybe it's the dew of the sea.

I could have said any number of things.

I think I did, actually. On and on, I went. Bloody hell – bloody nerves.

But still, you just sat there and listened. (Where were you sitting? I never asked you. Come to think of it, you were probably lying on your bed. And what were you doing while you were lying there, holding me to you ear, listening to me?)

So I told you how much I love being by the sea. Don't "keep fit", but I am fit and healthy. Don't have a car, or a cat. A bike and a dog.

Oh, yeah – I've definitely got a female shape. Don't know if the tits and bum are good, ho-ho, but they're there, all right.

Hello?

You were still there, still holding me, just listening to me yakking on, spilling out my oral history. I wanted the chance to show you what else I could do with my mouth.

* * *

After we'd spent our first evening together, I could have said: "I felt a vibration between us."

Except I didn't feel it, did I?

It was there all evening (you told me later), as we sat there, drinking our nerves away. If only I'd looked under the table . . . it's a wonder I didn't. After all, I was looking everywhere else – at my hands, at my glass, at your hands – anywhere, except into your eyes.

If only I'd known what was going on under that table, and what that told me about you, I might have risked a quick glance upwards.

So I should have risked a quick glance downwards. Under the table. At your legs.

We sat there for three hours, and I didn't look at your eyes or your legs. Either would have been a good idea, but for one I didn't have enough nerve, and the other, not enough imagination.

For three hours, you couldn't keep your legs still.

It's a funny business, getting turned on – it catches people in different ways. Why does it make parts of you go bone-dry, while others become unfeasibly wet? (One woman I knew used to get sweaty hands and feet.) And aren't our pupils supposed to open up, so we can see everything that we want to? I simply find it unsights me. All I can do is listen.

But with you, it's your legs. They don't stop moving. They twitch and bounce and jiggle. They open and close. They stretch and push. They dance towards me – an old-fashioned courtly dance, a ladies' excuse-me. May I have the pleasure?

My dance-card is nearly empty, so is yours. Not quite, but it's easy to change partners. I would have known how easy, if I'd paid attention to your fancy footwork. You knew the right steps.

"Don't you know by now? All you have to do to get somebody to go to bed with you is look into their eyes and ask them," you could have said.

And that *is* what you said.

So, I looked up from the table, and I looked into your eyes, and I said: "Would you like to come home with me tonight?"

I could have said, "Would you like to be near the sea with me, and hold me close to your ear, and listen to all the noises, and feel the spray on your face, and taste the saltiness?"

I can say it now, of course.

Now, you can hold me, and hear me, and taste me, and I feel your legs move, I watch them open and close, and stretch and push, and I may have the pleasure.

Sometimes we walk along by the sea, where we can hold hands, and you watch me while I look for magic stones. I find one, and I hold it up to you, and look through it, and I see your eyes and your face where the hole used to be.

I always knew they had magic in them.

RED ROCK

Lorna Stucki

She watched her in silence. Her soft black skin glinted in the moonlight as the small droplets of water rolled down the length of her body, tracing the curves leading gracefully in between her toes and settling into a puddle where she stood. Her hand reached out for her little piece of rag she used to wipe herself down and, as she stretched to dry her thigh, she dropped it carelessly on the ground. The river was still, as it mirrored her sleek tall frame bending down to where she dropped her rag, her ass, big black and round, the most perfect shape Castra had ever seen on another woman. Castra's tongue licked her moist thick lips at the thought of running it's tip along Marell's shoulders and down her spine to feel the ridges ripple beneath her skin. To carefully tease the small of her back and lick into the curve leading to her pert crack, searching for her dark whorl and rimming it until her love shook as if she had been taken over by the spirit of Voodoo.

A twig cracked below her foot. Her faithful shield, hiding Castra from her idol's every move, protected from her dark brown eyes, behind the bush. Where she hid. The ground squelched as Marell moved to see the branches sway in the midnight breeze, catching a glimpse of the candle-light far off in the distance at the big house. Castra held her breath, hoping that she couldn't be seen. Sweat on her brow slipped into her eyes, blinding with the sting of salt. Wiping them, she sighed quietly, whilst Marell returned to the small piece of rag she had dropped and continued to dry herself down. Castra yearned to help her but she knew she couldn't and that made her ache more. Marell had another at the big house; Castra couldn't compete with the power that this lover had over them all. Castra had watched Marell and her lover dance naked on the porch when the family was away, she had watched them make love until the sun rose, stirring them both from their sleep. That was the first time that Castra had seen two women love each other; that was the morning she knew what the strange feeling inside her belly was whenever Marell walked by and smiled.

The small rag, damp from the water collected from her idol's body was discarded onto the rocks close by. Marell stepped inside the pile of yellow sitting on the ground and scooped it up around her and began fumbling with the tiny mother of pearl buttons which ran the length of her dress. Castra lost her balance and slipped forward; she steadied herself quickly and then slapped her hand over her mouth to stop herself from squeaking with her own fear of being caught. With her eyes screwed shut to stop Marell seeing the whites of them, she ducked quickly as a cloud rolled passed the moon. Marell swooped around and scoured the bushes beyond; she couldn't see clearly but, with a smile, she tied a red scarf around her plaited hair.

"Castra, is that you?" The long clear southern drawl of her tender soft voice carried across the glinting water. Only the crickets answered. Castra stayed still, wondering what would happen if she ran into the arms of her dream. Her hand still pressed over her mouth, she watched as Marell puffed up her dress and dusted it down with a firm hand. The mud on her feet had dried in the warm night air and, with every step she took closer to the big house, the mud crumbled away. Castra sat staring into the darkness until the cloud that had guarded the moon passed and then she made her way to the red rocks where the rag of Marell's lay unwanted. She could see the candle-light through the cracks in the wooden slats beyond in the barn. If this small rag was all she could have tonight, then the months of watching Marell had been worth it. Castra settled on the rocks beside the water and watched as the crickets danced in the night along the water's edge. Castra lay down by the river and hitched up her dusty red dress around her creamy yellow thighs, she flicked her toes into the water's edge and watched the blackened clouds float by in the black sky, thinking of her darling, Marell.

"What's wrong, child? What's ailing you . . . ?" Castra giggled to herself and closed her eyes, picturing Marell's long lean body in front of her, as she was when she slowly surfaced out of the water. Every inch of her black glory wet and alight with the rays of the moon, every piece of her soft sweet black skin a goddess. Castra slid her hand under her worn cotton dress and slipped it between her thighs as her memory traced the image of Marell.

Her mound was damp with the sweat from crouching behind the bush for so long. The wiry hair tangled around her fine fingers as she teased the black silky mess and stroked through until she reached her moist secret. Her fingers slipped easily between her soft swollen lips; the juice trickled down between her ass-crack onto the red rock, marking a dark red trail in the rock dust from her cunt, snaking down until it reached the muddy earth. The heat from her pussy made her cunt-lips feel luscious to her touch. Pictures of Marell's breasts filled her head; she wanted to suck on them, pull hard on the black nipples until her dream begged her to stop. One long finger became two, then three as her hole welcomed more. Castra writhed, scratching her legs on the red rocks as she bucked up and down excitedly. Desperately she pulled at her own nipple, pinching the deep pink berry until it became as hard as a cherry stone; she forced her large, round breast up, out from under the cotton dress and squeezed it in her left hand until it was in the right position below her chin, close enough for her tongue to trace the cherry, close enough to suck, close enough to bite the tip hard until it made her shiver.

Castra twisted her head and suckled hard at her breast, her back hurting with the hardness of the red rock cradle beneath her, but the pleasure in her head made her go on, rocking herself, pounding her cunt hard and fast until her panting became so loud she thought she'd wake the spirits. Her nipple slipped from her mouth in a sigh, leaving warm saliva trailing down into her neck; she flattened the palm of her hand and pressed it firmly on her pussy-lips, teasing, circling her fingers in and out of her hot, swollen wet cunt, then pressing hard again with the flat of her hand, imagining that Marell was on top of her, their swollen clits slipping on each other's brown skin, sliding on soft thighs. Her pussy hungrily accepted the teasing pictures in her mind, making Castra's juice thick and sticky. Her legs splayed apart, moving her fingers up and down, exploring every warm crevice until her whole body ached with pleasure.

She smouldered at the thought of Marell's tongue slipping into her and prodding on her swollen sex inside her cunt.

Castra's cries became louder as she banged her ass uncontrollably hard against the rock, moaning Marell's name loudly. She hushed herself, filing her mouth with her wet fingers and sucking hungrily on them. In her head, she was comforting herself on her lover's breast, suckling desperately, craving for the pain in her belly to stop. Crazed with the image of Marell, she tempted herself into submission, to the burning rising in her.

Gasping for air, she rubbed her sopping cunt harder until her ass muscles squeezed tight and she raised up, arching her back, legs shivering; she held her breath as her passion rose like a fury inside her and exploded into a scream of madness as her whole body helped onto the image of Marell, burning deep into Castra's soul. The pictures replayed inside Castra's head; they tore right thought her body, liquefying into her blood, becoming part of her writhing on the red rock cradle. Castra's scream faded into a soft whimper as she rolled herself over tightly, pressing her legs together so as to feel the last few ripples of her thrill shudder through her. She closed her eyes and reached out towards the water's edge. When she was like this, the big house seemed so far away; there was no one who could control her here, no one to make her clean, or fetch their water from the pump, or to wash their pale white soft feet in a porcelain bowl.

In her hands, she cupped a few drops of water from the river and wet her face. She pulled her dress down over her legs to cover her yellow skin, closed her eyes, leaning against the warmth of the red rock she had made hers again that night.

The white rag, now dry, lay against Castra's flushed cheek; she pulled open her long, thick plait as she lay on the rocks, picking small pieces of twig from the curls. The heavy mop of hair covered her bare breast. Soon she would have to walk back to the big house and begin her chores for the day. But not just yet; the pictures in her head of Marell were flooding back and, as if by command, the clouds masked the moonlight again as Castra slowly reached down and pulled the skirt of her dress up around her waist. A warmth raged through her blood. The spirits wouldn't sleep tonight.

SLEEPING PASSIONS

Deborah Caplan

Quiet, peaceful, end of a long day at work, happy to be in bed, happy to be warm, knowing she loves and is loved, sleepy Simone. Quiet, hopeful, beginning of a long night of possibilities, happy to be in bed, happy to be warm, knowing she loves and is loved, aroused Ana.

Simone falls asleep, breathing slowly. Ana watches her, breathing quickly. "Not tonight, not again, three years and we're losing it, I'm not letting this happen." Night after night she has watched her friend sleep, fighting images of lovemaking, tormented by the hope that she would wake, overcome by desire and slip her fingers into Ana's wetness. Gently, carefully, Ana circles Simone's waist, traces the outline of her breasts, tickles her neck with her tongue.

"Where shall I take us? whispers Ana to her dreaming lover.

"Mm? Oh, to sleep, just let me sleep, I'm fucked."

"No, you're not, but if that's what you want."

Ana lets Simone sleep and steals into her dreams, caresses her pale nocturnal shadows. Silently, she calls out to her partner, asks her sleeping self to show her the hidden fantasies lying deep within. Ana seeks the colours of Simone's passion and sees only blue, the dark blue of blocked desire. She whispers insistently, "Come on, my love, show me."

Ana takes Simone's hand and guides her as they fall further and further into the night. The blue gets darker, then darker still as Ana travels deeper into Simone until they reach the place where black is full of light and images explode in an endless orgasm of shape and colour. Ana, blinded by the light, tries to focus. She sees the faint outline of two bodies, coming together, clearer now.

"Two women: what are they doing? I can see you, Simone; who's the other one? She's a bit plain. Why are you doing push-ups? Is she doing sit-ups? I know you're a personal trainer, but couldn't you dream something a little more exciting?"

Ana penetrates her pictures, inserts their bodies into her mind, and takes the place of the unknown woman. "You can train me, tonight. I'm a teacher; I'll teach you."

"Hello, I'm new here. I've come for the introductory session," says Ana innocently.

"No problem. We'll start with these machines here; these are basically for the thighs," replies Simone professionally.

"It's quiet, here, isn't it? Just us."

"Yep, well, you have to sit here and put your feet under this bar and push slowly."

"You have a lovely body, firm, but curvy, beautiful." Ana ignores her trainer's instructions.

"I'll show you. Watch me and then you can have a go." Simone ignores her client's compliments.

Simone sits on the seat and inserts her feet under the bar.

Ana sits behind her. Gently, carefully, she circles Simone's waist, traces the outline of her breasts, tickles her neck with her tongue. She feels her personal trainer melt into her, then pull away.

"What are you doing?"

"Teaching you how to train me."

Professional resistance is abandoned and trainer eases back into her client.

"Did you know the neck is one of the most neglected parts of the body?" Ana whispers, as she caresses it with her lips. "Bet you don't have any neck exercise machines: and these shoulders . . . you might be fit, but you're all knotted up. Let me give you a little massage."

Simone sighs in response and gives herself to Ana's firm fingers. They travel from her neck to her shoulders to her breasts, electric silk on velvet skin.

Her fingers continue their journey down, slipping inside Simone's shorts, finding her soft thighs, lingering, trapped by the beauty, the warmth of her. Ana has found a resting place but Simone is restless. She raises herself off the exercise machine and pulls Ana towards her. The two fall to the soft floor covered with mats, Simone on top.

"Don't forget who the trainer is. You mustn't stop, once you've found a rhythm. I'll show you how to work on stamina."

Simone pins Ana down on to the mat, little-known judo position, urgent lover. She pulls up her client's sweatshirt, frees her from her bra and runs her teeth along her nipples, biting gently. Waves of desire break over Ana, and she cries out, silently begging her trainer to enter her.

Agony and ecstasy wrestle intertwined as Simone runs her tongue along Ana's body, tiptoeing kisses until she finds the centre of her passion. She kneels at her entrance, and takes a sip. Another wave breaks and Simone laughs, salty water on her lips. Her tongue whispers secrets to Ana, deep in her seaworld, and the two women recover their language lost to the word of routine.

Ana cries out, unable to bear so much pleasure, and Simone escapes before her lover's final wave engulfs her. Ana, back to her surface, tastes her own seaworld in Simone's kiss, and craves the taste of her lover. She turns and descends to her thighs, warm and moist, approaches her shoreline and enters her ocean, liquescent. Simone simultaneously slips between Ana's legs, and the two are united. Ripples of desire, satisfied then born anew, swell in intensity, crash against their bodies, and then it comes, the tidal wave, releasing them from passion, returning them to peace.

Ana steps out of their dream world, satisfied, ready to sleep, but sleep doesn't come, and she hears Simone's silent call to come back. Her partner's dreams are now wide awake and Ana is dazzled by all the images dancing an orgy of colour. "My goodness, what have we done and where do I start? Lovely looking women in that sauna, schoolgirls slipping off their clothes in a field, two men in a shower, an all-woman music festival."

Ana surveys the multiple pictures of passion, tries to decide which one to settle on, when she sees a car driving through all the other images. She peeps in through the window and sees herself driving; it's a taxi, and Simone is sitting in the back seat, looking out of the window. Neither are talking. Ana merges with her character and enjoys the feel of the steering wheel beneath her fingers and the sound of the engine responding to her feet. She senses a new strength in her body, and tingles with the expectation of the pleasure she will bring to and take from her passenger.

They drive in silence for a while, watching the rain relentlessly falling on the windscreen, until Ana remembers that she is a taxi driver.

"Where to, madam?"

"Can you take me to White Cloud place, please?"

"With great pleasure," smiles the taxi driver.

"This weather is awful, isn't it?" says Simone.

"I love the rain. Special things happen in the rain," Ana replies, fixing her eyes on her passenger via the rear view mirror.

"I suppose so, but it hasn't been very warm lately."

"Warmth is felt in the heart and then the body. It has very little to do with the weather."

"Maybe," mumbles Simone, abandoning all further attempts at weather talk. She glances cautiously at the mirror and finds the driver's familiar eyes still fixed upon her. She lets herself sink into the seat and tries to fall into her thoughts and away from the green eyes which frighten and excite her. As she closes her eyes, a vision of the taxi driver comes to her. She is slowly undoing Simone's belt, unzipping her trousers. Before anything further can happen, Simone, aroused and disturbed, quickly opens her eyes and meets those of her driver.

"Don't be afraid of your fantasies. Open yourself to them. They will not harm you; they will only bring you pleasure."

Simone stares out of the window at the pouring rain, unsure whether the driver's words were spoken or imagined. The voice continues, sent through fingertips running up and down her back.

"So, what comes after I take down your trousers? Let me into your mind and your body."

Simone feels her eyes closing and an image of the taxi driver unzipping her trousers once again fills her mind, like a film she has paused and returned to. The car is still moving, yet the driver is kissing her now; tongues dance to the music of desire, and Simone feels the warmth of love spreading through her body.

Suddenly, they are naked, clothed only in each other's arms. Ana and Simone, travelling through the landscapes of their sexualities. Ana climbs her lover's breasts and nibbles her nipples, while Simone follows Ana's path down, stopping en route to rest at her stomach, her soft pillow thighs, a little further down to her flowing centre. She strokes her clitoris gently, asking to be let in. Ana's river rushes to greet Simone, who dives into her, deeper and deeper. Her fingers swim rhythmically through Ana, while her tongue finds her lover's tongue.

Waves of passion rise in delicate urgency as Simone's fingers and tongue bring Ana to near-climax and then withdraw in a futile attempt to make the instant timeless. She re-enters Ana's river and is sucked in to the whirlpool of her orgasm.

They lie calm with snoozing desire, while the car continues its journey.

"Come on, driver, wake up; we're not there yet. Can't you feel we're still moving?"

Ana stirs, feels the engine's soft purr and strokes her passenger, whose purring turns to a miaow. Simone rolls on to her back, opening herself to her lover and Ana tickles her tummy with her tongue, blows gently on her moist thighs. She hears Simone's cry that comes from deep within and answers, entering her, playfully penetrating, pulling back, penetrating, playing with her clitoris, deep inside her. They drive together, Simone's body directing Ana, showing her secret lanes, her hidden maps, her beauty. So much beauty, and they push to find more, go deeper, and further and more and beauty and further and don't stop, can't stop have to come, coming, we're there, we're there, washed clean, home, home.

LIGHT AND DARKNESS

Isabelle Lazar

She notices her across the bar.

The blonde one sits in the corner of the booth, jammed in there by her lover and the other adoring fans. The dark one stands off in a slight distance, temporarily obscured by patrons. In another instant, the view clears and she stands gazing at her desire, slowly smoldering into a fine ash. The blonde one looks up. The exchange is brief and silent, but speaks volumes.

Hello.

Hello.

Wanna fuck?

What?!

You heard me.

I guess I did.

I didn't hear an answer . . .

The blonde one looks to her lover. She kisses her lovingly.

I guess that's all the answer I needed. The dark one licks her lips dejectedly, smacking them lightly. She nods to no one in particular and forces herself to turn away. She finds an empty barstool, the one adjacent to her husband.

"Hi, honey!" He kisses her tenderly, breathlessly. She is the light of his life. He wonders what life was like without her, but he can't seem to remember. She cups his face and kisses him.

"Here's to the end of a long day," he says, raising a chilled glass of brew.

"Hear! Hear!" she echoes, deciding to forget her earlier lapse in sanity. "Cheers!"

The blonde one sat stunned for a moment, as if she'd just received a quick, stinging slap across the face. It still tingled, though she wasn't sure if it was pain or pleasure she was feeling. Did she really have that exchange with that dark-haired woman, or was her mind playing one of its old tricks on her? She had guarded against that for so long now. Be serious, she reproached herself. Don't imagine what is not there, you fool! Not again, not ever again! I won't let you! She thought she'd gotten over that juvenile stage of pulling petals off of flowers. She'd gotten her heart broken too many times to know not to play with fire. And the straight ones were the worst kind.

She looked over at her lover, her spouse. Maybe not by society's rules, but by our rules we are together forever. And she was happy. Happy to be out of the cold, happy to not have to wonder any longer, happy to be accepted and loved for who she is and happy finally be done with the chase.

She glanced back at the dark one sitting with her mate, perhaps her husband. His masculine arm was draped casually around her slim waist. It's easy for you, she admonished silently. You with your man. I wonder if you even like girls at all. Is this just a game for you? It's easy to play, isn't it?

Because at any time you can turn around and be the all-American family. So easy to blur the issue, that way; walk in any crowd, be anything you want at any time. It's too easy for you, the blonde thought hotly of the dark one, her insides churning. But life doesn't work that way. Nothing is that easy for anyone! I bet you wonder who you are, at times. Where you belong. And what does your instinct tell you? she wondered.

After some drinks, the dark one slides off her stool, excusing herself for a moment. She likes the effect alcohol has on her. So much of her days are spent on formalities, dignitary functions, ambassadorial smiles. She was taught to use just the right silverware, say just the right thing at just the right time. She smiles pretty. She is very cordial. She never says the wrong thing; she never even allows herself to think it. And she is never herself. Except, once in a while. When she let's loose a bit, has a few drinks. Never too many, though: can't have that. All of her conditioning goes against such lack of control. But just enough to feel good. To forget her troubles and the thoughts that haunt her late into the night.

She has had many male admirers. She finally settled on one with whom she knew she'd spend the rest of her life. She was happy. So why did her mind still wander to the other side? She could barely keep it in check any longer. Even on her best days, she knew something was missing. Some part, some missing link that would finally allow her to be the woman, the total woman she knew she could be. Could this be it? mused the dark one. Could she be missing . . . another woman, to make her whole? It was too incredible a thought. And anyway, she obviously had no idea how to go about achieving her plan. She clearly had just struck out. She thought she'd read her instincts correctly; that the sensuous blonde might find her interesting, too. But she struck out big time. Now she knew how all the guys felt when they had struck out with her. What a loser! I guess you're not as "irresistible" as you thought, she grinned to herself.

Rising to her feet, her knees crackle in the old familiar way. You old buggers, she reproaches them silently. She turns to go, but something beckons to her. She looks up to meet the gaze of the blonde.

The tables changed without her notice, throwing her a bit off balance.

What? she queries silently of her opponent.

You still want that fuck?

The dark one looks towards the ladies' room. Can't exactly escape there . . . though it is private. She looks at the blonde, contemplating. I've waited for this moment all my life. I am strong enough now. Are you? She looks towards the bathroom again and, without looking back, strides on. I call your bluff, she thinks taking the blonde on as if she were the Devil himself. Let's see what you got.

The heavy wooden door gives way to a lighted antechamber. Gilded mirrors, faux rococo style. Large basins. It would be perfect if the rest of the features matched. But the antiseptic, cream-colored doors of the stalls jarred one right back into the twentieth century.

The dark one walks to the basin to wash her hands. Maybe she'll come. No sooner she thinks this, the blonde enters.

She appeared to have walked there with a purpose, but that purpose clearly changed, the minute she stepped into the room. With a saunter, and a little jiggle of her hips, she falls back on the door as she closes it shut. Her hands are folded behind her. She tries to look bored; but she is anything but bored. Her eyes betray her growing hunger.

The dark one observes all this calmly through the mirror in front of her, enjoying the undulation of her opponent immensely.

"Who are you?" The blonde half-speaks, half-whispers. The question hangs in the air like dead weight.

The dark one doesn't answer, just continues to methodically wash her hands. When they are thoroughly cleansed, she shakes them off once into the sink and steps to the towel dispenser without turning around.

Finally finished with her ritual, she tosses the paper towel into the adjacent basket, and turns to face the blonde one.

They stand for a moment, sizing up the situation and each other. A gentle footfall coming from one of the stalls suddenly breaks through their reverie. The blonde is startled a little but doesn't move. The dark one's droopy lids bespeak her temporary annoyance. Don't move, she seems to say.

Walking silently over to the stalls, she assesses each one. Finally certain she's found the one she wanted, she kicks the door open, startling a rather large, fastidious patron sitting within.

"What the . . . !" The woman shrieks.

"Oops! I am so sorry. I did not mean to startle you." The dark one speaks quickly, picking up volume and speed with every word, as if she's had this speech prepared for years. She was making it very clear that she had no intention of leaving but would stand there for as long as it took, making the portly woman uncomfortable until *she* left.

"I'm sorry to have startled you but, you see, every other stall is broken and I am just so very ill! Please, I am going to be *sick*!!!"

The corpulent patron can no longer remain seated. Rising quickly, she scarcely gives herself a chance to finish her business before pulling up the stockings onto her hefty thighs as she bolts from the stall. By this time, the dark one is one knee in front of the stall, doubled over in what appears to be very believable spasms of excruciating pain.

The woman blows past the blonde in a flurry of skirts, tissues and lipstick, nearly knocking her over and sending her into peals of laughter. She shuts the door again, suffering to regain her composure and catch her breath. She looks to the dark one to see if she too is laughing, but that one's demeanor is far from jovial.

Looking up, suddenly the picture of composure as she half-crouches on one knee, the dark one finally speaks.

"Who am I, you ask? I am whomever you want me to be, whenever and wherever you want me to be it."

It's your move, the dark one muses. She stands motionless, holding tightly to her lover's hand. They were already lovers; this was just the necessary two-step, and they both knew it. They both knew it was the blonde's move, though how? why? who set up these rules? wasn't clear and didn't matter. The dark one waited patiently for a sign.

The blonde deliberates a second longer, and then tugs on the arm she is holding, pulling her lover into a passionate embrace.

That's all I needed. The years of longing culminating in instinctual actions, the dark one cups her lover's face, sucking deeply on her ruby lips, the sensation feeding them, swirling above and past them as if compelled to create one being out of the two. She feels her lover's breasts soft and full beneath her shirt. She holds her closer, pinning her against the door. The blonde moans in ecstasy, squeezing her thighs around her lover's leg. Their desire spilling, mingling, threatening to tear them apart piece by piece.

The dark one holds her lover ever closer, forcing, trying in vain to get inside her. I just want to be inside you, she thinks. Inside, where it's warm and safe. I love you, she thinks, for the woman that you are, for the woman that you're allowing me to be right now. I love you.

But the passion was stronger than both of them, overtaking them, taking them against their wills and with all their might.

"Let me touch you. I want to be near you," the dark one pleads. Letting go of her lover's face, she gently pulls her shirt out from her pants, their mouths never disengaging.

Her skin feels like silk as she runs her trembling hands over her lover's belly, up towards her breasts. She doesn't bother with the clasp. Simply sliding the bra up to her neck, the dark one lets her hands feel the weight of her lover's breasts, feeling their heat. She had looked too strong before to have such supple, utterly feminine features. The blonde one was now writhing in agony, begging for relief that the dark was only too happy to provide.

She let one of her hands drop to the waist line of the blonde's jeans. Deftly opening the button, she took only a second to unzip the pants completely, and slide her hand inside the to the deep, moist center. With her feet, she kicked apart the blonde's legs. The blonde clung to her, kissing her deeply, until their mouths mirrored the movement below.

"Bring me. Bring me," she whispered.

"Come," answered the dark one. "Come away with me, if only for a moment. Come; I will take you places you have only dreamed of."

The blonde tightened her hands around the dark one's breasts, suckling her neck, her chin, any part of her she could get. They rode this way, on the back of the oak door to the ladies' bathroom of McAlister's Tavern, until there was no more tavern, no more door, no more noise, no more world. Just they, two, alone, oblivious, riding the waves of passion. Free. Truly free. If only for a brief moment.

THE INTRANSIGENT PRESENCE OF PARADOX OR THIS IS NOT A ONE-NIGHT STAND

Maya Chowdhry

Picture two women in bed naked. One is studying a book entitled *Quantum Physics*, the other is reading *Tagore: Selected Poems*.

Let's call one of them "X" and the other "Y". Let's say that X was reading about physics and Y the poetry. Now lets zap them into hyper-space, into a type of hyper-reality created for conducting experiments in.

X says to Y, "I want to express myself in terms of my movements towards you."

And Y says, "In what way?"

And X says, "Unfold your arms and I'll show you."

And in a highly illogical way she licks her from one end of her naked body to the other, searching for satisfaction in the crevice of her elbow, the soft skin below her ear and other surprisingly fulfilling places. As her tongue lingers, tastes the scents of each pore, she ponders how skin without the "s" becomes "kin" and what secrets it could hold about belonging and body. They have only known each other for forty-five minutes.

Therefore: quantum sex is not a picture or a narrative that tells us how the outcome of an encounter comes about; it is a sexual expression that allows us to calculate what the outcome of an encounter will be.

Y says, "How did I become your lover? Why did I end up in bed with you, subsequent to a five-minute conversation where you interrupted me in the Halcyon whilst I had my head buried in Tagore? I mean, one minute we're talking 'favourite poem of all time' and the next your belly is resting on my arse, breathing with the waiting roll that keeps shaking me every five minutes."

X replies, "You haven't answered my question."

Y cuts in and X continues, "I was instantly attracted to your interest in Tagore and to the way your lips parted as you mouthed the words to *Unending Love* – 'Is it something not of the body that takes us there/To the bed of pining by the Manasa lake/To the sunless, jewel-lit, evening land/Beyond all the rivers and mountains of this world.' As I passed and breathed in your scent, leaning over your shoulder to confirm that it was indeed *Unending Love*, I felt a shudder somewhere around my belly (or lower) and decided that I needed to see you naked and hear your rendition of the poem."

At this point, Y interjects, "It was *The Meghaduta.*"

However, X continues unhindered, "the fact that you continued reading the book after I had seduced you puzzled me, but then confirmed my second observation about you."

"The second observation?" Y questions.

"Yes," X says. "That after we had exchanged dialogue about the poem and its virtues and I had invited you to bed with my eyes, you immediately became less innocent. In fact, decidedly uninnocent, which led me to believe that by leaning on the bar with a bottle of San Miguel and an open book of Tagore poetry, you were asking for it."

"It!" exclaims Y. "What exactly was I asking for? To be taken to task on my reading habits?"

"Perhaps," X finishes, removing her cheek from the cup of her left hand and sliding up the bed until her eyes are directly opposite Y's and, thus engaged, she regains composure. She finishes her sentence by kissing Y deeply, sucking her lips into her mouth and licking the corner of her mouth, assessing where her lips end and her face begins.

Therefore: "What we observe is not nature in itself, but nature exposed to our method of questioning" (Heisenberg).

Y says, "The more it hurts, the harder I want it," meaning love.

X says, "I thought you meant fu . . ."

The "ck" trails off and Y interrupts, "Harder!" cutting through the almost tenuous licks to get to where her tongue slides right into X's mouth and stops her putting the "ing" on the end of her word.

Cause and effect. Work it into the reality.

"You wear me easily," X says, disengaging Y and draping her over the pillows. "Like you would your jeans, hugging my hips with the double seam right up between my pussy-lips rubbing all the time I fold and unfold my legs in time to the rhythm of my chant of – What do you think is the difference between love and se . . . fucking?"

Y replies, with the unrhetoric answer in one of those long answers where "yes/no?" would do: "It's a matter of who's giving and who's taking and where you were when you took it/ were given it."

"Licking your arsehole," X gestures. "Remember?"

X says, "Sex is sex." Sliding her fingers into Y's cunt.

"Yes," Y muses, "It's to do with the hardness of the 's'. Take it away and you have finger. Was it two or three?"

Y's so wet she can't tell. The "s" in fist is harder, wider, it lingers on her tongue and the "t" that comes afterwards is short, abrupt, almost finished in her mouth before her lips part.

"I'm gonna come in your mouth," X spits out, enduring, enjoying the submission to hard come, to language: to the hard "k" in fuck; the bent-over "c", the inverted "u", almost horizontal; towards the "f", the horizontal position penetrating the smooth vertical line, watching the curve appear at the end of vertical, curving towards impatience.

Which is Y's impatience at the giving and X's greedy taking. Y wants to tell her. They have known each other for seventy-six minutes. She does not; she continues with the written narrative which was where she began: "In the conversation of physics, truth is largely procedural." (Gregory)

The ending: "Is the result of an extremely laborious process of adaptation: hypothetical, never completely final, always subject to question and doubt." (Einstein).

Y replies, reading from X's book: "Physical theories do not tell us how the world is; they tell us what we can predict reliably about the behaviour of the world."

X closes the book for her. "Some theory," she says, getting

out of bed and pulling her knickers on, almost in one complete action. "Is this a one-night stand then?" she says, snapping her knickers into place.

"Or somewhat of a paradox," Y replies, burying her head under the duvet, waiting for the next action.

STARLIT FINGERS

Berta Freistadt

Across the room, she is always across the room. One of them. Coming or going, never near. Always turning away from me, turning away. Inaccessible, inadmissible. Darling succubus; escaping, leaving, fleeing, flitting, flying away. Sometimes nearing me, me dying my little deaths alone on the tips of my fingers

Your head in my thoughts, my dreams, my reams of writing. Righting the wrong you did me, done me, left me unsunned; done you, unsung. Bird you are, never singing, never betraying, nor breaking. The pain, taking pains to shell yourself. Gird yourself tight, your loins, mine, never giving but one look, one kiss. One hot kiss on a bare shoulder, in a dirty dark room.

Your head, sharp carved. Medallion. Face cut, ravaged; eyes cut me, to the quick, my heart. Beat, beating to stifle. My breath away. Steal it away till I empty of air. Lungs pounding, crying out for quick relief. Lungs quicken with love; heart with pain. Old mother pain. The mother and father of betrayal. Old. So old and some older. Hold it, that's all there is. Hold fast. You faster, so quick, quicksilver. Slippery as a fish. Silver fish, fish on a line, rodded on a hook. Hooked on pain, both of us pain puppets, helpless, in motion with the current. Water weeds held by a thread, fish out of water. Bulging eyes, mouth agape, aghast. Gasping.

Your head with its face; its look, its eyes. Blue as the Virgin's robe, blue as a virgin's hopes, blue as the vein in my arm, as my bruised heart, soul, shoulder where forever your mouth is printed. Tattooed, cow-marked by your carelessness. Less care at your hands. Your hands. Those battered instruments of desire. Those bones of beauty, brutey, beastliness. Those skin-covered ends of your long rambling skeleton. Do I desire to be poked by your bone? Caressed by your carcass. Fingers of light, starlight points. Each nail a pink moon to rise up to, to set my ship to. A pink moon of some waxing and waning degree. Ten degrees to that compass. Time to tell by you, telling what, what truth or lie. Tell the time by you. By your coming and going. My calender girl. My night-time woman.

Which day was it? Which day is which? Which witch? Who cares. Most days were Sundays. Some days were any days. Any day I'd be yours. If you wanted. Just call. If you called

Called, not screamed. Just call and I'll be there. In your hair. Whisper a town away and I'll hear you, come to you. Come for you. Comfort you. Didn't I come? Bearing gifts? Beware of foreigners bearing gifts. Baring their all, their hearts on fire, their hearts on a sleeve on a festering shoulder, their needs.

Needing too much. I. Desiring too hard, waiting too long. Too long in time. Bad timing. Never could tell the time. Which is three and which is nine. Which is thee and which is mine. You were never mine. What's mine is yours. Give it me back.

Return to sender. Trial and error, all that anger. A hundred years of it; cruelty and hurt. In the dust, in the dirt. Fingers fingering it, scrabbling, low. So low down. On the ground. Longing for high. All that high lifted sound. The noise; the no. The no, no, no, no, no, no, no. Until I knew. Knew that was all you had for me. Had for me. Had me never. Never those long fingers, strong hands to lay me down. Never that lean face to lean on mine, that crying mouth to weep in my wet. Never the exchange of warp and weft; the slippery jigsaw never played nor pieced. The box not even opened.

Ah sigh, regret and loss and still can squeeze real tears like orange juice from then till now. Sweet juice in the mouth, pith in the teeth. Orange brilliance. Orange behind the lids as the sun explodes and white, white teeth. The T-shirt tight in the long leg jeans. the jeans of desire and length. Long length. The length of her from top to toe, stem to stern, hem to crotch.

I turn you round and hold you tight against me or you against me behind. Hold me all along your length, face at my neck, breath at my beck and call me. And all you have to do is undo me. Unbutton me. Buttons and your fingers, your hands are on me, in me, doing their stuff, taking the stuffing out of me with their knowing. You know it all, know it all. Palms on me praying. I'm praying for you to show me. I know nothing, am nothing, feel nothing without you touch me. Touch me, tingle me, take my breath away, mouth dry, all other moist, I gasp. Pull me to your sweet skin, your unknown breasts, your underjeans, your naked soul self. Breast to mouth and mouth to breast.

And we two clash. Titans tighten wrapped together, electric, charged. Horses we gallop in and through each other. Legs lassoed, lips lashed. Holding; holding up, holding on, holding down. Having, heaving, humping, hunting, helping. Whelping. Help me, dog tired, I give birth to the far shore. On the far shore where I swim, sick with passion, sick of your drawn loving, languid fingers, sighing breasts, cold white naked night practice. Sick of my desire to be taken. Take me again. Five times. In five different ways make me yours with your hands sparkling, your hips grinding, your loins flickering, your mouth amazing. Then hold me away from you and I'll do it again some more times alone.

Ah sigh, regret and loss, smiling at what was, what might have been. Seen. Parallel planet, stop still, stepping stones to ecstasy. Still dream of your body, using your body in the night, the hot, cold sleepless night. The sleepless half past two. The two, never one. More than once I use you, shameless. Shameless to steal you unawares, lover. Hover you above me, phantom of my heart, make you hard and loving, smooth soft and skinless. Weep into your ectoplasm. Long for you over again. Insane. Once in a while, once upon a time when we were there. Where? In the never-never possible land. Where impossible is just improbable and improbable is soon not sorrow, just sweetness on a spoon, tomorrow always jam tomorrow, maybe perhaps. The why not? Why not me? And you? Who knows it might, it may, but we know, never jam today. And it didn't.

It didn't for you fled it. Rabbit. Running scared and faster. Some disaster. Swift as a flea before I held on tight; tight through all your shape shifting. Through all your drifting wildness, monsters, bitter witches, poison fishes till you came you. Held you tight and gave you my heart to swap. Beads in a playground. Papier-mâché for gold. Gave you my heart to bleed for yours. My old, bouncing, juicy patched thing for your little shrivelled, full of holes. Wholly mine, I'd mend it. Blend it, sew it up tight, like a life jacket. Lend it back to you if you asked. Rabbit don't ask. Shiver their ears in the headlights. Wait for death and run from love. Run rabbit, run rabbit, run, run, run. Children sour, children's hour is over.

It's all over now, Baby Jane. Now I think of it. And I do. Of you. Keeping away. Just the thought the memory. Thanks for it. The kissed shoulder, broken hands, burnt out phone calls, the smiles, the miles, the car that nearly killed you, the red car, white roses, dark chocolates never given. The longing, the waiting, the leaving, the submitting; the urgent longing, the waiting, the leaving; the desperate longing, the waiting, the loss. The loss of you. February, month of thieves. A cold month for goodbyes. For cold mouths. For slamming doors, for scaring cats and mats. Me. Bats.

A cold month, cover up shoulders. And olders. A cold month for the old. All kissing done, all chance of kissing gone now. All gone, too late, too late. Too late now. Time for bed. A cold month for empty beds. A cold month for wet eyes icing down streets. A cold month at any time of the year. Dear. Dear me. Dear one.

Dear one, am I really forgotten? Dear one, do you never think of me in the long lost sleepless alone of half-past two with your starlit fingers that long for me? Starlit fingers that long to touch me. My long ancient places. My long hiddenness. Kept hidden. From view. Just you, I would have shown. Opened. By the light of your starlit fingers not so long ago, so very long ago, last year.

Still a tear. Precious as jewel. You are always near. Just across the room. Any room.

LITANY OF REMEMBRANCE

Sovereign Muse

out to touch, my libidinal impulses flipped over and backwards, turned inside out, opened suddenly to create a yawning hole of tragic and lonely desire.

in her absolute absence she was so close that i could feel warm ghosts of her kissing my neck; i could still imagine her perfume so acutely that i could smell its ripeness and almost taste her skin.

my lips became incomplete without their mirror match, magnet lips that would approach mine slowly before sealing a perfect wholeness with a familiar kiss – the grooves, lines and soft pouting of lipskin fitted perfectly to create a single loving mouth. so nice.

"i miss you"

"you didn't want me"
"i hate that you're fucking someone else"
"you didn't want me"
"i want to come home"
"you didn't want me"

each time i meet her she looks more radiant, beaming with the surety of new sex and attraction, overly generous in her physical affection towards me because she can afford to be. in our economy of love, she makes the profit while i make a loss. the transactions went thus: the currency of love ran high enabling wanton profligacy for the first few months. then she bankrupted me. then i bankrupted her. then she ruined me once more for good measure.

i see her everywhere as i look out the bus window. every blonde head catches my eye. every pair of swinging carharrt pants. increasingly now i find myself watching women's hands and remembering hers: fingers uniquely strong and broad yet also graceful and long.

for two years her body was mine.
mine.
my property.
mine to take home each night.
mine to play with each morning.
mine to revere.
mine to worship.
only i didn't.
i couldn't.

our bodies became our battlegrounds, the sites of anger and resistance, of offensives and defensives, where crimes were punished and transgressions resurrected over and over and played out incessantly. we trod deep inside each other's flesh and the scars will be difficult to smooth over.

i couldn't.

but if i could have her now, just for one afternoon, i would lavish her with love to hear her girlish laugh of safety. i would make her feel safe, safe to open up to me, to open her legs wide and honour me with trust. my pride swelling all the time that i could take this vibrant woman to the edge and watch her fall, knowing that she wouldn't land anywhere but in my arms.

the ellipses in our communication are heavily laden, soiled with dim recriminations where there should only be open silence. somewhere in the night the lines of our thoughts run into each other creating fragile interstices in the deep blackness, shading each other's dreams with fabulous tones and echoing soft words and phrases that evaporate even as our eyelids open. these ties ever evolve away from the organic intensity that was our shared bed and towards the steady stare of ice-cold strangers.

["nice to hear from you. so how are you?"

"great. how are you?"]

where once our menstrual cycles chased after each other to the very hour and our sleeping patterns shifted and grew to acccommodate each other, now all that's left of you in me are phantom responses that become more confused and impenetrable each day. our intertwined bodies adapt fast to forget each other.

loneliness is buying the small-sized can of baked beans at the supermarket.

["i wanted you"
"you never wanted me"
"you violated my trust"
"you never wanted me"
"i tried for so long"
"you never wanted me"

"i wanted you"
"you never wanted me"]

i catch you in a moment on the phone and suddenly i feel that i will journey to the end of this life with you, that how i love you will be transcendent.

i watch her swing her ass as she walks. holds herself well, alive with style, with attitude. a walk that's full of sexual promise. that lives up to her promise. that advertises who she is with one shoulder out and one shoulder back, and her head cocked to one side. bold enough to wear a t-shirt with the slogan: i like cock.

["that was the plan"
"you didn't want the plan"
"it was a good plan"
"you didn't want the plan"
"it just didn't work out"

You drench my dreams, lapping against them persistently until you swell and crash into them, submerging my very unconscious and sending sweet sprays to my morning awakenings. Dying love is so beautiful.

i remember your soft pale breasts hanging gently,
your silken milky belly,
your strong solid thighs,
your curved all-woman hips.
i remember your firm jaw,
your green eyes,
your sweet skin,
your square-set happy toes.
i remember your hairy shins,

the scar on your knee, the birthmark on your side.
i remember the colour and form of your lips,
your neat ears,
your flat wide fingernails,
your big nipples,
your golden pubes,
your salty cunt,
your beautiful hands.
i remember every inch of you.
this is my litany of remembrance, my dear.
eskimo.
butterfly.
kiss-kiss.
i wanted you.

ONE SIZE FITS ALL

Eileen Finn

Can't you come up with a better idea? I was whining at my lover, Kate, who decided she wanted to go shopping on our first day off in weeks.

"Come on, babe. It's just for an hour or two, and then maybe we'll go to the movies."

"So, now you're resorting to bribery? I hate shopping and you know it."

"Unless, of course, you are in one of your damn bookstores," she said sarcastically.

"That's not fair," I interjected, "because at least I don't drag you along when I go."

"Fine, stay home." She sounded pissed.

We were both standing in the middle of our living room, arms crossed, anxious to do *something* but, as usual, never able to agree. This was more than just a day off. Our seven-year-old son was staying over at a friend's house and wouldn't be coming back home until the next afternoon. It wasn't often we were free to spend a whole day and night alone with each other.

"All right." I was giving in. "If you promise we go to the movies tonight. I don't want to ruin this day with an argument." I reached out for her, but she kept her arms folded. "Come on, babe, don't be like that," I coaxed. Pulling her to me, I bent to kiss her neck. Her face started scrunching up in that way I know where she is trying to look mad but suppress a smile at the same time. Finally, her arms went around my neck and we stood there hugging each other. It felt so nice to do that without our son thinking it was time to wrestle and busting between us.

"So, where are we going?" I asked, dreading the answer.

"I want to go to the mall and see if Foot Locker has any good sales. Then maybe Carson's?"

"Jeeeez," I said, drawing out the word in my best Archie Bunker imitation. "Gimme a break here, hah?"

"Oh, c'mon, Archie . . . I'll get ya a beer," she said, playing along in her not-as-good Edith voice.

"Stifle," I said, on cue, and we both busted up laughing.

She bent down to grab her shoes, and I gave her a good crack on the ass. "Ow! Would you knock it off. You better be nice to me, if you want some later," she teased, grinning ear to ear.

"Oh, sure, more bribery. Tease the poor sex addict in the room. Maybe I should get some now, for agreeing to this whole thing," I replied, giving her breast a little squeeze.

"No, you don't," she said, pulling away, "that's for later."

Sooner than you think, honey, I thought.

Off we went to the mall. I was dragging along, bored out of my mind. I am just not the type to like typical shopping trips, especially with her. Half the time we end up getting nothing, and she buys cute little outfits for our son who has more clothes than both of us together. I must admit, though, he is one stylin seven year old. Anyway, my idea of shopping is roaming a bookstore for hours, or going into the city and finding one used record store after another, looking to add to my extensive jazz collection. For some reason, she finds that boring. Perfect match, we are.

After an hour of looking at the newest basketball shoes, the latest summer clothes for kids, and several pairs of western boots, we came across a new clothing store.

"Hey, look at this! When did this open?" she asked excitedly.

Yawning, I replied, "For all I know, it's been there for years."

"Oh, don't be so bitchy. Let's go see what they've got."

Happy, happy, joy, joy, I thought sarcastically, more fuckin' clothes.

She yanked my arm, and in we went.

"For God's sake, look at that woman," I whispered, pointing to one of the two sales people. "She looks like a barrel of fuckin' laughs." The sales clerk was sitting behind the counter, reading *Glamour*. Her hair was tied back in a bun so tight, I thought she would fit the part of Nurse Ratchet in a heartbeat. She had long red nails that looked as though they could slice meat. Her makeup was a little overdone. It wasn't exactly Tammy Faye style, but it sure bordered more on the whore side than the model side. The outfit she wore consisted of a black silky blouse with a lot of gold accessories, and a long black skirt which reached halfway past her knees. The clothes were completed by a pair of black, three-inch heels. I wondered absently how she could work a job standing on her feet all day with those things on. As we walked further into the store, we passed by her, and I saw a ring on her left hand with a huge diamond in it. Damn, prissy, straight woman, I thought.

I was grateful she didn't bother getting up to ask us if we needed her help with anything. I don't think I could've stomached that. "What a snotty-looking bitch she is," I said to Kate.

She elbowed me in response and quietly told me to shut up. I continued following her as she looked at the clothes and not really paying much attention. Suddenly, I slammed right into her as she stopped to pull something off a rack.

Startled, I said, "Dammit, woman, you need brake lights!"

"Well, if you'd pay attention occasionally and at least feign some interest, maybe you could walk and stop a little better than someone with a fresh lobotomy," she replied, annoyed.

"Hey, don't get snappish. What the hell are you looking at, anyway?"

She held up the clothes that caused this collision in the first place so I could take a look.

"Hey, that's actually kind of nice. You need a nice summer outfit for those parties coming up."

"Hello? That's why I wanted to go shopping in the first place."

"Excuuuuse me. My mind-reading skills are low today."

"Think about it. How often do we get to shop alone?" she asked, referring to our son, who was more impatient than me.

"OK, already. Go try it on."

"Come with me. I'm not walking out here to show it to you with Nurse Ratchet over there."

I snorted, "Ha! Ha! Ha! I was just . . ." She clamped her hand over my mouth.

"Shut up! Would you? She's looking at us."

"Should I give her the finger?"

"You're worse than a kid. Come on." She pulled me to the back of the store, into the fitting room.

I have to admit, these were some nice fitting rooms. They

had full doors, not those half things where little kids could crawl under and surprise you in a state of half-dress. It contained a bench seat, a chair, plenty of hooks, and a big full-length mirror. There was enough room to walk several feet back from the mirror to get the whole effect. We both went into the room at the end and shut the door. I sat down on the bench seat while she hung up the outfit and started taking off her clothes.

"Is this what it takes for you to take your clothes off for me? The promise of new ones?"

"Oh, yeah, baby," she said, teasingly, as she unbuttoned her shirt.

"Turns you on to shop, doesn't it?"

"Mmm hmm." Her shirt dropped to the floor.

"Do you need some help?" I asked, starting to get aroused at the sight of her.

"Maybe." She kicked off her shoes and unbuttoned her jeans. I reached out, unzipped them and pulled them down.

"How's that?"

She sat down on the bench next to me to pull her jeans all the way off. I leaned over and kissed her neck. Bending away from me, she picked her jeans off the floor and laid them next to her.

"Come on, honey. One little kiss?" I begged.

"Don't you want to see this outfit on me?"

"I like it better off you, right now."

"You are a such a horn toad," she said, smacking me.

"Yes, and you love it," I replied as I grabbed her hand and pulled it around my neck.

I kissed her full on the lips, waiting for her to smack me again, but she surprised me by kissing back. Holding each other, we continued to kiss, completely oblivious of our surroundings. After a few seconds or a few minutes, I'm still not sure which, I heard a female voice yelling, "Honey, would you go find me a size four in this? The five is just *way* too big, and it makes me look fat."

"Oh, gag!" I said, probably a little louder than I intended.

Kate started laughing, then mockingly, "Get me a size four, honey . . . what a silly bitch."

I grabbed her face with my hands and pulled her back to me again. The kiss picked up where it left off. With one hand stroking her hair, I used my other hand to gently squeeze her breast and tease her nipple.

Kate is not usually a risk-taker but, today, it was as though she were someone else. She pulled me halfway on top of her as she lay back on the bench. Moving my hands all over her now, I caressed my lover the way I had thousands of times. "Please, baby," she whispered. I slipped my hand inside her underwear and felt her wetness. What the hell? Why stop now? I thought.

I got back to a sitting position and yanked her underwear off. I stood up and pulled the other chair closer to the bench seat so they were in line with each other. As I did this, I got a glimpse of us both in the mirror. My face was flushed, and there she was, mostly naked, legs partially spread, waiting for me. It made me crazy with desire for her.

Kneeling down at the end of the bench, I took one of her legs and propped it up on the chair. She moved down a little more, so her ass was almost halfway hanging over the end of the bench. I pushed her other leg to the side, so now she was wide open and waiting for me. I didn't waste any time teasing her today. I knew I wanted her now, and I could see she wanted me.

Quickly, I slipped a finger into my mouth to use my own saliva as a lubricant, and then I pushed my finger deep into her. She moaned and grabbed on to the bench. Slowly, I slid in and out of her with one finger and gently added a second. Her eyes were closed, and she was rocking against me. I could smell the wonderful aroma of her desire as my hand motion became faster. Keeping my rhythm, I bent my head to her for a taste. God, she was so wet. I began licking her clit, covering her with my tongue. She was so close. I pushed the two fingers deep into her again and held them there for a second. Splitting my fingers open a little, I was able to slide my tongue in between them and into her. "Oh baby, that feels so good," she whispered, "I'm going to come. Oh, God, I'm going to come."

Letting my tongue slide from inside her, I moved once again to her clit. I covered it with my lips and sucked in. My fingers were still inside her, moving once again. With her clit in my mouth, I ran my tongue over it as fast as I could. The leg she had resting on the floor came up to rest on my shoulder. Now my face was buried in her as her muscles tightened and she burst into orgasm.

"Yes, baby, yes!"

I watched her face as she came, feeling overwhelmed once again at the ability to give someone so much pleasure.

After a minute, she rolled off the bench and onto her knees. Wrapping her arms around me, she whispered, "I love you."

Hugging her back, I ran my fingers through her hair. "Love you, too, babe."

After we collected ourselves, she did end up trying on the outfit. She hated it. We walked past the cash register, but there was no sign of Nurse Ratchet. Fleetingly, I wondered what happened to the old bitch. As we were walking out of the store, I stopped suddenly, all the blood draining from my face. This time, she slammed into the back of me. "Ow!" she said. "Now who needs the brake lights?" Then she saw my face and followed my gaze. In the front window of the store was a little sign: "Warning: For security purposes, this store contains two-way mirrors."

JOSIE'S RESTROOMS

Nina Rapi

Right, do I just start talking? OK, I'm ready, let's go.

I'm honoured, really I am. I mean, I wouldn't expect Dyke TV to be interested in the likes of me, but there you go. I must be worth something. I must admit I was taken back a little by the title of the series: *Sex: When Fantasy and Reality Clash*. Excuse me for being forward, but isn't that a bit obvious? Doesn't fantasy always clash with reality when it comes to sex? Well, it's done in my experience. And I've had lots of it, believe you me. I've got a PhD on sex, me. I can get a woman off, no problem, and no matter what she's into. No mean feat, I'm sure you'll agree, as most girls are hard to please. Not in my expert hands, though. I know all the tricks. And I'm proud of it. I'm Numero Uno. No one and I mean no one, right, can challenge me on that. All you have to do is ask all the girls I've ever had sex with. I'm ace. Period.

I was an early starter, see. I was thirteen when I had my first nookie. Now, that may not be early by some people's standards; I knew girls at the home who'd be at it from as early as eleven. That's diabolical, if you ask me. I mean, what do you know at eleven? Stay clean, girl, leave your little oyster well alone, at least until you're thirteen or fifteen or something. Then, OK, ready for action.

So, yeah, I've been around. And it's not all been girls, let me tell you. When you've got the kind of appetite I have – or used to have, I should say – you want to try the lot. And that includes bollocks, excuse my French. As long as you can find the right victims, of course, and I mean victims. Cos when it came to bollocks – sorry, blokes – it was only slaves I was interested in. Nothing else. Whip them to submission, that's what I say.

They loved it, of course. Me too, up to a point. But by the time I hit twenty-five, I couldn't face another dick, unless I got paid for it. So, why don't you, girl, I asked myself one fine morning. So, I did. I started charging them for it. Still gagging for it, they were. Earned quite a few bob that way, until I got sick with giving orders. It was strictly clipping after that. That was a laugh, but I started feeling sorry for the sods. Can you believe it? Time to stop this business, girl, I thought. You're getting sloppy and that can only get you into trouble. So, I quit. I'd also turned thirty, by then; and when you get to that age, you want to settle down and things, you want to get respectable, don't you?

That's why I became a toilet attendant. You laugh: I'm serious. It isn't exactly Top Notch, but it does have its perks, believe you me. If you're into business like me, toilets are where it's at, I'm telling you. I have plans, big plans, but more of that in a minute.

You want a shot of them driers? That's where a lot of the

action takes place – don't ask me why. Must be the vibrating noise or something. Yeah, over there in the corner.

Right, OK, on with my story. I've always liked having more than one girl at a time, me. It's not out of disrespect or nothing. It just sort of makes me feel like I have a family. I did have a family, once – well, just me and my mum, really. My mum only ever loved one person in her life and that wasn't me. It was my fucking dad, a man I never met. He went and got her pregnant out of wedlock, as they say – bad news back home, back then – so she came over here with me in her belly. He was going to join us later. But he went and threw bombs at some barracks instead. So. He got arrested. What did he expect? Stupid.

"He's a rebel your dad, a brave man," she'd keep saying. "He'll soon come out of prison and you'll love him, you'll see." There she was, wishing him home; and there was I, wishing him dead, so that she could love *me* for a change. Wicked, wasn't I? He did die, but I lost her with him.

Shit, when that letter came from the authorities saying that he did himself in at his cell, fuck me triple, they killed him, that's what happened, but that's another story, when that letter came, she gripped it so tight her knuckles nearly broke. She then lay down and never got up again. She went and died on me and I was only nine. That's why they put me in a home, see. Shit, mum, couldn't you hang around a little bit longer?

So, yeah. Girls. The more I have, the happier I feel. And they don't mind, either. I give them what they want, which is a good service to their fanny, and they're away. Me? I can't let them touch me: no way, mate. That's strictly private. Not to be interfered with. Besides. You let a girl play with your intimates, you've had it. *Finito.* She'll worm her way into your bloodstream and that's it, you're hooked. You'll never get her out of your system again, believe you me. Happened to me once. Never again. Ever. Period. She was something else, though . . .

Fucking bitch. Never mind. I shouldn't really swear. I did love the cow. I mean *really* loved her, which is what she wanted. But the moment she got it, she went all Ice Queen on me and that was that. Josie suddenly became the plague.

I saw a programme on telly about the likes of her, I did. They go and make people fall in love with them and, the moment they do, they dump them! Fucking sick, isn't it? It's revenge, they say, for what some fucker did to them when they were little. Charming. Can you imagine if we all went around taking revenge on innocent people for what some fucker did to us when we were little? Jesus. The world would be full of corpses. It's all an excuse, if you ask me; all they really want is to big themselves up by crashing you, that's all. There should be a law about this. They have laws about breaking into people's homes; how about a law about breaking into people's hearts, eh?

She's not getting away with it, though, oh no. I've got her all locked up deep inside me, I do. All locked up and no way out. That's her punishment. I haunt her in her dreams and in her thoughts all the time. She can't get away from what she did to me, oh no. Pulling me all in, then pushing me all out. I'm not a bloody yo-yo. No fucking way, mate. You can't do this to people. And if you do, you've got to pay for it. Fair's fair.

Where was I? Girls. Right. That's all you want to know, isn't it? Bet you do. What do you mean, how do I get off? I've got my ways. You want to know, you really, really want to know? All right. I've got this arrangement, see, with a friend of a friend. She's a cello player. Don't insult me. What do you mean "just surprised, that's all"? I may be a toilet attendant but I've got style, mate. Yeah, right. And I can stop this video diary any time I want, right? Right. OK. No, it's cool. I'm calm now. So. She comes to my flat every Thursday night and she plays music for me. That's right, music. All I ask is that she plays naked but wears a blindfold. She can play so well, she doesn't need to see the notes. And I ask her to do things with her cello while she plays. Rub her fanny, her legs, her tits with it, that sort of thing. Above all, she's got to play that cello as if I'm not there. She's got to give that out. I'm not there, you understand? That's crucial. She doesn't know I'm there, you with me? She loses that for a second, that's it, I'm a dead fish.

She knows how to pick her music, believe you me. It's like she can read my mind. She likes to tease me, at times, but we're always in tune with each other. I used to play in a band, me. I was a drummer, a good fucking drummer but it just didn't work out, too many drugs, mate. It did my head in, so I quit. Still, I know my rhythm. Her and me, it's something else, I'm telling you. She's got class, mate, you know what I'm saying? She's got class. So, yeah that's how I get off. Of course I pay her, what do you think? Not much, but she's worth slaving all week for, that's for sure. I pay her what I can afford and she knows that I'd give her all my wages if I could. So, no complaints. She's poor, I'm hungry, it works out for the both of us.

Sure, there's another way, too. You want to know, you really, really want to know? Bet you do. OK, here it goes.

It's getting a bit of a name this place, right? It's heaving in here on a Saturday night, I'm telling you. There are no straight ladies coming here late at night, right – well, not unless they're in the mood to get some of what their boyfriends can't give them, you with me? So, it's mostly dykes. Sassy dykes, you know what I'm saying? They've soon caught on what they could be using this place for, especially them baby dykes, so forward, I'm telling you. Well, it all started when I first caught them doing it over there by the driers. I just stood here and watched. They caught sight of me in the mirror. Did they stop? Did they mind? Pah! Not a bit. They went wild. They love showing off, they do. So, the girls are doing it over there, I'm getting off over here, it's getting a bit out of hand.

So, I went and did some thinking. Josie, girl, you've earned money from sex before. Move your arse and do it again. So. I started charging them a quid to get in and still they came in droves. This is working, girl, I think, time to get your act together, big time. So. I made some plans. Still with me? OK, that's how it goes.

Ready? Get a shot of my right profile, I look good from that side. Right. It goes like this. Gay men have their cottages, right? Why not dykes? You laugh, I'm serious. Now. This is a cottage with a difference, I'm talking about. Women don't want some poxy, dirty toilet. No. They want a nice environment, right? Right. Women want something hot and dirty but clean, you know what I'm saying?

Look at it this way. There are so many women out there who are dying for a shag with a stranger, no strings attached. But they don't dare do it. Why? Cos there's no safe place for them to do it in. You follow me? Also, they want a shag with a stranger but they don't want the girlfriend to feel left out. Why? Cos women don't like upsetting their girlfriends, do they, now? Well, not the girls I'm aiming this business for, anyhow. Dirty but decent, you with me? So, how can the girlfriend not get left out? If she does it, too, that's how. Now, if there was some place they could go, have their pick and fuck themselves silly, wouldn't they do it? You bet they would. But is there such a place? No, there isn't. Well, that's where I come in, see?

Here's the plan. I'll buy this place up; if you can buy PRIDE, you can buy anything, these days. So, I'll buy this place up, turn it into a Pleasure Dome, that's right, maybe that's what I'll call it. No, that's too obvious; I've got to be discreet. I might get into trouble with the law, I don't want that. Respectability, that's the name of the game. JOSIE'S RESTROOMS: that's better, it's got a ring to it, very English, don't you think? Yeah, that's it. This will be the toilet of the century, mind my word.

Imagine. A juke box over here, a small bar over there, rose petals coming through the water when you flush the toilet. Maybe a few poppers and disposable knickers on sale, too. I could have dildos for hire, and condoms and things, safe sex and all that. Not that anyone bothers with it, what with all these leaflets telling us lesbians can't catch it, but I've got to be responsible, don't I? Yeah. I'll make this place so hot, it'd be *the* place to be seen in. And the place to do and be done, too, you know what I'm saying?

I'll have fuck-me-rough and fuck-me-gentle cubicles, full of velvet cushions and mirrors on the ceiling. I'll have sleaze, I'll have class, I'll have variety. I'll have theme weeks, too: Roman, Indian, Greek, African, Egyptian. Maybe I'll add a couple of massage rooms, too, and kinky rooms and saunas and all sorts. When this place gets off the ground, I can expand my business and set up places like this all over the country. You laugh; I'm serious.

I'm no fool, you know? No. I might as well make some money out of what I'm good at. I'm hot-blooded; I can't help it, must be the Latin in me. All the girls go: "Fuck me, Josie, baby, fuck me, harder, faster, harder." I give them what they want and, as I said, I'm proud of it. But maybe I should now come clean and say: I've had enough. I'm not playing the fucking stud anymore. I mean, did they ever stop to think what Josie really wants? No, too busy looking after their pussies. Well, let me tell you what Josie wants. Love, that's what. You laugh; I'm serious. Fact is, I'd give anything to find the one who'll love me the way my mum loved my dad. Barking up the wrong tree, all this girls business. I might as well go digging for gold in a sewer. So. No more lolly, no thanks, mate. Go and fuck yourself, babes, Ice Queen and all, and I'll just watch. What's more, I'll get paid for it too! Now, that's what I call smart.

Aha, what have we got here? A sleek and shiny cockroach.

Hello mate, all right? Wait a minute! Don't run. *Oye*! Gone. Never mind. Most people hate cockroaches; not me. They're like family to me – always here, always looking out for me. And there's something about the way they're so cocksure of themselves that makes me really like the buggers. And they're fucking strong, mate. You know who'll survive a nuclear holocaust? That's right, cockroaches. And rats. But I don't like rats, no, too slimy. But cockroaches are OK. Where were we? I've lost my thread. Love, yeah, what about some fucking love, ah? No, that wasn't it. JOSIE'S RESTROOMS, that's it. That's the future, babes, sex for money. You laugh, I'm serious. Unless, of course . . . but that's another story.

CLASH OF THE TITANS

Karlyn Lotney

She gave up a Saturday night to come see me. Now, this may seem like no big deal, but when you are the featured dancer at the City's most expensive "Gentleman's Club", and fucking yourself in front of German tourists who use a flashlight to afford themselves an intimate view of your vulva, netting you a thousand bucks a show, Saturday night is, indeed, a big deal. She called to inform me that she was writing a paper detailing the status of women in Bolivian culture, and that she was coming over within the hour for my assistance.

"Be prepared," she commanded softly. She was my first femme top.

Taking her directive to heart, I busied myself around the apartment, falling into my traditional last-minute-a-trick-is-coming-over *modus operandi*, throwing the dirty clothes and papers into the closet, and collecting the dishes that had gathered since the last time we'd had sex. Luckily, I live in the Castro, so finding a decent florist is easier than locating a Frisch's Big Boy in the Midwest. I rushed out to the fanciest shop in the neighborhood and brought home a lovely arrangement of orange and fuchsia Gerber daisies, four perfect irises, and an enormous Cala lily. I know how to buy flowers for a femme.

Once these were placed artfully on my desk, I fired up my Macintosh Ilsi and found a generic entry on Bolivia in the Random House Encyclopedia software that came with my computer. I pulled a book on writing critical papers from the shelf, and set it next to a pad of paper adjacent to the computer. The flowers were placed sufficiently far away from the pad to keep from being a nuisance, yet close enough to inspire loftiness in her thoughts. I found the classical station, and turned the music down to a whisper, leaving just enough volume to produce an air of vague intellectualism in my converted little basement flat. Finally, I sat down on the couch and arranged myself in a casual pose, as though I lounged about my pristine living room, Cala lilies draped overhead, computer at the ready, Mozart playing in the background, incidentally poised to entertain the occasional errant stripper-cum-scholar who might randomly drop by my home. She was, after all, my first femme top.

The doorbell rang, and when I answered it, my carefully-composed mien of *suave casuale* went right out the door she was gracing. She stood there, nothing less than an impossibly perfect vision in BeBe, size two. Now, BeBe is the kind of clothier whose stock rises and falls with the relative success of flawless, high-priced call-girls everywhere, and she basically wore BeBe or nothing at all. Either state, BeBe-bedecked or nude, produces an effect in anyone who had at least a milliliter of either estrogen or testosterone, something akin to the force which sent Frankie Avalon reeling when the Gina Lollobrigida wanna-be did her famous hip swing. She was fine. And despite my carefully administered ministrations, I was made powerless to this Beach Blanket Babylon syndrome whenever she made her way into a room.

"May I come in?" she said, with a smile that conveyed enough amusement to acknowledge my hormonal subjugation, yet enough blasé to indicate the prosaism of my response.

"Oh, sure; please, uh, by all means. You look, well, really amazing. Ah, I've been checking out information about Bolivia on my computer, and there really isn't much there, I'm afraid. You probably have all the facts you need, though, I suppose. Oh, by the way, I have some oranges in the fridge if you're hungry." She snickered almost imperceptibly, and looked up at me with that same amused smile; this time it reflected the ridiculousness of my compensatory efforts to divert her attention from the fool butch blankness which was holding me hostage. She stared into my eyes, let her coat drop to the floor, and revealed the ebullient, lycra-covered lines that defined her perfect porn star body.

She cut a swathe through my flat like Moses parting the Red Sea, and made me feel like a man: all big and dumb and panting. I felt my internal butch cock harden and start its invisible levitation, and the part of my brain that concerns itself with floral arrangements, oranges, and perfect living rooms fell away, and the part that found its genesis in my father's collection of late sixties' issues of Playboy, benches 160, and answers to "Daddy", took over.

"I'm not hungry," she said as she swept into the hall and positioned herself against the wall opposite me, a few inches away from my body.

I must have been giving her one of those steely, hardass stares that appear inadvertently on my face after John Waters has vacated my psyche and porn legend John Holmes has taken his place, because she broke out of her femme top superiority stance long enough to angle her hips up slightly, look at me coquettishly, measure the effect of her proximity on me and ask, "Are you, hungry, baby?"

My phantom dick rises up further in response to the sound of her voice and the movement of her hips, and it bridges the narrowing gap between us. My breathing thickens as my desire lodges itself in my fingertips; every gesture is sexual. I lean into her and put these hands, throbbing and rough, on her waist, and its taut, shimmery tininess makes them feel enormous and iron strong. I encompass her ribcage in them, and move them slowly down the length of her torso. From there, I reach down quickly to the hem of her dress and expose her completely; one swift movement upward and she was bare. I returned my hands to her waist and spread my thumbs out from her stomach up to the nipples of her unbelievable 34Ds, kicked her legs apart, and lifted her up against the wall as she opened her legs and arms around me. I pulled her head back from the nape of her long, thick hair with one hand, and pressed my palm into the vulnerability of her throat with the other, as I kissed her violently.

I was her first butch top.

I lift her up against the wall and spread her legs so that they rest on my shoulders. Her ass is held up by my fingertips so that her snatch is about an inch and a half away from my face. It's shaven smooth, firm, and tight, and tastes so good it gives me a boner that could rip through my 501s. Her cunt smells like refined debauchery, and her pussy lips and clit hood are like perfumed velvet, brushing against my forehead, eyelids, and nose.

I move the heat radiating from her with my tongue, and

come excruciatingly close to her lips without actually touching them. She tries to maintain her composure – she can't do anything that might be construed as begging. My teasing is making her crazy, though, and she writhes around my neck and tries to rub her box on my rough, warm mouth. I have moved us both to pain with waiting; her body is shaking in front of me, and the promise of that cunt moves me to a violence that we both need. I throw her ass back into the wall, and spread her so hard, both her knees hit the plaster. Finally, she spreads her swollen clit and come-slicked lips in front of me, grabs the muscles in my shoulders, moves further into me, and mutters anxiously, "Oh, Jesus, suck it, baby."

She has made an offering of herself, despite her best intentions.

"You wanna be Daddy's hole, baby? You make me so hard, bitch, I could just split your cunt wide open with my big dick."

She smiled coyly and said: "Now, is that any way to talk to a teenager, Karlyn?"

Now, she's a seasoned nineteen, to be sure, but a teen nonetheless, and she likes to remind me of this fact at the most inauspicious times. And it's a bit of a shock to my Dayton, Ohio-grown sensibilities to think that my face is in the cunt of a girl who was still in her garanimals while I was fucking Tony Connors in the back seat of his grandmother's Olds 88. Yet and still, I sport more than my share of Roman Polanski-esque tendencies than the average bulldyke, so the thought that I'm fucking a girl within actual spitting distance of my Daddy/girl fantasies is, after the requisite flash of feminist guilt, actually quite the handy little fetish.

"I think it's an especially good way to talk to a teenager like you, Sugar. Now, grab onto my neck, keep your cunt spread, and straddle my face with that hot little teenage pussy of yours." She smiled down at me like it was her idea, and finally put her soft, sweet lips and swollen slit on my voracious mouth.

I take her in with my tongue all at once, my boots digging into the floor, and my hips thrusting hard against the wall as I rub her little girl cunt all over my face. I enter her and rip her apart with my mouth, lifting her up higher to thrust my tongue into her hole, all the while pounding my hips into the wall like a dog humping air. She rocks her tight little ass into me, and spreads her fine, fresh come all over my face and into my sucking mouth. Her girlish whimpers blend with my deep rough groans as I push her deeper into me by her ass, and furiously rub my own clit against the seam of my jeans. At once, she moves her hands from my neck and tears into my hair as she explodes into my face with several jerky thrusts.

"Oh God, Daddy! Oh, oh, yes, Daddy, take me!"

Come pours all over my chin and down the front of me, and as I let her post-orgasmic body slide down my torso, she looks at me with a bit of real submission in her eyes, and then some embarrassment. I think she was more surprised than I was at her sincerity.

I decide to make the best of my vantage point here, and treat her like a bitch for as long as I can; I know I'm on borrowed time.

"You wanna be Daddy's little bitch, don't you, baby? I know you do, girl, Daddy's here for you, girl."

I grab her hips roughly, bend her over, and spread her right there in the hall on all fours. Her face is in the carpet, her legs are spread as far as she can stretch them, and she has brought her Mac-shellaqued fingernails back to her cunt and is holding it open for me. I decide to take her ass first, barely touching her cunt. I coat my fingers with her come, and move her hands up to her ass, so she can open herself for me there. I hold her tight little body by the crook of her hip, my palm covering about half of her ass. I start rocking her slowly, massaging her hole, and then ease her back gently onto my fingers.

She lets out a high femme moan that makes me want to plow her, but I settle on kicking her legs farther apart and plunging my hand deeper inside her ass. As fortuitous happenstance would have it, a small bottle of lube was at the ready there in the hall: I coated my hand generously, and held her ass open while I poured some into her.

"Oh, Jesus, Daddy, my asshole is so tight! Take my hole, fuck it! Fuck me, Daddy!"

Now, these words uttered by a World Wide Federation wrestler would put me over the top, but hearing them from this stunningly gorgeous, high femme, hardcore top, bent over, with my hand inside her ass, incited me to excess. I pulled her head back by her hair, grabbed her hip, and pulled her hard toward me, and thrust my hand into her, first, three, then four fingers. I pump her furiously, and she moans and cries, and I'm sweating and fucking her intensely: her body bucks up as she climaxes hard and tight around my hand.

And then, the most curious thing happens – bubbles start flowing out of her ass. Suddenly, I went from Monster Top to Bobby and Cindy Brady after their mishap with the over-filled washing machine. What I thought was lube was actually the same company's brand of sex toy cleaner.

Only to me. Only I could have this flawless creature on all fours calling me "Daddy", coming and oblivious, while I'm behind her watching bubbles foam from her anus. I recover from the visual spectacle of it all in time to start scooping the bubbles out of her ass, and hold the scene together without breaking her concentration. Jesus, the non-oxyonol 9. I'm trying to rock this chick's world, and I'm going to end up numbing out her lower intestine.

"Give your little ass to Daddy, baby, I wanna make you feel real good," I say as I drop to my knees and start furiously sucking toy cleaner out of her, spitting the vile stuff into my hand, and then going back for more, like some pornographic take-off on a Laurel and Hardy bucket brigade. I felt like at any time Allen Funt might appear from behind my closet door to tell me I was going to be on the Triple X episode of "Candid Camera".

"Oh, yeah, that feels good," she said as I sucked out the last putrid bit of the detergent. I think I did it.

"That's a very good girl," I mumbled, and smiled as I tried to conceal the numbing effect of the cleaner on my lips and tongue, once she turned around in my arms.

We had spent three hours at my apartment, and had made no progress whatsoever in our scholastic inquires into the nature of gender amongst the Bolivians, and I was ravenous.

"Are you hungry now, honey?" I asked.

"I could be cajoled, I suppose."

"So I noticed," I said as reached down, squeezed her left nipple, and kissed her.

We decided to go to the corner restaurant for a bite to eat, which became increasingly feasible as the effect of the spermicide began to lessen. After dinner, we walked through the neighborhood with my hand slipped in between two of the front buttons of her coat, and inside the slit of the lycra dress that had earlier proved itself so amenable to our activities. I led her down Castro Street proper with two of my fingers in her cunt, and took her one block further to Collingwood Park, a place infamous for the sexual opportunities it affords the men of our famed district.

As we walked around the perimeter of the park, we were vaguely harassed as breeder spectators, due both to my high butch appearance, and to a lack of imagination on the part of the fags in attendance. She was a bit hesitant, but I moved us through their cruising territory, and right into the dead-center of the park.

"What are you doing?" she asked.

I gave her my John Holmes stare again and pushed her up against a well-lit fence; the ground around it was covered with broken glass and reeked of male piss. It was no Wuthering Heights, but it had its appeal.

"You aren't really going to, I mean, it's their park," she said, referring to the men waiting on the sidewalk like junior high school girls at their first mixer.

"We pay our taxes, don't we?" I asked as I kissed her and I held her tight against the fence. I unbuttoned her coat and thrust my knee between her legs to spread her. I shielded her body from the light with my own, grabbed the fence near her head, and thrust my hand between her bare legs, rocking the steel behind her. I kicked her legs further apart and her expensive heels scraped along the pavement, as I entered her, hard. I stuck my fingers down her throat so that she would have something to suck on while I pumped the come out of her still-wet cunt. I fucked her mercilessly there, in the middle of that park, four fingers pounding into her, my teeth clenched into her neck, and her fingernails digging straight through my jacket into the flesh of my biceps. She threw her head back against the fence, and then transformed a silent scream into deep bruises on my arms as she came in tight contractions that strangled my fingers. I cupped my hand around her abraded cunt, and held her like that for a while, there in Collingwood Park, before we walked back to my place.

Fucking another top is indeed a curious affair, which lends itself both to trepidation and paranoia. You see, no matter how amenable the other top may be to your ministrations in the moment, there is some little meter in her head that is constantly measuring the exact amount of domination and force to which you have subjected her, in order to repay you fully in kind at some later hour. Now this terrifies me, because, well, I just don't think many of my finest moments have been had with my ass in the air. I feel like a turtle on my back, and I have enchanted former lovers who have tried to flip me with a fetching "For God's sake, let me do it!" attitude that has more frequently moved them to tears than me to orgasm.

She wasn't having it; once we were back at my apartment, the hour of reckoning had arrived.

"Down."

In the intervening moments (which now seemed like light years) since I had her against the fence, she had apparently regained the high femme top fierceness that rendered me a slave boy at her feet. She demanded worship, and her body and bearing made it difficult to refuse.

"Excuse me?" I attempted to reel the words back into my mouth as soon as they escaped.

"What about 'down' don't you understand?"

This time, I dropped awkwardly to my knees, and looked up at her for further instruction.

"I think it's time for you to be naked." Like many butch tops, I cling to my clothes like a life raft during sex, and parting with them so unceremoniously was a trifle disconcerting.

"Take your shirt off, baby; let's see what you've got under there." I pulled off my black T-shirt quickly, like a band-aid, and revealed a serviceable white 42D Bali style 3208 underwire, sans floral cleavage decoration, which I had at no time regarded as a sex toy.

"Very nice," she laughed, and suddenly I was eight and shirtless on the basketball court in Robby and Phillip Miller's backyard, where a scandalized Mrs Miller returned home and brusquely corrected my impropriety.

"And in here?" I restrained myself from assisting her as my industrial strength brassière provided her with some resistance, but eventually she managed to unhook the contraption, and held my large breasts by the nipples for a moment before she freed them. She then had me stand up and take off my metal and leather belt, along with my poleclimbers, and black jeans. The latter had been concealing a huge boner I had packed in my jock strap before we had left, and was now bulging conspicuously before her.

"A present, I see. How delightful." I felt like I was living in *Emmanuelle III In 3-D.*

"Lie down, face up, now."

I complied and she took off her dress for effect, but kept those lethal, now damaged, stilettos on her tiny feet. She then rested the toe of her shoe on my cock, and said, "You look so pretty lying underneath my feet. I could keep you here forever."

She had, evidently, seen the bubbles.

She traced the outline of my shaft with the heel of her shoe, and I trembled as if it were attached by nerves and muscle, instead of leather. As she walked up toward my head, she traced the contours of my body with her heel, and upon arriving there, she planted her left foot next to my face.

"Lick it, boy."

I delineated her entire shoe delicately with my tongue, as though the thin leather were her pussy-lips, and I immersed myself in curve of her instep. She kicked my head away cruelly and thrust the heel into my mouth, and I sucked it rhythmically in response to her delicate thrusts. She then walked back to the middle of my body, slipped her foot between the divide of my legs, and pressed into my flesh with those heels of hers, stabbing at my cock before she made a slow and painful journey up to my chest. Once there, she extracted the retribution she evidently felt was due her, and dug the heel of her shoe into my sternum.

Jesus. The shoe-licking's one thing, but Good Lord, really, this is a bit much.

She looked down at me and laughed as though she was keeping score – and was winning.

I was shaking, as much from arousal as from pain and equivocation. She knelt down beside me, kissed the heel marks she had left on my body, and kissed my face in an almost maternal way.

"Now isn't this better, baby?" she said as she pinched my nipples and kissed me again before slapping me hard in the face.

Mother-fucking bitch. I stifled my tears; I wasn't going to let her have that part of me. She saw the frailty I tried to hide from her and laughed as she straddled my face with her perfect cunt and allowed me to suck come from her there. She ran me back and forth over the edge between trust and suspicion, and I trusted her just enough to make her dangerous to me.

She pulled away from me and let the cold air hit my come-wet face.

"There, baby. Get on your hands and knees, and keep your head down."

I wanted to trust her enough to let go, yet I was still wavering. I heard her rustling through my things, and when she returned, the first thing I felt was my own heavy leather belt doubled over, metal side out, caressing my inner thighs and the cheeks of my ass. She started whipping me, hard, with little ceremony, and it became increasingly difficult to stifle my tears as she persisted.

Jesus. Damn her, she could care less about how I feel. That's it. Just as I was about to pull myself up from the realm of bottoming and stop her, she dropped the belt.

"Had enough?" she asked, and I raised my red face up, trying hard to hold back the tears.

I've had enough, all right, you She-Devil.

"Poor baby," she cooed, only half-sarcastically. She directed me to lay on the bed face up, and I hesitated a moment before I obeyed the command I had just been ready to undermine. I could sense some contrition in her bearing, and we did have this tacit switching agreement. And then there was my remorse over the bubbles. I have instilled in me a capacity for guilt for which a team of Jewish mothers, working night and day through my formative years, would be proud. I once again acquiesced to her will.

She straddled my legs and began to massage the large bulge in my jockstrap. I felt at once enraged, rebellious, coddled, hard, and hurt. She talked to me in a mother's voice, and told me that she was going to make me feel very good, and started to rub her big soft tits over my cock and between my thighs. She asked me how old I was, and I looked up at her with a tattered, fledgling machismo, shaved twelve years off my age, and replied, "I'm 17."

She must have truly felt bad for whipping me so hard because she then did something she promised me she would never do – she started to give me a blow job. She eased herself further down the bed, so that her face was directly over my quivering cock. She then nuzzled the soft cotton of my bleached-white Calvin Klein jockstrap and asked me if any of my girlfriends had ever sucked my cock before, to which I replied, "Well, last summer, this girl who was a counselor at the day camp I was workin' at started blowin' me in the equipment shack, but some idiot kid came in right when she was about to start sucking on my rod, and then she was too freaked to ever try it again." I do a mean 17-year-old boy.

"Well, you're going to become a man tonight, baby, 'cause Momma's going to give you a blow job you'll never forget."

She peeled my jockstrap back gingerly with her teeth, and from the white cotton emerged the eight-inch Super Realistic I had packed in her honor; it felt all the more realistic for her sweet snatch poised above it. She pulled her body back and nestled her gorgeous face against my swollen cock head, and then slowly drew her tongue up the shaft and around, carefully covering every millimeter of this huge cock which had become my own. She went down lower, and sucked on each of my balls, and as she did, the rest of the dick balanced against her cheek, bouncing against her face like in porno movies scenes I replay in my head when I jack off. She drew the tip of her tongue up along the bottom of my cock until she was at the head, on which she placed a sweet little kiss which made me want to face-fuck her; naturally, I refrained. She slid her lips around the head of my cock so excruciatingly slowly that I had to restrain my hips from thrusting into her.

"What a big, hard dick you have, baby; you're bigger than most grown men. I bet you'd like to stick that big dick in Mommy's mouth, now wouldn't you?"

Well, I would indeed. I wondered briefly whether silence or a response would make her continue, and opted for the former.

"You want me to take your 17-year-old cock down my throat? Is that right? Well, OK, baby, I guess there are many forms of torture."

With that, she took the entire head in her mouth, drew the air from within her cheeks, and swirled her tongue around it while she began to suck. I wanted to slam my whole shaft down her throat, hard, but she corrected my instincts with a glare that told me to stay back on the bed and be seventeen. I fought against every impulse I had developed in my illustrious career as a butch top, and started practicing the stress reduction breathing techniques I had learned in my math anxiety seminar, thirteen years before. It may have improved my SAT score, but nothing could have prepared me for her deep throat artistry: she grazed the top of my cock head with her teeth before suddenly swallowing all eight inches whole down her throat. She closed her eyes as she had me there, all the way to the balls in her beautiful face, moaning like it was rubbing up against her G-spot every time she wrung it with her lips. Holding back was excruciating, and I was jittery and nearly hollow with desire. She looked up at me, measured my need, and smiled as if she owned me. She then went back to her sucking, moaning, and smiling, all the while holding me down with the slightest pressure from her index fingers.

I wanted to rape her.

She allowed my cock to slide slowly out of her mouth, and smiled down at me as she began to mount me, like she was an equestrian and I was her steed. She pushed my legs together so that the shaft stood straight up, parted her lips, and lightly grazed the head of my cock back and forth with the wetness of her pussy as she straddled it. She then moved up to my face and spread her lips, so that I could see the inside of the snatch I wasn't fucking. It was pink and smooth on the outside, and a deeper teenage rose color on the inside, which was coated with a slick, milky whiteness. Further inside, I could see she was contracting her walls for my benefit – alternating a slow, thick, cock-sucking motion with more rapid, squeezing movements.

"You want to fuck this, don't you? You want to ram your hard cock inside my pussy right now, you son of a bitch."

She really did have a certain flair for torture. She held herself just close enough to me that I could smell her cunt and feel its heat, but drew it out of reach whenever I lifted up to make contact. By the time she withdrew herself completely, my neck was sore, my hips were thrusting, and I had a hard-on that could have fucked through steel. She laughed at my predicament as if I had indeed been her animal; like she was taunting my hard horse-dick with her crop for her own amusement.

She lifted herself back so that her cunt was once more arched above my tortured cock. By this point, if there had been blood running through my balls, it would have been ice blue. She took my cock in one hand and smiled again at me, in my pathetic state. She never broke, but finally parted those velvet lips of hers, and held herself above me so that my cock was held lightly in her pussy. She slowly swallowed my whole head inside her, and though I quivered with the intensity of the scene, I was reluctant even then to give myself over to my desire. Then, in the same way she took the whole of my cock down her throat, she slid down my huge shaft until it amazingly disappeared completely inside her petite body. She closed her eyes and moaned deeply, and I put my hands on her smooth hips, started thrusting, and finally eased into the act like the million times I had done it before.

Or so I thought.

"Just what in the fuck do you think you're doing? Stay still and keep your hands where I put them." She stuck my hands under my ass and I laid there like a mummy, my body tight, an immovable, bound package, ready to come undone as she rode my cock. I was on the verge of leaving my body when a brutal slap stunned me across my face and woke me from my stupor.

"This is the way it will always be with us; this is the way that it should be."

Time moved in slow motion for a moment as I allowed the rage to register in my brain. How fucking dare she? That's enough. That is most certainly enough. I felt the blood swell in my face and my heart throbbing in my ears and I threw her off of me and yelled: "That's it! That is it. I've had it. You like it rough, baby? Well, you can have it rough, right here, right now, bitch."

I flipped her over on her hands and knees, and thrust my cock deep into her tight cunt, pulled her back by her hair and told her, "I'll be as vicious as you are long before you're as strong as me." I started fucking her like I had just been released from prison.

She signaled her consent to the rape by reaching back and spreading her cunt open for me as I shoved her face down into the bed. I grabbed her hips like they were handles and plowed her like a jackhammer. She had built a massive load up in me, and her cruelty and domination moved my topping pendulum so off the charts that I fucked her brutally. I kicked her legs apart, mounted her, and held her body down with my weight, while I pinched both of the nipples on her big tits with one hand. I gathered both of her thin wrists in the other while I tore into her tight slit with my steel cock. I ravaged her cunt continually and yelled: "You'll always top me? You will not always top me, bitch!"

All at once, her cunt became thick around my dick, I released my hold on her wrists and she reached forward, grabbed a pillow and screamed; her body heaved up in jerky movements underneath me.

I was far from done with her, though. The tension wrought up in me from bottoming to her made me a maniacal top. I turned her over while I was still inside her, put her ankles on my shoulders, and regained the momentum of moments before. Then I reached down and grabbed the steel of the bed frame and fucked her across the mattress for hours until her head bobbed off the edge, again invoking the skin flicks to which I jack off.

The rage in me began to subside, but the animalism remained; I grunted with every hard thrust into her. She received me with her entire body; her hips tilted upward, her legs wrapped around my back, and she sucked my dick tight inside her cunt until we were both dripping with sweat and our bodies were sliding across one another. Finally, my clit swelled until it filled the container of the cock inside her. She took a deep breath in, threw her head back, and I felt her pussy start to vibrate with orgasm around me. When she tore down my hyper-sensitive back with her long fingernails, I bolted into her with a brutal, cathartic intensity. I fell into the largesse of her breasts, and I swear to God, I saw a white light there which mirrored the explosions in my cunt.

I took my dick off, soothed my soaking wet, leather-worn cunt between my fingers, and climbed into bed, naked, next to her. She drew my head into her breasts for an eternity; my jaws went slack, and I released what felt like twenty-nine years of controlled pressure into her tits. I unleashed a powerful sigh into that mystical cleavage, and followed the white light I found there as if I were being led across the divide. Her tits were round and soft, and somehow teenager and Mommy at the same time. The power of them relegated me once more to a shy, youthful submission, but this time, when she asked me how old I was, I looked up at her bashfully, and said, "I'm eight."

"What a good, sweet boy you are. I bet you want to suck Momma's pussy." She spread her legs and parted her lips, and pushed my head down to her cunt, wet and sore from hours of fucking. "That's it, baby, come to me. Come back to me." I closed my eyes, discharged deeper from that taut reserve, and sucked her cunt as if it were all I needed to survive. I yielded to her in earnest there, between her legs, at her feet, under her control. I offered up my will in protracted gasps, and at once, a tight, archaic mass in me unclenched, and I was made free.

HOMAGE TO VI

Heather Murray

I'll huff and I'll puff and open the old front door with my thigh. Sigh. Music's turned itself on again. Automatic timer. Set since when? Least it's a discreet something medieval-like and won't bother Ramona downstairs. Though she's got her soap up high and is away in Venezuela. Or Paraguay, with the hair-dos, shoulder-pads and two-set melo-drama. Bananas spill out one downed shopping bag, ruptured over-ripes burst mulching around the bottom of the other. Time to turn myself on with automatic? Ooh, the stairs up to the flat (fourth floor!), what exercise for my varicose and ooh, the heat, always one to sweat (never could be cool, it's biological), the rivulets just flow and flow.

A good half hour to while away and unwind. Few swigs of soda fresh from the opened fridge door. Plastic bottle neck not the same as the old, cold beady glass ones. Sigh and knock the door to with thigh which jolts the goat into action, hum and loud drone, just enough muster to keep the chill at a minimum next to the permanent defrosting mechanism. Old fridge and outmoded lectric; when she starts up with a hiccup the other flat lights flicker and burp. Burr of the phone, but let the machine take whoever . . . Eva and it's urgent, over . . . Half hour.

If I lie down on the bed and use the double plug, the fan on high with a whirr and whoosh and the transformer to hoick up the current. Bedside cabinet door sticks but there she is inside, tossed willy-nilly among the gloves and sorry squeezed lube tubes.

Hi, Vi.

LadyFinger's in the drawer, now ignored, still in sock from the old days when she'd nuzzle amongst the knickers. Sock to slip over possible sensibilities. No competition for Vi. She's the business and she's seriously square, no sausage-shaped, battery-popping, shrill-buzzing, one-speed-if-you're-lucky-ducky for her.

It's been years now and still going strong. Not a murmur of discontent, even in those reckless early days of seven sessions daily. Gaily seven daily 'til I thought maybe she was getting out of hand and under my skin. Never put her in: she's not that type. She mows the mounds and tickles the lips and clits does Vi. Lickety-split.

Whoever the woman of the day, however much fleshing and delving, coming home to Vi always feels like a prized present, preferring this one private, not shared. Bearing the personal delight in political LadyFinger presents to all and sundry. Made for Sunday.

Unravel the cord and plug her in. Time to go slow, velocity down low, click her on and here we go. Plump up the pillow, lower the head, stretch out legs and grasp the handle in left, right wrist on pubic hump and gently ground Vi to vulva. Yeah. No wear and tear on her technique; she's finely tuned every time. Dip in the current and a momentary halt as the fridge shudders to another half-hearted start. There, settle lightly on the left ledge where the vibes begin to make their presence felt. Felt and velvet and rough hessian. Round and round the rugged rocks the ragged rascal . . .

Fan up high whirs away. Breeze blows through the window billowing the chubby angels on lacy curtain, leisurely pot-bellied and certain in their permanent pleasure. Hung-plants wave and waver. I love the green scene through that frame. Shame about the sudden police helicopter sound, *rucca rucca.* Pigs might fly. Back to the relative peace of the fridge, the fan, odd babble from Ramona's soap, and the high sigh of Vi. The days and nights of piling on the eiderdowns, upping the music, wondering if the neighbours might think I've an electric tooth-brush (for thirty minutes?) or a foodmixer (at 2 a.m.?).

Time to turn her up and move her a little lower to touch the disk edge between where the cheeks meet. Zmm. Mellow. Clench buttocks a bit. Start holding breath. My sister used to hold her breath, reading comics at night. Maybe she'd mistressed some between-leg-muscle-clutching and never let on. That or the Four Marys were fairies. Going from the plateau to early excitement phase I.

That book **For Ourselves**. This is the way our bodies work. The bare stages of orgasm where plateau sounds like a flat and barren landscape. Or a cake on a plate. Gateau. All those photos of fannies, pages of pubes and cunt close-ups! Another lesson in liberation. Better far was the girlfriend who presented me with a medical muscle massager and asked if I could guess its alternative and revolutionary use. That first hot hum, quick come and I was hooked. No book could outline the grinning grind of handle in hand and vibes on the up and up, along the plateau, sprint through phase I, II and III and away. Caught-up in thought.

Back to today and adjust the speed. Need that treble to drum deeper. Round she goes to pull skin over clit, pull skin over clit, back a bit and nestle there a while. Flex your calves, bounce the bum. A moan is good for the muscle tone. Joke or boast, I don't fantasize about it, I do it. With Vi, there's nothing to it. Guaranteed the speed to succeed. Flash of Liz Taylor's cleavage. Just creamy lines to a low V-neck. Tock of the clock. Already? Heady, steady, exert that lazy wrist, small twist and up the volume. Fridge gives a free voltage drop jolt. Sweat wetting sheets and trickling, tickling neck and filling belly button. Up the volume, drone is an insistent shriek, thighs alive for a life worth living, stick out belly and the warm sweat leaks down to pubic hill, through vulva valley and into my cunt as I raspberry ripple and plummet to the peak.

COCKTEASE

Deborah Kelly

This is story of stupendous naughtiness. Mine.

Cockteasing.

When I was a teenager, that was considered grounds for justifiable rape. Righteous, almost.

Usually, I feel guilty if men desire me. It makes me apologetic. It's usually an accident People think I'm flirting when I'm just being friendly. When I'm flirting, they tend to think I'm needling them. I am.

Anyway.

The story was begun to tell about a cocktease.

It was a warm night in April, I was going straight from work to another city by plane, to see my lover, I'd been breathless all day. It's a very steamy romance. Joyful. I had forgotten you could do that My last sexual relationship of consequence wasn't so much steamy, as sulphuric.

This one began, or was at least consummated, by the sea, on holiday, in salt air, with my sisters & friends around me. Love, all over the place. I thought the sex & romance part was an annexe to all this familiar & familial affection. Eventually, though, with much coaxing, & some gorgeous feasts of fucking.

(here I think of her sliding toward me at a bar, the night I realized that the disconcerting tickling feeling I was having about her was desire, and her saying nothing but, come and fuck.

Every time I think of it I feel it in my cunt Truly.

I wish it had happened. It didn't We couldn't find each other that night. It's what she had planned. How very bold. Boldness, my favourite attribute in a woman & shamelessness. I'm learning, myself, from example)

I came to be visiting her as often as I could.

Anyway.

You might think this goes too far in the practice of shamelessness.

For a grown-up woman. For a feminist.

But there I was, going to meet her. I felt like beautiful cat and I think it was written all over me. Flying off to be stroked. To have my fur ruffled.

I was in a hurry, had to run out of work. I got in the front seat of a cab. The driver, when I said airport, said business or pleasure? I must have purred when I said, the latter. He studied me for the length of a street and asked me questions in carefully gender neutral phrases. I responded in kind. He said, you're going to meet a woman.

Yes.

And are you really going in that?

My work clothes, not provocative. So I told him that I was changing at the airport. His eyes lit up: What into?

I decided he was my mouse.

I showed him, piece by piece, my long red silk skirt, restrained black cotton shirt which is, nevertheless, completely transparent, suede high heels, wide, hip-hugging, lace suspenders.

He swerved as he fell forward onto the steering wheel. I think he had a painful erection. We were, thankfully, very nearly at the airport. His voice was froggy.

Are you going to wear underpants?

No, I said, deciding then.

He couldn't look at me when I handed him the money. He couldn't sit up straight.

When I walked, *dressed*, out of the airport toilets, my clicking heels, my thighs whispering sedition to each over the stockings, I couldn't not twitch my ass, slipping against silk.

The whole way on the plane, I had to clench my thighs to keep from darkening the skirt with my wetness.

When I saw her, I was shy.

That's the end of the story, really.

But I wonder, if the taxi driver had asked me what she'd be wearing, if I'd have said, same kind of thing. That Bilitis thing, to please him.

Or, to please myself, the truth.

Being, jeans, T-shirt, pannel shirt, Possible building site dust.

Half smile like a scimitar. A cutlass. My pirate babe.

This makes me deeply uncomfortable. But that, as they say, is another story . . .

THE WEEKEND

Alex LeQuesne

A busy week came to a hectic conclusion. Friday evening at 7 p.m. and I was still in my office, pulling together some briefing for a meeting I had in Brussels the following Tuesday. It meant I was having to wrestle with photocopier technology and filing systems with which my position in the organisation left me quite unadept. Trying to persuade my clerical assistant to stay beyond four o'clock on any afternoon was a waste of effort and, by this time on a Friday, the entire building was almost deserted. I could hear the low rumble of male voices approaching and was actually pleased when my colleagues, Peter and Mark, stepped in and said enough was enough and why didn't we go for a quick drink in the Wine Bar? I was tired enough to prefer the peace and solitude of my flat but I also knew I'd get a buzz out of spending a little time with these jokers, so skilled in their wit and repartee. They were also some of the only straight men I knew who hadn't at any time tried it on with me or asked probing questions about my private life. I snapped the catches on my bulging briefcase, grabbed my coat and accompanied them along the corridor, down the stairs and out into the crisp November air.

Finlays was only around the corner from our office. You could never say with any certainty whether it would be quiet or packed to the gunnels. Tonight it was the former. The cold weather had no doubt driven the young executives scurrying home to "Commuter Close" and only a dozen or so people, mostly grey suited, anonymous-looking men and a couple of power-dressed women remained. We three leaned against the bar and Peter bought a round of overpriced drinks. Sipping at my white wine I subjected the place to a more detailed scrutiny, which was when I spotted Joan lurking in the corner, quite alone, nursing a glass of her own. Immediately I excused myself to the men and went over to her. Her head was down and she was buried in her own thoughts.

"Joan?"

She looked up quickly, guiltily. "Oh, Hilary. Hi! I thought you'd have gone home long ago." Why she should have thought this, I couldn't guess – in the three months she'd been working in my section, I couldn't remember her once staying very late. She was hard-working and career-orientated but no one was left in any doubt that her life with her partner, Barry, took precedence over everything else. She espoused feminist causes, trumpeted her independence, but always made sure Barry had a meal waiting for him when he arrived home.

I had liked her from the start; she was warm, honest and bright, We often lunched together, either eating or shopping, but suggestions I had made about going out after work had always been met with regretful excuses. These days, I didn't suggest any more and it was more than surprising to find her sitting there alone in Finlays Bar.

I sat down beside her. "I had to get the papers together for next week's meeting. To be honest, I'm bushed, but Peter and Mark asked me if I'd like a drink and I thought they might cheer me up a bit. Would you like to join us?"

She shook her head. "Thanks, but do you mind if I don't? I'm not really in the mood for male company, tonight."

"How about female company, then?"

She smiled at me. "Yes, I'd like that, if you can extricate yourself from Peter and Mark without offending them."

"Leave it to me," I said and went back to the bar where the men were so involved with the Premier League, they probably viewed my apologies as a blessing. They both knew how much I hated to talk about football.

I bought two more glasses of wine and returned to Joan. She flashed me a smile of appreciation but said nothing at all for some time after I'd sat down. I didn't want to ask probing questions, but nor did I want to pretend she hadn't made that remark about male company. If anyone was going to take the lead on this, it had to be her. Silently, we drank our wine. I remembered that I'd been too busy to eat much that day and the alcohol took an almost immediate effect. Looking closely at Joan, I suspected that she'd had quite a head start on me. Presently, she sighed and shifted her position slightly so that the top of her body was facing me. For a moment I recalled how disciplined I'd had to be when she'd first joined the section – she was very much my idea of an attractive woman but I'd made sure she didn't know that.

"Do you know what it's like to be really frustrated?" she asked with disarming bluntness.

"In what sense?"

She gave a mirthless laugh. "Sexually, of course."

Normally, the prospect of a discussion about sex would have thrilled me. It was one of my favourite topics when I was with my dyke friends but I felt much less at ease talking about it with a straight woman. "Well, I'm not—"

But she wasn't really interested in my reply. She just wanted someone to listen to her. "Maybe it's me. Probably it is. But no one has ever really satisfied me. I'm beginning to think I'm a nympho or something."

I opened my mouth to tell her that of course she wasn't, but she wasn't interested in my view on that, either. She went on, "I've been with quite a few men, and I've never hated sex with them, but always there's been something missing. The one before Barry was half-Italian. He'd got this sort-of stud reputation. Well he was just 'wham, bam, thank you ma'am' and the only time I had the courage to ask him if we could change the routine a bit he looked as if I'd questioned his manhood. He was so angry, he didn't talk to me for two weeks. Continued to fuck me, though." She gave a little giggle at this point.

I was transfixed. One of the things I'd found so entrancing about Joan was her air of innocence. "Fuck" was not a word I'd heard her use before. She'd struck me as the type only to "make love".

"And now there's Barry," she went on. "Do you know why I got together with Barry?"

I shook my head. I couldn't guess, but I was looking forward to finding out.

"Because he's gentle and kind and he respects me."

Seemed reasonable to me. I wondered what the catch was. Joan was about to tell me.

"Barry can't fuck. He's so bloody passive. Ninety percent of the time, he wants a blow job or mutual masturbation. On the rare occasions I can get him inside me, he's so slow I practically fall asleep. And he closes his eyes, which makes me suspect that he wishes it wasn't me lying there under him. D'you know what?"

"What?" I asked, dying for her to continue.

"I think maybe Barry's gay but afraid to come out. I wouldn't mind if he'd at least do something interesting like bugger me."

I'd taken a sip of my wine just before she'd said this. I spluttered most of it across the table then sat and choked for a minute or so. I wondered just how many drinks Joan had had to get to this stage of candour. I realized that what I'd known of her before was just the tip of a very interesting iceberg.

I couldn't think of a thing to say but, once I'd regained my composure, she continued anyway. With a lascivious gleam in her eye she said, "What I want is just good hot hard sex. All night long, if possible. I want someone to take me mercilessly. I don't even care much who it is, anymore. I've been having all sorts of peculiar fantasies – really smutty. Do you know what I mean?"

I knew only too well what she meant but I didn't want to elaborate. I wondered whether, on a smut scale, her fantasies could really be as kinky as mine. So I simply nodded and asked her if she'd like to go somewhere else for a drink.

She looked around the bar with a jaundiced eye. "Yeah," she said. "This is a dump. I bet you know somewhere much more interesting, don't you, Hilary?"

Her tone was intriguing, bordering on flirtatious. At that stage, I hadn't really decided how I'd like the evening to continue, but I knew that I wanted it to contain Joan for as long as possible.

Joan wasn't entirely steady on her feet as we left the bar but I was only too happy to support her. Back on the main street, I hailed a taxi and told him to take us to Jacob's Court. My hope was that "Ringers" wouldn't be too crowded or noisy, full more with drinkers than the bright young dancers who crammed in there on a Saturday.

As we travelled the London streets, Joan turned to me and said, "Where are you taking me?" with just a hint of damsel-in-distress, deliberately lacing her voice.

I resisted the temptation to make a suggestive remark and replied simply, "Trust me".

To my astonishment, she put her head on my shoulder and looked up at me with complete seriousness saying, "I do, I trust you completely."

I swallowed hard and stared ahead at the driver's mirror. He was looking back at us, probably thinking how he was going to tell his mates about the lezzos he'd had in the cab. When we arrived at the end of the narrow street that led down to the bar, I made sure that I got out first, as I couldn't be sure that Joan's exit wouldn't be calamitous. I really didn't want to see her sprawled on the pavement. Once she was safely decanted, I paid the driver, who surprised me by winking and wishing me good luck before pulling away, back in the direction of the West End. Frankly, I was embarrassed and relieved that Joan hadn't heard his remark.

She was staring up at the stars pensively. Gently I took her arm and led her along the street to the top of a metal staircase that led down to the basement of 17 Jacob's Court, aka "Ringers". It was a "dive", really, but a "dive" with atmosphere. A smell of stale cigarette smoke lingered, the lighting was dim and the bar furniture did not have a cherished look about it. But it suited me, particularly on a quiet night like tonight. From behind the bar Carol, one of the joint owners, gave me a wave. A couple of other women murmured greetings at me. I sat Joan down and went to the bar.

Carol smiled. "Hello, stranger. Haven't seen you here for a few weeks."

"I've been very busy," I replied honestly.

She looked past my shoulder to where Joan was sitting. "So I see," she smirked.

I pulled a face at her. "She's just a friend. A colleague actually."

Carol raised her eyes to the ceiling. "Oh, God, not another of your impossible straights, I hope," she said, referring back to a period in my life when I was forever getting entangled with straight women, with uniformly unsatisfactory results.

"Just give me two glasses of dry white wine, Carol and I'll take care of the rest, OK?"

She shrugged her shoulders, carelessly, though in fact I knew she did care about my happiness very much. She and her partner, Doreen, were some of my oldest friends. I'd loaned them quite a sizeable amount of money when they set up "Ringers". Within six months they'd paid it back, substituting, at my request, a case of wine for interest.

I went back to Joan, whose eyes were scanning the room and the women in it. The crowd was small tonight but fairly mixed. Over at the pool table a group of shaven-headed leather dykes argued about whether to nominate the pocket for the 8 ball. On the other side of the room were two or three women who were wearing office attire like Joan and me. I recognised Susie Crowhurst sitting in another group of women, dominating the proceedings as usual. She and I had clashed badly once at a caucus meeting to set up a new Lesbian and Gay political lobbying group. In a strident and humourless manner, she'd done her best to bully some members of the caucus into adopting a strict anti-SM policy as part of the new group's charter. I'd tried to use reasonable persuasion with her at first but her attitude eventually led to me calling her an intolerant bigot with a small but oppressive mentality. She'd swelled up with righteous indignation, but as the majority of the other people in the room agreed with me, her ship was sunk. She had flounced out, taking her two or three lackeys with her, and we'd never spoken since.

Now, to my horror, she had spotted me and was coming over to my table. She was such an aesthetic, with her corpulent body and sullen expression. I wondered if she ever laughed at anything. I thought I might try to disarm her by smiling and saying hello. Her face remained impassive as she stood sneering down at me.

"Still up to your revolting, fascist practices, are you, Copeland?"

Calmly, I replied, "I am not, nor have I ever been, a fascist and what I do in the privacy of my own home is nothing to do with you, Susie, so why don't you go and oppress someone else."

Her mouth had a particularly nasty twist to it as she said to Joan, "She's sick. I'd be very careful around her, if I were you."

The temptation to slap her stupid face was a strong one but I knew she'd react by suing me for assault and claim that my action just proved what a brutal pervert I was hiding under my veneer of respectability. So I just smiled again and said, "Fuck off," and fortunately she did.

Throughout this exchange Joan had sat rapt, blinking in astonishment. "What the hell was that all about? Who is that awful woman?"

"An old adversary," was all I could think of to say.

Joan frowned. "An adversary at what?" But before I could think of a reply she had resumed scanning the bar and then turned back to me saying, "Hilary, this is a gay bar. The women in here are lesbians."

"Hmm, yes."

She leaned forward. "Are you a lesbian, too?"

"I am."

She sat and thought for a moment before saying "Somehow, that makes sense. I know I've never really asked you about your private life but I've never been able to visualize you with a man. I can't see you putting up with their shit."

"Shit comes from all directions, Joan. Like friend Crowhurst over there," I said, indicating in Susie's direction.

"You're right," Joan said matter-of-factly, getting up to take our empty glasses to the bar. Considering how much she'd had to drink, she strode to it with remarkable confidence, as if she were quite at home in this den of queers. I watched her exchange some banter with Carol and I was conscious of the stirrings that usually foretold a bruised heart. Joan returned with two large brandies. My eyebrows shot up.

"Oh, shut up and drink it," Joan admonished, her words beginning to lack clarity. "It's not every night you get a chance to come out to a friend, is it?"

After that, she wanted to know what had caused the enmity between Susie and myself. I did my best to encapsulate the bones of a dispute that had rent the lesbian community in the 1980s. "Susie's very against certain sexual practices. She's convinced that sado-masochism is an extension of Nazism and full of racist overtones. I actually understand what's she saying and I don't doubt her sincerity but she doesn't want to give people the right to choose for themselves."

"So why have you crossed swords about it?"

I told her about the conference. She sat and nodded solemnly, swaying a little before asking me, "And are you into all this SM stuff, then?"

"It depends what boundaries you put on it. There are things I enjoy that some dykes would condemn, but I'm not into serious pain or humiliation, or blood, piss or shit. But if that's how others choose to get off then that's their business, as far as I'm concerned."

I could see then that Joan was starting to slump slightly and her eyes were getting glazed. She mumbled something about getting another drink but I reckoned we'd both had enough by then.

"Come on, I'll take you home."

"Whose home?" she slurred. "Not mine. I'm not going back to Barry tonight."

"All right. We'll go back to my place. It's actually not far from here but we'll take a cab anyway."

In the taxi, she slumped on my shoulder and appeared to fall asleep, even though the journey to my mansion block took under ten minutes. On arrival, she did her best to co-operate but it was as well that my flat was on the second floor and not the fifth. Unlocking the door, I bundled her in, at which point she surprised me by petulantly demanding to be shown around. There wasn't a lot to see: a hallway, sitting room, kitchen, bathroom and two bedrooms. All pleasantly decorated and furnished but nothing really to catch one's eye. It looked comfortable and lived-in.

"Do you live with anyone?" Joan called from the bathroom whilst I was making coffee in the kitchen.

"No," I called back.

"Why not?"

"It's a long story. I'll tell you sometime but not now, I'm too tired." I didn't have the emotional strength to dredge up my "Life with Angela" stories, with their tortuous ending as she bowed to parental pressure and vowed never to see me again. Of course she loved me but she loved the idea of inheriting a fortune even more. That was over two years ago. I'd had plenty of sex in the meantime but I'd not fallen in love, nor found anyone I thought I could live with.

I found Joan sprawled out on my sofa, legs akimbo, arms thrown back over her head. She looked hugely desirable. I could see that she wasn't going to be able to drink the coffee so I sat and drank both mugs, just looking at her helpless, intoxicated body. Then I went to telephone Barry to let him know where she was and that she was safe. It wasn't that I felt any obligation to him but I knew from experience how nerve-wracking it was to wait up for someone who didn't appear, to the point of phoning the police and local hospitals. Angela had played that game with me more than once. Barry laughed uncertainly and thanked me. He didn't actually sound as if he'd been too worried at all – perhaps he too needed a breathing space.

I went back and knelt at Joan's side. I stroked her hair away from her face and kissed her gently. "Joan, come on, I'm going to put you to bed."

She raised her head a little and squinted at me. "Yes, please," she said, a touch wantonly.

I helped her up and guided her to my bedroom. She fell backwards onto the bed and didn't co-operate much as I stripped her and manoeuvred her under the sheets. She had a lovely body, complete with appendectomy scar.

I turned to leave when she called out, "Aren't you coming to sleep with me?"

"No," I said gently, "I'm going to sleep in the other bedroom."

She gave a little giggle. "But I've always wanted to know what lesbians do in bed."

I knew that I was doing the right thing as I called back, "Well, you're not going to find out tonight. Go to sleep. We'll talk in the morning."

"Promise?" she cried, plaintively.

"I promise," I replied and walked honourably away. With a bit of luck, she'd have forgotten all about this by morning, She might even have forgotten that I'd come out to her. Then I remembered that I'd left a copy of *More Serious Pleasures* on the table by my bed. If she woke up and read that, she certainly wasn't going to need me to tell her what lesbians did in bed.

The following morning, when I woke up, I could hear nothing. I glanced over at the little bedside clock which told me that it was a quarter to ten. It occurred to me that Joan might well have woken up earlier and scurried off in disgust or embarrassment or both. The I heard the sound of the kettle boiling and a teaspoon rattling in a cup. I waited and presently Joan gently pushed open the door and put her head around it.

"You're awake. Good. I've made you some coffee."

She looked and sounded remarkably bright for someone who had really tied one on the previous night. She was wearing my towelling dressing gown, from which the belt was missing. As she came into the room, carrying a tray, she made a few half-hearted attempts to keep it together but then gave up and as she sat on the bed, it fell open, revealing all. What a way to wake up, I thought. I always slept naked so when I pulled myself up and leaned back on my elbows she had a clear view of my breasts. At first she looked away from me, uneasy about letting her eyes rest on my flesh but, by degrees, she stole glances and then feasted her eyes unabashedly. My nipples hardened under her gaze.

"Did you sleep all right?" I asked to break the tension.

"Yes, thank you. I woke up at about five o'clock with a raging thirst so I'm afraid I've polished off most of your orange juice and mineral water. Sorry."

"Don't worry about it. I can easily get more. I've got to go shopping at some point today, anyway. It probably helped you avoid getting a real hangover. Were you able to get back to sleep afterwards?"

She reddened slightly and looked at her hands before

replying, "No, I couldn't, so I read that book of yours, the one by your bed."

I felt the colour rise in my own cheeks. I decided to ham it up to try and make light of it. I fell back and pulled the duvet over my head, saying, "Oh God, no. Now you know my most awful secrets."

I expected her to laugh but she made no response at all. Slowly I re-emerged from under the duvet and looked questioningly at her. She was still looking down at her hands. It was hard to see what her emotions were. I wondered whether she was working up to telling me how revolted she was with me and that she didn't want to have anything more to do with me. Instead, she stunned me by looking round directly into my eyes and saying, "Hilary, will you make love to me?"

Instantly, I said, "No." A reflexive and defensive reaction.

Her eyes were pleading gently as she asked, "Why not?"

"A – because I actually like you rather a lot and I don't want to screw up our friendship. B – I'm not in the habit of helping frustrated straight women realize their fantasies." Not any more, I wasn't.

She'd gone back to looking at her hands. Softly she said, "I don't suppose it would make a difference if I told you that I like you rather a lot, too, would it?"

I learned forward and used a finger and thumb to gently bring her face back around to me. Our eyes met and I silently interrogated hers. I could do nothing but believe her. And I could do nothing but accede to her request. I pulled her head down towards mine and our lips met in a tentative first kiss that broke only momentarily before developing into something quite desperate and passionate. We kissed with frenzy and hunger. She was a divine kisser. My hands roamed freely over her breasts and she groaned into me.

She put her hands on my shoulders and pushed me gently

away from her. With a voice raw with lust she said, "Have you got a dildo?" Obviously she hadn't been joking when she said she'd been reading *More Serious Pleasures*.

I dropped my head down to her breasts and hissed, "Yes, yes, yes!" through the teeth I had clamped around one of her nipples.

Her head was thrown back and her hips were grinding on the bed. "Will you show it to me?"

By now, I hoped she was going to let me do more than show it to her. Mentally I was already more than half way to giving her the "hot, hard sex" she'd spoke of with abandon the night before.

"My bedroom," I rasped. "Get in there."

She acquiesced at once. It was as though we'd already tacitly drawn up the essential rules for a session of this kind. Her eyes told me that she trusted me with the power to give her body what it craved. I felt strong and powerful but tender as well. I knew exactly what boundaries were appropriate for this encounter. She wouldn't need to say another word. I encouraged her to stretch out in the middle of my bed and then retrieved my "toy box" from the bottom of my wardrobe. I removed the fabric cuffs and deftly secured her wrists to the bed posts. She licked her lips and wriggled with anticipation. It wasn't often that I had an opportunity to use the double harness but today it was going to come into its own. I stepped into it and brought it up loosely, almost to the top of my legs. Then I selected one of the plump pink silicone dildos from the box and smeared it with "Probe", a wonderful lubricant I'd discovered on a trip to the USA. I pushed it back through one of the harness rings then guided it towards my turgid flesh. With ease and joy I pushed its entire length into me and then secured the flap on the harness. I then took another dildo, greased that up and positioned it through the other harness ring and pulled the straps tight.

I doubted whether Joan needed any additional lubrication but I rubbed a little of the "Probe" onto her swollen red flesh anyway. At the touch of my hand, she whimpered. I got onto the bed and parted her legs enough so that I could kneel between them.

"Joan, look," I said authoritatively. "This is a dildo. I'm going to fuck you with it. Do you understand that?"

She raised her head and her eyes at once widened in surprise at the size of it. I deduced that it was considerably more ample than the tackle attached to "Mr Wham, bam, thank you ma'am" or the supine Barry. She gave a groan of surrender and let her head fall back. I pulled a spare pillow down and pushed it underneath her arse, to lift her slightly. Then I guided the tip of the dildo to the entrance of her wanting cunt. I pushed the head of it in gently, sensing that she would be tight but once I had effected the entry I lowered my body down smoothly, letting the tool slide untrammelled into her vagina. Almost at once it was buried up to its hilt and Joan gave a cry, mingling shock and pleasure. I caught her cry in my mouth as I brought it down to kiss her a little roughly. I kept still for a few moments so she could relax and then I withdrew about half way before pushing into her again.

"Oh my God!" she cried. "I feel like you're in my throat. I've never felt so full before."

I began a steady rhythm of fucking her then, drawing out almost to the tip and then plunging back in. She gasped with each thrust and shortly threw her legs over my hips in an attempt to pull me even further in. On and on we went, on a relentless see-saw until she managed to whisper, "I want to touch myself."

But I wasn't going to allow her to do that, just yet. She'd need to be screaming for release before I'd let her have that satisfaction.

"Not yet," I panted. "I'm getting fucked here, too, and it takes me a lot longer than this to reach the edge. You have to wait."

Cruelty didn't enter into it – if asked, then she would have only described the torment as delicious; my treatment of her firm but fair. I fucked her harder and faster for a few minutes then withdrew and, before she had a chance to ask what was next, I'd undone the cuffs and commanded her to turn over. Without bidding, she put her weight on her knees and presented her arse to me in a way I could only call perfect. Deftly I rubbed her anus with some of the "Probe" and then gently inserted a butt plug into it. At first she squirmed but, as it made its entrance, the only sounds she made were grateful ones. I re-entered her cunt with the dildo and she made inarticulate noises as the two-orifice penetration was completed. Her head down between her arms, I heard her say, "Oh, God, this is heaven. I've never felt anything like this before."

I only fucked her that way for a short time, just long enough to get her so excited that anything was possible and before she knew it I had withdrawn the butt plug and was gently easing the dildo into her tight little bum-hole. Her head came up and she gave a cry of, "Oh, shit" but there was no way she wanted me to stop. Slowly but steadily I filled her up, knowing that no one had ever fulfilled this particular fantasy of hers before. When the dildo's entire length had disappeared inside her, she initiated the fucking rhythm, pulling from me and pushing back.

"Touch yourself!" I commanded and she brought one hand gratefully up to a clit that I imagined was ready to explode, And it wasn't long before explode she did, crying out, "I'm coming! I'm coming!" in a voice so full of primitive release and raw passion that I felt moved by it.

Very gently, I withdrew from her and her spent body

collapsed flat onto the bed. I lay back myself and slipped a hand down to touch my swollen clit and achieved my own glorious release in seconds. I couldn't remember that I had ever felt quite so excited or satiated. As Joan lay recovering, I picked up the butt plug, slipped off the bed and into the bathroom where I undid the harness and thoroughly washed the toys. When I returned to the bedroom, she had rolled over and was staring at the ceiling. As I approached, I could see that she had tears running down the sides of her face, creating small wet patches on the pillow.

"Hey," I said, gently. "Don't cry. Or at least, if you want to cry, tell me what it's about." I bent over her and kissed away the tears.

She was silent for a little while before saying, "All those years I've been denying what I wanted. All those times I've told myself I was sick or perverted and now I know that I'm not. For the first time in my life, I've let my body experience true physical pleasure and I love myself for it." She looked up at me and murmured, "Thank you," rather shyly. My heart was lost at that moment. The power shifted to her and I began to feel that my fate was being prepared to hang in the balance.

I put on my dressing gown and went to make a post-coital coffee. I told Joan she was welcome to take a shower and the next time I saw her was when she came fully clothed into the living room, where the coffee and I were waiting for her. We drank in silence. Conversation on any level seemed impossible. She drained her mug and took it out to the kitchen.

Then she returned to stand in front of me and said, "I'm going home now. I'll see you on Monday."

I stood up to go to the door with her where she spontaneously hugged me and kissed me firmly on the lips. Her face was inscrutable. What had happened between us had triggered something off inside her and I understood that she needed space to think about it. I didn't say a word as she left.

Apart from when I went out to do the shopping, I spent the rest of the weekend alone in contemplation and, increasingly, regret. I recognized that I really did feel quite deeply for Joan and I was walking along that slim ridge that separates friendship and intimacy. Yes, I'd had one-night stands before, neither expecting nor wanting anything more than a few hours' gratification. But a part of me longed for commitment, for romance, for a soul-mate and I knew this didn't come easy. I'd envisaged a slow, polite, getting-to-know-you process with a woman with whom the path to love was gentle and unhurried but true and unwavering. I tortured myself with memories of what I'd allowed to take place between Joan and me. I tried to be objective about the state our friendship had reached before that Friday night and whether therein lay the basis for something much deeper. I agonized over the notion that I had simply been an experiment for her, a self-confessed frustrated straight woman, and envisaged her now taking her new demands to Barry or finding another man to continue what I had started. One thing was for sure: we were never going to be able to look at each other with quite the same eyes again and that both frightened and excited me.

I was sick with dread as I got in to my office on Monday. Joan and I didn't work in the same room but we normally greeted each other soon after arrival and hers was always earlier than mine. Gingerly, with my heart in my throat and my hands trembling. I went along the corridor to find her. As I put my head around the door of her room, one of her staff greeted me with the news that Joan was going to be in late because of an unspecified "domestic crisis". I immediately pictured her having wild early morning sex with a newly inspired Barry. My discomfiture was magnified a thousand times. Breathing normally became an effort, my breakfast threatened to reappear and my concentration was shot to pieces. I emerged later that morning from a pre-Brussels meeting, not having heard a word anyone else had said. I was just lucky that no one was choosing to disagree with the line I was proposing to take and so I could sit and be completely insular. As we left the room I was dimly aware of someone remarking that I looked pale and asking if I felt all right. From somewhere, I mustered a smile and said I was just a little tired before I went, like an automaton, back to my room.

On my desk was a note from Joan, ripped from one of those secretarial type notebooks. It said simply "When you're free, come and see me." I sat down and swallowed hard. What interpretation could I put on those words? There was nothing for it but to go and face the music. It took me a hundred years to walk the thousands miles of corridor to her room. Her mouth gave me the same smile she always gave me but her eyes said much more. I noticed then that there was a large suitcase by her desk.

"Oh, hi, Hilary," she said brightly. "I've got one or two problems in the flat just now and I was wondering if I might come and stay with you."

It was hard not to run to her and kiss her wildly there and then but I returned her controlled smile and said, "Of course, no problem. I'll be leaving here early this evening as I have to go to Brussels tomorrow. I can show you everything you need to know tonight."

"Great. I'll look forward to it," she said, in a tone the suggestiveness of which was not lost on me. I left the room, licking my lips.

ALL SHE WANTED

Debra Diana Blue

Another dream of being so close to her. All the lovely lesbians I could fall for and leave it to me to fall for a straight, married woman. Jacqueline works with me and she's my dear friend. I lusted for her grace, sweetness and her form. Only in my dreams did she feel the same way about me. The dreams were hot, but more on a sensuous level. We never actually touched, but I would wake up panting as if I'd known the full flavor of her body.

Jacqueline bounced into the office late and breathless, as usual . . . Explaining something about dropping her kids off.

"No need to apologize," I told her.

She took off her coat, revealing a form-fitting black sweater dress with dolman sleeves and the black velvet spike heeled pumps I adored. "You're quiet, this morning," she said. "Anything wrong?"

"Yeah, I had another dream about you that had my pussy throbbing when I woke up," I thought. "No, Hon, just planning my day," I replied. I was a bit embarrassed and probably blushing when she looked up and caught me staring at her.

"What is it?" she asked.

"I was just admiring your braids. How long have you had them now?" Nice save, Deb, I thought.

"About six weeks; it's time to get a fresh do, girl."

She had long braids just grazing her shoulders. They formed a frame around her pretty brown face.

She was caramel-colored, 5 foot 5 inches, probably about 130 lbs, tight body and didn't even work out. Damn her. She had a beautiful, oval face, never wore makeup, and didn't need to. A widow's peak and a sexy gap between her two front teeth. Sigh. Only in my dreams I thought.

"Did you make coffee?" she asked.

"No, Hon, I didn't think about it," I replied

"Good, let's make a pumpkin spice run," she said, smiling.

"That sounds damned good," I said, while getting my coat.

We let the secretary know that we would be gone for awhile. I love pumpkin spice cappuccino; it was a special blend most of the convenience stores and coffee shops served during the winter holiday season.

When she got in the car, her dress rose high above her knees. I patted her left knee and teased, "You'd better cover up those gams; don't want me getting too excited; remember, I'm single."

"O, girl, stop," she said, while pulling down her dress. She was silent for a moment "Seriously, Deb, would I be your type?"

I looked at her. "Type?" I said. "Honey, I don't have a type. I don't categorize women by type. I find you very attractive. Why?" I teased. "Are you trying to be my girl?"

"Stop, you're making me blush," she said.

We were riding in silence, when she said, "Hey, can you believe Whittman-Greyson sending us to the hospitality convention in Atlanta?"

"I know", I replied. "What were they thinking?"

We went into the store, picked up our coffee and some pastries. "So . . . are you packed" she asked.

"No way; I'll throw some things into a bag and be happy."

Friday morning . . .

I met Jacqueline at the airport; she was a nervous flyer and I was always as giddy as a child was on Christmas morning. We checked our bags, ate a light breakfast and waited till our plane was ready to board.

"So how's Ray going to fare alone with the kids? Will he be calling you every five minutes?" I asked.

She rolled her eyes. "Girl, you know my husband well."

We boarded the plane and I eagerly took my window seat. Jacqueline said she didn't see how I could stand it.

"Did you take your pill? I don't want you freaking out the passengers," I said.

She replied, "I'll be fine; I'm going to read my magazine until I drift off. You just hold my hand."

We started pushing back from the gate and Jacqueline closed her eyes. I took her hand in mine, kissed it and held it to my breast. "You're gonna be all right," I told her. Holding her hand against my breast made me tingle; I wondered if her thighs were as tender as I'd imagined. The plane started down the runway and I felt her tense up. "Relax," I said as I kissed her hand again.

I looked over at her and tears were streaming from her tightly shut eyes. Once we were airborne, she relaxed a little. I took a tissue and dabbed at her eyes. Our faces were close enough that I could have stolen a kiss.

"We've got to stop meeting like this," I said.

She cracked up laughing. "Thanks Deb, I needed that. I'm glad this is a direct flight," she said, beginning to relax.

I leaned back in my seat to see if I could catch a nap. We had to check into the hotel and report to the conference center at 9 a.m. Just as I was about to disrobe some scantily clad goddess, Jacqueline says "Deb, I'm reading this survey of married women who say they're safe, secure and happy. I bet they would trade all that in for one night of passion. I know sometimes I would."

I was stunned to hear her say this; from where I stood, it looked like she had it all. "You mean, Ray doesn't knock it out of the park?" I laughed.

"Shit, girl, Ray hardly comes to bat, if you know what I mean. And when he does, it's kind of methodical; I usually let him doze off and go do my own thing."

"O, stop," I told her. "You're turning me on." And I meant it. The thought of her waxing herself "poetically" was causing my pussy to throb.

"Since I've known you, you seem to have had a few passionate flings. Makes me think that you lesbians are having all the fun." She laughed.

"Well, yeah, I've had a time or two of passion – life is simpler since I've stopped searching for a soulmate. I guess you can't have it all, eh? I mean, you and Ray get along so well: you share everything."

She said, "I know, but I want the earth to move, I want for my eyes to roll back in my head, once in awhile."

I looked at her and said, "Jacqueline, you've got what counts; you've been reading too many Harlequin romances . . . kisses swept away with passion as the waves crash against the shore, yatta yatta yatta."

We both laughed, but I understood where my friend was coming from. A woman wants to be turned out, every now and then. I dozed off until I felt the plane touch down in Atlanta. I looked over at Jacqueline and saw she was relieved to be on the ground. We claimed our baggage and called for the hotel shuttle. In minutes we were checking into the beautiful Vista International Hotel in downtown Atlanta. Once in our room, we hung up our clothes and put out our toiletries.

The room was beautiful, of course, enhanced with all of our clutter. There was a balcony overlooking the pool and lush gardens. We had just enough time to shower, change, collect our conference material and get to the welcome seminar. We rode up to the eighteenth floor in stock silence; I was hoping that the seminar wouldn't prove too long and boring. I was watching Jacqueline and recalled seeing her jump out of the shower and unwrap and oil her braids. She stood there completely naked, unaware that I was watching her from behind the shower curtain. Her breasts jiggled deliciously and I wondered what they would feel like in my hands, what those pert nipples would taste like in my mouth.

I slid my soapy hands over my own breasts as I watched her naked body and wished I was lucky enough to be one of those beads of water running down her sweet ass. While I was squeezing my nipples, my clit began to stir. I put my hand between my legs and rubbed my soapy fingers over my clit and pussy to quench the fire that watching her had started. I never took my eyes off her as I was rocked by a very powerful orgasm. I bit my lip to keep from moaning out loud. As if on cue, she looked at her watch and announced that we had thirty minutes to get to the seminar. I emerged from the shower wearing a towel.

"You OK?" she asked. "You look flushed."

I almost thanked her for the delicious treat I'd just experienced.

"I'm fine, Hon." I brushed past her and stepped into my silk undies.

"Mmm, nice," she said, as she ran her hand over my stomach, causing goose bumps in places I didn't know I had.

"Quit it," I told her.

"Keep hanging with me and I'll have you all femmed up," she said, laughing at my discomfort.

"Bullshit," I hollered after her as she went onto the balcony.

We reached the eighteenth floor and entered a huge auditorium with a few hundred people. We looked like lost kids on the first day of school. Jacqueline and I made out our nametags and settled in for a two-hour lecture.

Two hours later . . .

"Girl, I could not wait to get the hell out of there," she said.

I nodded with a sigh of relief and said, "We're free until Monday. What do you want to do?" Before she answered I said, "Personally, I want to find some sweet thing and ravage her."

Jacqueline's face fell. "I know you're not gonna shack up with somebody and leave me all alone."

"I was kidding," I said. "Let's eat, I'm starved."

"Let's get room service and take a nap. I got up way too early." She yawned.

I looked at her. "I don't want to sleep. I can sleep at home. We can order room service and I'll check out the gym and pool while you nap."

"Good deal," she agreed.

We ordered salad platters with iced tea; the food took forty-five minutes to come. She had changed into shorts and a T-shirt; she looked so cute, almost like a college girl.

I know I was staring, when she asked, "What? Is my fly open?"

I laughed. "No. But mine is about to be."

Lunch finally arrived and we devoured tuna salad, devilled eggs, garden salad and crackers with cheese spread. She lay across the bed, reading her magazine. "Answer some of these survey questions," she said.

"No way," I replied.

"Oh, come on," she whined. "It'll be fun."

"OK," I sighed.

1. At what age did you lose your virginity?

"Nineteen," I said.

"Wow, late bloomer. Fourteen, for me."

"Remember, I had sexuality issues; besides, you were a ho," I teased her.

2. Ever had sex with a moss? (Member of the Same Sex)

"Duh, I'm a lesbian," I said.

"No," she said.

3. Would you be interested in sex with a moss?

"Pardon the pun but, damn straight," I said.

"Sorta," she said.

"What does 'sorta' mean?" I asked her, concealing my surprise.

"It means I'm intrigued by the idea," she answered coyly.

"Hmm, have you always felt this way, or did someone pique your interest?" I was clearly fishing.

"Someone piqued my interest . . . End of survey," she said, embarrassed by her admission.

I felt a little weird and agreed that it was a good time to end the survey. I threw some workout stuff in a bag and got ready for the gym. "Enjoy your nap," I said.

"Thanks," she answered, neither one of us making eye contact.

I left the room, wondering if I was being conceited by just knowing that she was talking about me.

I went to the gym and loosened up with a few stretches. The place was full of eye candy and I got an eyeful while riding the stationary bike and jaunting along the treadmill. I couldn't get what Jacqueline said out of my head. More surprising was her demeanor after what she'd said. I'd worked up a good sweat; I enjoyed a hot shower and decided to completely contradict it by going for a swim. The water was ice cold and had my adrenaline pumping. I swam a lap and jumped out of the pool to lie on a lounge chair and just relax. I put on my headphones, laid down a towel, put on my shades and enjoyed my music. I guess I was about to doze as someone touched my leg.

I opened my eyes to see Jacqueline, standing there in a black thong bikini. I shook my head because I thought I might be dreaming.

"I couldn't sleep," she said. She looked like a beautiful island girl. "Wanna splash around with me?" she asked.

I said, "Sure," trying to look unfazed. I was mesmerized; watching her sexy ass saunter toward the pool, I ached to touch it.

She got to the pool steps and inched in like a sissy; I dove in close enough to splash her with water.

"Show me your form, girl," I said.

"You know I can't swim," she admitted.

"What? What kind of a weenie are you? I'm gonna teach you," I threatened.

"Look, I . . ."

I cut her off. "OK, just learn to float and I'll feel better. OK?"

She walked/waded over to me. I made a cradle out of my arms. "Lie back." She was too stiff to relax. She almost fell backwards, but grabbed my neck instead.

"I can't," she said.

We were very close, basically because she was hanging onto me and would not let go.

"Honey, you've got to relax."

She was looking at me in a devilish way; I felt like everyone was watching us. What's wrong with this picture? I thought.

"Well, let me see what I can do," she said. She pushed away from me and back stroked to the end of the pool and back.

"All state high school champion, three years in a row," she announced, with her arms raised in the air like some Olympic medalist.

I just stood there, too stunned to move. "Thanks for nothing," I said and got out of the pool. I was humiliated and embarrassed; not to mention pissed off. I got my things and headed for the elevator.

"Deb, come on, Deb, I'm sorry . . ." she was shouting after me.

I just kept walking.

She caught up with me before the elevator doors closed. "Deb, I'm sorry; it was a joke. I was kidding."

"I don't appreciate being made a fool of, Jacqueline. That was totally unnecessary." I leaned against the wall, I was so mad.

We got to the room and I went straight to the shower; I didn't want to be in the same room with her. The water hit my body and somewhat calmed me down. I knew Jacqueline didn't have a malicious bone in her body, but I had always hated being made to feel stupid. Here I was, concerned for her safety and comfort in the water, and she can swim rings around my dumb ass.

She knocked on the door. "Deb, can I come in?"

I wanted her to go away and respect my hurt feelings. "Give it a rest, Jacqueline; I need to cool off," I said coldly.

"Deb, I feel awful. I need to talk to you." She sounded tearful.

I figured it was another trick; she had shaken my trust. "Then wait till I come out," I said in my nastiest tone.

I took forever in the shower, almost wishing that she would be gone when I came out. I knew she wouldn't be. I opened the door and went to the bedroom; I was still pissed off. She was sitting on the balcony. Looking forlornly out at the city. "Deb, I—"

I cut her off. "The shower's all yours."

She took some things into the bathroom. I sat at the vanity and combed through my went hair. I really wanted to get past this; we had four more days to be here and I didn't want to be miserable the rest of the time. Thirty minutes had passed and I was starting to feel better. The phone rang; it was Jacqueline's husband, Ray.

"Hey, dude," I said. "Yeah, it's all that and a bag 'o' Doritos; she's in the shower. I'll call her. Jacqueline, Ray's on the phone." I tried to sound normal.

She came out in a white terry robe; she'd obviously been crying. I handed her the phone. "Hi, honey . . . nothing, kinda tired. How are the kids?"

I tried not to stare or listen to her conversation.

"No, it's Ray Jr's week for trash and Tiffany's week for dishes. Honey, they're having fun with you." Her son was twelve, her daughter ten. They were adorable.

I looked up and into the mirror; I saw her looking at me. Her eyes were locked on mine.

"Yes, Ray" she said. She looked into me. She walked over and started rubbing my shoulder, sensuously. "Sure, Ray." She moved her hand down to my right breast. I leaned against her. "Uh huh," she said. I was looking into her eyes through the mirror. "Yes, honey," she said in a detached tone.

I put my hand on hers and guided it to my other breast. Her touch was heaven. I turned around on the bench and pulled her to me. I opened her robe and kissed her smooth stomach.

She caught her breath as she said, "Yes, Ray."

I stood up, put my arms around her and kissed her. "Mm hm," she moaned into the phone. I could hear him talking; she pulled her mouth away from mine to say "Ray, I have to go."

She put the phone into its cradle. Never taking her eyes off of mine, she took her robe off and backed toward the bed. I dropped my robe to the floor and climbed on top of her. I kissed her as deeply as I had in my dreams.

She kissed me as if she'd been having those dreams, too. Her mouth was sweet and hungry. I devoured her, but I wanted to savour the lover I had ached for. I stopped kissing her and looked into her eyes. I kissed all over her face, her chin, and her neck. I circled her nipples with my tongue; she moaned, "Yyyes." I rubbed her soft ass, her stomach; I wanted to love every inch of her. I kissed between her breasts. Sweet, perfect breasts. I put my hand between her legs and gently touched her mound. She pushed against me, urging me to explore her deeper. I ran my fingers along the length of her slit while shoving my tongue into her mouth. To say that this is a dream come true is an understatement.

Her pussy was wet and inviting, I stopped kissing her long enough to bring my wet fingers to my nose and put them into my mouth. I closed my eyes and tasted sheer ambrosia. I had to taste her. I slid down her body; she lay back and closed her eyes. I planted tiny kisses in her public hair then I parted her lips with my tongue. I breathed her in, and then I blew my warm breath on her clit. She moaned her approval; I kissed my way down to her asshole and back to her precious love bud. Finally I touched the very tip of it with my tongue and flicked it back and forth a few times. She gasped as if in shock. I wanted this to last forever. I wanted to taste and inhale her for an eternity. I moved down to her pussy to taste the nectar that was escaping her. Nothing could be sweeter at this moment than inhaling her musk and tonguing her juices.

She whispered something in French.

I buried my face in her pussy, I ran my tongue from her clit to her asshole, and I stuck my tongue into her copiously flowing pussy. I was carried away as she undulated her wetness against my face; I was lost in her. As sweet as my dreams had been, they had not come close to what we were experiencing at this moment. I was covered with her flow. I put her rock hard clit in my mouth and ran my tongue over it; I sucked and licked it. Marveling at the hardness of it in my mouth. By this time she had grabbed my hair and was riding my mouth. She was in control, moving toward her moment. I was in awe of her passion.

Sensing the closeness of her orgasm, I reached up and grabbed her nipples, pushing her completely over the edge. She stiffened up, to an almost sitting position. My mouth was her seat. She held her breath, tightened her fingers in my hair and screamed – no, wailed – long, loud, lascivious. She threw sparks in every direction. Her heavenly sounds completely filling my head. She was pumping herself against my face in short tense bursts as her voice trailed off. As wave after wave hit her, I squeezed her nipples, causing her to moan gutturally. When it was over and her pleasure subsided, she fell back to the bed, completely wiped out. I lay beside her and gathered her in my arms. She kissed my mouth, and my face.

She said, "About earlier: all I wanted was for you to save me." And then she was asleep.

PETRA AND OTHER IDENTITIES

Carolyn Gammon

My relationship with Frau Klein did not develop quickly. For the first six months, in fact, she couldn't remember my name. It was just as well as I was working for her under an assumed name. But when she did remember it, she would use it with great zeal.

"Peeetraa!" Calling me down from upstairs. Then, before I could turn off the vacuum cleaner, I'd hear the next "Peeee-traaa!" even more drawn out, almost sung. I'd rush my feet in short-clipped anxious steps. "Petra," said Frau Klein, pulling me in tightly with one long arm, "Petra, these blinds need dusting." She would point to the blinds as if they were a view of the Rockies, her long fingers tracing the peaks. "There, you see, there, Petra." Then, taking my hand and leading me to the vast array of solvents, vinegar-based cleaners and environment-friendly acids, "I think, Petra," she'd say, "I think this will do!" She selected a spray bottle with the attention one might give to selecting an engagement ring. We would then hasten back to the waiting, pouting blinds and Frau Klein would show me how until the job was almost done. Perhaps she really liked cleaning better than selling real estate, but the former was my job and the latter hers, so there remained only these orchestrated ways she could get around to it.

"And, Petra," she added.

"Yes, Frau Klein?" I'd answer, and in fact had said little else in six months.

"Petra, would you *please* turn off that vacuum cleaner when I'm on the phone."

Now, I liked to please Frau Klein. At fifteen Deutsch Marks an hour, anyone would, but frankly I often couldn't hear the phone when I was upstairs with a motor in my ear. Nevertheless, I once again answered, "Yes, Frau Klein," knowing in some way she needed one thing to complain about. In six months, I'd perfected the office cleaning job to an efficient art.

Frau Klein was two meters high and wore six-centimeter heels, thick heels, so she could still rush over freshly washed bathroom tiles and never slip. She wore a hand-sized gold heart on a thick chain about her neck. Her dresses were multi-layered, multi-textured and bright black or stabbing pink; her makeup was also multi-layered-textured and crimson. I wore jeans, a T-shirt and no makeup. Her gloves were fake leopard-skin; mine were real rubber. Her voice was loud, fast and emphatic, often verging on chainsaw stridency with certain male clients. I spoke in monosyllables and we got along.

I'm not sure exactly why we got along. Nothing promised it except my weekly salary. Maybe because she more or less left me alone, except when she huggingly wanted to show me some small task. I appreciated not being asked questions, why I had a German name and couldn't speak much German. It had never occurred to her to ask. Why I sometimes didn't recognize my name when she called it, she didn't seem to notice. Why my address didn't correspond with my telephone number or the birth date on my job contract with my looks. All of this was water off a swan's neck to Frau Klein. Somehow, in six months, we'd developed a good working relationship.

But then, one day, Frau Klein held onto a hug. Maybe it had happened before and I'd not noticed but, one day, the amount of dust on the computer screen just did not correspond to the long-armed squeeze around my shoulder. Frau Klein herself seemed confused, looking from the screen to my crushed body, to the screen, repeating three times that only the well wrung-out leather chammie was to be used on the screens. I felt her fingers press into my biceps as she looked directly into my face for something.

"Yes, Frau Klein," I said, to make her more comfortable. "I couldn't find the chammie today," I added, trying to diffuse her perplexity.

"Petra," she said, turning to face me and hold me by both shoulders, "Petra, I know nothing about you!"

Frau Klein seemed truly taken aback. So was I.

"What did you say?" I asked, always using the polite and distanced form of "you". Whenever I didn't want to hear, I pretended I'd missed the German.

But Frau Klein was a straightforward business woman, not easily dissuaded. "I know nothing about you, Petra," she repeated. "Now, sit down; I'm going to make us tea and you will tell me about yourself."

"I just want to finish the upstairs bathroom," I told her, to stall for time.

I could have left, I suppose. The pressed part of my biceps knew what was coming. I could have never come back to the job. All she had on me was a telephone number and a false name. But the money was good and I'd had a hard time finding other illegal work. So each day when I was finishing up but still on paid time, Frau Klein made tea and sat me down to chat. My German became purposefully even more limited and basic. Any question I didn't want to answer, I said simply I didn't understand. But, bit by bit, Frau Klein was casing me out. She may not have even known she was. Her life seemed so beyond contact to me. I cleaned her house, too, and wondered how anyone could live in a place which they never really touched. Even meals she served guests were catered. When I would tell her about a light bulb that had gone, she treated it like a strange, almost wonderful phenomenon and would ask me immediately to go buy another one. At the office, no one would ever guess that two-meter Frau Klein, the boss who had brought her real estate business from a home operation to a penthouse suite in Schöenberg, was fascinated by the changing of light bulbs. But later, when the room was lit, she would thank me and exclaim what a good job I'd done – as if she couldn't have herself.

Somehow, Frau Klein had lived forty-five years in Berlin and never met a dyke. And she wasn't about to meet one too fast.

"Petra," Frau Klein would ask, "what do you do after work?"

My life, as told, sounded so nondescript that she must have thought I checked into a convent. But by the fourth or fifth week I must have said "my friend" rather than "a friend" one too many times.

"Petra, tell me about your friend."

My friend, too, ended up sounding like a generic student, a frame with no picture. Frau Klein would sit across the spotless glass tabletop and stare at me as one might stare at a window rather than the view outside; then she went on to something else.

I couldn't have know, it was coming. Maybe I should have because that day she'd taken off her spike-toed weapons while we sat.

"Petra," she said, "I'm looking for a bit of . . . excitement," she finished, lowering her glasses to look at me directly.

I held my hand to my brows, covering my eyes as if from too bright a light.

"Petra—" she reached across the table and touched my chin, startling me "– I want—" she paused again "– more than this." She took her hand away and gestured at the mahogany furniture, the indoor manicured winter garden, the buzzing phones and computers.

I was quietly pushing my chair back when she continued, "And, I'm prepared to pay."

I made a date with Frau Klein. Suddenly the roles were switched and I was the one pointing. "Lower heels," I told her. "Less makeup, a plainer dress." I'd seen her wardrobe many times. I knew her plainest dress would still not pass but I wanted her to feel somewhat herself.

She walked into Pour Elle at nine, one Friday night. I was seated. I'd planned things to be in control. She looked bewildered but, on seeing me, strode over.

"Petra," she said immediately, "I've passed this place so many times and never knew!" Her eyes were shining. "Petra," she added, "you look lovely!"

I was wearing my new button-up black Levis, a white shirt, tailored suit coat and leather tie. My long red hair was freshly washed, the bangs blown back. Frau Klein had on four-centimetre heels and a black dress which pulled tightly at the waist and flared in many pleats. No one stared; no one else was in the bar.

"So *this* is where you meet," she said, looking in awe. "I like it," she added. The plush velvet cushions on the couch where she sat were not so different from those in her own house and the chrome-framed furniture was the same style as in the office. She was about to go for an inspection when the waitress came by. Frau Klein appraised the lesbian like a diamond, her hair shaved on one side with a triangle mound remaining, a flip wave over the front, a starched white blouse and a nose ring.

Frau Klein eased back into her chair and ordered a double martini. I ordered orange juice. Frau Klein was excited. She took my hand and squeezed it under the table.

As the evening progressed, Frau Klein became more and more excited. We hardly spoke, she was so engaged in thoroughly surveying each new customer. "That one," she would say, pointing or nodding her head discreetly, "is she really?" I would raise my eyebrows and smile. A grey-haired bar-goer with a short blunt cut wearing patchwork flannel asked her for a light in passing. Frau Klein leaned in conspiratorially. "Her, too?" Flannel meant nothing to Frau Klein.

By midnight, the jukebox had run through Tina Turner's entire repertoire one too many times.

"Frau Klein."

"Please, call me Antya."

"Frau Klein," I continued, "we have to go now." She didn't question my authority. I helped her into her coat, she helped me into mine and, arm in arm, we walked out.

She wanted to drive me home but I insisted on taking the U-Bahn. "That's five hundred Marks please," I said.

She didn't hesitate and had a stiff new bill prepared.

"See you Monday," I said, using the polite form.

"See you, then," she chimed, using the familiar.

* * *

Nothing changed at the office. We still had tea. Sometimes between roadrunner bouts on the phones, I caught Frau Klein smiling to herself or at me. The other office workers were oblivious. They even joined us for tea, occasionally.

A month went by before she asked me for another date.

"Petra," she announced, one special day, when she had bought a four-layered cream cake worth more than two hours of my salary, "I would like to meet women."

I wondered why she didn't go back to the bar herself.

"I would like to . . . Petra, you know what I mean."

"Yes, Frau Klein," I answered. Well, I didn't quite know if she meant that night, with me, or what, but I proposed another meeting place. Two a.m., I told her.

This time, I met her outside. We were buzzed into Lipstick after being inspected through the peep – hole which surely only reached Frau Klein's chest. The bar was smoke and body-thick as I led my date to a table where we could see the dance floor. She ordered a double martini, I ordered an orange juice. We danced. Frau Klein was clearly the tallest on the floor, the one with the most bracelets and make-up and the one most at ease in heels. She seemed to encourage the accidental bumping with other dancers and came off the floor perspiring and smiling. I didn't know how Frau Klein was going to meet other women. Everyone seemed coupled and I didn't know how to introduce my date. Hello, this is my boss. Hello, you must meet Frau Klein. Hello, hello. Finally I suggested she visit the bathroom alone.

Returning, she was almost breathless. "A bald-headed young woman offered me ecstasy!"

"Did you take it?" I asked.

"There!?" She was astonished. "Look, there she is!" She nudged me enthusiastically.

The dyke joined another with leather chaps and heels almost

rivalling Frau Klein's. I recognized her as a woman I'd mistaken for a man one time when I had walked into a unisex toilet at a lesbian dance. She had been peeing standing up.

"Don't you want to get to know her?" I asked.

"Oh, yes!" Frau Klein said decidedly, "but not tonight."

At four a.m., the crowd was thinning. I told Frau Klein that the U-Bahn wouldn't open until six. She took my hand in both of hers, pressing crisp notes into my palm, five hundred and twenty for a taxi.

The next time, I proposed a date. When Frau Klein arrived at the Women's Centre, I was busy in the back and someone else ushered her in. The dyke at the door later told me that she had said "keep the change" when paying twenty Marks for a four-Mark entry. When I came out, it was five minutes before show time. I was wearing a dress, a tight black polyester wool which clung to my body like a snakeskin to a snake.

"Oh, Petra! You look lovely!"

I had very little time to concentrate on Frau Klein and told her the performance would begin soon.

She held onto my wrist. "Petra, where am I?"

In a Women's Centre, I told her, suddenly wondering what she thought a Women's Centre was.

The organizer introduced me and a translator worked with me as I presented my erotic poetry and my book. I didn't dare look at Frau Klein the entire performance. In the question period, I had no choice.

"Petra." She was the first to speak. Everyone turned to look at her. "Petra," she repeated, seemingly having forgotten that I had been introduced by my real name and the poster on the wall near her head clearly announced that my name was not Petra. "I think that was just great!" she said clapping her hands together long after the applause. "But I have a question . . . is it true that the lesbian women, like in that "Bad Lesbian Sex" poem, is it true that they sometimes don't talk to each other and have bad sex?"

"No, I just wrote that for poetic effect," I answered.

Everyone laughed except Frau Klein.

"No, really, I wrote that poem 'cause it's mainly experiences I've had. There's a lot of sex happening that's not so healthy but if we talk about it, then there's hope that we can have really good, life-affirming sex with each other."

Frau Klein thanked me for my answer.

I didn't notice when she left but, after the discussion, she was gone. The bookseller said she had bought ten copies.

Frau Klein and I never went on another date. I kept cleaning at the office and at her home and we still sometimes had tea. She occasionally remarked on how nice I looked that night. Sometimes she wore her four-centimetre pumps to the office. Sometimes she seemed tired in the mornings, as if she'd been out late, as if real estate wasn't the first thing on her mind. But I never saw her at any of the bars. And the ecstasy woman had many partners but not Frau Klein.

Long after my job had ended, I had another reading in Berlin. On my way into the Lesbian Archives to prepare, an organizer handed me a bouquet of flowers. Inside the tiny envelope, a card: "*Viel Glück*" and a crisp folded five hundred Deutsch Marks.

A STORY FOR LOUISE

Julie MacLusky

Louise and I were breaking up, slowly but surely. A good sign was that, instead of spending this gloomy, dark Saturday afternoon in bed, we had brought work home and were sitting at the dining room table, in front of our computers. She was writing a treatment about the sighting of angels for her documentary company, and I was supposed to be fixing my departmental budget to the year 2003. The spreadsheet was glowing on the laptop, but I was not working.

Looking across at Louise, intent on her writing, I felt sorry for the passion we had lost. The window behind her was smeared with relentless rain. Moving the spreadsheet to one side, I started writing Louise a story.

The ferry chugged slowly around the coastline of southern Crete. Glancing up between the pages of my book, I noticed that the land was slowly changing.

The gravelly beaches of the West, which were overhung by dark cliffs, were being replaced by small farms dotted with olive trees.

On a table close to me, a mother was slicing feta cheese, tomatoes and thick Greek bread and making sandwiches for her family. The sunniest part of the ferry's deck was crowded with couples and groups of backpackers. Some played backgammon or chess on tiny magnetic traveling boards, other played cards, and some were content to doze, topping up their tans, sipping cold beers.

The bench I sat on offered the only shade on this part of the deck. Having fallen asleep on the beach on my first day, I still needed to cover my shoulders with a beach towel, and avoid exposure to the relentless Mediterranean sun.

After so many years of traveling with this girlfriend or that, I was enjoying being alone in a crowd. A straight crowd, too, with no distractions. My main goal on this trip had been to work through a pile of paperback books, and move every two days.

The ferry chugged through the sea with a comforting, rolling rhythm, giving out the oily smell of a well-tended, old engine. Even on this short trip to Matala, I was determined to read and maintain an expression stern enough to discourage the chance of any connection with strangers. However, being alone for six months, or perhaps something about the boat, was making it hard for me to maintain my solitary reading habit.

For amusement, I caught myself imagining what each of the women on the deck would look like when they came. Some were noisy, some looked pained, some froze, some were drama queens, all were beautiful at the moment of abandon, giving up their control to me.

Putting my book down, I walked into the dark shade at the far end of the deck. As I took deep breaths from the salt-churned air, the breeze made the hairs on my forearms stand on end. Then, cooled down, I made my way back through the sunbathers to my seat. Back to the book. The author was travelling by train through Poland and finding the people kind.

Something moved past my book. I looked up to see a pair of lithe brown legs squeezed together to avoid touching mine. Only a serious stretch of time on the islands could produce a tan that deep. I wondered what her tan line would look like, if her skin was a light olive in the bikini area, or if she'd been sunbathing nude, and baked dark brown all over.

She was wearing an ankle chain so thin that I only saw it because the sun hit the gold as she searched for a seat amongst the backpackers. The ankle chain helped me get back into my book, dismissing Miss Tanned Legs as just another straight woman thinking that an ankle chain would make her seem sexy, exotic and loose.

Back to the travel book, where the author was eating cold greasy potatoes. I thought about exchanging the book in Matala, when something flashed on the edge of the page – a glint from the ankle chain, which was up on the seat next to me.

"Wow, look at the island!" the owner said.

I looked. The same view. Olive trees and farms. What was much more interesting was the slim brown calf, only about six inches from my elbow.

"Yeah, I've been in the islands six weeks, in case you were going to ask."

For the first time, I looked up at her face. Her eyes were the same azure blue as the shallow patches in the clear sea which rolled beneath us. Aside from the ankle chain, she was wearing binoculars around her neck, a blue sundress, and well-worn leather sandals.

"No, I wasn't going to ask. I might have been wondering, you have such a good color, I'll admit it."

She leaned over and ran a finger along my book, then turned it over to see the name of the author.

"He's good but he seems to hate everyone he meets."

"Good for me, right now."

"Oh, yeah? What could be more interesting than Gorky?"

"Gorky?"

"Yeah, you can see it from here; d'you want to look through my binoculars?"

She sat next to me and the sun-heated skin of her forearm touched mine. My mind was working, fast. I did not want her to think she could take the initiative here.

She fixed the binoculars on the Roman garrison and handed them to me. I focused them on the shoreline, the point where the sandy beach was visible through the bulging sea but, when I tried to move them inland, it became a blur.

"No, like this."

Her cheek was almost touching me. She put her hands over mine and moved the binoculars. Suddenly I could see a miniature city on the hill.

"They built it there, so that they could see us approaching and, from a boat, we couldn't see them. They had time to prepare their defence."

A small boy ran up to us, followed by a straight couple who sat next to her. She squeezed closer to me. I took a chance.

"D'you fancy a beer?"

"Sure, but you have to tell me your name, first."

I told her my name. She said she was called Sandrine, after her mother, who was from Belgium.

"Let's go to the downstairs bar, get out of the sun."

The bar was on the lower deck. It was lined with dark varnished wood and, as we entered, my eyes could only make out the blurred shape of the counter. As they adjusted, I could see that we were alone apart from one other customer, an old truck driver, dozing over an almost empty bottle of retsina. We settled into a corner booth.

She was so beautiful I just wanted to kiss her. She said, "If you like, you can kiss me; you don't have to ask."

For the moment, I pretended not to have understood properly. I leaned into her hot body, stretched my arm along the seat behind her, and asked her how she knew so much about the island. It was important to keep her talking so that I could prolong the physical contact. She was studying archaeology, spending her summer going from site to site with a friend from college. She was passionate about her subject and determined that I should be able to look at a pile of stones on a hill and see a thriving Minoan city. The island was magical to her. Her favorite sites were pre-classical; she was on her way to the most isolated Minoan palace, near Vai, on the far eastern tip of Crete. This city was only just being excavated, its streets revealed to the sun for the first time since an earthquake hit the island, or the shower of ash from the volcano at Santorini buried it.

Through all this I was watching her pulse, racing, in the skin on her neck. I pushed a tendril of her damp black hair back, and saw the pulse quicken.

We kissed. She had plump, juicy lips, a taste of cold beer. My fingers touched her side, the tight skin just above her waist, and she shuddered. I ran my fingers around under her breast and her nipples reacted, jutting out through her thin dress.

She kissed my ear and whispered, "No one can see."

I took my cue and reached for her swollen nipples, through the cloth. Impossible that they could become more prominent but they did. I eased the fabric back and exposed the nipple, moved my lips towards it, kissed it at the side, and pulled the fabric back up.

"God, no."

I kissed her again. She parted her legs, so willing and desperate, which is exactly how I wanted her.

She put a hand on my knee and started to circle it up my inner thigh. I took her hand firmly and held it back while I leaned over, slipped her thin shoulder straps off and pulled her dress down so that I could suck on one nipple while brushing the tip of the other with my palm.

Then I took her hand and lead her so that she was sitting astride me. This way, I had easy access to her breasts. She had not been sunbathing topless – her breasts were a soft gold color, with darker nipples. The perfect size for squeezing together on my cheeks, licking my way up and down the skin between them, while teasing the nipples.

The ferry started to roll more deeply as it turned across the waves and headed towards the port.

She was grinding up and down on my thigh. I moved her to the center, so that I could slide my hand up the inside of her dress. Once I reached the softest skin, on the inside of her thigh, I realized I wouldn't have to ask. As soon as I got to the edge of her pants, I found her juices had spread right through the fabric and made the surrounding skin slippery to the touch.

Inside the cotton pants, she was very hot. I traced the outer, delicate folds of skin first, around and around the slippery clitoris then over and over it when I'd worked out how much pressure she wanted.

Once she was breathing very hard, I pushed my thumb up inside her and said, "Move."

She was surprised, but started gently raising and lowering herself, almost experimentally, following the rhythm of the ferry, which was struggling through deep waves towards the shore.

Finding she liked it, she began to move faster and harder. It can take a while to hit the G-spot just so and, when we did, hot liquid squirted out of her, soaking my hand, my legs and forming a pool on the bench.

She grabbed a paper napkin and said, "Will this help?"

I took the beach towel from my shoulders and said, "No, but this will."

The ferry had almost come to a stop, easing its way through the calm waters of the harbor towards the dock. She scrambled back into her dress and grabbed a pen and a napkin from the bar.

"Here, I'm staying at the Sitia Tavern; please call by for me. I have to catch up with my friend."

She ran to fetch her bags. I climbed back to the upper deck and watched the passengers scramble to get off. Amongst the crowds making their way up the quay, I recognized my towel wrapped around Sandrine's neck. Even at a distance of fifty yards, it still looked wet. She was hurrying to catch up with her friend. She didn't look back, but the men gathered on the dock all turned to gaze as she passed, at her walk, which was that of a satiated woman.

Folding the note with Sandrine's hotel address into my back pocket, I thought maybe it was time.

A warm breath on my shoulder warned me that Louise was leaning over me to find out what I was writing. I didn't have time to pull up the spreadsheet to cover my writing.

"I see," she said. "Not working. You don't change."

But I had changed, and I gave the story to Louise, as a farewell present.

LAST TIME

Jo Fisk

So you lie on your back to be fucked? I could imagine it, but won't.

Shock, nausea, pain, jealousy have all given way to Revenge.

We joked about packing my last night on the island, that night we kissed – knowing we would not be together . . . for a while. Not without the unpredictable energy that is anger. The heat coming from your cunt amazed me, standing at the bar, touching lips so softly, the softest hint of breath overwhelming my whole body with desire frustrated.

It's been a few weeks and it's not going to be another post-mortem – no more recrimination.

Don't ask about my life. No longer open for discussion: past or present.

Strange that the door opens with your key that is still in my pocket. Your hallway is fantastically huge and beautiful. Banal, vaguely musical notes and sweet steam drift out as I push the familiar wooden door to the first floor of this grand old building – your floor.

You look OK, nervous, exhausted, compelling me with your eyes. There is no way we're going to eat now. I turn the oven off, stick Glenn Gould's Bach in the CD, light some candles and switch off lights.

I hold you at arm's length for a few seconds and look at you. You took trouble. The gel above your ears, the deep blue shirt. The rest of you blurs as I fix on your eyes.

You start to talk about wine. I raise an eyebrow, like "does it matter?", and you shut up.

I push my body against you hard but quickly so that you sense my body again. You try to touch me and I turn away.

Your wrought iron sofa glints in the street-glow from the window. I take some thick black leather restraints from my jacket and attach them to the corners. I lead you over, hold the back of your neck and bend you forward in order to ease your wrists into place.

Once fastened, you must lean over. I take off your belt and tell you to shake your Levis off. It takes a while and you're getting impatient and confused. Not my problem.

Once they're at your ankles, I take out my anger on you with your belt. Twelve or so red welts cross your ass and thighs. You are too proud to cry out until the last stroke, when you mutter, "Fuck."

I have not spoken a word since I came in. Me, the wordy one, jettisoned in favour of sexual conquest with or without consent.

Shall I rename us? Your "real" name never did suit you; I forgot it once, way back when.

Your sofa consists of contorted welded metal and some well-stuffed white cushions which I rearrange to support your body. You'll need it.

I am keeping all my clothes on. Never again vulnerable here; cynical, brutal – believe it. The safe word is Doubt.

After this I'll be gone, for good, keys through the mail box.

Very slowly, I allow the length of my hard worked-out body to rest on your back, shoulders, legs. You like the tenderness after the naked exposure to the blows of your belt.

To me, it's a dance of contrasts, no emotional engagement. I can feel my straps digging into my muscled ass pulling the silicone I'm packing against my clit, just exactly the right pressure. I could come, standing here, simply moving inside my thick tight black Levis, aware of your desire.

I've been there (sub) – but not with you – exhausted by an unexpected turn of the night, hot wax searing into welts all over my back and legs, the softness of a naked warm body on top of my wounds like a shot of morphine for all the pain exhumed from my grave of a child's mind. No longer "here". Gone to that utopian ecstasy which belongs to those who drink, snort, fuck or starve to oblivion, day-in, day-out, haunting our railway stations and memories.

Don't ever again dare to ask me to speak to you about me, my history, my fears and hopes. Why would I trust?

I am only in this moment, this wanting to come. But there is more. I want to come in you, in the tightest, most sensitive place.

Do I care if it causes pain? No. I care only that there is no lasting damage, no evidence of assault.

I reach for the lube, spilling fat globs all over your naked back, into your very penetrable crack, pulling your Calvins aside, pushing right up inside your asshole with two lube-soaked fingers, hearing you moan in that detached-from-reality sex-craving way of those who have let go. Your pain-threshhold elsewhere.

I could lick you, touch you, even push you now into orgasm, so easily – you are delicate, truly on that edge. Do I pull you back with pain, kisses of leather; or let you stay where you are? My watch: due home ten minutes ago. I unbutton myself and force black silicone into your nervous ass, the angle perfect, still dripping lube onto you and all over the length of my dick, each movement forward bringing me so close to coming, I wonder if I'll collapse. I push harder and you moan in aroused protest.

I fuck you to my own inexorable rhythm. Nothing else matters but this all-absorbing surge through my neck, nipples, cunt, toes. You are no longer here . . . I am totally lost in my own exquisite body-waves, heat and sweat running over my skin, muted breaths, violently shuddering against you.

Seconds pass. I pull out, back away. I sense the want in your body. I lean over your back, undo one of the restraints, leaving your hand in it and you as you are. I check that I am as I was when I arrived, leave your apartment, walk out of the main street door, lock it and chuck your keys in the mail box.

SPEAKING IN TONGUES

Emma Donoghue

"Listen," I said, my voice rasping, "I want to take you home but Dublin's a hundred miles away."

Lee looked down at her square hands. I couldn't believe she'd only spent seventeen years on this planet.

"Where're you staying?" I asked.

"Youth hostel."

I mouthed a curse at the beer-stained carpet. "I've no room booked in Galway and it's probably too late to get one. I was planning to drive back tonight. I've to be at the office by nine tomorrow."

The last of the conference-goers walked past just then and one or two nodded at me; the sweat of the *céilí* was drying on their cheeks.

When I looked back, Lee was grinning like she'd just won the lottery. "So is it comfortable in the back of your van, then, Sylvia?"

I stared at her. She was exactly half my age, I reminded myself. It was not the first time I had been asked that question, but I had thought that the last time would be the last. "As backs of vans go, yes, very comfortable."

The reason I got into that van was a poem.

I'd first heard Sylvia Dwyer on a tape of contemporary poetry in Irish. I'd borrowed it from the library to help me revise for the Leaving Cert that would get me out of convent school. Deirdre had just left me for a boy, so I was working hard.

Poem number five was called Dhá Theanga. *The woman's voice had peat and smoke in it, bacon and strong tea. I hadn't a notion what the poem was about; you needed to know how the words were spelt before you could look them up in the dictionary, and one silent consonant sounded pretty much like another to me. But I listened to the poem every night on my walkman till I had to give the tape back to the library.*

I asked my mother why the name sounded so familiar, and she said Sylvia must be the last of those Dwyers who'd taken over the Shanbally butchers, thirty years before. I couldn't believe she was a local. I might even have sat next to her in Mass.

But it was Cork where I met her. I'd joined the Queer Soc in the first week, before I could lose my nerve, and by midterm I was running their Chocolate-and-Wine evenings. Sylvia Dwyer, down from Dublin for a weekend, was introduced all round by one of her exes in the French Department. I was startled to learn that the poet was one of us – a "colleen", as a friend of mine used to say. Her smooth bob and silver-grey suit were intimidating as hell. I couldn't think of a word to say. I poured her plonk from a box and put the bowl of chocolate-covered peanuts by her elbow.

After that, I smiled at her in Mass once when I was home in Shanbally for the weekend. Sylvia nodded back, very minimally.

Maybe she wasn't sure where she knew me from. Maybe she was praying. Maybe she was a bitch.

Of course I had heard of Lee Maloney in Shanbally. The whole town had heard of her, the year she appeared at Mass with a Sinéad O'Connor headshave and a T-shirt with women's symbols all over it, like some kind of post-modern Virgin Mary. I listened in on a euphemistic conversation about her in the post office queue, but contributed nothing to it. My reputation was a clean slate in Shanbally, and none of my poems had gendered pronouns.

When I was introduced to the girl in Cork, she was barely civil. But her chin had a curve you needed to fit your hand to, and her hair looked seven days old.

On one of my rare weekends at home, who should I see on the way down from Communion but Lee Maloney, full of nods and smiles. Without turning my head, I could sense my mother stiffen. In the car park afterwards, she asked, "How do you come to know that Maloney girl?"

I considered denying it, claiming it was a case of mistaken identity, then I said, "I think she might have been at a reading I gave once."

"She's a worry to her mother," said mine.

It must have been after I saw Sylvia Dwyer's name on a flyer under the title DHÁ THEANGA/TWO TONGUES: A CONFERENCE ON BILINGUALISM ON IRELAND TODAY *that my subconscious developed a passionate nostalgia for the language my forebears got whipped for. So I skived off my Saturday lecture to go to Galway. But only when I saw her walk into that lecture theatre in her long brown leather coat, with a new streak of white across her black fringe, did I realise why I'd sat four hours on a bus to get there.*

Some days I have more nerve than others. I flirted with Sylvia all that day, in the quarter-hours between papers and forums and plenary sessions that meant equally little to me whether they were in Irish or English. I asked her questions and nodded before the answers had started. I told her about Deirdre, just so she wouldn't think I was a virgin. "She left me for a boy with no earlobes," I said carelessly.

"Been there," said Sylvia.

Mostly, though, I kept my mouth shut and my head down and my eyes shiny. I suspected I was being embarrassingly obvious, but a one-day conference didn't leave enough time for subtlety.

Sylvia made me guess how old she was, and I said "thirty?", though I knew from the programme note that she was thirty-four. She said if by any miracle she had saved enough money by the age of forty, she was going to get plastic surgery on the bags under her eyes.

I played the cheeky young thing and the baby dyke and the strong silent type who had drunk too much wine. And till halfway through the evening, I didn't think I was getting anywhere. What would a woman like Sylvia Dwyer want with a blank page like me?

For a second, in that Galway lecture hall, I didn't recognize Lee Maloney, because she was so out of context among the bearded journalists and wool-skirted teachers. Then my memory claimed her face. The girl was looking at me like the sun had just risen, and then she stared at her feet, which was even more of a giveaway. I stood up straighter and shifted my briefcase to my other hand.

The conference, which I had expected to be about broadening my education and licking up to small Irish publishers, began to take on a momentum of its own. It was nothing I had planned, nothing I could stop. I watched the side of Lee's jaw right through a lecture called "Scottish Loan-Words in Donegal Fishing Communities". She was so cute I felt sick.

What was most unsettling was that I couldn't tell who was

chatting up whom. It was a battle made up of feints and retreats. As we sipped our coffee, for instance, I murmured something faintly suggestive about hot liquids, then panicked and changed the subject. As we crowded back into the hall, I thought it was Lee's hand that guided my elbow for a few seconds, but she was staring forward so blankly I decided it must have been somebody else.

Over dinner – a noisy affair in the cafeteria – Lee sat across the table from me and burnt her tongue on the apple crumble. I poured her a glass of water and didn't give her a chance to talk to anyone but me. At this point, we were an island of English in a sea of Irish.

The conversation happened to turn (as it does) to relationships, and how neither of us could see the point in casual sex, because not only was it unlikely to be much good but it fucked up friendships or broke hearts. Sleeping with someone you hardly knew, I heard myself pronouncing in my world-weariest voice, was like singing a song without knowing the words. I told her that when she was my age, she would feel the same way, and she said oh, she did already.

My eyes dwelt on the apple crumble disappearing, spoon by spoon, between Lee's absent-minded lips. I listened to the opinions spilling out of my mouth, and wondered who I was kidding.

By the time it came to the poetry reading that was meant to bring the conference to a lyrical climax, I was too tired to waste time. I reached into my folder for the only way I know to say what I really mean.

Now, the word in Cork had been that Sylvia Dwyer was deep in the closet, which I'd thought was a bit pathetic but only to be expected. However.

At the end of her reading, after she'd done a few about nature and a few about politics and a few I couldn't follow, she rummaged round in her folder. "This poem gave its name to this conference," she said, "but that's not why I've chosen it." She read it through in Irish first; I let the familiar vowels caress my ears. Her voice was even better live than on the old tape from the library. And then she turned slightly in her seat and, after muttering, "Hope it translates," looked over her silver-rimmed glasses and read it straight at me.

> *your tongue and my tongue*
> *have much to say to each other*
> *there's a lot between them*
> *there are pleasures yours has over mine*
> *and mine over yours*
> *we get on each other's nerves sometimes*
> *and under each other's skin*
> *but the best of it is when*
> *your mouth opens to let my tongue in*
> *it's then I come to know you*
> *when I hear my tongue*
> *blossom in your kiss*
> *and your strange hard tongue*
> *speaks between my lips*

The reason I was going to go ahead and do what I'd bored all my friends with saying I'd never do again was that poem.

I was watching Lee as I read *Dhá Theanga* straight to her, aiming over the weary heads of the crowd of conference-goers. I didn't look at anyone else but Lee Maloney, not at a single one of the jealous poets or Gaelgóir purists or smirking gossips, in case I might lose my nerve. After the first line, when her eyes fell for a second, Lee looked right back at me. She was leaning her cheek on her hand. It was a smooth hand, blunt at the tips. I knew the poem off by heart, but tonight I had to look down for safety every few lines.

And then she glanced away, out the darkening window, and I suddenly doubted that I was getting anywhere. What would Lee Maloney, seventeen last May, want with a scribbled jotter like me?

I sat in that smoky hall with my face half-hidden behind my hand, excitement and embarrassment spiralling up my spine. I reminded myself that Sylvia Dwyer must have written that poem years ago, for some other woman in some other town. Not counting how many other women she might have read it to. It was probably an old trick of hers.

But all this couldn't explain away the fact that it was me Sylvia was reading it to tonight in Galway. In front of all these people, not caring who saw or what they might think when they followed the line of her eyes. I dug my jaw into my palm for anchorage, and my eyes locked back onto Sylvia's. I decided that every poem was made new in the reading.

If this was going to happen, I thought as I folded the papers away in my briefcase during the brief rainfall of applause, it was happening because we were not in Dublin surrounded by my friends and worklife, nor in Cork cluttered up with Lee's, nor above all in Shanbally where she was born in the year I left for college. Neither of us knew anything at all about Galway.

If this was going to happen, I thought many hours later, as the cleaners urged Sylvia and me out of the hall, it was happening because of some moment that had pushed us over an invisible line. But which moment? It could have been when we were shivering on the floor waiting for the end-of-conference céilí band to start up, and Sylvia draped her leather coat round her shoulders and tucked me under it for a minute, the sheepskin lining soft against my cheek, the weight of her elbow on my shoulder. Or later, when I was dancing like a berserker in my vest, and she drew the back of her hand down my arm and said, "Aren't you the damp thing." Or maybe the deciding moment was when the fan had stopped working and we stood at the bar waiting for drinks, my smoking hips armouring hers, and I blew behind her hot ear until the curtain of hair lifted up and I could see the dark of her neck.

Blame it on the heat. We swung so long in the céilí that the whole line went askew. Lee took off all her layers except one black vest that clung to her small breasts. We shared a glass of iced water and I offered Lee the last splash from my mouth, but she danced around me and laughed and wouldn't take it. Up on the balcony over the dance floor, I sat on the edge and leaned out to see the whirling scene. Lee fitted her hand around my thigh, weighing it down. "You protecting me from falling?" I asked. My voice was meant to be sardonic, but it came out more like breathless.

"That's right," she said. It occurred to me that I didn't think I had ever heard this child say more than a dozen words in one go.

Held in that position, my leg very soon began to tremble, but I willed it to stay still, hoping Lee would not feel the spasm, praying she would not move her hand away.

Blame it on the dancing. They must have got a late licence for the bar, or maybe Galway people always danced half the night. The music made our bones move in tandem and our legs shake. I tried to take the last bit of water from Sylvia's mouth, but I was so giddy I couldn't aim right and kept lurching against her collarbone and laughing at my own helplessness.

"Thought you were meant to be in the closet," I shouted in her ear at one point, and Sylvia smiled with her eyes shut and said something I couldn't hear, and I said "What?" and she said, "Not tonight."

So at the end of the evening we had no place to go and it didn't matter. We had written our phone numbers on sodden beermats and exchanged them. We agreed that we'd go for a drive. When we got into her white van on the kerb littered with weak-kneed céilí dancers, something came on the radio, an old song by Clannad or one of that crowd. Sylvia started up the engine and began to sing along with the chorus, her hoarse whisper catching every second or third word. She leaned over to fasten her seatbelt and crooned a phrase into my ear. I didn't understand it – something about "bóthar", or was it "máthar"? – but it made my face go hot anyway.

"Where are we heading?" I said at last, as the hedges began to narrow to either side of the white van.

Sylvia frowned into the darkness. "Cashelagen, was that the name of it? Quiet spot, I seem to remember, beside a castle."

After another ten minutes, during which we didn't meet a single other car, I realised that we were lost, completely tangled in the little roads leading into Connemara. And half of me didn't care. Half of me was quite content to bump along these lanes to the strains of late night easy listening, watching Sylvia Dwyer's sculpted profile out the corner of my right eye. But the other half of me wanted to stretch my boot across and stamp on the brake, then climb over the gear stick to get at her.

Lee didn't comment on how quickly I was getting us lost. Cradle-snatcher, I commented to myself, and not even a suave one at that. As we hovered at an unmarked fork, a man walked into the glare of the headlights. I stared at him to make sure he was real, then rolled down the window with a flurry of elbows. "Cashelagen?" I asked. Lee had turned off the radio, so my voice sounded indecently loud. "Could you tell us are we anywhere near Cashelagen?"

The man fingered his sideburns and stepped closer, beaming in past me at Lee. What in God's name was this fellow doing wandering round in the middle of the night, anyway? He didn't even have our excuse. I was just starting to roll the window up again when, "Ah," he said," ah, if it's Cashelagen you're wanting, you'd have to go a fair few miles back through Ballyalla and then take the coast road."

"Thanks," I told him shortly, and revved up the engine. Lee would think I was the most hopeless incompetent she had ever got into a van for immoral purposes with. As soon as he had walked out of range of the headlights, I let off the handbrake and shot forward. I glanced over at Lee's bent head. The frightening thought occured to me: I could love this woman.

The lines above Sylvia's eyebrow were beginning to swoop like gulls. If she was going to get cross, we might as well turn the radio back on and drive all night. I rehearsed the words in my head, then said them. "Sure, who needs a castle in the dark?"

Her grin was quick as a fish.

"Everywhere's quiet, at this time of night," I said, rather squeakily. "Here's quiet. We could stop here."

"What, right here?"

Sylvia peered back at the road and suddenly wheeled round into the entrance to a field. We stopped with the bumper a foot away from a five-barred gate. When the headlights went off, the field stretched out dark in front of us, and there was a sprinkle of light that had to be Galway.

"What time did you say you had to be in Dublin?" I asked suddenly.

"Nine. Better start back round five, in case I hit traffic," said Sylvia. She bent over to rummage in the glove compartment. She pulled out a strapless watch, looked at it, brought it closer to her eyes, then let out a puff of laughter.

"What time's it now?"

"You don't want to know," she told me.

I grabbed it. The hands said half past three. "It can't be."

We sat staring into the field. "Nice stars," I said, for something to say.

"Mmm," she said.

I stared at the stars, joining the dots, till my eyes watered.

And then I heard Syvlia laughing in her throat as she turned sideways and leaned over my seatbelt. I heard it hissing back into its socket as she kissed me on the mouth.

When I came back from taking a pee in the bushes, the driver's seat was empty. I panicked, and stared up and down the lane. Why would she have run off on foot? Then, with a deafening creak, the back doors of the van swung open.

Sylvia's bare shoulders were wrapped around the blanket that covered her body. She hugged her knees. Her eyes were bright, and the small bags underneath were the most beautiful folds of skin I'd ever seen. I climbed in and kneeled on the sheepskin coat beside her, reaching up to snap off the little light. Her face opened wide in a yawn. The frightening thought occured to me: I could love this woman.

"You could always get some sleep, you know," I said. "I wouldn't mind." Then I thought that sounded churlish, but I didn't know how to unsay it.

"Oh, I know I could," said Sylvia, her voice melodic with amusement. "There's lots of things we could do with a whole hour and a half. We could sleep, we could share the joint in the glove compartment, we could drive to Clifden and watch the sun come up. Lots of things."

I smiled. Then I realised she couldn't see my face in the dark.

"Get your clothes off," she said.

I would have liked to leave the map-reading light on over our heads, letting me see and memorise every line of Lee's body, but it would have lit us up like a saintly apparition for any passing farmer to see. So the whole thing happened in a darkness much darker than it ever gets in a city.

There was a script, of course. No matter how spontaneous it may feel, there's always an unwritten script. Every one of these encounters has a script, even the very first time your hand undoes the button on another woman's shirt; none of us comes without expectations to this body business.

But Lord, what fun it was. Lee was salt with sweat and fleshier than I'd imagined, behind all her layers of black cotton and wool. In thirty-four years, I've found nothing to compare to that moment when the bare limbs slide together like a key into a lock. Or no, more like one of those electronic key cards they give you in big hotels, the Open Sesame ones marked with an invisible code which the door must read and recognize before it agrees to open.

At one point Lee rolled under me and muttered, "There's somewhere I want to go," then went deep inside me. It hurt a little, just a little, and I must have flinched because she asked, "Does that hurt?" and I said "No," because I was glad of it. "No," I said again, because I didn't want her to go.

Sylvia's voice was rough, like rocks grinding on each other. As she moved on top of me, she whispered in my ear, things I couldn't make out, sounds just outside the range of hearing. I never wanted to interrupt the flow by saying "Sorry?" or "What did you say?" Much as I wanted to hear and remember every word, every detail, at a certain point I just had to switch my mind off and get on with living it. But Sylvia's voice kept going in my ear, turning me on in the strangest way by whispering phrases that only she could hear.

I've always thought the biggest lie in the books is that women instinctively know what to do to each other because their bodies are the same. None of Sylvia's shapes were the same as mine, nor could I have guessed what she was like from how she seemed in her smart clothes. And we liked different things and took things in different order, showing each other by infinitesimal movings away and movings towards. She did some things to me that I knew I wanted, some I didn't think I'd much like and didn't, and several I was startled to find that I enjoyed much more than I would have imagined. I did some things Sylvia seemed calm about, and then something she must have really needed, because she started to let out her breath in a long gasp when I'd barely begun.

Near the end Sylvia's long fingers moved down her body to ride alongside mine, not supplanting, just guiding. "Go light," she whispered in my ear. "Lighter and lighter. Butterfly." As she began to thrash at last, laughter spilled from her mouth.

"What? What are you laughing for?" I asked, afraid I'd done something wrong. Sylvia just whooped louder. Words leaked out of her throat, distorted by pleasure.

At one point I touched my lips to the skin under her eyes, first one and then the other. "Your bags are gorgeous, you know. Promise you'll never let a surgeon at them?"

"No," she said, starting to laugh again.

"No to which?"

"No promise."

When Sylvia was touching me I didn't say a single one of the words that swam through my head. I don't know was I shy or just stubborn, wanting to make her guess what to do. The tantalization of waiting for those hands to decipher my body made the bliss build and build till, when it came, it threw me.

There was one moment I wouldn't swap anything for. It was in the lull beforehand, the few seconds when I stopped breathing. I looked at this stranger's face bent over me, twisted in exertion and tenderness, and I thought, yes, you, whoever you are, if you're asking for it, I'll give it all up to you.

In the in-between times, we panted and rested and stifled our laughter in the curve of each other's shoulders, and debated when I'd noticed Lee and when she'd noticed me, and what we'd noticed and what we'd imagined on each occasion, the history of this particular desire. And during one of these in-between times, we realized that the sun had come up, faint behind a yellow mist, and it was half five according to the strapless watch in the glove compartment.

I took hold of Lee, my arms binding her ribs and my head resting in the flat place between her breasts. The newly-budded swollen look of them made my mouth water, but there was no time. I shut my mouth and my eyes and held Lee hard and there was no time left at all, so I let go and sat up. I could feel our nerves pulling apart like ivy off a wall.

The cows were beginning to moan in the field as we pulled our clothes on. My linen trousers were cold and smoky. We did none of the things parting lovers do if they have the time or the right. I didn't snatch at Lee's foot as she pulled her jeans on; she didn't sneak her head under my shirt as I pulled it over my face. The whole thing had to be over already.

It was not the easiest thing in the world to find my way back to Galway with Lee's right hand tucked between my thighs. Through my jeans, I could feel the cold of her fingers, and the hardness of her thumb, rubbing the denim. I caught her eye as we sped round a corner, and she grinned, suddenly very young. "You're just using me to warm your hand up," I accused.

"That's all it is," said Lee.

I was still throbbing, so loud I thought the car was ringing with it. We were only two streets from the hostel now.

I wouldn't ask to see her again. I would just leave the matter open and drive away. Lee probably got offers all the time; she was far too young to be looking for anything heavy. I'd show her I was generous enough to accept that an hour and a half was all she had to give me.

I let her out just beside the hostel, which was already opening to release some backpacking Germans. I was going to get out of the car to give her a proper body-to-body hug but, while I was struggling with my seatbelt, Lee knocked on the glass. I rolled down the window, put *Desert Hearts* out of my mind and kissed her for what I had a hunch was likely to be the last time.

I stood shivering in the street outside the hostel and knocked on Sylvia's car window. I was high as a kite and dizzy with fatigue.

I wouldn't ask anything naff like when were likely to see each other again. I would just wave as she drove away. Sylvia probably did this kind of thing all the time; she was far too famous to be wanting anything heavy. I'd show her that I was sophisticated enough not to fall for her all in one go, not to ask for anything but the hour and a half she had to give me.

When she rolled down the window I smiled and leaned in. I shut my eyes and felt Sylvia's tongue against mine, saying something neither of us could hear. So brief, so slippery, nothing you could get a hold of.

I'VE SEEN HER BEFORE

Twiggy O'Connor

She's always late, is Jill, and this Sunday morning is no exception. My first cappuccino is just a memory, a chocolatey crust round the rim of the cup and a few bitter grounds in the bottom and my second is going cold by the time I spot her bleached-blonde head through the steamed up window of Ragazzi's.

Even if she didn't have hair like a dandelion clock, it would be hard to miss Jill. She doesn't just walk along the street, she bounds. It's quite distinctive. No other woman I know can cover so much ground in one stride, which is odd, because Jill isn't particularly tall. Maybe it's because she used to be a dancer, and still teaches the odd class sometimes.

She'll be here in a few seconds, so I down my chilly coffee in eager anticipation of the bacon, sausages, chips, beans, toast and mountain of scrambled egg we'll be ordering – but where is she? The blonde head's gone, but Jill hasn't come through the door yet.

Then I spot her bright hair again. She's crossing back to the other side of the road. Not walking, not bounding, but positively *bouncing*. It's no good, I have to see what she's up to. I get up, wipe a clear patch on the misty window. She's waving to someone up the street, not just her arm, but both legs as well, leaping in the air like a puppy. Hitting the ground, she spins round a few times and lands up against the window of the secondhand dress shop, where she hops on one leg for bit, hugging herself and then comes springing back across the zebra crossing.

She bursts through the door as usual, bringing a gust of icy air with her.

"Marf, babe, how you doing?" Several chairs are flung sideways as she unwinds her scarf and fights her way out of her sheepskin coat.

"Starving."

"God, am I late again?" Jill looks completely unrepentant. Her eyes are shining and her hair is positively vertical. "Cheer up, Marf," she says, and gives me a hug. Her cheek is icy, but her touch is like an electric shock, crackling with vitality.

Eventually, when she's settled in a chair and we've got our food and eaten our way through most of it, I ask her what's got into her.

"In what way?" she says.

"Jill," I begin. "When I came into Ragazzi's this morning, I walked like this." I get up, and walk to the door and back again. Eyes on the floor, shoulders droopy, a bit stiff in the lower spine. Typical post-Saturday-night, just-got-up, feeling-a-bit-fragile gait. I lower myself into my chair with a fraction of a sigh and rest my chin in my hands.

"So?" says Jill, eyebrows raised. "What's new?"

"And this, Jill, is how you came in." I do my best to imitate her crazy, bouncing walk, finishing with a little jig on the spot before leaping into my chair. Jill squeaks helplessly, which is her way of having a good laugh.

"Just what is your secret?" I say. "What are you on, at this time of a Sunday morning? Do tell me, please." I jump up as if I'm going to carry on leaping round the café.

"No, no, no, Marf!" she squeaks. "Don't! Stop it!"

"Tell me, then! It's abnormal to be leaping about like that. You're six years older than me but I feel like your aged auntie . . ."

"Oh *Martha*! Lighten up! You are only fifty-seven, after all."

This is Jill's standard response to any mention of the fact that I'm finding the approach of my thirtieth birthday is making me feel, not exactly unhappy, but just a bit thoughtful.

"What is it, Jill? Why don't *I* bounce when I wake up on a Sunday morning? What am I doing wrong?"

"Martha," says Jill, suddenly very serious. "Can't you guess? I've met someone."

Since Jill and I stopped being lovers more than four years ago, she's had a new girlfriend at least every couple of months. Some of them seem to be fun, and some don't. None of them ever really have much effect on Jill. I can't even remember the names of more than a couple of them. I hope Jill can.

"No, really," she says, seeing my cynical expression. "This is it, Martha. She's stunning. She's really, really special."

Even though we're not touching, I can sense the thrill that rushes through Jill's body.

"Really, it's better with her than I could ever have imagined. It's amazing," she is saying, her eyes like stars. Then she sees my face and shuts up for a moment.

Even though we've enjoyed nearly four years of easygoing

friendship since I was a humble wardrobe girl strapping Jill into her *Rocky Horror Show* corset and shoving her onstage to strut her stuff – and then, after the show, rushing back to her digs to make love in front of the sputtering gas fire, I still feel a little chill of jealousy.

"Martha, don't look at me like that. You should be pleased for me."

"I am pleased for you," I say, trying to smile.

"Oh, Marfs. I wish *you* could find somebody really special."

"I wish I could, too."

And then Jill gets a look in her eye that I've become only too familiar with over the last few months. Since she gave up full-time dancing, she's got very into New Age stuff. It's something different every month or so, but it's always the same, slightly fanatical expression on her face. And be it aromatherapy, rebirthing, eating macrobiotic food or moving the sofa into a more auspicious position, it's always going to sort her life out completely and forever. (And mine, too, if I would only listen to her.)

"Two things, Martha," she's saying. "And the first is, you must never say I wish. Wishing gets you nowhere. Wishing's for sad people who never get what they want. You've got to *intend.* And then you've got to *visualize.*"

I wonder which self-help book she's got that from. Her bookshelf is overflowing with them. At least she's not telling me to get in touch with my inner wolf, which was the message of the last weighty volume she couldn't put down.

"You've got to *see* the woman you want, *touch* her, *smell* her . . ."

I glance over my shoulder and notice that Maria, wiping down the counter behind us, is earwigging like mad.

"Thanks, Jill." I say. "And what's the second thing?"

Frowning earnestly, Jill tells me: "You've got to make *space* in your life for the woman you want. She's out there, just waiting to meet you, but you've got to make room for her."

"Oh, look. My life's all space at the moment. You know I'm not working right now. I've got all the time in the world . . ."

"I don't mean that kind of space, Martha. You've got to clear out all the old stuff from your life. Throw all those horrible old clothes you've been hoarding for years away."

"Don't be silly," I say. I am deeply attached to the contents of my wardrobe, as well she knows.

"Martha – it *works*!" Jill is thumping the table. "I tidied up my flat, and then I emptied out half of my chest of drawers and half of my wardrobe so there was some *space* for another woman to put her things. And then along came Simone!"

Simone. She must be French. I can just picture her. Probably a butch version of Simone Signoret, the French movie star of so many grainy, arty black-and-white films. Earthy, husky-voiced, red-wine-drinking, nicotine stains on her long fingers from chain-smoking. Full lips, heavy-lidded eyes. Ever so, ever so sexy. I can see her folding up her silk stockings (no, no, her *Levis*, Martha, don't be daft) and placing them in Jill's top drawer.

Oh well, that's life. I think to myself. We can't all meet up with our dream lovers all at the very same time. There'll always be someone who's feeling a bit left out, and today it's my turn.

Jill can see that I'm a bit grumpy, and spends the rest of our time together trying to make me feel better. But she just can't keep glowing with joy and I can tell she's itching to jump up out of her seat and go bouncing off back to her new love. And I don't for minute wish her any less happy, but I can't say that it isn't a bit of relief when we part company and I make my way back along the cold pavement to my flat.

I love my flat. It's almost, but not quite, an artist's garret. One huge room right up under the roof on the top floor of a converted house. It's a bit of mess, but I've painted it in the bright colours I love, and it's full of my bits of junk that I've picked up touring the provinces with various shows. Working in wardrobe like I do, you never know when a wacky pair of seventies platform shoes, or a forties tailored jacket, or a twenties silver cigarette case might come in handy for some little theatre production with a tiny budget and no resources.

Right now, the flat is freezing. I'm unemployed, and I can't afford to have the heating on during the day. There's nothing for it but to dive into bed and hide under the covers.

I think about Jill's advice. Visualize the woman you really want in your life. I'm not feeling very sexy. The huge Sunday breakfast is lying very heavy in my belly. And, for some strange reason, all that comes into my mind is the fairy that used to sit on top of our family Christmas tree. She was a small doll, with hard china flesh, pink cheeks, soft, fluffy dark hair and bright blue eyes. She wore a white and silver frock (one of the first things I ever made and pretty successful, considering I was only six at the time) and little shiny black boots which didn't go with the frock but which couldn't be taken off because they were painted on her feet. I loved her dearly and it was always my job to get her out of her box at Christmas, refurbish her silver frock and stick a new star on the end of her wand.

Sliding my hand between my legs I try to conjure up a hot flesh-and-blood woman. But my fingers are icy, and I remain obstinately dry. The doll's smooth, sexless china crotch and relentless blue stare keep getting in the way of any other fantasy. My head aches and there's a cold feeling round my heart. Eventually, I stop shivering and fall into a heavy sleep.

When I wake, it's getting dark outside. I feel warm and comfortable and I realize that I'm thinking about Jill and smiling. I understand how much she really cares for me. She's nutty, but all the weird advice she gives me is well meant.

And I'm really pleased that she's gasping her lungs out in ecstasy in the arms of her lusty Simone Signoret lookalike. She may be unreliable, she may be irritating, but there is absolutely nothing bad, nothing mean, nothing unkind about Jill at all. She is the best friend I could wish for, and she deserves the best lover going.

And as for our time together – it was great, but it was right for us to split up when we did. We were just too much the sun and moon. Her leaping round the room shedding rays of energy everywhere, and me lying in a foetal position on the sofa daydreaming. So there are no regrets, just that special closeness that you only get with an ex-lover.

Later, when I'm up and about and I've made a cup of tea and decided to go mad and switch the heating on, I try the second part of the plan of action Jill outlined for me in the café. It seems to work much better than her first suggestion.

I get a roll of black plastic sacks and start going through my drawers. Oh no, not throwing out all my beloved oddities. But just all the nondescript clothes that I don't like wearing any more. The baggy leggings worn thin between the thighs. The frumpy skirts that are too long, but not long enough. The Marks and Spencer jumpers my mother's given me, with the odd moth hole here and there. The jeans that are far too tight for comfort and never looked that good anyway.

It takes several hours. I never realized how many things I've been holding onto that I never wear and really have no use for. Of course, there are things that I don't wear much, but I simply can't bear to part with, like my antique black lace dress with very thin shoulder straps, and the little red hour-glass corset I made myself when I was at college. I may never fit into it again, but just to see it lying in the drawer is a turn-on.

I end up with three large empty drawers and a couple of free hangers in the wardrobe. It's now 2 a.m. but I'm feeling great and I attack my "living room" space with vacuum cleaner and feather duster. I clear all the empty shopping bags, receipts and dirty plates off the sofa, and rescue my one and only comfy armchair from underneath a pile of unironed washing. Then I light some candles and sit on the sofa.

The room looks warm and welcoming. And, just for a moment, I get a sensation, as if someone is sitting just opposite me in the armchair, looking at me in the candlelight. And I realize that I have been alone, and lonely, for a very long time.

Oh yes, there have been lots of women in my life. I've bumped into them all over the country on tour, and all over London when I'm at home. So many girls I've bunked up with, shagged, gone down on, fought over the duvet on cold nights with, brewed bitter get-up-it's-time-for-you-to-go early morning coffee for. So many girls loved and lost, loved and left. But looking back, it's as if I have always been alone, enjoying or enduring a series of chance encounters.

Recklessly leaving the ancient central heating boiler to thunder on into the dawn, I fall asleep on the sofa, relaxed and peaceful and *warm*, for the first time in many nights. When I wake, the phone's ringing with an offer of work – standing in on a West End musical for an ex-colleague who's gone down with the flu. I have to get up right away and go into the theatre – not exactly what I was expecting, not what I was trying to visualize when I cleared up the flat, but a blessing and a bonus all the same.

When I get home in the early hours of the morning, after a hectic day and a hair-raising evening learning my new job, the answer-machine is blinking at me. I press PLAY and for a moment I don't recognise the husky voice on the tape. "Martha! Where are you? Are you OK? Call me!" and then another message: "Oh, Marfs! *Are* you all right? Call me! Call as late as you like. Simone's not here. We've been in bed all day but she's had to go tonight and I miss her so much. And I'm really worried about you. You looked so miserable yesterday. Are you listening to this? Call me!" It's Jill, of course. I should remember how her voice drops a couple of octaves after a long session of really good sex.

There aren't many people I would call at 1.30 a.m., but if Jill says "Call me late," she means it. At first, all I can get out of her is a moan.

"What's the matter, Jill? Did I wake you up?"

"No . . . noooo," she groans. "I'm just feeling so good. Where have you been?"

I tell her about my surprise job.

"Oh, that's great!" she says, gravel-voiced. "I'm so pleased for you. You deserve a break."

"And I don't need to ask what you've been up to all day. And all last night, too," I say.

"It's so good," sighs Jill. "She's my soul mate, my body mate . . ."

"And where is she now?"

"Oh, she had to go and do a gig. I told you she's a singer didn't I? Oh, Martha, her *voice* . . ."

"Don't tell me, it comes right out of her boots . . ."

Jill squeaks. "Oh, her *boots* . . ."

Jill has always had a weakness for a well-booted woman. Do Frenchwomen wear Doc Marten's? Or maybe the voluptuous Simone goes for something a bit more designer, with a lot of laces and a bit of heel.

"And, Martha, her hands . . ." Jill is saying.

"No, Jill, please," I say, with a vision of those nicotine-stained fingers sliding into my ex-girlfriend.

"I'm just trying to tell you what she's like!"

"Spare me the details. You don't need to tell me how gorgeous she is. I can hear it every time you speak about her. She's big, she's butch, she's French. It sounds like a marriage made in heaven," I say, trying to banish the black-and-white, flickering image of Simone Signoret's sultry, sensual mouth in *Room at the Top* from my mind's eye.

"Martha, hang on a minute. She's . . ."

"Please, I don't want to know how she looks and how she fucks. I expect I'll meet her soon enough and I'll make up my own mind."

"Oh, babe, you're just jealous."

"I might be."

"You should try what I was telling you about yesterday."

"I did."

Jill can't believe I have actually taken her advice, for once. "Did it work?" she asks.

"Well, it got me a job, which isn't exactly what I was after," I say, ironically.

"You can't have been doing it properly. You've got to be very precise with visualization." Jill is getting back to her more normal self again. "Otherwise the results may be unexpected."

I laugh at her and tell her about the Christmas Fairy. Jill isn't very impressed.

"You've got to make a proper list, Martha. Write it down. All the things you want from your ideal woman. Sex, brains, glamour, money . . . It's time you stopped picking up all those tatty lame ducks."

"*Jill!*"

"Well. You know what I mean. Get yourself a classy broad, for once." And Jill suddenly yawns hugely. I tell her to go and get some much-needed sleep and put the phone down.

I'm physically tired after my day at work, but my mind is buzzing. OK, I think to myself, I'll make me a list. Jill's found her soulmate. Why shouldn't I find mine? I light the candles again, looking round my tidy room with pleasure, find a ballpoint pen (in the correct place – the pot by the telephone – for once) and get writing.

After all, if I can't inspire myself with a session between the sheets, maybe I need to be completely prosaic. I'll write myself a shopping list of all the best qualities I can think of in a woman, all the things that would most turn me on and make me happy. Have I ever even thought about this properly before? Suddenly, what I am doing – thinking about myself and my own desires – seems a wonderful, indulgent luxury.

The blank page sits in front of me for a least ten minutes before I realize that I need to draw up some categories. Why not begin with physical? That's where I always seem to start from.

Well. Number one. Dark-haired, like me. That's very important. Maybe not as dark as me. My black hair and black eyes look more Spanish or even Arab than Irish, which is what I am, way back, on both sides of the family. But definitely dark hair. Even Jill, with her bleached mop of hair, is a dark-haired woman where it matters. I have been out with fair-haired girls, but it's the dark ones that really get me going. I like the smell of their skin more . . .

Much to my delight, I find that I'm starting to get very horny. And I have only put one item on my list. I could gladly jump into bed and finish the list in a much more pleasurable way, but I force myself to sit on the sofa and keep writing.

Eyes. Well. Could be brown. Or could be blue, at a pinch. There's something about a really sharp blue glance that can make me go a bit wobbly at the knees. A look to penetrate the soul . . .

Now I have to cross my legs to keep myself sitting still on the sofa. Body. Not too tall, not too heavy. So I can be underneath her without having all the breath squashed out of me. So I can move her round and put her where I want to. But I'd like her to be quite tough, so that she can give as good as she gets. And soft where it really matters, so she can take it and take it and take it.

By now, I'm shivering with lust. And I haven't even thought about her personality. With a shaking hand, I jot down a few things, like "good sense of humour", "being creative", "not being freaked out when I have to go away on tour", and then I can't hold out any longer and I rush over to the bed, shedding garments as I go.

I start with the inside of my ankle. That oh, so sensitive and oh, so neglected spot that never fails to set me on fire, if touched in the right way. And as soon as my fingers brush my ankle bone, I'm flooded with warmth and lost to the world. It's most inspiring, the most exciting, the most extraordinary session of making love to myself that I have ever had. (And also, probably, the longest. The winter sky is beginning to show light by the time I surface.) It's as if it isn't me touching myself, but I'm being caressed by another's warm, sensitive hands. The sheets wind themselves round me like warm limbs, and the pillows stroke my face and soak up my kisses and my cries of pleasure. As my desire gets hotter and hotter, it's another's finger that slides in and out of my mouth and another's hand that dives in between my legs to drive me to distraction.

It's lucky that I don't have to be at the theatre until eleven o'clock, next day, because it gives me a chance to snatch a few hours' sleep. I am completely distracted all day at work. The list I began last night is growing and growing. But I am not writing things down any more. It's as if the lover I have created for myself has taken control of her identity. She is becoming more and more real as the day goes by, acquiring a body, a face, a way of walking . . .

She keeps showing me bits of herself in the people round me. A slim, strong thigh in tight jeans waiting on the crowded Tube platform in the morning. A schoolgirl's cloud of dark, wavy hair hurrying to school. The fierce, ice-blue gaze and taut cheekbones of the young Russian dancing master who bumps into me at the stage door as he's leaving after taking the morning class for the cast. The small, high breasts of the leading actress who's washing under her arms in her dressing room basin as I drop off her freshly laundered underwear before the show.

I can't wait to get home and have my dream woman all to myself again, and, by the time I do, she's become, physically at least, complete. A slight, supple, strong woman with high cheekbones, dark hair, vivid blue eyes, a soft, curving mouth and an electric, performer's presence. Where that last bit has crept in from, I don't know. It just seems to be an integral part of her. I get enough and more of the "artistic" temperament in my line of work. Not all the "turns", as I sometimes disparagingly call them, have got Jill's sweet nature. There's a lot of very badly behaved and selfish folk around in show business. But I guess I do just love that performer's energy. The sparkle, the pride, the passion that a good actor or singer or dancer radiates is unbeatable. And my dream woman has it.

Sitting on the sofa, that night, I can feel the warmth she gives off. Her presence is more intense, more powerful than any real human being who has visited my room. It's as if she's sitting in the armchair, several feet away, but I can still feel her glow on my skin.

Later, when I go to bed, I feel more terrified than turned on. What have I done? Am I going out of my mind? Am I being possessed? And suddenly I find myself laughing hysterically. Black hair, blue eyes, lovely white skin. What have I done but brought to life the fairy on the Christmas tree? I laugh until I am weak with exhaustion, and I'm about to fall over the edge into tears, when I feel two warm, strong arms catching me and holding me in bed. I should be even more scared by this odd sensation, but instead I find it very comforting and I fall deeply and safely and dreamlessly asleep.

Over the next few days, my dream lover stays with me – but the intensity of those first nights fades a little. She's there, in the back of my mind, growing more familiar. When I get back to my flat I can feel a warmth in the room, as if she had just been there a few moments before. I still keep seeing her in the people around me – her mane of dark hair; her supple, powerful walk; her wicked blue glance. At night, even after I've been making love to myself, exploring the secrets of her body and my own, and I think that I've extracted every little bit of desire from myself, I often wake, deeply aroused, and with a name I don't yet know trying to burst out of my lips as I ache for more of the touch that has pulled me out of sleep. But in the morning, when it's time to get up, I feel relaxed, refreshed as if I have been loved and cared for all night long.

My secret sensual life carries over into the daytime a little bit, too. When I catch my reflection in the bathroom mirror, my eyes are gleaming and my skin is clear and bright. Sometimes, just for a moment, I feel a twinge of fear. It isn't a real situation that is making me look so good, feel so fulfilled. But the panic subsides very quickly. It is as if someone puts a hand on my arm and whispers: "This is real. Trust it. Enjoy it. Everything is working out for you . . ."

I am very busy and very pressured at work, but people are nice to me. I get thanks and hugs and words of appreciation from my colleagues in the wardrobe and from the cast, too. It's as if I have that special glow which people get when they're in love, and which is attractive to everyone around. When the woman I have been replacing phones in to say she is well enough to return to work Alice, the wardrobe mistress, doesn't want me to leave. She asks me if I'll stay on and help her out with some costumes she's making for a TV show.

I phone Jill in my teabreak to tell her the good news.

"Hi, babe," she yawns.

She says she's pleased for me, but I can hear that she is half asleep and not really listening.

"How are things with you?" I ask.

"Oh, good, good. Yeah," she says, with another mammoth yawn.

"I've been doing my visualizations."

"What? Oh right. Yes. Have you met anyone yet?"

"Not exactly. But I've been having a great time."

"Good old Martha," says Jill. "Keep it up, you never know. Hey, look, I'll call you in few days, OK?"

I am longing to tell her about the incredible time I'm having, but I feel a bit foolish. And it doesn't feel like the right time. Jill doesn't sound like her usual self. The two of them must still be deep into their honeymoon and suffering from serious lack of sleep.

That afternoon, cutting out white silk for an evening dress and pinning it into a rough shape round a tailor's dummy under Alice's supervision, I think how pleasurable it would be to wrap the fine material round my dream lover's narrow waist. I've never made anything beautiful for a lover before, just for the sake of it. But on her a dress would hang perfectly, a leather corset would fit like a glove.

"You've got such a feel for fabric," says Alice, peering over my shoulder. "I would never have taken it quite like that under the bust. But it's going to look lovely. Just right."

The next day is Sunday, my only day off. I wake up with that sense of ease that a working girl only feels on a Sunday morning and, as I'm rolling around under the covers, wondering how it can be that I feel as if I've been caressed all over when in reality I've been dead to the world all night, I realize it's now a fortnight since I last saw Jill.

She seems to have disappeared off the planet – presumably lying in bed all hours with the sultry Simone. I can't say that I have missed my gossiping sessions with her. I have been enjoying my work, and my sensational fantasy life too much.

I call her, but there's just a rather cross-sounding message on her answer machine. So I decide to go for my breakfast at Ragazzi's on my own. Still warm with the glow of my dream lover, I pick at my food and happily indulge in a bit of chatting up with Maria, who isn't a dyke but is so bored that she will flirt with anyone who'll pay attention to her.

"I saw your friend, the other day," she says. "Is she sick? She looks awful."

I explain that Jill is just knackered from being in love, but Maria doesn't look entirely convinced.

"She should come and and have some good breakfast. She looks bad," she says, gloomily.

After breakfast, I decide to take a stroll in the park. The weather is beginning to show hints of spring today, with fluffy white clouds racing past in a blue sky. But it is still cold, and there aren't too many people about. I stride along, pulling fresh air into my lungs and feeling impossibly well and happy. Life has improved so much for me in just a few days, and I feel in my bones that the process is going to continue.

A couple are walking towards me along the path. At first I don't recognize Jill, because she's wearing a hat and she isn't bouncing today. But she calls my name and, when we get close to each other, I can see that she's looking tired, but very happy to see me.

I don't take much notice of the slight woman standing beside her, wrapped in a huge scarf and with a floppy hat pulled down on her forehead. I suppose I'm expecting someone taller, bigger-boned, more striking. A sophisticated older woman with a Gauloise between her lips.

"Martha, Martha, great to see you. Hey, this is Simone!" says Jill.

And the woman beside her looks up at me with the bluest eyes I've ever seen. I am struck completely dumb. She smiles at me. Her mouth is soft, upward-curving, her cheekbones high. And under the brim of the shapeless hat, a curl of dark hair escapes.

She takes my hand in a soft, warm grasp, still smiling at me, though I am not only dumb, but unable to move a muscle.

"Martha," she says, in a soft, slightly husky voice. "Jill tells me so much about you."

My knees have turned to water. How can I tell her that any introduction is superfluous, that I know her already? That her face is more familiar to me than my own? It's just about all I can do to hold on to her hand without falling over.

"You know that I am a singer?" she is saying. I stare speechlessly into her blue eyes.

"I have a big gig – is that it? – coming up. I would like you to make for me a dress to wear . . . something beautiful, that looks good for me. I know this is what you do."

With a superhuman effort, I look across at Jill. Does she have any idea what I'm going through? What a horrible, mean, unfair trick fate has played on me? On all of us? By some strange, evil twist of telepathy, I have tuned into my best friend's psyche and fallen in love with her lover. Jill looks strained and rather unhappy. Maybe she's just worrying that Simone and I won't get on.

My gaze is drawn back to Simone's face again. She *is* my dream lover, there is no doubt about it. Even if I shut my eyes I would still know her, by the touch of her hand, by the warmth that seems to radiate out from her body. But looking at her, drinking in every detail of her, I realize that the real woman isn't exactly the same as my fantasy. She's looking at me with open interest, but there is something guarded in her blue eyes. Her soft skin has some fine lines – she is a bit older than I thought – and there's a little twist to her mouth that hints at defensiveness, at irony. But the real woman touches me in a way that no dream could. I feel a great rush of complex emotions. Protectiveness. Fear. Shyness. Passionate curiosity.

"So what do you say, Martha?" Jill is saying. Her voice sounds rather thin, as it does when she's getting a cold. She's looking at me anxiously, and I know that she badly wants me to make the right response.

But what is the right response? What else can I do but walk away from the situation as fast as I can? Simone is still holding onto my hand and I am unable to pull away from her. Surely Jill must be able to see what's going on between us.

I look at Jill again. She looks lost and left out and my heart aches for her.

"Martha?" she says, hungrily.

And I do the only thing I am able to do.

"Of course. I would be happy to make a dress for you," I say to Simone. "You must come over and I'll get your measurements and you can tell me what you want."

And suddenly all the tension is gone and I know in my bones that I have done the right thing. The guardedness drops from Simone's eyes and her whole face lights up. And Jill is smiling for the first time in our encounter and now I can see that her sadness, her anxiety have nothing to do with me. That maybe, could it be, the honeymoon is over and things aren't working out for them?

And as for me, I can move my limbs again (though I don't quite trust my voice to say very much) and as I stumble off alone down the path back to my flat, I know that it won't be easy, that it's a complex situation, that marrying my dream to reality will be the biggest challenge I have ever faced – but that I have taken, am taking, the first steps towards the most wonderful experience of my life.

In just a few short hours, I'll be winding my tape measure round the woman of my dreams. And after that, who knows?

PIRACY

Rebecca Rosenskjøld

I can hear her mouth curved into a pirate's smile.
Glinting in the dark
she says,
let me tell you a story,
she says
she wants to fuck me,
she says
she wants to fuck me slowly surely deeply
w i t h   a   d i c k
to move over me pushing it against my cervix, into me, to
slide through me, to have my feet meet around her my hands
pressing into her handsome ass to push her, to push her dick,
into me, to make me feel this, to edge me to annihilation
there conscious senses alight complicit present
in this: with this hijacked artefact

stories history culture performance.
could I be?

I'm butter on the bed, astonished & lustful, hammering blood.
I melt into the crevices of the pillows, in awe of her audacity
her voice dripping honey & brimstone so close in the darkness.
Her hands find me, leave phosphorous trails across my
skin. My ears burning.
She says, as I fucked you, you would feel like coming, it
would engulf you, you would cry & babble into my mouth, you
would push yourself against me, I would drive you, push you
into the bed, turn you over to clutch the bedhead while I
found your clitoris with my free hand & fucked you with the
contraband cock & fucked your mouth with my fingers &
you'd
come weeping & shuddering
but I wouldn't,
because
the dick's plastic.

W e g i g g l e , n a u g h t y g i r l s .

I say, astounded I can hear myself over my heart in my throat,
astounded I can hear myself sounding relatively relaxed as if
people say this to me often, or as if I have even ever heard
such a thing before, or as if I can imagine speaking at all in
the wide wake of her buccaneer's tale,
you could find one that touched you cleverly & would make
you feel & the thought of her aroused, crying out, fucking me
like this turns my bones to paste my cunt opens listening I
have to keep instructing myself to
b r e a t h e .

* * *

We speak of other things. She falls into the grace of sleep,
suddenly she's little, lithe & delicate in my arms in her stripey
pyjamas, tenderness undoes me finally & I have to slip out
from our tangle into the cool night air & smoke & grin at the
crooning birds & the fat moon hanging in the trees.

A STRUGGLE FOR PEACE

Mercia Schoeman

May months in South Africa can be smoulderingly hot, even though the smooth winds and fiery colours of autumn are usually only a few days away. It was on a scorching day in May 1971 that South Africa commemorated its tenth year of being declared an independent republic. That day at school we did not attend classes – instead, everyone marched down to the sport stadium to join neighbouring schools for the celebration ceremonies. We waved miniature flags in the orange, white and blue colours of the new republic and a rosette of the same colours was pinned to my grey school uniform. It looked like a flattened rose. The flag and rosette became proud possessions that I treasured in a shoebox for years.

The school's principal, Mr Van der Merwe, made a speech in rapid, enthusiastic bursts of sentences, telling us in his coarse voice about our ancestors' battles for autonomy and the subsequent freedom from British Imperialists. In the relentless heat I became aware of the slow dawning of nausea and a headache sweltering through my body. We, the children of this country, had the proud legacy of freedom that rested in our hands and we had to guard it against foreign and dark forces that might claim this God-given right from us, we heard. I was twelve years old and believed what I was told to, although the seriousness of the occasion left me with a diffuse feeling of anxiety and confusion, intermingled – of course – with my swelling nausea.

Much later in my life I learned about another event that took place during May 1971. A few days before the declaration of the new republic, a non-violent national strike led by Nelson Mandela and supported by millions of oppressed people in South Africa took to the streets. This historical strike challenged the creation of an exclusively white man's republic on African soil and the supremacy of white rule. Africans were called on to refuse to co-operate with the new Republic. The Union Defence Force left its barracks in full strength and violently suppressed the strike. More than ten thousand Africans were arrested and any further meetings were banned. After this event the freedom struggle mobilised underground.

Anyway, that day at the sport stadium, we stood to attention as the parade of awkward military vehicles rolled past, followed by the stomping of heavy army boots and fed-up sunburnt faces of young men behind the shiny display of their R1 machine guns. Then we sang patriotic songs. Though my head was swirling by the time that thousands of young voices carried the last notes – a long-winded "*aaaa*" at the end of South Africa – high into infinity, I thought that the songs were the most beautiful I had ever heard.

When I decided to write a story about us, my love, it was this incident that flooded my mind and refused to leave. I am not exactly sure why, but I can speculate up to a point that would put Freud to shame. Perhaps it was the first amorphous beginning of my collective identity as a citizen of a country of which I had to be proud without ever knowing or questioning why. At the risk of sounding inapt, I can also insinuate that on that specific day I made my first connection between the peaceful sham that the apartheid regime made me believe in, and the undercurrent of pain and violence that ran well concealed and parallel to most South Africans' lives. I still cannot grasp the full symbolism, but I do recall that my headache became worse, settling intensely behind my eyes as if someone was pouring lead into my skull. I tried to swallow the thick sweet smell, but eventually it was so unbearable that I emptied my stomach over my black school shoes. Let it be sufficient then to say that, for some reason or another, I could not write our story without relating it to the incident of the shoebox with the little flag and rosette and the lead in my head before I threw up.

When I met you round about 1982, you already had a sturdy reputation in underground circles as a political activist and freedom fighter. It was also known that you were a lesbian and that your lover was killed in a township skirmish with the South African Defense Force, although her death was never reported by any news agency. My role as sympathetic bystander to the freedom struggle was clear and simple. At that stage, restrictions were imposed on people who were suspected of being involved in the struggle or having connections with underground cells of banned political parties. House arrests became frequent, persecutions were spreading and people disappeared either behind bars or in shallow graves in desolate areas and were never heard of again. Even today some bodies have not been found. Freedom fighters retaliated with acts of sabotage. Some left the borders of the regime to be trained in supportive foreign countries as guerilla fighters. There were times that you would have needed a safe place to stay over and lay low before moving on, and that was where I came in. Whenever you called, I was to give you shelter – no questions asked.

Your first call came, quite coincidentally, on my birthday. Half past one in the morning, the telephone rang. I offered you some champagne, which you declined with a tired flicker of your eyes. A conversation of polite questions and answers followed. Then you made a few telephone calls. Even today I remember how I immediately noticed the casual and generous movements of your hands. Yes, your hands definitely exuded the temperament of an exceptional dancer. I was sure that you could move like shimmering satin billowing in a gentle warm wind, with your hands framing the curving movements of your body. Once I caught you staring at me from across the table, unabashedly holding my eyes for the few seconds that it took me to look away and empty my champagne glass.

As I later passed your bedroom I heard you shuffling, then you clicked off the light and sighed. For a moment I stood in the dark, pretending to hear you breathe. Perhaps it had only been my imagination, but I was sure that I could hear your breath slowly filling the apartment. I immediately felt closer to you, as if I possessed some private knowledge about your life that was usually only reserved for sharing during intimate moments.

After that first sojourn, you continued entering my life like a wave freeing itself from the deepest indigo of the sea, bringing to shore all kinds of secrets and debris. And at the appropriate time you swiftly and quietly retreated, leaving nothing but a glittering trace that soon disappeared in the sand. Until the next wave. Often you only stayed for a night, or you left boxes of leaflets smelling of printers' ink with me for safe-keeping, which other comrades would collect just as mysteriously as you had left them.

Every time I remembered something different about you. It started with your dancer's hands and the click of a light switch followed by a sigh. But soon my head was filled by the way in which you held a tumbler moments before you sipped, or your shoes tainted by rain while travelling on remote roads between tropical green villages. Also the way in which you frowned when trying to elude any emotional reflections in your eyes, the way that the bed and cushion slightly preserved the shape of your body, your fingers teasing a candle flame. Ah yes, of course, your hands – there was so much passion in the way that you moved your hands.

You were continuously on the move and sometimes disappeared for months on end. Often you arrived exhausted at my apartment with fragrances of foreign countries and desolate places surrounding you and persistently inhabiting your body – even after a hot bath. Through you I inhaled the yellow desert sand and copper sunsets that nested beneath your skin, or the vapor of pine needles after a thunder storm, or herbs and leather from outlandish craft markets and *souks* entangled in your hair. Once I caught the crude iron stench of dry blood and bones, burning hair and sticky flies – it must have shown on my face, and for a moment I thought that you were going to say something.

It was probably a mixture of similar images that were continuously clogging your dreams, eventually immersing your mind and spilling over into nightmares. Night after night I woke up to your terrified screams. I would go to you, gently woke you and stayed with you until you were asleep again.

One night I heard you open the backdoor to the small balcony and close it again. You were probably afraid of having another nightmare. From my bedroom window I watched you sitting with your back against the wall. You shoved your hands deep into your jeans' pockets. I could see your breathing deepening until your body became uncomfortable with its own yearning. Then your one hand moved to your jeans' zipper, teasing and stroking, skilfully disappearing deeper into the front of your pants. I saw your fingers kneading yourself in a gentle and kind way under the heavy material of your jeans, and I could hardly breathe. Then you looked up at the skies. Silver stars pricked through the purple and black hues of the night. You became impatient; I could see agitated lines forming around your mouth and a vein rising across your forehead. You started moving your hand violently, sucking your lips, licking, gasping and softly moaning, but apparently without any release. I went back to bed and waited for you, but you never came. You left early the following morning. I heard the key turning in the lock and once again thought about the raw and painful country we were living in.

After a long absence, the doorbell rang one morning at three o'clock. You appeared tired and frail at my doorstep, your turbulent eyes imitating the swaying movements of grass in a fervid wind. I noticed that your hair was sun-bleached and you smelled like gray smoke and disinfectant. That night, you did not wait for the nightmares to unfold. You simply got into my bed as if it was the natural thing to do. I felt no surprise. Rather, despite the daily violence ripping through the country, I felt a strange peacefulness while holding you. Your body relaxed in my arms and you smiled in your sleep.

The following morning you told me in a thick and sleepy voice about a woman who was set alight in the township by being doused in petrol. Violence breeds violence, you said, and people were turning against each other. Apparently the woman was suspected of being a traitor. I could feel your breath on my cheek while you were talking, your words against my face. I wanted to cry. You got up and ran a bath.

Afterwards you came into the bedroom with a towel wrapped around your body. Your shoulders were bony and sharp. Then you dropped your towel and sat on my face. Your eyes were closed as you moved yourself into my mouth, your fingers strangled in my hair. I opened you up with my tongue, licking and prodding until my face was covered with your warm moistness. The strong muscles of your buttocks rested like a half moon in my hands. Then time accelerated. Moons and millenniums flashed by, exploded and revived themselves again under a new firmament where the breeze carried the rich fragrance of musk and jasmine through my head.

"That is why I need to love you now," you said as you got up.

A week later a bomb went off in a restaurant in a well-off white area. A boy lost his sight and a pregnant woman miscarried under a table while waiting for the ambulance. You disappeared for over six months. When I saw you again, you seemed older. Folds of aging lines around your mouth made your voice seem sluggish and sometimes you got caught up in your own words. You also smoked more than you used to. I helped to bathe you and noticed that your hands were chapped and hardened. Your fingers seemed scarred and spongy, your fingertips hard and unconscious.

Then you sat down, took my hand and told me that your flight to London departed at 8:30 and I had to take you to the airport. A national state of emergency was just declared and the regime's security forces were closing in on you. I still remember the hollow scream with which your airplane lifted its stump nose and swallowed its wheels. Fragments of the wing- and tail-lights flashed further and further and then faded into the night. It was cloudy, I noticed, the stars were far apart from each other and vague, the moon a pale cold glimmer.

"Remember that I will always love you," you said at the airport as I was overcome with sorrow. "So many people had been forced to choose between this country and their loved ones, so many people . . ." Before I could think of anything to say, you were gone. So I decided to write this story.

In April 1994 Nelson Rolihlahla Mandela was elected as the president of South Africa. It was the first general election in South African history where all citizens were allowed to vote. I am sure that you voted on a grey and rainy morning in London. Most likely your hands were so cold that you could hardly hold a pencil and an icy wind pierced your eyes so that it almost seemed as if you were crying. Through mutual friends I heard that you visited South Africa twice after the elections, and that you were granted political amnesty. You never contacted me. Perhaps you could not bear the familiarity that my body would hold, the memories that would be invoked every time that we made love. Even though we shared a deep found peace in my apartment, we were always aware of the struggle raging outside the windows. We both knew that you would never be able to separate your memories of peace from the violent images of the struggle. We had to let all memories go.

But, my love, African summers still swell with a heat that wakes me up early in the mornings and warms my body with yellow rays. At night I sleep next to a woman who is kind and soft-spoken and knows me well enough not to ask certain questions. And sometimes, when the phone rings at an ungodly hour, I still think that it might be you, smelling of sun-dried wheat and burnished copper.

I still need my time alone. And during these times I am an expert in pleasing my own body. Then I recall your face, imagine the way that you closed your eyes as your body waited expectantly for my tongue to open you up, the way your back arched as you moaned for more and the sensitive way in which your hands danced through my body. But most of all, I remember the peaceful feeling that followed as you fell asleep in my arms. And I can still recall with uncanny detail how vulnerable you used to look early in the mornings.

SUMMER'S COMING

Julie MacLusky

Winter, London, England

A kiss on the lips woke Helen but she rolled away, feigning sleep, and waited for the the door to slam shut behind Sara. Helen's heart beat fast because today was the day she was going to commit the crime. At least, she and Sara, both the daughters of nosy mothers, had agreed long ago that reading each other's journals or letters was a crime. In fact, it would be grounds for breaking up. But today Helen was well beyond caring. When she was sure Sara would not return for keys, or something else forgotten, Helen scrambled under the bed, pulled Sara's letters out of their box, and started reading.

Even though she knew it was wicked, it felt good, very good. Helen's senses were flooded with adrenalin; her palms were wet, and she could hear nothing but her own heart kicking against her ribs. She had known that Sara was seeing someone, but not who, as Sara refused to talk about Helen's paranoid and pointless jealousy of her "good friend" Paul.

As Helen read she felt at a strange distance, intrigued by Paul's writing as she read. To her surprise she became annoyed at how rarely her own name was mentioned in the correspondence between these two. It was humiliating to find out how little she registered in their world.

Helen had found out what she wanted to know in the first letter but kept going until the very last in the stack, then folded each one carefully into its envelope and hid the box back under the bed.

That night was to be their last night. Sara was supposed to come home early but called in the middle of the afternoon to say she would be working late. Helen let the answering machine take the message, then went to see her old friend Harry, who said all the right things. That he'd never liked Sara, that she was treacherous, that Helen would meet a better woman during her year's study in America. And also one sad thing, that it was only the first love that kills you, and everything that came afterwards would be easy in comparison.

Later in the evening, Helen asked Harry if he thought she was far gone enough to act the drunken husband with Sara. Harry gave Helen enough vodka not to have to act at all, and sent her home in a taxi.

When Sara slipped into bed with her, Helen realized the vodka would be no protection. Sara laughed at finding Helen fully dressed and, thinking it a new game, stripped her roughly. Helen gave in rather than have her clothes torn. She hoped Sara might let her sleep once she was naked, but the pain of Sara sucking roughly on her nipples made her yell, and Sara smirked, "Ah, you are alive!"

After that, Helen lay quietly, too drunk to argue, and too tired to begin a fight, hoping for it to end. She was surprised at the effort Sara would make with her numb body. The slick hot patch that she made on Helen's hip as she slid would once have delighted Helen, but now made her nauseated. She dozed until Sara came, folded her hot damp body around Helen's, and slept.

Lying awake, Helen waited for the blind to lighten from black to gray so that she could get up and have a bath, fly from the English winter into the Californian version of it, and never, never do such a thing again.

Some months later, California

Helen drives home from work to the weekend at the time when a gauzy saffron haze falls between the city and the Santa Monica mountains. Taking the longer coast road, she slows her car to catch the red lights, so that she can watch people gliding by on the beach track. She loves to spot the tanned girls who skate in just bikini tops and shorts, with the brazen confidence that they will not fall, that they have never fallen. As the sun slips towards the northern mountains, its russet light is still strong enough to heat Helen's skin, newly exposed to the sea air after the long winter.

At home, Helen finds it is warm enough to sleep with the windows open. Turning constantly, she becomes tangled in the sheets, unused to their lightness. Her attempts to fall asleep again fail, disrupted by the warmth of a breeze from the garden, carrying in perfumes from the blossoming trees. Sometimes when she wakes, Helen feels a body close to her, a hand sliding gently over her stomach, pulling her back. Sara always needed the whole naked length of her body against Helen's, all night.

Each time Helen rolled over in her sleep, Sara would roll, too, and since they parted, Helen has found it hard to rid herself of the physical imprint Sara made on her body. She turns again onto her stomach and spreads her legs wide, expecting to be able to hook into Sara's body; but there is no body to press against, just the flat expanse of bed.

She still gets long, long airmail letters from Sara who says she loves her but she's living with Paul, who needs her, who she thinks she might love. To explain why she left, Sara says the affair with Helen is not what she wanted, and that the whole thing was too scary for her, the terrible "L" word. Sara says she can never accept being called by that name, and Helen must try to understand, this is her way of coping. All Sara's letters end with a request that they should remain friends, and asking Helen to please reply, soon.

In the hours before dawn the temperature drops. Helen falls into a deep sleep and wakes late. She takes an elaborate breakfast into the garden: brioche, coffee in a French press, and fruit. The food reminds Helen of all the other times she has eaten in the sunshine; for her the fledgling summer has a promise in its skies, of endless days eating outdoors, as though the fresh air could squeeze onto the food an extra piquancy, as sharp as lemon juice.

Nothing in Sara's letters has cured Helen from checking the sky constantly for jet-trails, reminding herself that Sara is only ten or fifteen hours away, that the Atlantic is not that wide any more. And wishing herself on each and every plane.

On the way to check her mailbox, Helen hears her phone ringing. She stops and listens to hear a message from Isabelle, a French woman whom some friends had tricked Helen into sitting next to at a party.

"Hi, I am joining some people at a club tonight, I remember you said you liked dancing. If you don't want to come along, let me know, otherwise I'll call by for you at about eight and we can get something to eat."

Her friends meant well, but Helen does not consider herself ready to start going out with anyone. She feels irritated by the sound of Isabelle's voice. Dropping her mailbox keys, Helen grabs the phone.

Isabelle asks, "Did you hear the rest, is that OK?"

Helen can't think of a good enough excuse in the couple of seconds Isabelle gives her to answer, at least not one good enough to warrant hurting Isabelle by rejecting the invitation.

"Sure, see you at eight."

Helen opens her mailbox and finds another letter from Sara. For the first time she hesitates to open it, fearful of the injury its contents might do. Instead, she places it unopened with the other letters under her bed.

Helen's day becomes dominated by the imminent outing. She dresses down on purpose, hoping to prevent Isabelle from getting any ideas.

Isabelle has dressed very well.

Helen asks, "Is this all right? I don't know what kind of place it is."

And Isabelle smiles, "Sure, you'll do."

On the way to Isabelle's house they have to stop off and buy things for a salad. In the car, the talk between them is easy but slightly edgy . . . Helen is aware that she is weighing too carefully what she says, and that physically she is curling herself up as small as possible to avoid contact with Isabelle. While Isabelle keeps her eyes on the road, Helen enjoys covertly taking in Isabelle's angular face and smutty eyelashes. Then, as Isabelle ends one sentence, she turns and catches Helen looking at her, and Helen is surprised by her eyes, which are brown with flints of green, and dilated.

Their last call is at Isabelle's favorite French bakery, partly for the sake of its loaves and partly because Isabelle can chat to the staff in her native tongue. Isabelle negotiates to buy a large, pale loaf, the crusty dimples of its surface outlined by a dusting of flour, and some croissants for breakfast. Helen is fascinated by the care taken with the marbled counter display, which offers a vast selection of cakes, whose golden folded layers reveal strawberries, apricots and apples, set off with a glaze, or chocolate icing and cream. The neat rows of pastries stop Helen from even worrying about how many croissants Isabelle has bought.

Once out of the shop, she asks Isabelle to carry on speaking French, because she adores the sound of the language, but Isabelle refuses, suddenly shy.

At Isabelle's house, any awkwardness between them is covered over with the preparation of the food. Isabelle slices fresh tarragon leaves and sharp basil brought in from the garden, then mixes them into a paste with mustard, before adding vinegar, for a dressing which she dribbles over a large leafy salad. Helen chops up the bread and mixes up a jug of pressed apple juice and ice. Then they take the food on trays down to a table in the sun-dappled garden. The chairs have to be arranged so that Helen can be warmed by the sunlight, which she can never take for granted, having grown up in the frozen north of Europe, and Isabelle, who spent her childhood hiding from ever-present Mediterranean sun, can sit in the shade.

After the meal, Isabelle sits a little too close to Helen and it should not matter but it does, it disturbs Helen, and as Isabelle's leg touches hers, Helen's skin burns along the length of its contact with Isabelle's, and she gingerly changes her position, hoping Isabelle hasn't noticed. As she curls up her legs underneath her, Helen wonders if it could work, if the burning means that she could be attracted to Isabelle. Helen is still worried that sleeping with another woman would be final treachery, that Sara has only betrayed her with a man, and that doesn't count.

When Isabelle gets dressed for the club, she lends Helen a long backless dress, and they get ready in separate rooms. While dressing, they have a little wine, which Helen needs for courage. They talk through open doors and, leaning out of the bathroom to be heard over the running of a tap, Helen catches a glimpse of Isabelle in a black silk patterned bra and is surprised by the contrast with Sara, who wore only white cotton, and would never exchange it for anything as frivolous as Isabelle's.

Walking into the club is like walking into a dark bath of women, music and lights. The bass notes of the dance music, which are being amplified through Helen's chest, take the place of her heartbeat.

The two women make their way through to one of the platforms overlooking the dance floor, to find a seat. Helen goes up to an empty table but just as she pulls back a chair for Isabelle, two women dance over to them, to let them know those seats are taken. The women look like twins, with identical, almost waist-length dark hair, spaghetti-strap sprayed-on black dresses, and unfeasibly high, sharp heels, the kind that would sink deeply into a lawn.

Helen asks them if she and Isabelle could sit there until they get back, and one of the women says, "You're so beautiful, how could I say no?"

Isabelle pulls anxiously at Helen's arm, wanting her away from these seats before the dancing women return, and leads Helen over to some stools at the far side of the bar.

As she sits down, on Helen's right the whole wall of the club is made up of a window which gives onto the inky orange sky and live mussel bed of the city. Isabelle starts telling Helen a story, of how she got married to escape her first girlfriend, and why it didn't work at all. Helen enjoys Isabelle's voice, which is breezy and low, with an accent which seems to tweak and stretch every English word she speaks in a sensuous direction. She leans closer, pretending to have trouble hearing but enjoying the vibration of Isabelle's voice against her earlobe. Isabelle touches Helen very lightly, placing one middle finger on her shoulder, and then brushing her long hair back. The heat from Isabelle's body unsettles Helen; she doesn't know if she likes to have anyone but Sara that close.

As Helen listens, she finds Isabelle's touch has brought back a physical memory she has of a time when she had just showered and was supposed to go straight to work but Sara was still lying in bed warm and naked and said, "You can't resist, can you?" and Helen slid her body cold and wet all over Sara, to get dry. Helen knows that her pupils have dilated and she can hardly concentrate on Isabelle's story.

Isabelle is wearing a long silk blouse and, as she leans across the table with the light behind her, Helen can see her breasts a little, at least the curve of them and she thinks, I wonder if they are like Sara's? and thinks that she'd like to slide her palms up Isabelle's ribs and over the flesh to get to the nipple, and she can almost feel the sensation on her hands.

Soon Isabelle and Helen have finished their beers and a waitress turns up and puts her arm around Helen and she loves it, the warm touch on her side. Some nights she might think of it as an invasion, but never tonight, in this mood.

They do some dancing and Helen begins to wish she was alone. Trying to shake Sara from her mind, Helen offers to go to the bar for more drinks. As she wriggles through the crowds, there is a rare natural blonde with milky coffee-colored eyes who is watching Helen as she passes. Helen wishes the woman would engineer to touch her accidentally, to give them an excuse to start talking, but Helen has already moved on, past two black women leaning up against a wall necking; then she notices the dancing women whom they nearly got talking to earlier, who are now back in their seats, and gesture to Helen to join them. She waves to them and carries on to the bar, where she has to press through a throng of women's bodies, and Helen realizes how much she's enjoying the flirting and thinks, Good grief, they like me, even though in the end Sara didn't.

For a moment, she wishes she could stay at the bar, checking out the women standing in groups round the dance floor. Squeezing herself back into her place next to Isabelle, Helen has a moment of blissful happiness. The night has become a gift to Helen from Sara, an impossible event, without Sara's rejection.

Helen says, "Let's just drink a toast to the fact that we are here!" and, as they clink bottles, she's also drinking her own private toast to Sara, who will never come to a club like this now.

Isabelle leans close to Sara and asks, "You look so happy, and pretty; can I kiss you?"

What can Helen say? Of course she wants to be kissed; she can't say no but she tries to warn Isabelle again, about Sara.

The beer is working on Helen's memory like developing fluid on a photograph, bringing images into focus. As Helen looks at Isabelle she can only see Sara walking her backwards onto the bed. Helen could never, until the last night, refuse or get out of it once Sara had kissed her just there. Looking into Isabelle's eyes, Helen thinks it awful and horrible that this strange woman wants to do that to her, wants to know the weak spots.

Before she can find words to warn Isabelle of how she feels, Helen has been shut up with a kiss, and of course she loves it, it's been so long and Isabelle has got her warm hand inside the back of Helen's dress, sliding the fingertips up across her ribs and she can't wait for it to go higher. Now they're not talking any more, just kissing.

Isabelle breaks free and asks, "Will you come back and stay with me?"

Her straightforwardness surprises Helen, who wants to linger a little longer in the club with all the beautiful women, watching their bodies, enjoying their covert gaze, because they are too tactful now to look at Isabelle and Helen for long. Waiting for Helen to reply, Isabelle explains, "I wanted to kiss you earlier today when you first got into the car but I didn't dare."

Helen wants to say, "I'm glad you didn't, because I wasn't attracted to you at all then." But instead, she says, "I'm glad you waited."

Then Isabelle kisses Helen's neck just there, the patch that is wired directly downwards, that makes her feel like she is being kissed all over.

Helen tells Isabelle, "You should know I'm the walking wounded, right now."

"How so?" Isabelle breaks off from kissing.

"Boring story; I'll tell you later," Helen says, while thinking, Well, how can you be disciplined and say no when you are enjoying it so much?

Isabelle is stroking the fabric of Helen's bra, working her way up towards the nipples, and asks, "So, are you going to come back with me?" She looks into Helen's eyes and, at the same time, slips a finger under the lace of Helen's bra to brush one of her nipples directly. When Helen doesn't reply, Isabelle reaches for Helen's other nipple. Helen smiles yes to Isabelle and reaches for her coat.

Back at her house, Isabelle has sobered a little and is shy and says, "D'you want to go to bed, we don't have to do anything?" and Helen is disappointed: she had been thinking of lots of things she'd like to do to Isabelle during the drive there. Helen pretends to go along with Isabelle's coy plan to lend her pajamas, and then strips off her own and Isabelle's, as soon as they get under the sheets.

Later, Helen looks up and sees her brown legs sprawled far apart, at forty-five degree angles each side against the white sheet, which forms her current horizon, and wonders at the heat of Isabelle's skin all over her, and how she came to be doing this, feeling totally exposed with a stranger. Isabelle is determined Helen should come but she fights it long and hard. Helen has decided that Sara must be bed with Paul on the other side of the world, at that moment, and she feels Sara's ghost is lying next to them in bed, watching, and asking sarcastically, "What do you think you are doing?"

Helen is still worried that this would be the final treachery; coming with someone else will be the end of anything, of any hope she had with Sara.

But Isabelle is finally taking the orgasm from the outside into Helen and she feels it has been forced upon her, that her body has deceived her by giving into the pleasure against her will. As she comes, Helen cries out in grief and despair, as if that is the moment when she has let go of Sara. The sound she makes seems to come from a hard place inside, the same place that makes women cry out in labor, and over death, a voice which doesn't belong to her, which is beyond her control. Isabelle has one hand inside Helen and one over her mouth to stop the neighbors hearing. She holds Helen tight and tenderly. They do not speak, and Helen is aware that Isabelle is waiting.

Out of good manners, Helen rolls Isabelle over and starts kissing her and Isabelle's passivity inspires her to be bold. It's easy, almost too easy for Helen to get her hand inside Isabelle. She's hot, small, and juicy, rippled inside, and Helen likes to control Isabelle's breathing, making her groan, likes the power of knowing that it is she who is making Isabelle's heart beat so very hard against her chest.

Helen likes to take her fingers out and up and round one side of her and back down and inside her but Isabelle just wants the surface stroked lightly and guides her . . . She starts shaking a little with tiny twitches in her legs which Helen absorbs into herself. Then there's a longer, more intense shudder and Helen's body sympathetically contracts inside as Isabelle's does. Just after this, Isabelle goes over the lip of it and comes, and is still.

Helen wraps her arms around Isabelle and wonders, How long will I have to hold her? and feels guilty just for thinking this.

In the morning, Helen wakes and pulls the sheet over her head and groans, "Oh, no, what have I done?"

Isabelle tugs at the sheet and laughs at Helen, "You Anglo-Saxons with your after-sex guilt, come here!"

As Isabelle starts kissing Helen she thinks, No, it is not guilt, it's because I've woken and you can never be a substitute for Sara.

Helen rolls over to avoid looking at Isabelle's body.

Isabelle asks, "What do you want to do today?"

As Isabelle talks, Helen looks out of the window; she can't bring herself to look into Isabelle's dark eyes, eyes which she imagines will have the smug look of a conqueror.

Meanwhile, Isabelle dips a finger into Helen and, delighted by how wet she is, circles the juice on her nipple and kisses it all off.

Putting Isabelle's image out of focus, Helen escapes by rolling away and asking, "Can I make you coffee, after all your hard work?" She then hurries into the kitchen to avoid any more sex.

While the kettle boils, Helen wanders through all the rooms, like an animal checking that a new home is safe. Helen is concerned that there might be something awful, one object that would suddenly change any friendship she could have with Isabelle. But Helen has discovered nothing that jars: quite the reverse. She is now keen to find out the answers to several puzzles: how Isabelle's parents got through the war, why they lived all over Europe, how she got hold of that fifties oil painting of Collioure in the south of France, and why she likes to paint woodwork in the turquoise blue that Helen has only seen in the Cycladic islands of Greece.

Coming back into the bedroom with the tray, Helen does get back in with Isabelle and they lie close, but Isabelle leaves it up to Helen to initiate things and she doesn't.

They dress and go out walking around Isabelle's neighborhood, on a path alongside the dazzling sea, to have lunch in the sunshine. As they walk, their fingers brush accidentally and Isabelle takes Helen's hand. Helen begins to enjoy being with Isabelle, who tells her stories about her childhood in France, how her father was captured by the British and made a prisoner of war so he avoided fighting, and how the longest time they lived anywhere was with the artists' colony in Collioure. This talk distracts Helen and she begins to think that Isabelle could make her forget. Helen, to her surprise, is enjoying looking at Isabelle's profile as they walk, her eyes softened by dark shadows she earned in the night.

They stop at a café on the edge of the beach and Helen faces the sea so that, while they talk, she can watch the surfers showing off. As they carve out perfect lines on the sparkling water, the surfers seem to display an irrepressible joy in living, not caring that each wave will finally smack them down in the shallows, bobbing back up from the froth every time, and fighting their way out to a good depth again, to wait for the next wave.

Turning to follow Helen's gaze, Isabelle notices the surfers and, smiling broadly, says, "Joie de vivre!"

Helen is eating an omelette stuffed with spinach and gruyère cheese, and the cheese has melted deliciously into a golden slime, juicy and ripe, and she's drinking strong coffee with honey. She and Isabelle swap some of their food and Helen thinks, This is where I should have been all my Sundays, this year; what a fine thing to be sitting with a lover, eating lunch.

Helen feels as though she has been nourished all over, had every pore of her skin fed though contact with Isabelle. She takes a long time over her food, because she is being distracted by graphic flashbacks of the way Isabelle's body felt under her, and thinks what a thrill that was, what a lovely treat Isabelle is.

Isabelle confesses that she didn't sleep all night, and Helen is sure it is because she is only the second woman that Isabelle has slept with. But when Helen asks Isabelle what she thinks the reason is, Isabelle makes up some lie and Helen, for now, doesn't challenge her about it. She's thinking that maybe they will have time, after all.

Isabelle drops Helen home in the late afternoon. Helen is intending to work, but feels too happy to settle to anything, and wanders around her rooms, distracted by Isabelle's farewell kiss, which she can still feel on her lips. She looks out at the patch of sky over the trees at the end of her street, and realizes that she hasn't noticed a single jet trail in two days, and hasn't wished herself on a single plane.

Turning from the window, Helen grabs the stack of letters from under her bed and takes them outside. She makes a neat pile on the concrete patio, then gently touches the edge of each letter with a match to spread the flames. Helen sits gazing into the greedy fire until every scrap has been reduced to charred black flakes. Then she sweeps the ashes onto the lawn, where their dust leaves a gray smudge on the blades of grass. Back inside the flat, Helen opens all the windows, to encourage the early afternoon breeze inside, and welcome the summer home.

CAROL

Kathleen Bryson

You squirt it on your pussy, which sort of burns now. The sting of perfume always makes you squirm. You have lipstick in your travel bag, too, "Wine" lipstick. You remember how you wanted to put some on when you were walking up the hill, and you take it out now, unscrew it and paint the areolae of your nipples. They stiffen immediately around the colour. You start to sing *Paper Moon* to yourself. You rub just a taste of the lipstick on your lips for colour; you don't want someone to refuse to kiss you because of lipstick plastered on your face, it's happened before.

Stop. Goes your brain. Stop. But your mouth keeps going in song – the truth is, you can't think what Nicky will say when she comes back from her walk.

You had walked fairly slowly back to the hotel room where you're now waiting for Nicky. It is a strange, dirty little hotel, set in a neighbourhood above downtown Seattle. You think about Nicky, she looks great now that she's got her hair cut properly. Just how you like it, a really sexy bob. It suits her. You wonder if Nicky is pleased with the bleach job you did on your own hair – it's hard to know, Nicky rarely tells people what she thinks of things, even you. She's always been like that and you suppose that at one point you just got used to it. Usually you even guess wrong if you try to guess what she's thinking. That's why people think Nicky's so weird – because she's so hard to read.

It's been about three days since Nicky kissed you in the woods back home. That had been a wonderful day, and you're pleased you took those photos in the woods. Just as a souvenir of sorts. She hasn't tried once to kiss you since. You've known Nicky forever but lately, since the kiss, you've been looking at her in an entirely new light. You wish she'd try to kiss you again. You'd close your eyes; her lips would be soft and sexy, like the skin of a ripe apple, like that favourite lipstick colour of yours, "Wine". Nicky's lips stay perpetually red; she doesn't need lipstick like you do. Maybe Nicky loves you. But you don't know; she hasn't said anything about it. You had felt yourself tingle down between your legs when you had walked back up to the hotel. You haven't felt like this since Mark, the one Nicky hated so much. True, he turned out to be a bit of a jerk, but sometimes you would go even further and make up things, just to watch Nicky's eyes narrow. God, she was so possessive. She used to pretend she couldn't remember his name. It really got to you, sometimes.

Guys had whistled at you as you walked up the Seattle hill to where you are now, in the hotel room. You were wearing a tight white tennis dress and you had ponytails on either side of your head. Guys really go for the little girl look, you had thought to yourself, taking care to put one foot in front of the other and, just like you had heard, it seemed to make your hips sway. You had wondered if Nicky would like this look. Maybe you would do that Marilyn Monroe trick soon and cut off one of the heels to give you just a bit more of a wiggle. You could see the birthmark on your left thigh with each step, each step bringing you closer to the hotel, closer to Nicky.

What is lesbian sex like? you wonder. Probably just lots of cunnilingus. Maybe girls putting their fingers up each other. That would be OK with you; you like that. You like it when boys' fingers get all wet. You're such a tart, they say, look at you, you're such a tease. And then you squirm and put your finger in your mouth and look up at them with big eyes. They like that, too. You wonder if Nicky would like that. Maybe Nicky doesn't like you at all in that way; maybe she's not a lesbian at all, the way you suspect she is.

Maybe you'll have to kiss her, first. You can't do that. Maybe you're the one who's gay, really, not Nicky. That's why you've been thinking about the kiss for three days straight, when obviously she forgot about it since it was just a joke. Usually when you start to think like this you go and put some more lipstick on or go flirt with a boy – because that way people won't be able to tell that it's really you who's gay.

You had kept walking up to the hotel where you had left your lipstick, so you couldn't put it on right away. You had wondered whether Nicky would be there when you got there. Would she grab you and kiss you now that you were finally alone together? If you were to kiss her first, she might think you were disgusting, too forward. Sometimes in the past boys have said that to you when you try to kiss them first. But Nicky's not a boy. Sometimes she acts like a boy, though. She won't wear makeup and she won't laugh right.

It had felt strange just walking along up the hill, being away from your parents and in a big city. You'd never been on your own, without adults before. You could go eat a couple pints of ice-cream now, just because you can. But this meant there are no rules . . . so you *could* kiss Nicky, couldn't you, if she wanted to kiss you, too. You're thousands of miles away; nobody knows you here. Several cars had beeped their horns at you when you were walking up. You had smiled.

Back at the hotel there was no one there; Nicky seemed to have gone for a walk or something. Thank God you had dropped off the other two who had driven down the Al-Can with you, this morning. The four of you had driven shifts and straight through the Canada nights and made it here in five days. Now it was just you and Nicky.

You had taken off all your clothes and checked yourself out in the mirror. You had wished your hair was longer, just a few more inches and you could sit on it. You had reached your hand behind you and pulled on your hair in front of the mirror. You had pretended it was Nicky pulling on your hair. Knock, knock. Who's there? It had been hot in the hotel room and it still was.

You had gone to open a window. Your breasts had brushed against the sill as you forced up the stuck window. Off in the distance, nearly two blocks away, you had seen someone you had thought was Nicky walking towards the hotel. You had wondered whether Nicky liked big breasts, the kind you have.

Maybe you should have put your clothes back on. Maybe not. Your heart had already started beating quickly. There was a haze in the room, a sunlight haze, but it was already darker here in Seattle than it would be at this time back home. They have dark nights here. That's what you had remembered about Seattle and the rest of the Lower 48. It was so hot – you had looked out the window again and seen that the approaching figure was Nicky for certain, but she had only progressed about a block. There had been about another block to go. You had grabbed your perfume from your travel bag. It was a really decadent, heavy, trashy scent – *Paris*, and you knew it never failed to turn Mark on when you wore it. But maybe Nicky would recognize it. Maybe she was sick of it.

The perfume is still stinging slightly. You put the lipstick back in the travel bag, go to the bed and sit down on the edge, crossing your legs and facing the door. The rouged nipples make you feel powerful and now you feel confident of the situation. A little bit of colour has perked them right up; forget that ice-cube shit you once read about. You don't know why you have this little catalogue of sex tips in the back of your head and you don't know where the catalogue comes from, but you know it serves you well. You are hyper-aware of your protruding scarlet nipples; you put your hands behind you and wait.

Nicky opens the door. She just stands there in the doorway, looking at you. She appears shocked. Maybe you've made a mistake. You look down at your purposefully sluttish nipples and again you feel a burst of courage. Without raising your head, you look up at her from underneath your eyelashes. "Hi," you say, "come in and shut the door."

"I've just been out walking," says Nicky.

"Your shoes are wet," you observe. You can be as cool and casual as you want because, in the end, it is going to be she who makes the first move. Maybe she doesn't think this is shocking, you think; I'll mention the nudity. You'll draw her attention to it, so she has to notice, even if she doesn't want to.

"It got so hot in here, I couldn't help myself," you say. "I had to cool down."

Nicky looks nervous. Is she gay or isn't she? Most guys would have been all over you, by now. But you've been naked before with each other before this, for chrissakes. You've known each other since you were kids, after all. Maybe she thinks you actually *did* get too hot. Maybe she thinks this is all perfectly normal. But you aren't. You're perfectly abnormal.

"Just a second," says Nicky. She walks over to the thermostat. "Well, no wonder it's hot," she says. "It's turned way up to 90°."

You do hope that she didn't read last month's *Cosmopolitan* with that little trick. Of course not: who are you kidding? Nicky would never read *Cosmopolitan*.

"Come over here on the bed," you say. "I want to talk."

Nicky comes over and sits some distance from you. She's trembling. So she *is* nervous about you, after all. Now you know what to do. You swivel your upper body towards her, keeping your pelvis where it is. There, that can be a bit of a tease. You absent-mindedly look at your hand, then let it brush across your tits; her eyes follow your hand, as whose wouldn't? But you are talking to her.

"I'm scared," you're saying. "I've never lived Outside before."

"That's not true, Carol," she says. "You left for a while, the summer before our senior year."

"Yes," you agree partially, "but only extended vacations. Now we're living down here, Nicky, and it could be completely different. Maybe they'll think we dress funny. Maybe they'll think we talk funny."

"That's also not true, Carol," says Nicky. "You know we talk just the same."

She's so literal. You look at Nicky until she breaks the gaze and then you let your eyes fill up with tears and spill over.

Nicky looks at you again. "Oh, Carol, don't cry," she says and she tries clumsily to hug you. As soon as she touches your flushed skin, you know you are going to win this one. Your lips and Nicky's lips are so close that she kisses you quickly on the lips again, just like she did in the woods that time. She pulls away and starts to apologize, but you give her your brattiest and most charming smile, the one she couldn't resist from you, even when you were kids. She looks stunned and then smiles back and pulls you to her, like James Dean, even though she's a girl. You close your eyes and imagine James Dean kissing you. Then she starts taking off her clothes while you put your hands behind you and lean back on the bed again, watching her. You will remember this moment. There are points of time you remember clearly for years.

There are points of time you remember clearly from before they locked you up, such as the snow. You loved the hard spruce needles of the forest. It was a forest with thick canopied leaves like pale green lace. And if you touched it so it trembled, the lace fell down delicately. When she reached the place where you slept, her hand moved into your bed and coldly on your neck.

Nicky puts her mouth down against your pussy, and you move your hand onto her neck, but she doesn't lick or probe any further. Your body towers over hers, the kneeling body. *Can she smell the Paris?* You are turned on. You smell like sweet water and you taste just as good. You know it. Then Nicky begins to lick you, just outside your lips, but working towards angling in, if you catch the meaning. At first it feels good and, while she does it, you run your hands up and down the designs of bone on her spine, up and down. You let your hands rest on her back for a moment, like you are doing that laying-on thing in church, and you look up at the ceiling. You imagine what you look like sitting there, your head back, your hair behind you brushing the bed. Your face is tan, a fact of which you're well aware, and it probably looks very beautiful.

Then it starts to feel bad, it hurts where Nicky holds you far too tightly, and even though Nicky now has her tongue up you and even though you are getting wetter, it hurts. You don't know the right way of telling Nicky how bad the pain is. So you stand the pain of a too-tight embrace on your sex and you grip Nicky's back and you stare up at the ceiling. You come actually, surprisingly, and it is not that long after you come that the pain in your pussy stops.

You know that you and Nicky are going to have to look each other in the eye and talk about it. But that's exactly it, because it is Nicky you hold in your arms – and only because it *is* Nicky, and no one else – you know that it can't be just another screw either of you just blow off. Just another screw for you, you mean; you don't know if Nicky actually has slept with anyone before. You've never seen her with a boyfriend.

At that precise moment, Nicky gives you a wide, beautiful smile, and that's how you know Nicky is the one. The do-till-you-die, heart of your heart one. And you are going to be hers, too, only she doesn't know it yet. You know right then that you don't have to wait for a knight on a white charger to sweep you away, to defend you, to protect. Because Nicky will do all that. You don't care if she is a girl. In fact, it might be even better; the two of you could maybe understand each other better than if she had been a boy. And plus, she can make you come. She doesn't know that yet, either. She has to ask you afterwards, on the bed, while you lay petting and talking and stroking each other's bodies. It irritates you when people have to ask you.

You talk about Seattle that night, and of Oregon and of the whole Lower 48 and what you are going to do with your lives and where you are going to go, but all you really remember of the whole night is the dream-like wonder of having Nicky in bed beside you, actually *Nicky*, with her hair so sharply cut and hanging in her eyes and pretty, and you with that little voice in your head saying, now I have someone I can be sexy for, now I have someone I can be slutty for, now I have someone for whom I can try out my whole bag of tricks and it actually *means* something. You feel vulnerable, like the wind coming from the still-open window is rushing through each one of the un-guarded gaps between your bones.

That night, the two of you make the inside and the outside of your sex hurt again. It has become raw. The colour over Nicky's cheeks is deep red – not the scarlet colour that often hurts your eyes, but instead the tone that soothes your eyes and makes your stomach feel hollow. You are slow . . . You wonder if your own lips are as swollen as hers, soon they are, she kisses them so they swell puffed up, then she kisses you, then she kisses you . . . When you wake up, you are both in love. She doesn't say it yet, though. You know you aren't the first two young lovers in the world, but it feels like it. You know it's stupid to say you feel like you're going to be together for ever after, but it feels like that, too.

The window still stands open in the morning. You have lain there all night, kissing and pushing everything further, and you have the taste of Nicky smeared all over your mouth. You detach yourself from her hold and stretch out in the patch of sun on the bed. You can still see the artificial raspberry tint on your nipples and you tease them, the left breast, then the right, until Nicky takes notice again and buries her mouth over them in the same order, the left breast, then the right. While her apple mouth works away on your right nipple you take in a breath; it is like you notice the curve of your breast for the first time and the nipple, the nipple is made up of dozens of globe-like tiny segments, like many tiny salmon-eggs. It is disgusting.

It may sound stupid to say you have never really looked at your breasts before. But it is true. And now you don't want to look too closely; the fear is you will become sickened. Especially as you do not know what else you will find when you look too closely.

When Nicky's head next comes up to your own – you think she is intending to kiss you – you dodge her and quickly adjust your body to a sitting position. People always like you more if you withhold something from them.

"I'm hungry," you say. "Aren't you hungry?" She's ravenous. "Let's go find one of those cute little cafés down the road I saw when I was walking up," you suggest.

Nicky first gives you an intense look – and your heart beats rapidly with that gaze – until, nodding, she agrees in a calm voice which belies, you feel, the obvious electricity between the two of you. And she doesn't even know yet how in love with you she is.

ONE NIGHT IN PARIS

Jill Gardiner

"Pat, do me a favour," you said. "Come and ask Joy for a dance."

Your eyes met mine. Dark, open, appealing: how could anyone resist eyes like yours? I'd checked out the rest, believe me, and you were by far the most attractive woman at the party. I looked down at my glass, took another sip of Chardonnay.

"Must be ages since you and Joy split up," I said. "I mean, you and Fran have been partners for ever, haven't you?"

"Ten years." Your hair, always unruly, suddenly tumbled across your cheek. "Joy and I were together before that, when I lived in London. She used to be great fun: she's just been a bit down since her girlfriend left her. It's time she enjoyed herself again, let herself go."

I wanted to lift the hair out of your eyes, but I resisted.

"Well, there's nothing like dancing to take you out of yourself, is there? I love it."

"Come on, then," you said, and took me by the hand, led me out of the kitchen and through the crowds of women. You walked the same as you dressed: casual but not careless. Dark leggings and T-shirt. Your thighs so slim. The gentle curve of your hips. You had, I realized, the most beautiful bottom in Brighton. The nape of your neck was tantalizingly bare. I had a sudden image of us lying naked in each other's arms, stroking each other's faces and taking our time. I would caress your back with a feather touch, flickering lower and lower, until I would cup my fingers around your buttocks and pull you against me. You would sigh deeply and kiss me over and over, your lips exploring my neck, my breasts, my nipples.

But here we were in the front room, with Tina Turner blaring.

"This is Joy," you said in my ear. So that was her: the one with the Cheshire cat grin.

What a disappointment: she was nothing like you. Tall where you are petite. Bosomy, not boyish. Crisply ironed cream trousers. A face without a freckle. Improbably neat curls. But she was smiling at me, with a definite glint in her eye. She liked what she saw, didn't she? And she was unattached, wasn't she? Fran smiled approvingly, perched on the sofa, her eyes on you, as you got Joy and I going on the dance floor. Then you melted away, back to Fran's side.

Joy could move, all right. I was away as usual, arms everywhere, and here was a woman who could actually keep up with me. I had that starched jacket off her in no time. She gave me a twirl or two, made sure I'd caught a good glimpse of all she had to offer. Her long legs leapt back and forth, and she lunged her bottom towards me, then bounded away. I advanced. She retreated. I backed off. She moved forward. And so mirroring, then deliberately opposing, each other's movements, we danced ourselves into such a frenzy that women cleared a space around us, and when the music stopped there was a round of applause. Pink and flushed, she smiled bashfully. I understood why you had once wanted her. I was wondering if I could want her myself when she turned and left the room without a word. When she finally came back she ignored me, and badgered you to take her back. Fran was exhausted, so you were outvoted. You hugged me goodbye, and I could feel the shape of your breasts against me. My nipples grew. Fran kissed me, in all innocence, more warmly than I deserved. But Joy was outside already, squirming and giggling like a schoolgirl on the doorstep. I blew her a kiss, but she poked out her tongue and ran down the road.

"She likes women to treat her badly," you explained. "God knows, I did, and it took her years to leave me."

"Good luck, Pat!" said Fran.

"We'll work on her," you promised, winking at me. I felt a sudden tightness between my legs. I caught my breath and turned it into a cough.

"We'd better be going," you said. "Thanks a lot. Take care."

Six weeks later, I was on my way out to dinner when the phone rang.

"Hello, you gorgeous, sexy, creature."

"Sorry?"

"Where have you been all my life, you beautiful thing? I'm dying to see you again."

"Excuse me, who is this?"

"It's me, of course, sexpot! You haven't forgotten me already? You fickle old flirt, you. I did get your messages, darling, all of them: I just haven't had a minute."

"Joy?"

"Joy by name and Joy by nature, that's me. Now what are you doing next weekend?"

"Well . . ."

"Whatever it is, cancel it. I've got this irresistible urge . . ."

"Oh, really?"

"Yes. All this work's driving me crazy: I've just got to have some fun. Lights, music, action; wine, women and song . . ."

"Mmm?"

"Which is where you fit in, sexpot. How d'you fancy a weekend in Paris?"

"Paris!" No, no, no: too excited. "Well, I'll, er, have to check my diary. I'm really not sure, hang on . . ."

"Now, look here, sexpot, this is me offering you a weekend in Paris: just drop everything. Oh-h-h-h! What a ravishing thought. Drop everything, you gorgeous thing, you, and come fly with me. Don't even hesitate, just say yes."

I said I would phone her back.

By the time I did, her cat had been sick and she couldn't leave him in case it was something serious. Then her mother's pressure cooker exploded, and she was on decorating duty for the next fortnight. Inhaling all that Mellow Yellow for Kitchens and Bathrooms left her with a persistent cough with which no French doctor could be trusted, should it turn tubercular. Once she had recovered, the next weekend was your birthday and you might invite her over. When you didn't, she finally flounced down to the travel agent's and I raided the last of my savings and sent her a cheque for my ticket. By then, we had been out together a number of times in London, and romance was definitely blooming. She needed to talk, she said, and I was a good listener. I needed to have fun, I said, and she made me laugh a lot. While I always caught the last train home, we had got as far as long lingering kisses in doorways, so it could only be a matter of time, and where better to seduce her than Paris?

I could hardly believe it when we were finally on the plane. I offered Joy the window seat. It was a perfect sunny day, the waves glistening far below us. Beaming all over her face, she said, "Do you know, I'm so happy with my life. I've really got over Pauline leaving me."

"Oh, that's wonderful. I'm so glad."

"Yes, it's great to be free of it all. You know, it's just so much better, being celibate. No hassle. No upheaval. That's it, I've decided. I shall never have another lover."

"Oh, really?"

"No."

"Never?"

"No. Well, I'd only consider it if she was French."

"French?"

"Well, foreign, anyway. And dark, olive-skinned. But preferably French: they are so passionate, the French. I had this girlfriend once, Sylvie . . ."

Foreplay, I thought, sipping my gin and tonic. If I hadn't been blonde and fair-skinned, she would have been telling me how she yearned for an English rose.

And when we were finally in the back of a taxi, darting in and out of the Parisian traffic, I risked a squeeze of her hand, which she returned, turning her face to me with a blissful grin. I paid the taxi driver, dealt in confident French with the receptionist, and tipped the porter who'd staggered upstairs with her case. And then we were alone.

"I'm dying for a bath," she said. She hung her jacket in the wardrobe, sat down and slipped off her shoes. Loosening her belt, she eased off her trousers. How vulnerable she looked: her long bare legs, smooth, tanned, very naked. She began to unbutton her blouse. I went into the bathroom, turned on the taps, and returned to find her bouncing on a bed, wearing nothing but her bra and knickers. Virgin white. Lacy. Distinctly new. "We're all girls together: what the hell!" she said. I looked away, breathing faster, pretending not to watch while she bounced on the other bed.

"Hah! I'll take this one. You have that one."

Then she stood up. Her stomach was firm and gently rounded. I longed to kneel at her feet and explore her navel with my tongue. I would caress her hips, ever so gently, and kiss every inch of her stomach, very slowly, and then her breasts. And when she could hardly stand for wanting me, I would sit her down on the edge of the bed, kiss the soles of her feet, then flicker my fingers slowly up her legs, stroking her, oh, so gently, lingering with my lips as long as she could bear it, longer, on the tender flesh along the inside of her thighs.

I smiled at her, dreamily. Joy turned her back, glanced over her shoulder with a flirty grin, then took off her bra. It was too much. I stepped forward to take her in my arms but, with one hand across her breasts, the other clutching her sponge bag, she leapt, whooping, from bed to bed and into the bathroom. Click! Defeated, I tried the door. There was a hoot of laughter above the rush of running water. I lay on my bed, picked up the *Independent*, and was still there, fully clothed, indifferent, when the bathroom door creaked open. There was a smell of steam, then the faint and tantalising sound of talcum powder being rubbed into bare flesh. There was a scent of rose gardens and then a whiff of clean white linen. I sensed her glancing at me, furtively, like a love-bird expecting admiration, but the paper entirely absorbed my attention. Suddenly a squirt of perfume hit the back of my neck, and I turned, caught hold of her and pulled her down beside me. Her face was glowing, her hair damp, and a peach-pink bath-towel was wrapped around her. She scrambled free, squealing, and clutched at her towel as it came loose with a flash of breast. She really was tanned all over, and her nipples were erect.

"You are so sexy," I said, goaded beyond endurance. "Oh, Joy! Oh, rapture! Come to me! Come to me!" I caught hold of her waist, and parody succeeded where all else had failed. A yielding look came into her eyes. I stroked her hair, I caressed her cheeks, I kissed her neck over and over, and oh, so gently, I didn't rush her for a moment, but just when I could feel her body responding, she thrust me away.

"What on earth," she demanded loudly, "makes you think I'm that sort of girl?"

Everywhere we went that evening, I opened doors for her. When she was cold, I gave her my jacket. When she was hungry, I found us a candlelit table for two at a typically French restaurant in the Latin quarter, and ordered Chablis and oysters. We strolled along the Seine by moonlight and I declaimed French love-poems in the shadow of Notre Dame. When she tired of Baudelaire and Verlaine, I whisked her off to Montmartre, and we lingered over original paintings on the stalls of the Place du Têtre. Then we strolled over to the Sacré Coeur, and stood at the top of the long white flight of steps, the city spread out before us, an endless sea of glittering possibilities. I suggested going clubbing but she wanted an early night, so I hailed a taxi. While I was in the shower, she got into bed, turned her back and started to snore. When I finally managed to fall asleep, suddenly there she was, flicking a towel in my face, bounding around in nothing but her knickers in the early morning light.

"Come on, sexpot! Time for croissants and coffee! Wakey wakey!" I reached out to caress her, and my fingers made contact with warm flesh, but she slapped my face and slammed the bathroom door behind her.

That day, I decided never to see her again. Well, you know how she can be. The one time I tried to slip my arm through hers in the street, she was off, off and away, leaping into the distance like a gazelle, glancing back at me under her lashes, laughing. So we stayed at arm's length, hour after precious hour. We saw the Impressionists in the Galerie D'Orsay. We sailed in a bateau mouche along the Seine. We took the lift up, up, up to the summit of the Eiffel Tower, where the city buzzed below us with all its energy and dreams. How could anyone resist its romantic appeal?

"It's an incredibly beautiful view, isn't it?"

"It's bloody freezing up here," she said. "Let's go and get a cup of tea."

By evening, the streets were full of women, elegant and beautiful, with long brown legs, their breasts pressing against crisp cotton. The market traders on the Rue Mouffetard called out the price of passionfruit and pomegranates. Young couples in shorts, their thighs firm and bronzed, wandered the streets, their arms about each other's waists, each slipping their fingers inside the back pocket of the other. I felt as if I was sixteen again, with that first buoyant, amazing sense of sex, free-floating and everywhere, breathed in like oxygen, till it seemed that no one on earth could be thinking of anything else. When we saw the crowd on the corner, we stopped to listen too. He was a brilliant busker: played Spanish guitar, a passionate, yearning sound.

Suddenly I saw her in the crowd. Elegant. Blonde. Mature. Short chic hair. Cream suit. Trousers. Expensive looking. Very French. Parisienne, without a doubt. Her eyes met mine and looked, unflinching, till I glanced away. I was in confusion. I felt myself breathing faster. I glanced back and she was still staring. Her eyes said it: she wanted me. Instantly. Just like that. I had read of such things but never experienced them. Before. I didn't know where to look. I looked anywhere but at her, yet all I could sense was her eyes on me. She was exploring every inch of my body, mentally undressing me, I knew it. I looked back and she parted her lips slightly. I was not imagining it. What the hell was I to do next?

Suddenly she leaned forward and spoke to me, in a low languid voice.

"*Vous êtes anglaise?*"

"*Oui.*"

"*Vous aimez les femmes?*"

"*Bien sûr!*"

"Here, what's she's saying?" Joy demanded.

"*C'est votre amie?*"

"*Non, non, une camerade seulement* . . . She just wants to know if we're English."

Where did she live? I wondered, and she told me: not far from here. We stared at each other and she smiled, knowingly. I imagined myself on my back, naked on a vast fur rug while she trickled champagne over my nipples and licked it off. I could see her at that moment, in stockings and suspenders, and those creamy silk French knickers, wide enough for me to slip my hand inside. She would pour champagne through my eager lips, and kiss me with such force that I would cry out. Then she would tell me how she wanted me so much that she was afraid she was too passionate for me and I would tell her that I adored her passion and not to hold back for a moment. "Lie back," she would command me, and then she would pour champagne all over my stomach, and my thighs, and it would dribble in rivulets all over my body, and down between my legs, and she would lick it off, all over me, like a cat devouring cream.

"I'm starving," said Joy. "Let's go and eat."

"*Viens avec moi, chérie, ma belle rose anglaise.*"

I turned towards my femme fatale, and she gave me the most seductive smile.

"What are you doing?" asked Joy. "Who is that woman? What's she saying to you?"

"She asked if I liked women."

"No! What did you say?"

"I told her, of course I did."

I had never seen Joy so animated.

"So what are you telling me? Are you going off with her?"

"Well, would you care if I did?"

Glancing back at the seductress in the cream suit, anxious not to lose her, I caught her whispering fiercely to a middle-aged man beside her. Would you believe it?

"So that's how it is," I said to her. "Well, in that case, *au revoir*."

"*Mais, attendez!* I invite you both, for a glass of champagne, you and your friend, in a spirit of Anglo-French amity."

"Yes, I bet you do," I said, and took Joy's arm firmly, and marched her away. She could talk of nothing else all evening. When we got back to the hotel, I made no move at all, and even that failed to seduce her. I spent a restless night, dreaming of fur rugs and lithe women with tireless tongues, serenaded by the sweet sound of Joy's snoring.

Once we flew into Gatwick, I left her to struggle with her luggage trolley, protesting like a demented bluebottle further and further behind me. When, red in the face, she caught up with me in the Green Channel, I said casually, "Well, goodbye then," and walked away to catch my train without so much as a shake of her hand.

Within hours, she was on the phone. Within days, she was on her way down. Within the week, she was lying back on my bed, giving me a long seductive look. I said I was going to make a cup of tea and she pulled me down on top of her and slipped my hand inside her bra. When we paused for breath, I said perhaps she would prefer coffee. She took my hand and slipped it down her knickers. "Hot chocolate?" I murmured and she moaned unmistakably, lifted her shirt and thrust my lips against her stomach, and while I was so engaged, wriggled out of her trousers.

The rest you know. That was the evening when we finally arrived at your party, and you answered the door. It was gone eleven, and, if you remember, you were decidedly merry. I could not help noticing: you still had those extraordinary eyes. Your hair had that dishevelled, end of the evening look about it. There was a sound of whooping inside, and the music pounding:

Girls just wanna have fun
That's all they really want . . .

Joy's cheeks were still flushed as peonies. I suppose mine were, too. Before we could begin our careful explanations of what had kept us, you took one look, and said, "Ah, this calls for champagne."

"I don't know what you mean," said Joy, flouncing past you.

You winked at me, and went to fetch the bottle.

ALL OF IT

Joan Nestle

Ten years have passed since I crossed the seas. Ten years of work and play and then so much loss. Now I hold the renewed passport in my hand. All because of you, because you insist on hope, a hope that sings in your upturned phrases, that sits perched on your backpack sharing its bumpy ride down the streets of Havana, London, Melbourne, New York, Beijing. You make a home in whatever city your work takes you, your true home being the ideas that shape your vision of a world more equitable in its securities while still thriving with difference.

Wherever there is a desk, you live. I have watched you work, my black slippery coat with its gold dragon draped around your shoulders, books and papers piled around you as, hour after hour, you read through texts, always looking for the insight that will move your work along, that will push into place the next step of your argument. The huge shadows of your antagonists hover over you, the governments and the banks, the soldiers and the courts all pitted against the fall of your red hair, the squareness of your copied words. I turn to look again as I go back into my room to put my own words on paper, and see the frail strength of the future, your comrades, like yourself, working in so many places in the world, trying to chip away at the stolid face of unquestioned, unquestioning power.

I am afraid to leave what I know, to leave my home. I am afraid to take my body with its fumbles and mysteries into countries where I have never lived. And then you lay me down, and laugh gently in my ear. "You're a funny old thing," you say. I cling to you, to the difference of you, your sounds and smells from so far away, too far away. I weep into your shoulder. "I'll be back," you always say before leaving.

But now you are here, your hand moving down my belly, your hair trailing its red fingers over my face. I tense with waiting for the homecoming, and then you reach me and pause before my hunger. This is another kind of power, one that leaps from your hand into my heart. You pull your head back so you can watch how I will take you in, how I will arch with pleasure, my head thrown back with the wonder of the first thrust, and then all my will sinks to my hips and I call to you to never stop, to keep entering me with your difference, with the worlds you carry on your fingertips, to paint my caves red with your travels.

I hadn't thought it possible or wanted it. The night before you were to leave for England, the day we heard the news that Marjorie had died her cancer death, we made love as if all the days and nights ahead of us were lost in darkness.

You were lying against the pillows, your red hair spreading across them, your lipstick making the blue of your eyes even sharper. I get caught on those eyes; I think I see in them the seas

I will never see – the endless blue on the map surrounding the continent of Australia, a blue I fear because it is as vast and unknown as death itself. You turned toward me when I entered, your body urging me to hurry. "I want you," you said as I bent over you, taking you in my arms. I was deeply moved by your direct request and by my knowledge that I could meet your need.

I kissed hard and then light, kissed your neck and shoulders and throat. I wetted your nipples, my mouth pulling on them through the sheen of your nightgown. I buried my head in your hair, pushing your face to one side with my cheek. I just wanted to touch you, to taste you, to make up for years of fear, of deprivation. Your breasts swelled to my mouth and I pulled them free of the gown, rounding them in my hands, resting my head against their swell. Here was an ocean I could survive.

I slowly caressed the wetness out from between your drawn-up legs, opening you up, making love to every fold and crevice of your sex, knowing just what I was doing, and letting you know that I held your need in my hand. I was making love as much to your belief in me as to your body.

I leaned over you so my mouth could pleasure you, and I could see so clearly the movements of my fingers, the redness of your cunt, taking me in. I entered you, pushing against the swollen flesh until it gave way; then slowly, I moved in and out while I sucked you into my mouth, all of you bursting in my mouth like all things hot and moist and deep. You were all around me, your thighs like high walls keeping me in, your breasts above me still hard with want, your sounds, small moans, sharp intakes of breath and I was in all of you. You came in the way I had come to know, first small gripping of orgasms, and then as I kept on, not fooled by these first signs of pleasure, you pulled up into yourself, your moans becoming a hot wind above me, and roared your full giving into my mouth, on my fingers, through my soul.

Then your broad shoulders rose into the night, and your face looking down at me became my total vista. You smiled as you untied my black silk jacket. I asked you to turn the light off, and a sadness flickered across your face. "I will, darling, if you want me to." You leaned across me and the room fell into darkness. Now I could allow all to happen.

You kissed me deep and full, the kiss I had such a hard time accepting when we first started to explore our desire. Like the whore I sometimes was, kissing was the gift I did not give away. After such a drought, I was afraid of the intimacy of kissing, not of fucking, but of the hungry touch of mouths. One day in Riverside Park, with the sun falling into the river, you had held my head so I could not turn it away and forced me to take your kiss, your tongue. Now I raised my head in hungry pursuit of your lips, wanting more and more of you.

Your large, strong body, the assurance with which you maneuvered me under you – you surprised me. This woman, who was so languid an hour before, who half- draped her eyes with receptive want, now bent over me, holding me, teasing my nipples until I moaned for relief. I could feel your smile moving over my body as you spread my legs with your knee. "You keep open for me," you said, and I did not move. I felt you reach for the small bottle of lubricant we kept near the pillow. You kneeled between my legs, bathing your hand in the slippery lotion, your shadow large against the moonlight. Suddenly, very quickly, before I could contract with resistance, I felt your hugeness enter me. Your hand, sleek in its liquid coating, pushed past the guarding muscles, and you had me, all of me, waiting on your smallest move, longing for your thrusts. Not even breathing was as important as your next motion. "This is what you will remember each day I am away," you whispered, forcing the turn of my head by your grip on my hair. And you thrust into me with such power that my whole body moved into the air. "And this," you said again and again. Five times you took me with your hand, five times, one for each day you would be away. Then you stopped and I trembled in your arms, and you lifted me, held me, against you. I was emptied, or so I thought.

We lay in the darkness, my head on your shoulder, waiting for calmer breaths, the air still heavy with our need. You asked me to enter you. I did. And then you entered me, not all of you, not like what had come before, but enough so my swollen clit could feel you, and then you said, "Now fuck me," and I started to move my fingers in you. With all my focus on you. I did not realize for the first few seconds that you, too, were moving inside me, on me, that our bodies were moving together, pushing toward the same pleasure. This was something I would never have allowed, this sameness of penetration, this blurring of bodies, and you had known that. Before I could take in what was happening, I was coming in bursting waves upon you, and you, pushed by my movements, came with me.

Too exhausted to move, too amazed at what had happened, I just lay alongside of you. "You see, Joan," you said, your Australian accent incongruously crisp in the sex-scented night air, "it is all possible for me, for us, all of it."

THAI SILK

Bente Clod

"Fucky fucky?" A little boy in a starched white shirt tugs at our sleeves. Startled, Lisa lets go of the duffle bag she has just hoisted on to her shoulder. "Is he suffering from delusions of grandeur?"

"Sister, beautiful sister," the little tyke insists. He has an ugly sore at the corner of his mouth. For a moment we watch the skinny seven-year-old boy struggle to get the next bit of English out. Then I gently grab him by the collar and the seat of his pants, and send him off with a slap on his backside.

"No fucky fucky."

The boy turns on his heel and tries his luck with some of the other tourists.

We are dripping with sweat. Of course we'd heard of the humid Bangkok heat, but that's not the same thing as being right in the middle of it. Thank goodness that the travel agency's bus fought its way through the traffic and spared us from having to find our own way. It's taken almost an hour to get to our hotel, only a few miles from the airport, and we are completely wilted. I'm having my period, and the heat seems to augment my flow. When we finally end up in our air-conditioned hotel room, we throw ourselves onto the bed, exhausted. A twelve-hour trip. We've only had a few hours' sleep since yesterday.

"Fucky fucky!" We're rolling around on the bed. "Fucky fucky." We've been gently caressing each other for the last few hours on the plane. Our bodies are still tingling from the euphoria of the flight. Lisa rings room service for a bottle of cold champagne.

"It hardly costs anything out here," she claims, and pulls me into the shower. Before we can get our clothes off, the cold water splashes all over me and I'm screaming, grabbing a towel in defence. She runs into the room, taking refuge behind a bamboo chair, begging for mercy. At the very moment I wallop the towel across her guilty back, there's a knock at the door. A lovely little figurine opens the door and sticks her head in:

"Champagne?"

We're standing there like two guilty schoolgirls, me with my sopping wet clothes, and Lisa covering herself with the chair. The Thai girl sets the table gently and begins to struggle with the cork, but Lisa protests resolutely: "We'll manage that ourselves. Thanks, thank you very much."

The Thai smiles charmingly and turns at the door, curiously: "You on holiday?"

"Er, we're visiting a friend," I gulp, trying to wipe away the drops of water, "and to do some research".

The woman is unbelievably beautiful. She has dazzling, white teeth and a golden mother-of-pearl complexion. Her permanented curls are short and coal black.

"She looks like Cher," Lisa mumbles, rising from behind the chair.

"She's more beautiful," I snort.

"You – eh – tomboys?" the beauty asks, cautiously, clearly nervous now about her own boldness.

We look at each other and then back at Beauty.

Her face is lit up with a shy smile that discloses a pair of fascinating dimples. Lisa clears her throat; she likes to have everything out in the open. No hiding around in the closet, everything directly and clearly spelled out.

"We – er – love each other."

"Oh!"

The way the pink mouth takes the shape of the oh made us salivate. She nods, throwing her curls around, and declares, "You tomboys." Then, with two fingers, she waves coquettishly before she disappears with an even bigger smile. There will be a lot of talk down in reception now.

Lisa picks up the champagne bottle, screwing the wire off.

"Do you think that could be their word for lesbian: tomboy?"

"It just means a boyish girl in plain English, you dummy. There probably aren't many lesbians in Bangkok. I mean, aside from in the nightclubs. But in the sex bars you could probably get any number of possible propositions, not to mention impossible ones."

The cork pops off the bottle and the white foam spills onto Lisa's dry zebra-striped leggings and the little braided bracelet I gave her on the night of our engagement.

"It would be exciting to meet a real lesbian from Thailand."

"Maybe we have met one."

"Really?"

I put the bottle to my mouth and slurp the foam up. Now that I'm sopping wet, we might as well forget about glasses. In danger of upsetting the rest of the bottle all over me, I start licking her skin all over where the champagne is glistening.

Five minutes later we're high on champagne and naked and thoroughly giddy. Lisa has removed the bedspread and placed four of the hotel's thick white towels on the bed so that it will not get drenched. She seems to have clean forgotten her sociological research for her thesis on economic opportunities for young women in Asia, which has brought us here in the first place.

"Fucky, fucky?" I sputter with my face buried in her bush. She drills a heel into my behind and makes me plunge into her tiny precious spot. Not that I have seen thousands of pussies – I have seen some – but none of them are as beautiful as Lisa's. She has lots of black curls and the outer lips are as darkly pigmented as the rest of her skin. But the inner ones are much smaller and the prettiest pink. I envy Lisa's lovely flesh. My own pussy is a real flabby snatch, a colourless thing that just hangs there. She claims that it is the eighth wonder of the world, but when I hold a mirror between my legs, I'm not impressed.

I lick and suck on her little pink wings while I keep eye-contact with her, that lush. My eyes gazing all the way up past her soft belly and navel, through her cleavage where no cavalier has ever ridden, up past her chin and her nose, to meet Lisa's half-closed, delighted eyes. She reaches down and tickles my ears, puts a sneaky finger into one ear. It sounds like doomsday. I squirm it out again, put my mouth to her slit, and blow into her with all my might. She howls and pounds me on the head, pulling me up to her. We kiss as though we were trying to engulf one another. I put her hand on my breast and she takes hold of it.

I love the way Lisa takes hold of my breasts. I mean, Debbie used to handle them as though they might fall off, and Isabel used to suck a bit too hard.

Sometimes when we went out to Café Rose on Thursdays, it was as if my breasts were leading the way. But I never listened to what they were telling me until the time I danced with Lisa. Or, rather, until I went home with her later that night. That was the first time I had someone grasp and massage them with lots of kneading and squeezing. That was when I realized what they were for. Lost of hugging and squeezing.

Now it's my turn to moan. Usually I am not much of a sexpot when I have my period, but the champagne and the heat and Lisa's lovely hands are doing their work. And we're on vacation. A wonderful, long, exotic vacation in the East, where all I have to do is to assist my honey while she interviews enchanting Thai girls about their incomes. All this gets my hormones going.

Lisa bends down and sucks me so I quiver. "Now I *could* give back all that air you blew into me. But I don't do nasty things like that. I only do good fucky fucky."

She gently caresses my bush – I refuse to call it a Mountain of Venus, even though Lisa claims that it is the only proper word for it – and my pussy. Our attention goes towards my sore bottom. She slowly puts her sneaky finger inside. I wince, "Uh-uh. I'm sore."

The fingers pat the flaps back together again. It prickles as sweetly as a pin all the way up along the pea pod and closes it for now. She concentrates on my breasts; they open up to her hands, massaging and squeezing so the nipples stand up, and I tingle all the way down to my pussy from her hands, singing a song about Bangkok.

Lisa climbs on top of me like a frog with a leg on each side of my straight legs and squeezes herself against me, with confidence. Guess who doesn't have her period today, says her little pink pussy. Guess who's very horny right this minute. Guess who loves you. I'm near exploding with excitement, worming a finger between her thigh and pussy to help her wet place to weep.

I have never seen anyone produce as much fluid as my little Lisa. I mean sure, Debbie used to get wet, and Isabel used to have orgasms you could hear a block away, but that soaking wet little snout of Lisa's is almost frightening. Her pink flower petals produce enough dew for a whole field. I got a bit scared, the first couple of times. Later I made myself ask whether she had what they call female eja-cu-la-tion. She screamed with laughter. Then she admitted that Barbara had also been quite upset that she never could get as wet as Lisa, back then when they were together. That calmed me down.

"Take it as a compliment," she suggested.

Her dew is running down my thigh now. I have my fingers on her nipples, pinching firmly. We're kissing each other to pieces, right down to the bottom of our dreams where I can feel her getting ready for orgasm. It begins to shake her, a foot twitching. I send loving sounds into her, sucking my way over her lips towards her ear. When I start playing Walk-Lady into Lisa's pink shell of an ear, she gives a long ah. Coming now, she shakes as violently as one of these voodoo men in a trance. I mean, Debbie used to coil up like a spring, and the wall of Isabel's pussy would press and clutch at my fingers so I could hardly get them out afterwards. Lisa quivers and quakes her orgasm forth. All the goodness in her boils over, seethes over the edges. She is my little immersion heater, I whisper into her ear. My own little Thai immersion heater.

We fall asleep and wake up to an enchanted city. Outside, the city lights are sparkling, shining in the dark. A yellow moon is hanging low in the sky. We shower, get dressed and stand at the window in awe before we get going out into the sultry night in search of dinner. Before leaving we call up Eva on the phone, making her explain how to find her house the next day. She gives us the address of a good restaurant nearby. With a firm grip on each other's hand, we venture forth into the crowds on the street.

There are throngs of people, walking, driving, blasting their horns and streaming around us. Even though it's nine o'clock at night, the streets are swarming with bicycle taxis, real rickshaws and countless motorcycles. We ask directions, take a wrong turn, laugh and retrace our steps.

"Eva said we should watch out for the parallel street, lots of chauvinist clubs there."

"Here it is, Kathy."

The front of the place is lit up with a golden dragon spitting neon flames. Outside, the doorman keeps guard with a stone face. he looks at us, looks away, looks at us again and seems to swallow a ghost. Without the slightest change of expression, he holds the door curtain aside so we can step inside.

We freeze, as if hit by lightning.

The room is very dark, lit only by pink lotus-shaped lamps. The walls are lined with tables and there's a round stage in the middle of the room. Men of all ages, but mostly older ones, are smoking, drinking and slapping each other on the thighs, or keeping to themselves, one hand in their pocket. Some are accompanied by Thai girls in miniskirts, who seem to be about twelve and a half years old. Everyone's staring at the girl in the middle of the floor – our lovely Thai chambermaid.

She has dressed up in a leather thong tied around her waist and nothing else, except garish green spangles on her nipples. She is about to go down on her knees. Slowly, her perfectly shaped porcelain legs bend until her knees are pressed onto the floor. Then she tightens her thighs and begins to sway and bend backwards, like a snake in its basket.

Lisa grabs me by the hand. I squeeze back. Fascinated, we're staring at the performance, our dinner completely forgotten. It hurts to see that fine little person coaxingly reach out seductively first to one, then to another of the fat drunken Europeans old enough to be her grandfather. I can feel the sociologist rise up in Lisa. The rich world's exploitation of the beautiful people of the East.

At that moment, the dancer notices us. Her eyes open wide and, as graciously as a queen, she makes a deep bow toward us. A spotlight, which has been circling the room, hits our faces. We freeze.

She lifts up her head and sends us an adorable smile. She bows deeply towards us, arms crossed over her chest. For the rest of the show she directs all her attention to us. She keeps her seductive eyes on us while kneeling, she arches her back right over in a limbo position, resting on her knees, making lots of circling movements in front of her abdomen. Her pussy is a delicate golden brown with fine, short hair, and a violet ribbon suspended from it. We look at each other. She pulls the ribbon seductively, looking around the room that is filled with applause. She pulls a little more, and the applause grows. Now most of the men are standing up, cheering while her conjuring hands circle around her pelvis twirling the silk ribbon more and more. The place is boiling with excitement. Suddenly, with a quick little flip of the fingers up her pussy, she triumphantly pulls out a row of shiny metal plates, tied to the silk ribbon.

"Razor blades," Lisa moans, "she's pulling razor blades out of herself."

I get the chills in the middle of all that heat. The men around us are clapping and cheering and throwing money at her. The place is hopping and our little friend with the dimples turns toward us to receive our applause.

"We've got to save her," says Lisa, breathlessly.

I look around. The crowd is not exactly wild about us getting all the attention of their dancer. I quickly pull Lisa out through the hanging in the doorway, past the motionless doorman, who doesn't bat an eye at the sight of our beet-red, bewildered faces.

Outside on the sidewalk, Lisa paces back and forth, heedless of the people hurrying by and pushing. She thinks we should report the case to the UN. I figure we should wait and talk to Eva tomorrow and find out how ordinary this is.

"She'll chop her pussy into hamburger meat before she's fifteen and a half. Are we just going to stand by and watch her destroy herself? Then we're no better than those stupid assholes in there."

"How does she do it? I mean, she had real razor blades in her cunt!"

"She wants something from us. She was appealing to us for help. We can't let her down."

"OK, you're right. It's revolting. She could get blood poisoning. We'll notify the UN and the Human Rights Commission tomorrow."

"Right."

"Now I want something to eat."

We collapse at a coffee house a few blocks further down the street. It turns out that they serve simple, elegant food – three kinds of soy sauce on lots of vegetables flavoured with ginger and coriander. We kiss each other and order some tea.

Lisa frowns, "No. I just have to call Eva. I can't stand the thought of those razor blades."

I nod. But she comes back to the table with no result. The telephone is out of order. The waiter brings us dessert and an extra treat: two oranges with twigs and a few leaves still attached. The oranges let go of their peels with a silky sound. Long white threads hang down the soft arched lips. A drop trickles between two segments, the juice spraying out of the flesh. I let a finger glide into the meat of the fruit. Through half-closed eyes, Lisa watches how it sinks deep into the fruit and makes the sticky juice run down my hand. My finger continues down between two segments and splits the crisp fruit flesh so that the matte membranes burst, and the sun-coloured, taut sections of flesh are revealed. I pull out segment after segment and put them into my mouth, crushing them with my tongue so the juice runs down my chin. My tongue finds the smooth seed; it is hard and slides away under my tongue, the next orange tree hidden inside. Now Lisa attacks her fruit; sticks her thumb between two segments and wedges the flower open so that the segments fan out and the juice sprays her face. She licks the taste off her lips, opens the connected segments so the matte membranes get wet and the juice flows down her hand.

"I love you so much," she tells the orange. "If only we could be together forever."

We're strolling back to the hotel. The crowd around us seems to be thinning out. Handsome pairs of tourists in expensive clothing walk lazily among the small busy Thais and groups of red-complexioned men of the kind we have seen in the club. When an empty rickshaw cycles past, I put out an arm and hail it.

"I have never kissed anyone in a rickshaw," I assert into Lisa's warm mouth. The footsteps in front of us waver a little. Then the rickshaw stops in the middle of the street. The yellow face turns to us with a crooked grin. "Fucky fucky? You want?"

Now my beloved is really furious.

"I'll give you fucky fucky," she shouts fiercely right into the man's terrified face. "Come on, run, get going, you lazy beast! We've paid for this ride."

I hint that she's revealing an imperialistic attitude. She fumes in silence in her corner and keeps away from me for the rest of the lurching ride.

The first thing we see when we get to the hotel and go to the desk for our key is a grin splitting the receptionist's face wide open. He goes into the office behind him and makes a remark that gets an older woman to come out and stare at us openly. We clear our throats and ask for our key again. Then someone comes in behind us.

The exquisite little thing is tired. She's wobbling on her high heels, wrapped in a silk coat. She must have been drinking with the cheering men at the nightclub. The clock over the reception desk shows two a.m.

At the sight of us, our child of sorrow lights up as if we were old friends.

"Why you go away? Make me sad."

Lisa thrusts a hand into her hair so that it stands straight up. "How can you *do* that?"

"What?"

"That – that – razor blade thing."

"Oh, that's easy. I show you. How take care. No hurt. Mostly no hurt. I show you."

"No, no, no . . ."

"I do special night for you two," she winks. "In your room. But now I sleep. Very tired."

Woozy, we watch this little sensation receive a parcel of clean laundry and wobble off homeward.

Lisa is tearing at her hair, "Do you think she wants to do it with us? Is she a whore? Is that what's going on?"

"It's – er – well, you can't rule that out as a possibility."

My feminist sociologist lover has always had this secret dream of buying herself a prostitute. Sex for money. Of course it could only happen with the complete, unqualified consent of the whore; there would be no coercion or exploitation here. But to go out and buy a wild time has always fascinated my darling Lisa. I later wondered whether this could have been – wholly unconscious, naturally – partly the reason why we ended up in the world's Number One land of prostitution to do our sociological research.

We stagger up to our room and Lisa calls Eva.

"Do I know what time it is? Listen here, I said she had razor blades in her vagina. She pulled them out . . . What? No, not champagne corks, just razor blades. No, no barbed wire, we're not talking some hardware show, she . . . Sleep? How can we sleep when we've just seen a woman expose herself to mortal danger and humiliation? Eva? Eva!"

"What'd she say?"

"She said she would explain it all to us tomorrow."

"OK, honey. We have to gather our strength. We haven't slept for twenty-eight hours." After a while, I get her calmed down, undressed and tucked under the single sheet that serves as a coverlet. The last thing we hear before we drop off is the sound of the motorcycles in the street.

The next morning there's a knocking at the door before we wake up. Long before. It feels as though we've only had an hour's sleep when the door opens and our special friend minces in, wearing heels and balancing a full tray.

"Breakfast," her mother-of-pearl face whispers.

Heavy and crumpled with sleep, we emerge from under the top sheet, trying to pry our eyes open. Her white blouse looks newly ironed, the little skirt under her apron is smooth, and two tiny turquoise drops hang from her earlobes.

"Don't you ever sleep?" I yawn, astonished, while she sets things on a table that can be slid over the bed, right under our snoring noses. Lisa has fallen asleep again. "Sit down," I encourage. At that moment I feel an urgent need to go to the bathroom. A warm stream is on the verge of running out of me when I sit up. She sits on the edge of the bed, shyly.

"I sleep – afternoon."

"That – show – er . . ."

She smiles proudly.

"But it's dangerous! You could get infections. You could cut yourself."

"Oh," she shrugs her shoulders. "It happens. It's better than – than – I mean other things more dangerous. Much, much dangerous!"

"Other things?"

Lisa turns onto her back and snores loudly. We laugh. The Thai girl remembers her duties and pours the coffee into our cups. It smells wonderful, good and strong.

"Is better than . . ." she looks at me and blushes, looks away, studies the wallpaper, looks at me again, and makes sure I understand her before continuing, ". . . men. Fucking men."

I swallow my coffee and blink. Here it is, the one thing we want above all for our project. A genuine lesbian. A woman who earns her living by something other than exposing herself to life-endangering contagion through intercourse with men. I can hardly believe my own ears.

"You never – with men?" I ask.

"Oh, yes. But not in club."

So she only wants to avoid germs.

"Are you married?"

She blushes. "Two children."

I stare at the child before me. "*Two* children?"

She nods proudly, reaching into her apron pocket. Proudly, she holds out a photo of two little toddlers with teddy bears in their arms.

"Sister has six."

I smile and look and give Lisa a good poke. "Take a look, you sloth. A native takes us into her confidence and you just lie there and snore. Coffee-time. And baby pictures."

Lisa opens her eyes with difficulty, squinting at the two

babies and their teddy bears. Slowly, she swallows the tail end of her dream and hauls herself up to a sitting position.

I continue my conversation with the Thai. "What does your husband say about that show?"

The word husband has the effect of a bucket of cold water on Lisa. She stares, wide awake and thunderstruck, at the girl. The little porcelain figurine squirms.

"No, no husband. Brother owns club."

"Is she married?"

"Listen here, Sleepy, I'm going to get the mattress soaking wet. I've got to get to the can. I'll wrap the sheet around me."

"You want me to lie here stark naked in front of this nice lady? Are you crazy, Kathy? She'll be shocked."

But I have already pulled the sheet around me and Lisa gives a shriek. The hell with the consequences; I have to get to the toilet.

Lisa whimpers. The Thai woman hides her face in her hands – but not so thoroughly that she can't get a good look at Lisa's stunning body. At least, that is Lisa's account of the scene. I'm wiggling my way out with tiny steps, tightly wrapped in the top sheet, with a long stripe of red down to my toes, achieved quite without the help of razor blades or barbed wire. According to Lisa, our Cher now shakes her finger at us, teasing: "Oh, you tomboys!"

"Please!"

Lisa gets hold of the bottom sheet and pulls a corner of it over a quarter of her body. The chambermaid hands her a kimono, but she does not leave. She looks at Lisa slyly. "You want show – here – tonight?"

Lisa chokes on her coffee. Then she carefully sets the cup down. "No thank you. We go today."

"You . . . *go?*" Her face expresses such surprise and grief that Lisa claims it was touching.

"Yes. To stay with friend here."

The Thai starts to butter some lovely mouthwatering toast for us. Then she looks at my darling:

"I make show – now? Special for you."

"No, no, no."

"Yes, special for you, my friends."

"But we don't want . . ."

That was when the little lady put her tiny cool hand on Lisa's thigh. Not on her arm or her shoulder, but on her thigh. She put her porcelain hand on Lisa's broad thigh before she pronounced three little words: "I like you."

And then the feminist in Lisa surfaced. If there is one thing of supreme importance, it is a woman's feeling for other women. A declaration of love from one woman to an other has enough power to bring about world revolution and shake the foundations of life itself. It is nothing to be sneezed at.

The woman still has her hand on Lisa's thigh and they're melting into each other's eyes. I'm still in the bathroom, rinsing out my panties and putting the towels from last night in to soak. When I finally open the door to the bedroom again, arrayed in a short T-shirt and clean panties, I behold a scene that makes me stop in my tracks.

The Thai's opened her blouse. She's sitting on the bed with her blouse open and Lisa is staring hypnotized at one of her fingers, which is circling a dark brown nipple.

To interrupt would be like breaking into a holy ritual. No interruptions would be tolerated, I can see that. It's now or never if we ever want to have a real live prostitute at our bedside. At the moment, it is impossible to communicate this to my dearest Lisa. She is bewitched.

The girl can tell that she is making quite an impression. She smiles, showing her lovely dimples, and rolls her shoulders slightly so that the blouse falls to the floor. Then she reaches back and loosens the bow on her apron strings. Her little doll breasts jut right into Lisa's face. I can hardly breathe. The butter on our toast practically melts when Beauty drapes her apron across Lisa's body. With exaggerated gravity, she gently and strategically adorns Lisa's pale European body with the little frilly thing.

We are giggling. The Thai is giggling. She laughs until she has tears in her eyes, she curls up and puts her head down into the apron, overcome by laughter, she lies there like a playful puppy while we also start helping to arrange the apron, joining in the game, and before we know what is happening, the stranger has lifted the apron and begins to caress Lisa's flower. Her little supple fingers stroke and massage the rose petals, making Lisa close her eyes in bliss. Her little mouth puckers in the direction of Lisa's "Mountain of Venus". But it is me she is gazing at. I am the one who is drowning in her liquid almond eyes. I do not know whether I'm coming or going.

Suddenly, the Thai's hand slides down to the zipper of her skirt. In a fraction of a second, she has pushed the breakfast table away, wrenched her panties off, and laid herself down between us on the bed.

She nods and smiles at me and pushes herself over Lisa's thigh. Then she concentrates on Lisa's rosebush with her back to me.

I have a view of porcelain buttocks and under them, two tiny pillows. I have to admit that my temples are pounding. I've never been to bed with such a fine little body. Debbie was big, taller than me, and Isabel was stocky. But an Asian mother of two, the sister of a nightclub owner, equipped with razor blades in her cunt, this I have never – and never again will have . . .

My hand cannot help reaching out. My finger cautiously

draws a line down along her backbone She shudders and emits sounds of pleasure into Lisa's pussy. My fingernails begin to make circles, as light as a feather on her back and her buttocks. This is the nicest thing Lisa ever does for me just before I fall asleep. It makes me feel heavy, contented and blissful to have my back tickled like that. Up to her neck, all the way down under her buttocks . . . Whoops, my finger has slipped into her little clam shell; it is truly wet and warm in there – almost a tropical atmosphere. The muscle there holds onto my finger tightly, begging it to stay.

Lisa begins to utter long ohs and ahs. I bend down to kiss her. We both have closed our eyes. This is a situation for closed eyes, not that there is less pleasure in it than the things we usually do together. It's just so much more strange and dangerous. I must have forgotten Cher's soft little cushions for a moment because her behind pushes against my lap and digs into my stomach entreatingly. But she does not let go of Lisa's temple of Venus, and, from the sounds, it must be absolutely scrumptious. I try to fight my jealousy with lechery – and it works, more or less, until I find Lisa's hands on *my* Thai back. They seem to be out on the same errand as mine are; our hands collide on the crest of the backbone. They stop still like rival spiders that lift their tentacles at one another before they charge and tangle to join the rest of us, entwined in each other and the Thai girl, sweating and moaning. I have my thumb inside the Thai's pussy, and Lisa has a finger in her rectum and at the same time we kiss with unbelievable passion, more than we've ever known before. I mean, we've done plenty of experimenting in bed together, just the two of us. But to share a stranger's body is more exciting than any of that.

Our lover is beginning to shudder, she's vibrating; in fact, so is the porcelain behind. After all, she has two of my fingers in her cunt and Lisa's finger up her end, and apparently it's not all that bad; the beautiful body writhes between us and utters little porcelain shrieks, little yehrr's, grrry's and eeh's. Then her body is shaken by spasms, she scratches Lisa's belly and Lisa's body shakes, too. I'm so excited that there is nothing else for it: I lay Lisa's hands on my breasts and by reflex, she reacts: pressing and kneading and squeezing until I come in ecstatic gasps, my blood mixing with the transparent viscous fluids that keep me alive. It rises and erupts out of me in small slurps. I can hear that Lisa is far away in Orgasmland now. The little girl between us has thrown her head back into the pillows so her damp hair has got into our open, kissing mouths, and we smile at each other's mouths – having opened our eyes for a moment.

Then we shut them tight.

I'm sure that the Thai also closes her eyes and that her head is as empty of thought as mine. At any rate, the three of us lie there in that red hot room, gasping quietly, listening to the ceiling fan rotate above our sweating bodies.

We eat breakfast afterwards, and we make an appointment to visit her family. We write down her address, overwhelmed by all the favours she has so generously bestowed upon us here at the hotel. We've heard that the Thais are a proud people – they have never been colonized, I think – and that they're extremely hospitable. But this is more than you could expect.

Finally, our lovebird gets out of the bed and slips into the bathroom:

"Work!"

We nod understandingly, hold hands, sink back, and listen to the sounds of the city and to each other's heartbeats. We do not look at one another. The sociologist in Lisa is absolutely silent, and so is the feminist in her, I can tell. The Thai girl runs the shower and puts it off. Then she comes back in to us, newly starched and ironed, coolly genteel again with her apron on.

"Fifty dollars, my friend," she says with an enchanting smile, slipping her sandals on. "Special price for you. I like girls. My brother tell me you nice – remember little boy, 'Fucky-fucky'?"

A WINE-DARK NIGHT

Boz Thomas

Hayley is walking home through east London. It's Sunday morning, early, and a long dusty walk though the sun is bright. The shops are all closed and there's not too many people about. Which she is grateful for, because this morning her whole body feels as if it's been taken apart and rearranged. The sensation is strongest in the root of her belly, where a dull, sweet ache is pulling. Is it alcohol from last night, or the memory of love-making? Or is it desire building up again after just a few hours? Her legs feel heavy large like trunks of wood. Sometimes a hangover makes her body ache, sometimes lovemaking leaves echoes of pain, of pleasure – but this is different. Her lips, nipples, fingers, labia seem to be swelling softly in the morning sun. They're like new, delicately veined young leaves, unfolding in the light.

Am I turning into a tree? she thinks, with a shiver, and

words heard long ago and then forgotten surface in her mind. "You don't just pick a style off the tree. The tree's growing inside you all the time." Who said that? A musician. A black jazz musician talking on TV about his music. His name's gone, but his face is still vivid for her. Could it be the same with lovers as it is with creating music? That you don't just "pick them up" but your readiness for them grows inside you until you meet them and suddenly the sap's flowing and your body and soul are ready to burst into life, new shoots and leaves swelling out into the world?

When did the tree start growing for me? I didn't even know it was there, inside me, growing away all this time . . . The thought brings Hayley to a halt. She's standing outside a fabric shop. Rolls of cloth with vivid, African designs piled haphazardly behind the grimy window, waiting for Monday and potential customers to rifle through them. Or maybe for Monday, and for no customers, just another day lounging in the dusty sunlight.

There's one particular fabric, red, with an aggressive, spiky pattern which draws her eye. It's like the huge red curtains in the school dining hall where she sat fifteen years ago and suffered the smell of sour baked beans and chocolate custard. It's a memory that hasn't surfaced for many years. Disturbing, unsettling, and emerging from Hayley's subconscious all too often, recently. Why now? Why should she remember the noisy, violent hell of school. The bitter soil she grew up in?

And now, shivering, Hayley's plunged back into the bedlam of school lunchtime in that grubby, dark hall, under the red curtains. Girls shouting, throwing food, pulling each other's hair, slinking out to smoke and fight in the toilets. Shrill white girls with roughly highlighted hair and chipped nail polish. Or raucous with cropped hair and smudged mascara. Asian girls bunched together, talking and laughing, making plans, as if the tempest round them didn't exist. Proud black girls with long legs and big shoes and hair extensions and rolled-up skirts looking around aggressively, in case someone was looking at them with disrespect.

It was an environment where the best bet was to stay out of trouble. Keep quiet and you wouldn't get punched or scratched or kicked or verbally abused. Keep yourself to yourself, and you wouldn't have to get involved if you saw any of those things happening to someone else.

Hayley always took sandwiches to school. Oily fishcakes and stringy meat with tubes poking out of it were not for her. Impossible to eat a big meal in the midst of such gut-churning turmoil. Hayley tried to keep out of things at lunchtime, finding a quiet spot in the shadiest corner of the hall, under the lurid curtains, which always remained drawn so that girls passing down the corridor on the other side of the glass wall wouldn't be tempted to look in at the mayhem within. Those curtains, with their brooding orange and red abstract design, which looked like nothing so much as a forest of spears on a bloody battlefield.

I wanted to be alone. But was I? Hayley shivers again. Most times – and this has lain forgotten for many years – she had a companion. Another solitary, sandwich-eating girl would often be at the same table. A black girl: shy, silent. Hayley never knew her name, or if she was West Indian or African, or why she didn't hang out with the other black girls. She never thought about her, but she was always aware of her presence. She was a big girl, with a gentle face and rounded shoulders, as if she was trying not to stand too tall. Her hair was short. Not braided or shaved in a fancy style, just short. She wore a perfectly correct school uniform, nothing added, nothing missing, though the navy skirt was shiny and baggy with wear. Hayley noticed every time they sat together that someone had put together a packed lunch for her with care. A ham sandwich. A circular Wagon Wheel chocolate biscuit, a bottle of brightly coloured pop.

Hayley and her companion didn't speak, they barely made eye contact for more than a moment. But around them and between them was an island of calm and safety. An unspoken refusal of the anger and strife around them. A place of quiet where they could expand and relax and look at each other's packed lunches. Natalie's spartan Ryvita and boiled egg. Her friend's luxurious pink fizzy drink and foil-wrapped chocolate biscuit. No words, no physical contact. Just kindness in the agony of school life where conflict, violence, cruelty, abuse went unacknowledged and unchallenged.

Hayley struggled to pull herself out of the past. Why did I think of her? I never knew her name, and I never spoke to her, even though we must have spent hours and hours together. And what am I doing here, leaning my forehead against this dusty window? Hayley straightened up, and the memory of last night rustled through her leaves like a summer breeze. Natalie. Tall, thin, noisy, outspoken. Black – well, mixed-race. Hayley's friend and now Hayley's lover.

She came into the office where Hayley worked from a computer consultancy, to help with the teething problems of a new systems installation. And as she burst through the door, navy suit unbuttoned over a white shirt, short hair in a wild black cloud, briefcase swinging from a long arm, Jonesy and Frank and Joe and Judy and Lara scattered, like sheep who have smelled a wolf, leaving Hayley to face the intruder.

"Would you like some coffee?" said Hayley, having discovered who Natalie was. Judy, the receptionist, was nowhere to be seen. Her usual perch, a trendy plastic stool behind the silver artificial flowers on the white reception console, was conspicuously empty.

"Great," said Natalie. Her eyes were golden brown. She wore no makeup, her white teeth were ever so slightly irregular and the arch of her left eyebrow was pulled out of true by a scar.

"Actually, it won't be very nice," said Hayley, remembering with embarrassment that the real stuff was all used up. She hurried to explain: "There's only instant. I mean, it might be OK, but I never drink it so I don't know."

"Why are you offering it to me, then?" said Natalie, sharply, to which Hayley could think of no reply. "I'd better get on. Where's the boss? Or is it you?" Natalie peered at something which seemed to be scribbled on the back of her hand. "No. You don't look like a Mervyn Jones to me." And she smiled suddenly, wickedly at Hayley. "More like a Samantha." Hayley felt herself blushing. Long, blonde hair, pointed chin, blue eyes. Typical Sloane, you might think, if you didn't know that she was born and dragged up in the badlands of Tooting Bec.

"Hayley. I'm Hayley," she said, and went to excavate Jonesy from the men's loo.

After that, Natalie was in the office nearly every day. The new sales programmes were complex, and there were many problems to iron out. She knew her stuff, but people were a bit afraid of her. A small office, where everybody knows everybody and the routines of teasing and badmouthing are long established, doesn't take kindly to someone different upsetting the status quo. And Natalie's brusque manner, her sharp wit, didn't help to endear her, especially to Jonesy and Frank.

"What a dog," Hayley heard Jonesy mutter one morning when Natalie turned up to deliver some software, dressed in jeans and a sweatshirt. And, with a touch of shame, she thought, not for the first time, that her own slim, blonde looks, that somehow made everything she wore look as if she had just picked it up from Harvey Nicks, were what had got her the market research post, and were what kept Jonesy keen to stay in her good books.

Market research was not a priority for updating, so Hayley had very little to do with Natalie at first. But she was always vividly aware of her presence, even if she was tucked away in one of the box-like, windowless private offices, rejigging the computers there. One morning, Natalie put some popcorn in the office kitchen microwave. The half-sweet, half-savoury smell flooded the office, drowning out the ubiquitous dry smell of carpets and the sour tang of old air-freshener. Hayley's mouth watered, driving her crazy with thoughts of lunchtime, still two hours away. The columns of figures on the screen in front of her wobbled, breaking up as her concentration wavered. She pressed the keyboard. The columns wobbled even more, the screen flushed rose-pink, and all the data dissolved. Is it me, or is the machine? she thought and after a few minutes' futile rebooting made her way to the kitchen.

"Still speaking to me, then?" said Natalie, perched on the kitchen counter and licking popcorn from the bottom of the bowl. "Or not? You're so other-worldly, it's hard to tell."

Hayley, at a loss for words, saw that in the bright sunlight from the kitchen window, Natalie's irises, light brown in normal light, shone vivid gold.

Natalie suddenly grinned her wicked grin. "You're a Halien, that's what you are. Hayley, the alien. Halien, I shall call you."

"That's fine by me," said Hayley, pulling herself together. "Just so long as you fix my computer, you can call me what you like."

"I will, babe, believe you me, I will." And Natalie hitched herself off the kitchen counter, dusting off bits of popcorn. "Show me the way."

Frank looked sourly out of his room as they passed, his public school tie all crooked. "I'm still down in here," he said, crossly.

"And that's where I like to see a man. On his knees," said Natalie swiftly, under her breath. "I'll come and sort you out in five; just keep your pants on," she called to him.

"Can't I even take a coffee break?" she added, as she sat at Hayley's desk in her little pale-grey-walled office. "So, Halien, what's up with it? Oh, seeing life through rose-coloured spectacles again . . ." And watching her strong, sensitive fingers slide over the key pad, Hayley thought, she's really good at this. And she really loves it. She's much better than the usual bored blokes from the consultancy.

"What's wrong with it?" she asked.

"It's not your machine. Just too much overload on the system. It'll be sorted in a day or so. Just run one programme at a time, for now." Natalie paused, sitting very still in Hayley's chair. "Do they know about you, Halien?" She inclined her head at the outer office, where Frank was now talking to Jonesy. It was gloomy in Hayley's room, in spite of the halogen lighting, and Natalie's eyes were dark, not gold any more. "I saw you, didn't I? Clubbing, a few weeks ago. With a red-haired girl. It was you, wasn't it? Not many girls who look like you on the scene."

"No. I mean, yes." Hayley was stiff with shock at the sudden exposure. She had never properly come out at work. She had never lied about her sexuality, but she never talked about it, either. It was too easy just to keep herself to herself and go along with the office flirting. Sometimes Jonesy would tease her and call her a dyke, but did he really mean it? Was he just being crabby because she would never go out for a drink with him after work? Hayley had never been any good at working out what men were really thinking. "Yes, it was me. But I don't . . ." She began.

Natalie's forehead was creased in a frown and Hayley realized that she was frowning too, struggling to get her words out. But there was no need. The moment passed, Natalie was grinning again: "OK, babe, all done." And she sprang up, her usual brusque self, and loped out of Hayley's room.

Maybe it was then that the memories started coming back. Tuning in to Hayley's slight feeling of insecurity, of something just around the corner waiting to blow her cover and rip her apart. She waited for Natalie to approach her again, but beyond a friendly grin – much warmer than before – she kept her distance.

After a few days, Hayley took to going to the kitchen in the mornings. She stood leaning against the wall and watching Natalie crunch popcorn and swig coffee, but mostly, apart from "Hello" and "Thanks for sorting out the printer" and suchlike, they hung out in companionable silence, soaking up sunlight in the one place in the partitioned, divided-up office where the rays could get in. It had been a long, cold spring, and the warm light was like a drug, inducing instant relaxation and peace.

And then it was May, and Hayley took a few days off, returning the day after the Bank Holiday. The weather suddenly turned very hot. Hayley had intended to go to the sea with Gina, her red-haired ex. But Gina had found a new lover and was preoccupied with her. So Hayley stayed at home in her small studio flat and managed to get some sunbathing in by sneaking up onto the roof. Lying in the gully, hidden from prying eyes, she had brazenly taken off her top and stretched out in the first real sun of the year.

Though blonde and blue-eyed, Hayley's pale skin was sallow, a legacy from her Welsh grandmother, and she tanned quickly and easily. When she got back to work after the Bank Holiday, it was obvious that not everyone was so lucky. Jonesy, in rolled-up sleeves and red braces, sported fushcia pink forearms, matched by the bridge of his pointed nose and his bald patch. Every inch of Frank's fair English-rose complexion was a raw shade of beetroot. Judy, the receptionist, elegant in her tight black plunge-back top, had a neat white cross on her pale pink back, legacy of a Bank Holiday sundress. Only Lara, who never went anywhere without an arsenal of cosmetics and protective creams, and Frank, whose olive skin and straight dark hair indicated Asian ancestry, were unscathed by the early sun.

Natalie was late in, that day, but she barged in to the ladies as Hayley was washing her hands. "Why do white people try to get brown?" she said, sharply. "They just end up with pink patches everywhere. It looks crap."

"Not me," said Hayley, quickly, aware that Natalie was looking at her neckline.

"Don't lie to me. You've been in the sun." Natalie looked tired and cross. She was wearing white shorts and a white, unironed shirt. She seemed out of place, as if she should be sitting on a hot beach somewhere, not coming into work.

"Yes, but I do it all over."

"What? Oh, really?" Natalie was fumbling in her bag, not really listening.

"Look!" Boldly, Hayley pulled down the shoulder of her blouse. As she did so, the top button came open, leaving her breast exposed too, soft and vulnerable, its warm honey colour washed out by the harsh lighting and the acid lavender paintwork in the ladies.

The door of the ladies flipped open at that moment and Judy came in.

"Very nice," said Natalie, drily, and disappeared into a cubicle, Tampax in hand.

"All right?" said Judy, looking sideways at Hayley. "Had a nice break?"

"Yes. I've been sunbathing." Hayley buttoned herself up quickly.

"So I see," said Judy, peering in the mirror and applying lipstick. "I've caught the sun, too. We went on the river."

I wonder if she's seen her back view and she knows about her lovely white cross? thought Hayley, and made good her escape from the ladies. Judy was probably too busy rerunning the little scene she had just walked in on to care. Strangely, Hayley didn't feel too bothered about what she might be thinking. Normally she would have been agonizingly embarrassed. But she could only wonder if Natalie was angry with her. Or did she just think she was a fool? Or was she just having her period and feeling off colour? When Hayley went to look for her, later, in the kitchen, Jonesy said she had gone home, feeling ill. "Fine thing, too, with my e-mail down and all the holiday backlog," he grumbled.

When she saw Natalie again, there was no time to hang out together. It was Natalie's last day. She was desperately busy ensuring that all the work was done, everything up and running smoothly.

"Will you be back?" said Hayley, as Natalie scooped up her papers and stuffed them into her bulging black briefcase.

"I doubt it. They'll send round one of the other guys if you need any back up." Natalie was backing towards the door. "See you round, babe." And she was gone, leaving Hayley feeling very lonely and out of sorts, and everyone else relieved to settle back into their old routines. As for the incident in the toilet, Judy must have kept quiet about it. Maybe she didn't have the imagination to read anything into it. Or maybe she was just selective about who she told. Hayley got some very sour looks from Jonesy for a while, and no offers of after-work drinks, which was his usual way with her at least twice a week.

May drifted into June and June scorched into July, and the air in the office was unbearably dry and lifeless. Hayley felt distant and bored at work, sitting in her little grey box. But she couldn't help noticing how well the new system worked, and how both sales and enquiries seemed to be going up and up. Jonesy was so pleased with the figures that he applied to head office for permission to appoint two new staff. All the current staff got a mid-year bonus, which was unheard of, and Jonesy announced that he was going to give a party, to celebrate his birthday, and the outstanding performance of everyone in the office.

"Bit of a shortage of girlies," said Frank, who had just split up with his most recent girlfriend, Tara. He grinned at Hayley.

"I'll sort it out, don't you worry," said Jonesy, huffily, noticing the grin. Oh dear, thought Hayley. He's getting jealous. He'll start asking me out for drinks again. And I'm so bored, I might just say yes.

"You could ask that computer bird. What's her name. Marianne?" said Joe.

"Natalie," said Hayley, quickly, too quickly, and hoped no one had noticed how she had suddenly lit up for a moment.

"Are you serious?" said Frank.

"She's got great legs," said Joe, cheerfully, tossing his black fringe. "She did a great job, too."

"I'll sort it out," said Jonesy, asserting himself.

Which means he won't ask her, thought Hayley. Because he doesn't like her.

He seemed to have got over his sulk with Hayley, however. "Going to get yourself a little black number from Harvey Nicks?" he said, when she asked for a day off before the party.

"I've got one already." she said.

"I bet you look great in it," said Jonesy, hungrily, and Hayley shrugged and slipped away before he could invite her for a quick one round the pub.

When the day of Jonesy's party finally arrived, Hayley didn't want to go. It was a hot day, too hot to be comfortable dressed up, too hot to spend hours making polite conversation while trying not to get too drunk. Jonesy's little Islington pied à terre with its tiny flagstoned terrace and bijou kitchen/diner would be crowded and noisy. She didn't even take the little black dress out of the wardrobe. What would I wear on a Saturday night if I only had myself to please? she thought. And put on an old blue cotton vest and pair of ancient, baggy jeans.

Later that evening, sat on Jonesy's lumpy sofa, wedged between Judy and Frank, who were flirting drunkenly across her, with the party well under way, Hayley remembered the ordeal of the school Christmas dance one year. The headmistress had arranged for the boys from the local boys' comprehensive to be invited, and the result was chaos, a noisy whirlpool of sexual competition and aggression. Hayley hid herself amongst her classmates, desperate to avoid attention, until one by one they paired off, and she fled to the kitchen where she hid amongst the tea-urns until it was time for her father to come and fetch her.

Now, sinking fast after five glasses of wine and with her head aching evilly, Hayley longed to be at home. When the doorbell rang, she retreated further into the sofa. It could only be more of Jonesy's noisy friends. But it wasn't. It was Natalie. Natalie almost unrecognizable, slim and sinuous in a tight, red, very short dress, her hair slicked back, gold hoops in her ears and gold dust glinting round her eyes. The seething partygoers shuffled back to make space for her, a tiger in their midst. Hayley's mouth was dry, her legs trembling. She had never felt so frumpy, so ill-prepared. I've missed her, she thought. Until just now, I didn't realize how much. And she is so beautiful, I can't bear it.

Natalie was talking to the guys, showing off her long beautiful neck, lapping up their attention. Jonesy seemed to be talking business to her, waving his hands as if explaining how things were going at the office, and she was smiling at him, cool and proud. If only I'd worn the black dress, thought Hayley, I could go and join them. She just couldn't stand up in her faded, unironed vest and old jeans.

"What a tart," said Judy, nastily, glaring at Natalie's legs. Natalie looked over and caught Hayley's eye.

"Excuse me," she said, swooping across the room and neatly shoving Judy to one side. "Halien, how are you?"

"Oh, well. You know. OK." Hayley felt Natalie's bare thigh against her leg, very warm. Her eyes glinted gold where they picked up the light from the candles, and her mouth – Hayley had to look away, it was so soft and inviting. Struggling to keep her eyes on Natalie's face, she found herself looking at the crooked scar, highlighted by the gold dust round her eyes.

"What's the matter? You're frowning," said Natalie.

"I was wondering how you got that scar."

"My foster brother hit me with a golf club when we were kids."

"Oh, no!" Hayley winced, in sympathy and in embarrassment for having asked.

"Great chat-up lines you've got up your sleeve," said Natalie, heaving herself up from the sofa. She went back to the men on the other side of the room and Hayley felt deserted, all contact broken. She tried to pretend that Natalie wasn't there, that she didn't matter, but it was impossible. Her red dress and her gold earrings lit up the room.

Frank, still sitting beside her, put his hand on her knee. I'm glad I wore the jeans after all, thought Hayley. Let me just fade into the background, let me become as the sofa, inert, upholstered, insensitive. "What's up?" Frank was saying, breathing heavily into her ear. Turning to look at him, Hayley realized he was touching her with concern, not lechery. It was Judy he had the hots for, not her.

"I always say the wrong thing to people I really care about. I'm such a fool," she said. "I just asked her a really personal question and I've upset her."

"Don't be stupid," said Frank. "She's your mate. She really likes you. Anyone could see that. Go and have a word with her. She likes you."

Hayley went to join Natalie. Blond Frank, hugely drunk, was holding her by the arm and boasting about his sales technique, of all things.

"The best people to sell to are West Indians. If you can get your foot in the door, you're in there. D'you know what I mean?" he was saying.

Natalie, who in her heels was almost as tall as Frank, gave him a cool look. "I wouldn't know. My mother came from Ghana," she said.

Frank looked at her as if she might as well have come from Mars.

"I think Lara needs a drink," said Hayley. Elegant Lara, unimpressed by the male company on offer, was leaning on the sideboard, looking bored. "Be a love, Frank; go and look after her."

"I'm sorry," she said to Natalie. "I didn't mean to upset you." Natalie leaned against her for a moment, their arms touching. Hayley had never realised how sensitive her upper arm could be. The contact was more intimate and comforting than a hug.

"You didn't. I'm just doing my party thing, that's all. It's good to see you." And they stood for a few moments, quiet and still and close in the centre of the party.

And though they separated and talked and drank and laughed with other people, Hayley could feel the contact between them. Every time she looked at Natalie, which was very often, Natalie looked back and met her gaze. And Hayley stopped feeling frumpy and tired and felt just like herself, happy and warm and sexy and relaxed, with not even a whisper of her headache left. It was as if the little island of closeness between them was expanding, encompassing the whole party, so that wherever she went she felt strong and bright and at ease.

Later, when they had both found themselves sitting on the sofa and the party was beginning to break up, Natalie slid her hand into Hayley's.

"Come with me," she said.

Hayley felt a rising panic. "What?"

A shadow of Natalie's tired, cross expression flitted over her gold-dusted face. "Come home with me, stupid."

"No," said Hayley, fighting off a sea of fear and confusion. The feeling of warmth and expansion was gone and she was back inside herself, alone and afraid. It was all too much; she couldn't handle it. Everyone would see them. Natalie was too abrupt, too scary, too unpredictable, too beautiful. "I can't."

Natalie took her hand away and stood up, leaving a cold space behind.

Don't go! thought Hayley, biting back the words. Natalie was waiting. "It isn't far," she was saying.

And Hayley, missing the warmth of her more than she had ever missed anything, got up and got her bag and went with her.

They walked through Islington together, not talking much, touching shoulders sometimes. It may not have been far, but it seemed like a long, dark walk through streets of shops and then streets of houses and estates. Not many people about, except a group of teenage girls on a corner.

Hayley remembered walking home from school one winter evening, with her friend Sharon. Sharon was going to have tea at her house. Sharon was a mixed-race girl; her father was a musician, West Indian, and her white mother was a singer. As they passed the bus stop, where a horde of their schoolfellows were waiting, Hayley could hear them making comments. "She doesn't know if she's black or white," said one girl. "Can't make your mind up, can you? Don't know who to stick with, do you?" and she pushed Sharon with her shoulder, hard. Hayley felt a gobbet of spittle, probably meant for Sharon, land on her bare ankle. The two girls ran the gauntlet in silence, inching their way past the dreadful bus stop.

Hayley felt awful, as if it was her fault for asking Sharon home with her. She had no idea what to say to try and make the situation better. Tea was an uncomfortable affair. Sharon spent most of the time talking to Hayley's mum, who had made a very special effort for their tea, with three different kinds of cold meat, and four kinds of cake. Hayley didn't like to ask her again, and after that Sharon seemed, while not actually avoiding Hayley, to melt into the background and disappear out of her life.

The girls on the corner were laughing and shouting. Natalie was walking on ahead of her. She didn't look round for Hayley, just kept on walking. Hayley's guts were turning over, but she kept walking too, trying not to flinch when she felt something touch her ankle. But looking down she saw it was the sleeve of the jacket she was carrying. A roar of laughter went up from the girls, and Hayley told herself, don't run. Don't look round, and then she was past, and she was following Natalie up some steep front steps, and through a front door and then, finally, they were off the street and inside Natalie's flat.

But the contact between them was gone. Hayley was stiff with fear, the school bus stop more real to her than the big, untidy bedsitting room, than the bedside lamp glowing through the red cloth thrown over it, than Natalie, tall stranger in a red dress, pulling off her earrings and throwing them on the dressing table.

"What's up?" she was saying. "Don't you like my room?"

"I'd better go," said Hayley, icy cold, thinking about Sharon. If it was bad for me, in that divided hell which was my community, the soil I was raised in, what can it have been like for her? Why didn't I talk to her about what happened? She was my friend and I just let her go. And Natalie. How can I ever know her? All the things she must have been through . . .

The warmth and joy and closeness of the party had turned into a hard, cold stone around Hayley's heart. The memory of Natalie's touch was painful, not a pleasure. I can't bear it, she thought. I'm being pulled back into that noisy hell, into all that conflict, and this time there'll be no staying out of trouble. I won't be able to protect myself. I should go away now . . .

With a huge effort, Hayley focused on where she was, standing in Natalie's room. It was very quiet, the soft red light reflecting in a large mirror, a faint smell of spices and perfume. Natalie was watching her with a frown, no gold lights in her eyes, just darkness. She went out for a moment and came back with a bottle of wine in her hand. She took a slug of it. Still holding the bottle, she stood in front of Hayley. Too close, but to move backwards would mean that Hayley was on the bed. So she stayed where she was.

"Are you sure you want to go? Because the door isn't locked," said Natalie, matching Hayley's coldness. She took another slug of wine, then leaned forward and kissed Hayley. Her lips were warm and soft, not cold at all. Then there was a sudden gush of liquid in Hayley's mouth, warm at first, then cool as it spilled out over her lips and chin. It was the red wine Natalie had been holding in her mouth.

Natalie drank again, and kissed her again, pushing her backwards onto the bed, and the wine ran over Hayley's front, chilling her nipples and sliding cold wet fingers under the waistband of her jeans. She was so hot between her legs that the cold was shocking, a painful, sweet sensation. Natalie pulled the little red dress up over her head and threw it on the floor, pressing herself against Hayley and bumping the wine bottle into her mouth. Hayley drank, and then slowly, so slowly, let the wine slide out against Natalie's skin, watching the gleaming rivulets slip down her body into the darkness below her stomach. And then the only thing to do was to try and catch them with her tongue, tasting Natalie's salty skin and the sourness of the wine, until Natalie snatched the bottle back, and wrapping her legs round Hayley drowned them both in wine. But nothing could put out the heat that was burning in their joined bellies, evaporating the alcohol, burning up the past, feeding itself and growing until Hayley no longer knew her body was her own, only that she was flying further and higher and faster than ever before, and as Natalie's long fingers slid inside her, that she had no secrets left, no place to hide, and nowhere that she wanted to be except here and now.

Later, surfacing, washed up in darkness with her cheek resting between Natalie's legs, caught up in her wet essence, breathing in her smell, soaking up the kindness and vulnerability of her warm sex, Hayley feels empty and perfectly at peace. A peace that is flowing between her and Natalie but is somehow far bigger than the two of them. Not an island any more, but a whole world.

And then it's a new day and Natalie's face is swollen and soft with sleep and wine in the bright morning sunlight, a sheen of sweat on her brow and shoulder as Hayley struggles awake, aware of the comfort of Natalie's body, and the discomfort of the damp, wrinkled sheets. Above her, on the off-white ceiling, spots of what could be red wine are scattered. She tries to pull apart from Natalie, easing her sticky thighs away, and Natalie wakes.

"Jesus Christ, what time is it?" she says.

Hayley fumbles under the bed, finding her trousers and her watch. "Half past ten."

"I've got to play football." With a huge yawn.

Hayley feels a little shock of fear. Natalie is drawing back from her. The contact is broken again. She wants Hayley to go. Best to get away, get herself out of there first. Natalie buries her face in the pillow, groaning and yawning.

Hayley makes herself small, prepares to make herself gone, fumbling into clothes that feel rough as chalk squeaking on a morning blackboard, falling over her bag, trying to smile but not quite making it.

Natalie rolls over, watching her, yawning, as if waiting for her to go. Then says: "You've wrecked my bed."

"Me?" says Hayley, adding quickly: "Sorry."

"You'd better go, hadn't you?" Natalie rolls her face back into the pillow, yawning her guts up. Or is it a grin? "Before I have to give you a good seeing to."

It is a grin. Hayley puts down her bag. But Natalie keeps talking. "Even for you, Halien, I am not giving up my football. But if you're not busy later, baby, you might like to give me a call. I've got a bottle of champagne in the fridge."

Hayley is smiling, but speechless. Natalie says, "It's a shame I don't have any champagne glasses. But I expect we'll manage." And she turns back into the pillow, rubbing her eyes.

Hayley's out the door and halfway down the stairs before the memory hits her. The end of the school term, no – the end of exams and the end of school forever, and a woodland picnic deep in the wild part of the common. Three girls partying before they go off to college and the old safe world is gone forever. A bottle of champagne but they've forgotten the glasses. And Hayley goes first, daring to drink the fizzy wine from the neck of the bottle, and it froths and foams against her lips gushing again and again in irrepressible waves into her mouth, almost too fast to swallow, wave upon wave of freedom and wickedness and excitement.

And all the way walking home (for she doesn't trust her new self on the bus, she wants to be alone, savouring all the new sensations), she's looking forward to the evening, and remembering old stuff like the school hall, and wondering how it will be when she goes back to work and everyone will have seen her leaving with Natalie, and what will they say?

And Hayley is not afraid any more. Her whole body shivers all over with new growth, with delicate, fresh green leaves, sprouting and reaching for the sun. Each leaf a new thought, a new word, a new weapon against fear, against sadness, against the cold. Each leaf spreading boldly out into the unknown, drawing warm and living Hayley after it, so that whatever happens to her, she will never be the same again, never be able to step backwards and undo what she has grown into.

THE MISSIONARY POSITION

Astrid Fox

Ber-ring!

The doorbell blasted through my sweet dreams of sugared pussy melting in my mouth. I lifted my head blearily to look at the alarm clock, then fell back on my pillow with fatigue and irritation and stared up at the ceiling. Eight o'fucking clock on a Saturday morning.

Ber-ring!

I shrugged on my bathrobe and ran my fingers though my short dreads. "I'm coming, aren't I?" I growled out.

Ber-ring!

As I reached the hallway, the bell sounded again. You know, I thought, I am not going to be a happy bunny when I answer this door.

I pulled open the front door and tried to glare and focus at the same time. "Do you know what time it is?"

A chirpy bright-eyed girl of about twenty with pale-brown skin, neat cornrows and a blue blazer stood beaming at me. "Good morning! I'm sorry to have woken you up so early, but I wondered if I could talk to you about religion for a –"

"No." I was already closing the door, but she stuck her foot in it, with more aggression than I had expected.

"Couldn't I come in for just a moment and show you some of our magazines? You never know, you might change your mind."

I looked at her again, this time more closely. She was very pretty with ink-black eyes framed by long lashes, what looked like a curvy body under that horrible blue blazer and with a real glow to her cheeks that had to be the result of religious fervour, I decided. The name-tag on her blazer read *Helena.*

"All right," I said, as a wicked idea struck me. "Come in, Helena."

The girl followed me into the front room, commenting politely on my house.

"Tea?" I asked.

"Yes, please," said the girl, and started to lay out reams of papers, religious pamphlets and magazines on the floor.

I returned and set her tea down on a side table. "Here you go." The girl looked slightly nervous – I wondered if she had noticed the bookshelf crammed with books, many of whose spines read in part "Lesbian".

"Do you want sugar with it?" I said softly, and moved very close to Helena. I could smell a musk coming up from her – fear or arousal, I couldn't tell. But it was sweet.

"No," murmured shy Helena, not raising her eyes to mine.

"Is something wrong?" I lifted her chin softly with my hand and innocently looked into her bright, dark eyes.

"No, no, there's not . . ." she demurred, and tried to look away, but I kept her chin in my hand.

"Maybe this?" I pressed my lips against her own full rosy lips and, to my surprise, she opened them and I was kissing deep into her wet, sweet mouth. My hand went beneath her blazer and ran over her crisp white shirt. "Or this?" I undid the first two buttons, so that I could now see the black lace bra sheathing her gorgeously full tits. "Or even this?" I bent my head to suckle at one nipple pressing through the lace, and could feel it swelling through the fabric.

God, I must be horny, I thought, seducing a religious evangelist. I wondered what her pussy would look like, wet and smooth and juicy, already slick for the touch of my hands. As I thought this, Helena moaned and my hand inched up her pleated skirt to her thighs, and then rested on the plump curve of her arse. She wasn't wearing panties. Hmm – missionary girl wasn't as pure as she presented herself to be. She moaned again, and my hands shifted on her lush arse, trembled at its hole, and then moved to the wet cleft further on. Heaven.

Oh, God. My own clit was throbbing and I was wet, myself. "Oh, *God*." I said it aloud and Helena nodded, no doubt mistaking the phrase for an invocation.

I slid my fingers into her lovely wet cunt and Helena sighed, and then I lowered her gently to the floor, on top of the confetti-spread of religious paper pamphlets. My fingers still working her pussy, I twisted three of them inside her and drove them in harder now, plunging into her wet sex. God, I wanted to fuck this girl. I wanted to put my hand inside my robe and touch myself, too – I was so wet – but I didn't want my attention to waver from the virtuous Helena, who was raising her hips up, raising her arse up so I could fuck her the way I wanted to: deep and fast.

She was tight around my fingers as she – almost coyly –

snaked her hand down to rub her clit. It was so hot to see the little do-gooder wanking in my front room, her face so flushed I thought she'd burst and her cunt tightening wet and firm around my fingers.

I wanted to touch myself badly, but I knew I couldn't stop.

"Christ!" Helena's pretty face screwed up as she came, and my hand was slick with her honey. I was surprised by her blasphemy, but I continued pumping my hand into the hot liquid velvet of her cunt until she motioned for me to stop and I was sure she'd finally had enough.

I was still aroused as Helena rose dazedly, pulled down her skirt, dusted off her blazer, murmured a quick thank you and headed out the door.

Her tea hadn't been touched and was surely cold by now, I thought, as I leant back groggily on my sofa and looked over the array of slightly damp religious pamphlets strewn over the floor of my front room. I wondered if she'd come back for them. I picked one up, and fumbled through a vitriolic discourse against homosexuality before tossing it in the bin near me. I had a feeling she'd soon be back again, and then I would receive my due satisfaction. Conversions are not easy, but the reward once a single soul's been saved is *always* worth the effort.

I MARRIED MADAM PART II

A Work In Progress

Daphne Adams

"Meryi Streep, eat yer heart out!"

"What?" The booming voice prompted Anna to twist round so suddenly that she almost turned her ankle. She wasn't used to wearing shoes with a heel.

"In that get-up you look just like her, in that film *Passage To India.*"

"*Out Of Africa,*" Anna corrected. "And I don't remember her being dressed like this."

For the umpteenth time, she inspected herself in the long bedroom mirror. She touched her russet-coloured satin dress, admiring its delicate patterned ochre and lime flowers, their centres inlaid with mother-of-pearl. Anna could feel her ivory silk corset underneath. God: she felt sexy. There was something about the touch of the finest natural fibres against skin . . .

She snuck a sideways glance at Joan, whose secret admiring looks reinforced Anna's belief that she looked good enough to eat. But if that was true, it would be Marlene's prerogative.

Briefly, Anna fantasized about Marlene taking her into a field and pushing her down into the long grass. Marlene would be rough with her (with the right mix of eagerness and experience, of course) . . . Marlene's hand thrust up her dress . . .

The pupils of her eyes widened in surprise as she moved her fingers along Anna's stockinged thigh to her suspender belt and the beginnings of a boned corset . . .

Her mouth twisted into a feline smile as she felt the soft bare flesh where she'd expected lace panties to be . . . and she . . .

"*Mea culpa!*" a voice barked.

"Oh, bloody hell," Anna swore, dragged firmly back into reality just as everything was getting juicy.

"I said, a thousand pardons for being so wrong about the damn film . . . an earth-shattering error on my part." Joan, seemingly chastized, bowed her head – but only so far down that her mouth could make contact with a lit ciggie she'd been holding between her opened legs. "No, not Meryl Streep." She shook her head. "In fact, *Passage To India* is right, because you resemble a dotty old dowager from the Raj. And," she added caustically, "when you stick that straw bonnet and beige cardy on, you'll look just like Margaret Rutherford digging her garden!"

Joan waited to see how Anna would respond to the jibe about her expensive silk cardigan and designer hat, both of which she looked splendid in.

"Well," Anna sparred, "if I'm 'Mem Sahib', you must be 'Pukka Wallah'!"

"Fifteen all! Well done!" Joan laughed. "Mind you, many a true word spoken in jest, angel: someone's got to escort you on the bus to Epsom. Trussed up looking like Princess Di, you'll be in serious need of some protection." She stood up. "I believe I am the right woman for the job."

Joan thrust her chest out like a bantam cock and strutted a few paces round Anna's bed.

"You amaze me," Anna exclaimed. "How you manage to inveigle your way into everything. It's like picking a juicy plum from a tree and biting into it only to find that a fat, grey little worm has chomped her way through the best flesh. Marlene invites me to the Derby – tickets for the Royal Enclosure no less – and . . ."

"*Quel horreur*! You lie!" Joan jumped onto the bed. She faced Anna eye-to-eye and waggled her finger under her nose. "Dietrich-Dyke is bringing a pal with her and she said you could do the same. I am your oldest and bestest friend. In choosing me, there should be no hesitation on your part *whatsoever*."

Anna was silent.

"Why," continued Joan, "when she offered to send a black cab to pick us up, did you have to decline . . . to insist we meet them outside the racecourse? Instead, we've got to sit like a couple of nit-wits for two hours on a bus because we can't afford an alternative."

"Because, O Wise Gonk, we don't want to be beholden to them. We might not like them. And at least we can go home when we want."

"But if Marlene's pal is half-fanciable, she'll do for a quickie," Joan winked.

"You are a depraved bitch on heat," Anna snapped. "If you

think you're going to score wearing that suit, shirt and tie, then you need to know something . . . you look like Quentin Crisp's Siamese twin. Now who's going to be the one in mortal danger on the bus?"

Joan stepped off the bed. "Exactly my point! *Quis custodiet ipsos custodes*? Who will guard the guards themselves?" She raised her right eyebrow. "One for the road?"

"No. It's only ten-thirty in the morning. Don't be such a vile old lush. Let's get on with it or we'll be late." Anna laughed as she rammed the fetching hat over her sun-bleached hair.

"Hallelujah!" Joan's plimsolled foot kicked open the bedroom door, Kung-Fu style.

Marlene and friend Monika looked radiant in black haute couture suits.

"Versace and Armani no less. Are you sure they aren't Mafiosi?" Joan asked as Marlene sashayed up to them. Her whole body said: Here I am, open and waiting for you, as she reached out to kiss Anna sensuously on the cheek. Anna blushed furiously as she remembered her fantasy from earlier that day.

"Velcom. You vill be my guests for ze afternoon."

"Charmed." Joan extended her arm and, upon shaking hands with Marlene, quaffed, "Who's this spirited filly, then?"

She gazed so intently at Monika that Anna realized her friend was seriously attracted to this woman. It was more usual for Joan to stare rudely through or past someone in order to spy out the nearest watering hole! Anna also knew from experience that these seemingly revolting manners were really a test to (as Joan would say) "sort out the wheat from the chaff". Anyone she liked the look of who could come up with a suitable retort to her charming introduction immediately became a candidate for serious respect and copious amounts of obsequious chat-up lines.

"A pleasure," Monika retorted. "I've always wanted to cop off with a real-life Sister George."

Everyone burst out laughing. Joan was obviously suitably impressed because she clapped her hands and exclaimed "Marvellous!" It was going to be a fun day.

After the first race . . .

"Do you really think she'd like me, you know . . . in that way?" Joan looked expectant. "Monika, the hornier version of Nana Mouskouri. If one adds to this the fact that she's classy, has brains and, most importantly, the wit of a viper . . . ooo-er." She shivered. "I think I've met my nemesis."

"If love is blind, then anything's possible," Anna replied sarcastically. She knew she was being selfish but she hoped Joan would be offended enough to leave her for a while, because she wanted to spend some time alone with Marlene, not waste the afternoon trying to fix her little friend up with the improbable again. To Anna, it was clear Monika wasn't interested. She was just being polite.

Joan wasn't used to Anna continuing to quip when she had plainly shown her serious intent. She was a little hurt at her friend's indifference and failure to offer moral support, and stomped off in dramatic fashion to signal her discontent. This action had little effect on her pal; Anna seemed miles away.

Joan left Anna's world, allowing her to dreamily savour her surroundings. She had never been to a race before. In fact, she'd never placed a bet. Anna was fascinated by the proceedings.

When a race went off, nothing much happened where she stood. For a while, women (many were wearing this year's fashionable black ostrich-feathered hats) continued to amble aimlessly. But in reality Anna knew every step taken was one of utter calculation. They revealed their true quest via spiteful and dismissive glances at their counterparts. Style Queens, Anna thought; they'd fit in well on the gay scene. If only they knew how close they were to the lifestyle they professed to despise.

She became aware that an imperceptible change had occurred, like a light breeze changing direction . . . suddenly, you hear and feel it: a murmur in the crowd followed by mass concentration. The swaggering stops and they stand to attention . . . Style becomes forgotten as substance (one's potential winnings) comes to the forefront of their thoughts . . . The Queens' arms gesticulate wildly, their gloved hands moving strips of fluttering paper up and down like railway signalling.

Turning up the slope, Anna watched the flock of women: black-feathered birds practising synchronised swimming, but on dry land. And for what? A small gap in the crowd revealed a flash of equine moving parts. Seated on these horses were miniature jockeys, whips in hands; shadow puppets.

It was all over. The atmosphere banked down. Limp, torn tickets were discarded and the sizing up began all over again.

"Sorry, I was miles away. Did you win?" Anna linked her arm through Marlene's.

Her companion smiled. "No, dahrlink. But zis is not a problem."

Disengaging herself, she opened her Louis Vuitton handbag and extracted the longest cigarette holder Anna had ever laid eyes on. Opening what looked like an antique jewel-bedecked Cartier cigarette case, Marlene selected a Turkish cigarette, inserted it smoothly into the holder with the tips of her fingers, then snapped the case shut and placed it back in her bag. Anna shuddered. She didn't know why.

"Cartier?" she asked.

"My grandfather's," Marlene teased noncommittally. "Let's get some fizz."

"Helloowww, Bum-Fluff." Joan tipped her glass in greeting. (Luckily, the cognac in it had long since been emptied down her gullet.)

"How many have you had?" Anna stared accusingly at Monika, who shook her head.

Joan snorted. "Only two doubles, Mrs Goebbels. I'm enjoying myself far too much to get tiddled." She leered at Monika. "We should bet. I fancy . . . this one." Smacking her hand against a name in the paper, she winked at the object of her desire.

"Adam's Apple. Yes, that sounds good," Anna agreed.

"That settles it, then. Sod the horse's form; if the name's right, it'll be OK." Joan attacked. Behind her back, Monika rolled her eyes heavenward in sympathy.

Anna grabbed Joan and took her to one side. Whispering through the side of her mouth, she asked, "What do we bet? I reckon those two can afford £50. It's going to be embarrassing, but the most we can do is a fiver."

Joan started her deep-throated chortle. "Oh, Little One. If only you paid attention to your brain rather than your gonads. They've been putting a fiver on each way!"

Whatever the significance of that remark was, Anna decided to tackle her friend about it much later. She certainly had no complaints about their escorts. Marlene had been absolutely charming. No woman had ever treated her in this way before: the attention she had paid Anna over the champagne and picnic lunch; the interesting people she bumped into and the way she made Anna feel important when she introduced her to the influential politicians, media and business people. How did she know so many? The way they deferred to her . . . really, Marlene must be very important.

At one point, Anna had asked her sheepishly, "What do you do?" She knew she sounded inane, as if she were trying to make conversation, but she really did want to know.

"I had a little company that did rather well." Marlene seemed vague. "I suppose you could call me a 'lady of leisure'." She smiled serenely.

"I want to go somewhere I can press myself into you," Anna whispered after the final race. She sucked in fresh air as if it would give her Dutch courage and grabbed Marlene's arm a little more roughly than she'd wanted to; perhaps to force a positive reply from her?

Marlene grinned. "I thought you'd never ask. The Jazz Bar it is!"

"*Ausgezeichnet*!" Joan burped, in perfect time to Sarah Vaughan.

"House-gay-what?" Anna stopped. What was the point in getting a translation? Joan was very drunk. Anna knew, because her friend had failed miserably to light her last cigarette. The lit match and dead roll-up had refused to mate because Joan's coordination had deserted her.

"When all words fail me because I'm having such a marvellous time, I have to resort to the language of my forebears." Joan hiccuped.

No, please, Anna prayed – not the story that takes three hours to tell. Not the one where your great-great-great-great-great-grandfather was the bastard son of King William of Orange. Not the one in which, but for a quirk of fate, you would be Queen Joan I of Great Britain and Northern Ireland . . . "Spare us all from your family history, please," she begged.

Anna sat back in her seat to find it cushioned by Marlene's arm. Relaxing into the muscled comfort, she placed her hand on the other woman's knee and shivered with excitement as she felt Marlene's body tense. Slowly, she moved her hand up the leg until she reached the inner thigh. She stopped.

It was a moment to savour, like the exploration of a strange fruit you instinctively knew would taste delicious at the first bite.

Suddenly, Marlene's hand clamped over hers and she turned and kissed Anna. The move was sudden, but its gentleness came as a surprise. The kiss was soft and opening, yet hinted at the passion to come.

Joan cast a bleary, beady eye over her subjects. "Anything to prevent you two babes from continuing to drool over each other. It really is sick-bucket time." She proceeded to imitate (with such realism they couldn't be sure a bit of bile didn't escape her lips) someone being sick into a bucket or similar receptacle.

"*Omigod,*" Joan shrieked.

So this is it, Anna decided. She's twigged Monika isn't interested so she's out to ruin everyone else's evening. She can't get what she wants, therefore neither can we. I'll kill her when she's sobered up. "Ignore her," she hissed at a concerned Marlene and Monika.

"Shit. Blimey what-a-to-do." Joan tried to get out of her chair. Forgetting that her legs had turned into brandy-flavoured blancmange, she fell flat on her face with a loud crash.

"That's it, you rotten bugger. Into a cab. *Now.*" Anna yanked Joan to her feet.

Her little pal was by now nearly hysterical. She gibbered: "D'yer see'er?"

"What?" Anna failed to understand, but followed Joan's shaking index finger . . .

"Bloody hell." Anna paled and dropped Joan.

"What is wrong?" Marlene exclaimed. "You look like you've seen a ghost."

"I think I have," Anna trembled. "It's my girlfriend Vicky."

Marlene was clearly embarrassed. She moved away from Anna.

"Sawright. I don't think. She didn't see us," Joan burped.

"Oh, no, darling. You're very wrong. I think she's more than aware we're here," Anna said, too calmly.

So: the moment she had always dreaded, but half-expected too, had finally arrived. Anna suddenly realized that this was how her death would be. One day there would be no more time ahead of her; the escape route life provided would be removed. Then she would find herself facing her deepest fears about the unknown. Sheer terror and then blackness? But at the moment her life ceased, she would embrace the inevitability of it all and welcome it as something familiar that had been lost and found again . . .

Anna got up.

"Please trust me." She didn't look at Marlene, but sensed her stillness was a sign of acquiescence and understanding. She walked over to the table where Vicky sat, and lightly touched her hunched shoulders.

"I feel truly wretched," Anna said as Marlene ushered her into her flat. "She was so graceful about it all. She's agreed to my suggestion that, under the circumstances, I should stay away for tonight. I've given her my word that we'll meet up for dinner tomorrow. Thanks for letting me stay with you," she added. "I'm grateful for the thinking space."

"Really, it's no trouble at all." Marlene ushered her into a wide hallway hung with exquisitely-painted watercolours. Anna made a mental note for a later date to ask Marlene who'd painted them.

"You know," she continued, "that's exactly what the problem's always been about . . . that word grace."

Marlene was silent; waiting.

"I've never wanted a relationship with a nun, someone who radiated that . . . that otherworldliness that made me feel as if they were walking six inches above the ground, whilst I was firmly stuck to it," Anna spat bitterly. "It was as if I couldn't touch her. If I'd tried, it would have been wrong, because I hadn't reached that state of grace myself. But how could I? How can I even know what grace is until I've fallen from it?"

She paused expectantly.

"What do you want, then?" Marlene was smiling, Anna noted. It was a little disconcerting. Was she teasing her?

No: Anna sensed that Marlene knew exactly what her role would be. Subconsciously, she also recognized that the German's accent was less pronounced than before.

"Someone who is of this earth, and is . . . grounded, not ethereal," she responded. "Someone I can smell, someone who'll let me press my fingers into their skin. To be able to pull them towards me . . . to hold them fast, stroke them, bite them . . . to be alive: that's what I ache for."

Marlene steered Anna into her bedroom.

"Bed," she stated authoritatively.

Anna felt the capable arms lightly around her waist. God, she felt tired. It was as if she had been travelling for a long time and had finally reached her journey's end. She had nothing to prove. She smiled at the irony of it all: there would be no sex tonight, only the most proper sleep she'd had for months. The release from pressure was overwhelming.

Dimly she took in her surroundings. Marlene's bedroom was large: twenty foot square at least. The walls and carpet were red velvet, something that would make her acquired taste buds shudder in ordinary circumstances. Around the edge of the room were totally incongruous pieces of furniture. As her eyes became accustomed to the half-light, she realized that they formed what looked like a pair of mediaeval stocks and a long rack from which chrome chains dangled. Just like London Dungeon . . . or was it Warwick Castle? She was so drained, she felt detached from it all anyway.

The centrepiece was Marlene's bed. She kicked the ankle and wrist restraints away from view and pulled back the black leather bedspread to reveal a set of bluebell-printed sheets. Anna wanted to laugh at their absurdity.

"Come," Marlene commanded. Anna lifted her arms above her head like a little girl to ease the removal of her dress. Before she knew what had happened, she was lying snug in a pair of outsize brushed-cotton pyjamas covered with dogs wearing red bow ties. She surveyed her surroundings once more.

"A little hobby of mine," Marlene soothed. "Collectors' items which appeal to my sense of humour."

It isn't important, Anna decided. No matter how bizarre things might seem in the morning, she vowed to remember just how she felt at this moment . . . that she had come home.

She felt Marlene slide into bed beside her. Her body was enveloped in a warmth that was simultaneously exciting and comforting. Briefly, Anna drifted between sleep and conscious thought. As Marlene continued to spoon her, she allowed herself to fall into unconsciousness.

There would be much to tackle tomorrow. Things would be said and done that would make her happy and sad. She smiled to herself. Whatever was to come, she knew above all else she could say, "Dear reader . . . I married Madam!"

BIOGRAPHICAL NOTES

DAPHNE ADAMS grew up in Worcestershire. Having both obtained a degree at Warwick University and realised she was gay, Daphne arrived in London seeking work, romance and the meaning of life. More than ten years later she is ensconsed (with partner and black cat) in Dorset. She has a nice car and a worthwhile job as a local government officer. She waits for her talents to be discovered: her dream . . . to be the Jane Austen of the gay twenty-first century.

PATIENCE AGBABI, 33-year-old wood snake virgo open to astrology and crazy about numerology, with a no. 1 destiny and a no. 5 expression: seriously into trains, planes and platform trainers; crushed velvet and stretch satin; rap, jazz and northern soul; good food and fine wine seeks fame, fortune and fun.

AMAZON was born in New York in 1968, raised in Newcastle and is currently living in South London. She writes "poetry you can understand", as well as short stories and the occasional article. She's inspired by the works of Sapphire and Jean Binta

Breeze and hopes to have her own collection published some time in the next millennium.

THEA BENNETT's earliest memory is of her father painting his face green and sticking a hook nose on before playing the Witch in pantomime. When she grew up, she was happiest following in his footsteps, treading the boards in theatres, pubs, schools, car parks and even, once, in a cave. But the theatre is a cruel mistress, very sparing with her favours, and in between acting assignments she has done just about every job under the sun, met scores of extraordinary folk and discovered that life is truly stranger that fiction. Now, she earns her living writing all sorts of stuff, and would like to thank the wonderful birds in North London and Northamptonshire for their top-class inspiration, love and support.

DEBRA DIANA BLUE is a writer of poetry, essays, commentary and short stories who lives with her two sons in Forestville, Md, USA. Her work has appeared in *Les Talk Magazine* (currently named *Kolors*), the Boston Bi Women's Newsletter, *THOTH* Literary electronic magazine, the BiNetwork DC newsletter and also DC's premier gay weekly, the *Washington Blade*. She is currently working on a book of poetry. She is currently serving as Fiction Editor for the Binet USA Quarterly Newsletter and Contributing Editor for the web-based guide, *Suite 101.com*.

BENTE CLOD achieved literary acclamation for her writing soon after starting out on her career in 1975 as a provocative feminist debater and, in 1981, was nominated for the prestigious Scandinavian Literary Award for her poetry. She has published eleven books of fiction, prose and poetry. Her guidebook for writers-to-be and her writing workshops on prose, poetry and erotic writing have made her widely known throughout Scandinavia. *Thai Silk*, translated by Margareth Hellmen, is taken from *Ex hibition*, her 1997 collection of erotic stories for grown-up women about grown-up women. The story was first read aloud by the author in the Gay Pan Bookcafé in Copenhagen in November 1996, making the crowd laugh a lot and at least one person come.

SHARI J BERMAN has completed three novels and numerous short stories. *I do! THE QUARANTINE CHRONICLES* is a novel in progress. She took first place in the Lavendar Life fifth anniversary short story contest. Episodes of her lesbian fiction serial, *The Selena Stories*, appear online at *http:*wowwomen.-com/visibilities/fiction–1998/index.html. She also contributed the title story for an upcoming parody anthology from Alyson Publications. After two decades in Japan, she has settled in Hawaii with her lover of seventeen years and two Westies who braved quarantine.

KATHLEEN BRYSON was born on the northern Arctic coast of Alaska in December 1968, but at the age of two her family moved "south" to central Alaska. In 1987 she moved to Sweden, and since then she has dug up Viking graves, moved to Seattle, held numerous telemarketing jobs and played electric Hawaiian slide-guitar in a Riot Grrl band called "Thommy Goes Down". At twenty-five, she began a post-graduate acting course in London, and followed this up with an MA in film. She spends most of her spare time writing, painting and acting. She has written one full-length literary novel entitled *Mush* and several plays – as well as poetry and erotica – and is a commissioning fiction editor at Virgin Publishing.

DEBORAH CAPLAN is a 33-year-old lecturer in Latin American Literature and Spanish at the University of Portsmouth. She has a doctorate from King's College, London, on contemporary fiction by Mexican women, and has published a number of articles on this subject, including one on lesbian fiction in Mexico. She has recently begun writing fiction herself.

MAYA CHOWDHRY: As a teenager poetry was my lifeline. Now it's an occupation (dangerous?). Poems/fiction has been published in anthologies including *As Girls Could Boast*! Written five radio plays and six stage plays including *Kaahini* (Red Ladder Theatre & Birmingham Rep) and *An Appetite for Living* (West Yorkshire Playhouse). Currently working on a collection of poetry: *The Seas of Neptune* and completing new work for theatre and radio.

EMMA DONOGHUE is an Irish novelist, playwright and historian who is based in Canada. Her books of fiction are *Stir-fry*, *Hood*, and *Kissing the Witch*; her work on lesbian history includes *Passions Between Women* and a poetry anthology, *What Sappho Would Have Said*. In 1998 she published a biography of two Victorian lesbian poets, *We Are Michael Field* (Absolute Press/ Stuart, Tabori and Chang), and a vaudeville play, *Ladies and Gentlemen* (New Island Press). She is the editor of *The Mammoth Book of Lesbian Short Stories* (1999).

STELLA DUFFY has written three crime novels, *Calendar Girl*, *Wavewalker* and *Beneath The Blonde*, all published by Serpent's Tail, and two other novels, *Singling Out The Couples* and *Eating Cake*, published by Sceptre. She has written thirteen short stories, a one-woman show for herself, a musical cabaret *Close To You* and the script for Gay Sweatshop's dance/theatre piece *The Hand.* She is also a performer and writer with the comedy company Spontaneous Combustions and recently toured Britain with *Lifegame* for Improbable Theatre. Stella lives with her girlfriend in south London. Purely because it annoys north Londoners.

EILEEN FINN: I am from Chicago, IL and consider myself a proud, "South Side Irish" girl. I live with my partner, Kate, and our eight year old son, Adam. We have been together as a family for seven and a half years. I started writing short stories a couple years ago for the entertainment of my friends. I grew to love it more every day as I became more confident in my abilities. I recently began my first novel. My goal is to become a self-sufficient writer and be able to lose my "day job" which is Controller for a food distribution company.

JO FISK is a Londoner and a lawyer.

ASTRID FOX: 31, fond of blood-red lipstick and bright green hair, had her first erotic novel – a historical Viking fantasy in the style of *Xena Warrior Princess* and *Red Sonja* – published by Virgin's Sapphire imprint in June 1999.

BERTA FREISTADT is a Londoner and a teacher with some pretentions to being a writer. An only child, her fantasy world is strong and easily accessible. The product of a dysfunctional family, her eroticism can often be banally tinged with melancholy, but a natural GSOH usually comes to the rescue. Her therapist is having a field day . . . Berta is a poet and a short story writer, published in anthologies and magazines, including *Diva*, and has had many of her theatre pieces performed in Britain, Australia and Canada.

CAROLYN GAMMON, east coast Canadian, was invited to read her erotic poetry at the Berlin Lesbian Week in 1991, theme of the week: Lesbian Sex in the Year 2000! Keeping with the theme, she fell in bed and in love and has since lived in Berlin with her relationship going strong into the turn of the century. She has lived by hook and by . . . innumerable jobs including cleaning, caring for the elderly, teaching English, working as a tour guide, etc. Her book of poetry, *Lesbians Ignited* (gynergy books, 1992) documents, among other themes, the thrills and spills of lesbian sex. She is currently writing a novel and glad to be living legally in Germany!

JILL GARDINER: lives in Brighton. Her previous publications include poems in *The North*, *The Margot-Jane Memorial Prize Anthology* and in Brighton Poets' *Ice on the Wing*. A long-standing member of Brighton Ourstory Project, the oral history group, she helped edit *Daring Hearts: Lesbian and Gay Lives in 50s and 60s Brighton* (QueenSpark 1992). She is currently working on a history of gay women's lives in the era of the Gateways Club (1945–85)

MARY GERIDEAU was born in Oxford in 1963. After a first degree in history, she qualified as a solicitor, and subsequently worked in publishing as a warehouse packer and sales assistant. She currently divides her time between working in a bookshop in the Charing Cross Road, London, and writing. Her poems have been published in *Language of Water, Language of Fire: A Celebration of Lesbian and Gay Poetry*, published by Oscars Press in 1992.

AVA HINES: 34. Mother of two. Singer. Songwriter. Poet. Currently lives in Sussex where she came to do a degree in

Economics and ended up writing songs for other people and eventually performing both poetry and music herself. She has recently branched out into short story writing and is beginning work on her first novel.

ILSA JULE is a writer currently living in New York City. More often than not she is referred to as "a purveyor of smut". (Just the other day she was called the John Steinbeck of smut.) Her most recent work, *Pornography for Miss X*, can be found in *The Best Lesbian Erotica 1999* (Cleis Press).

DEBORAH KELLY: *Cocktease* is my second story. I'm much more a visual artist/activist. I'm creative director of a progressive advertising agency, a daydreamer, 37, eldest sister of seven girls; my nephew Liam Wanunga is the light of my life. I'm involved in campaigning around Aboriginal Land Rights much more than anything in the queer community . . .

MARY-KATE KELLY grew up in a rural Irish landscape that taught her all she knows about Love. Writing and art are her means of showing who she is inside, they are tools for survival in this world. At just twenty-seven, she shows signs of growing up already! But her heart will never grow old.

MAISIE LANGRIDGE is a lecturer in Theatre and Performing Arts at a Further Education College. She writes prose, poetry and plays and is currently involved in displacement activities as a substitute for starting The First Novel. Her literary aesthetic aims for a fusion of semantics and style. She is a qualified Iyengar Yoga teacher, has short hair and a sharp wardrobe, loves eating and the country and cats, GSOH and has been described as "small but perfectly formed".

ISABELLE LAZAR's work has appeared in numerous periodicals, magazines and anthologies but Literary Erotica is the ember that smolders dangerously within her at all times. She's currently at work on her first full-length book of erotica entitled *Intimate Confessions of a Proper Young Lady*, from which the piece *Life's Breath* was showcased in Alyson Publications' *Early Embraces II*, and *Light and Darkness* appears here. She lives in Los Angeles, CA.

ALEX LEQUESNE (pronounced Le Kane) lives and works in London, England. She has somehow managed to rise to being a senior civil servant in a large government department despite making no real secret of her sexuality. Given half a chance though she'd be a full time writer and has completed one "slushy" novel and is working on a political thriller with a strong lesbian theme. She lives in a "becoming beautiful" Edwardian House with her partner who didn't approve of *The Weekend* at all and three cats who expressed no opinion.

KARLYN LOTNEY, aka Fairy Butch, produces and emcees *In Bed With Fairy Butch*, a campy erotic cabaret, leads instructional sex workshops, and publishes her advice column, Ask Fairy Butch in *Curve* and *Creampuff* magazines. Look for her book, *The Ultimate Guide to Dildo & Harness Sex for Men & Women*. Contact her at *fb@fairybutch.com* to receive her free sex tip/event e-mailer and check out her web page at www.fairybutch.com!

JULIE MACLUSKY is a writer of fiction and screenplays, living in West Hollywood, Southern California. She worked as a broadcast news journalist in England before winning a scholarship to study screenwriting in the USA. She now teaches Screenwriting at a major University, whilst writing short stories and scripts, two of which are in development for production. Another short story, *Hunting*, is being published in a forthcoming Women's Press collection.

ROS MARINUS is an evergreen, native to the south of England, though remembered in many other regions. Though sex has played a large part in her life, this anthology is the first real chance she's ever had to write about it.

SUSANNAH MARSHALL: Fresh from a previous life as a pirate, it was almost predetermined that my present life would be unusual. While pregnant with me, out in Africa in 1968, my mother was bitten by a monkey. Subsequently, I was born in the Chinese New Year of the Monkey, sporting a birthmark in the shape of a monkey's paw. In earlier times, I was kicked out of school for climbing on tables and throwing bananas. These days, I channel my monkey energies into more creative ventures, namely painting and writing. My murals can be seen around my hometown of Bradford, and I have had a number of short stories and poems published in small press publications. *A Feather* is for my wonderfully inspiring partner, Rona.

HEATHER MURRAY: Large nose is an outstanding feature. Born in Lancashire, England, but pretty soon went running from the rain to the Mediterranean and has lived and loved in Barcelona since 1985. From books to life and back, singing and song-writing among the experiences under the belt.

SOVEREIGN MUSE is a 27-year-old writer/singer/academic who earns her living as a book editor. She has spent her years between Limerick and London and is passionate about literature, music, swimming and marijuana.

TWIGGY O'CONNOR came to London from Ireland to attend art school in the 1970s – an experience she is probably still recovering from. It was there that she acquired her faultless sense of bad taste, slept with her first woman, and baptised herself Twiggy. A hopeless romantic, O'Connor now teaches part time – textile design and the history of costume. She writes fiction for fun and has a long list of friends and acquaintances waiting for her to make them the corset of their dreams.

NINA RAPI is a playwright and writer. Her plays *Dance of Guns*, *Dreamhouse* and *Ithaka* and her monologues *Johnny is Dead*, and *Dangerous Oasis* have been staged at Riverside Studios, Oval House, Kings Head and other London venues. *Ithaka* is published in *Seven Plays by Women*, Aurora Metro, which won the Raymond Williams Award. Radio work includes *Catch The Ball Baby*, Anna Livia Station, Ireland. Her latest play is *Edgewise*. She is currently writing *Angel State*, a new play, funded by the Arts Council of England. She's had numerous critical articles published and is co-editor of *Acts of Passion: Sexuality, Gender and Performance*, Haworth Press, N.Y. 1998.

ROSA RILEY is a pen name taken here to protect both the innocent and the guilty. She is a poet and a short story writer, published in many anthologies and magazines.

REBECCA ROSENSKJØLD farms organic soybeans in the mountains of Tasmania and provides shelter to injured rock wallabies. She has published stories in the UK & the US, but not Australia. She was a founding member of the Feminist Urban Guerilla Movement in the mid-eighties in Melbourne. She will stand for election to parliament when Australia becomes a republic.

MERCIA SCHOEMAN was born and raised in South Africa, where she works as an adult educator. She was actively involved in the struggle to entrench equal rights for gays and lesbians in the South African constitution and was a founder member of several activist organisations. As an adult educator, she has presented workshops on racism, sexism and homophobia. She is currently living in Nelspruit and writes full time.

STEPHANIE SELLIER: born in 1968, studied German, Philosophy and Latin at the University of Cologne, editing work for several German publishers since 1991, started writing in 1996, publishes her stories, articles and book reviews in the nationwide German lesbian magazine *lespress* since this time, co-organizer of the first nationwide German lesbian literature festival which took place successfully in Cologne November 1997, her first book *Frisch aus der Hölle* (*Fresh Out Of Hell*) appeared in March 1998 (Konkursbuch Verlag, Tübingen 1998), from which *Tea and Sympathy* comes. I'm most interested in recent American and English lesbian and gay writing; my favourites are Sarah Schulman and Edmund White.

MARJORY SMITH: I'm 37, a Capricorn with Scorpio Rising, Neptune and Venus in Scorpio on my ascendant and an Aquarius Moon. Though I had lesbian incidents in my childhood, I came out properly when I was eighteen and started trying to make a space for myself where I could exist. I was born in the Highlands and didn't see why I should have to leave just because of my sexuality. After six years of fairly hard work revolutionizing the Highlands for dykes(!) I did leave for a year of abdicated responsibility in Edinburgh. Pollution returned me from whence I came, where I now live with my partner Maureen and three cats.

SUSAN STINSON is the author of the novels *Fat Girl Dances with Rocks* and *Martha Moody* (The Women's Press), and the poetry collection *Belly Songs*. She has both a novel and a non-fiction project in progress. Stinson has been awarded fellowships from the Vogelstein Foundation, the Blue Mountain Center, and the Wurlitzer Foundation. She frequently reads from her work in what IKON magazine called "a stunning, energized performance." She lives in Northampton, MA.

LORNA STUCKI: Born to a Swiss mother, Jamaican father, I consider myself to be a big, bold, loud, creative Black dyke who has a varied interest in all visual arts. My ultimate aim is to have more work published for lesbians of all nations to enjoy.

BOZ THOMAS escaped from the rat race to the country more than a decade ago. She now shares her life with two beautiful couch potatoes, retired racing greyhounds, Tonker and Princess – or perhaps it's closer to the truth to say they allow her a few square inches of the sofa . . . Boz's work as a therapist allows her plenty of time for her hobbies – sex and gardening – and her passion, writing.

KAREN X TULCHINSKY is the award-winning author of *Love Ruins Everything*, a novel, and *In Her Nature*, short stories. She has edited numerous anthologies, including *Hot & Bothered: Short Short Fiction on Lesbian Desire*, *Queer View Mirror*, *To Be Continued* and *Friday the Rabbi Wore Lace: Jewish Lesbian Erotica*. She lives in Vancouver, Canada.

RUBY VISE: Came to England from New Zealand in the mid-1980s and forgot to leave. She lives in an unfashionable part of

North London with her two cats and plays football for Hackney Women's Football Club. She has had a couple of other short stories published.